A Touch of Love

Regina Jeffers

White Soup Press

A Touch of Love (Book 6 of the Realm Series)

ISBN-13: 9780615893594
ISBN-10: 0615893597

White Soup Press

A Touch of Love

He caught the bowl she carried and set it on a small table. Her defiance enflamed him as no woman ever had, and Carter was not certain if his heated blood came from his ire or his desire. Either way, he was lost to her closeness. She was not the sort of woman to whom he was normally attracted. With the golden highlights framing her face and the changing color of her eyes, she reminded him of a pixie set upon mischief. The thought brought a wry smile to his lips, but he swallowed his thoughts when a flash of irritation crossed her countenance.

He watched with interest as the lady pushed a stray curl behind her ear. Carter murmured, "Perhaps we should start again." He gently brushed her hand away before catching the loose strand between his fingers. Slowly, he wrapped the hair about his finger. "There is no need for us to be ill friends." He leaned closer, where his lips might graze her temple. His was a primal need. A slow, easy smile tugged at his lips' corners when he heard the delay in her breathing. It was satisfying to know his presence disturbed her as much as hers did his.

"I should go," she said on a rasp, but rather than reaching for the door's handle, the palm of her hand slid up the front of his jacket. He wondered whether she planned to push him away, but she fingered the thread of his badly worn costume.

Carter turned his head to slide his lips along her cheek. "Must you?" he said huskily. "You have yet to forgive me."

Her eyes closed in anticipation. "Forgive?" she whispered, as if she held no knowledge of the word.

Carter used his fingertips to raise her chin. "You are so beautiful." Her eyes blinked several times in an unknowing response, and he used the moment to claim her mouth. Gently. Encouragingly. Testing. A soft sigh of expectation. When she leaned toward him, Carter slid his arms about the lady's waist. The taste of her lips brought the blood to his erection. Although she was tentative, Carter recognized the signs of her desire.

Members of the Realm and Their Ladies

James Daniel Kerrington, Viscount Worthing (Future Earl of Linworth) – the group's "unofficial" leader; resides at Linton Park in Derbyshire

Lady Eleanor Agatha (Fowler) Kerrington, Viscountess Worthing – Kerrington's wife; Brantley Fowler's sister

Brantley William Fowler, the Duke of Thornhill – resides at Thorn Hall in Kent

Velvet Elaine (Aldridge) Fowler, the Duchess of Thornhill – Brantley's wife and distant cousin

Marcus Alexander Wellston, the Earl of Berwick – resides at Berwick Hall in Northumberland

Cashémere Adele (Aldridge) Wellston, the Countess of Berwick – Velvet Fowler's younger sister; twin to Miss Satiné Aldridge

Gabriel Luis Crowden, the Marquis of Godown - resides at Gossling Hill in Staffordshire

Grace Anne (Nelson) Crowden, the Marquise of Godown – former governess for Samuel Aldridge, the Aldridge girls' paternal uncle and guardian for Cashémere Aldridge

Aidan Colin Kimbolt, Viscount Lexford – resides at Lexington Arms in Cheshire

Mercy Elizabeth (Nelson) Kimbolt – the Viscountess Lexford; Grace Crowden's younger sister

John Isaiah Swenton, Baron Swenton – resides at Marwood Manor in York (occasionally uses the courtesy title of Lord Shannon)

Sir Carter Stephan Lowery, a baronet; resides in London, as well as at Huntingborne Abbey in Kent

Lucinda Isabella Rightnour Warren – a war widow; attended the Come Out balls of Eleanor Fowler and Velvet Aldridge as the Duke of Thornhill's guest

Other Characters Important to the Story Line

Aristotle Pennington – the Realm's leader; the group refers to him as "Shepherd"

Murhad Jamot – a Baloch warrior who has been sent to England by the tribal leader, Shaheed Mir, to recover a missing emerald

Rhamut Talpur – Jamot's former partner; was killed by James Kerrington during a kidnapping plot against Brantley Fowler

Sonali Fowler – Brantley Fowler's daughter by his first wife, Ashmita

Captain Matthew Warren – Lucinda's late husband; died during the Napoleonic Wars

Simon Warren – the five-year-old child of Matthew Warren by his first wife

Gideon and Ruth Warren – Matthew Warren's parents; resides in Devon

Colonel Roderick Rightnour – Lucinda's father; passed at the Battle of Waterloo; second son of the Earl of Charleton; resided at Merritt Hall in Devon

Sophia Carrington Rightnour – Lucinda's mother; died of consumption some 5 months after Lucinda married Matthew Warren; was the fourth daughter of Viscount Ross

Lord Gerhard Rightnour – Lucinda's uncle; resides at Charles Place in Lancashire; the current Earl of Charleton

Lawrence and Arabella Lowery, Lord and Lady Hellsman – Carter's brother and sister-in-law; future Baron Blakehell; resides at the Dowager House at Blake's Run in Derbyshire; married in "His American Heartsong" from *His: Two Regency Novellas*

Ernest and Louisa Hutton, the Earl and Countess McLauren – Carter's oldest sister and brother-in-law; resides at Maryborne Park in Lincolnshire

Campbell and Maria Laroche, Viscount and Viscountess Sheffield – Carter's middle sister and brother-in-law; resides at Field Hall in Staffordshire

Stewart and Delia Roxbury, Viscount and Viscountess Duff – Carter's youngest sister and brother-in-law; resides at Roxbury Manor in Warwickshire

Niall and Fernalia Lowery, Baron and Baroness Blakehell – Carter's parents; resides at Blake's Run in Derbyshire

Mr. Dylan Monroe – Carter Lowery's assistant with the Realm

Charles Morton, Baron Ashton – resides at Chesterfield Manor, near Manchester; is the maternal uncle for the Aldridge sisters; former Realm member

Miss Satiné Aldridge – the twin sister of Cashémere Wellston; traveled to the Continent to escape an earlier scandal; was raised by Baron Ashton after her parents' deaths

Hugh Dymond, Viscount Ransing – son of the Earl of Holderman and Lawrence Lowery's long-time enemy

Prologue

Love consists in this, that two solitudes protect and touch and greet each other.
- Rainer Maria Rilke

" I will come for you when this is over." Every time Carter Lowery closed his eyes, he heard the deafening rattle of the explosions, which had raged about him. It had been three months since Waterloo–three months since he had taken a bullet in his thigh–three months since he had promised the boy he would return for him–three months since he had tasted failure.

Carter lazily turned his head to take stock of the situation. This was his first assignment since Belgium, and he meant to prove himself worthy of being one of "Shepherd's flock," which was what the others fondly called their band of the Realm, a secret covert operation of the British government.

Resting upon a low-slung chaise, Carter hoped to portray the appearance of indifference. In reality, his heart pounded loudly in his ears. He had always felt quite invincible, but Waterloo had taught him the fallibility of too much pride and the physical pain of facing his own mortality.

A shuffling of feet off to the left told him something had changed. As casually as possible, he stretched his neck and back in a manner, which would permit him to determine what was amiss. Marcus Wellston and John Swenton exchanged hurried whispers, and Carter followed Wellston's gaze with anxious anticipation.

He swung his legs over the chaise's edge to sit. With another covert stretch Carter palmed a double-edged knife hidden in a pocket of his boot. He could not see clearly what it was that interested Wellston and Swenton so intently, but he knew from the alert slant of their shoulders, it was something of import. Looking to the others, he discovered Gabriel Crowden, the future Marquis of Godown, had slipped into the shadows, while Aidan Kimbolt impatiently palmed a deck of cards.

Carter swallowed his growing fear. Until Waterloo, he had easily engaged in confrontations with the ignorance of youth. He was only a few months older chronologically, but emotionally he felt ancient.

He heard Brantley Fowler say, "I believe I will take a walk. Stretch my legs," and Carter had instantly understood the apprehension found on James Kerrington's countenance. Kerrington "captained" their group and possessed the most experience in the ways of the outlaw bands they sought. Through his service, Carter had found admiration for a man, who still grieved for his late wife. He often thought, *It must be difficult to love so deeply.*

Fowler, on the other hand, irritated Carter. The future Duke of Thornhill was too impetuous—too self-centered, and too anxious to prove himself a hero, which explained what Fowler now intended.

Their Realm band were "guests" of Shaheed Mir, a shady Baloch warlord. Their mission was to secure Mir's cooperation in protecting British outposts along the Indian border with Persia. They had been in the Baloch camp for three days, and for two of those days, they had witnessed Mir's men repeatedly abusing a young girl, likely no more than fifteen years.

The woman's screams had torn at Carter's heart, but he had refused to risk his friends' lives to save her. *Concomitant damage. Just as the boy.* A cold shiver ran down Carter's spine. Was the boy really expendable? If not, was also the girl? The unknown brought bile rushing to his throat.

Before he could wallow further in his misery, chaos erupted. One of Mir's men warned Fowler's steps aside when the duke set a course for the girl's tent. In the blink of an eye, Fowler struck the man with the heel of his hand to the nose, sending the Baloch sprawling upon his backside, while Marcus Wellston shot one of the charging Balochs in the knee, and Crowden knocked another across the width of the tent.

Carter scrambled to his feet, only to be flipped over a Baloch's brawny back. He rolled to the left as his attacker pulled a curved sword from a sheath tied about the man's waist to hack away at Carter.

The blade hissed closed to his nose, missing Carter's face by mere inches, before he reversed his path, rolling to the right. The scene would have been quite comical if part of a theatrical farce, but this was not low comedy: This was life and death. The man jabbed at him before Carter took cover beneath a low table. Despite his many attempts to escape, he remained ineffective, his knife useless against the Baloch's swords.

Then, miraculously, Mir's henchman sprawled beside him on the dirt floor, knocked unconscious. Carter looked up to see Aidan Kimbolt reaching a hand down to him. "No time to rest, Lowery," Kimbolt declared over the din.

Carter angrily shoved the badly damaged table aside before accepting his friend's assistance. "You're a prat, Kimbolt."

"Now!" Kerrington's voice boomed above the melee, and they each broke for the tent's open flap.

"I have it," Carter yelled as he shoved Kimbolt through the opening. He turned to slit the arm of one of their pursuers before flipping the knife over to stab another. Wellston and Swenton rushed past him, while Carter guarded the exit.

"Go!" Kerrington ordered as he and Crowden cut several more of Mir's men low.

Carter turned to race toward the waiting horses. Up ahead he saw Fowler swing into the saddle, while Wellston assisted the girl to the future duke's arms. Lowery caught his stallion's saddle and pulled himself to the seat. Capturing the reins, he turned the animal in a tight circle.

He heard Crowden's call of "Lowery!" Instinctively, he kicked the animals' flanks. He and Crowden would draw Mir's men away so Fowler and the girl could escape. Their band would meet again at the safe house in Bombay in three days.

"Were you injured?" Crowden called over the sound of gunfire.

Carter squeezed his horse's sides with his knees. It would be a torturous death if the Balochs managed to unseat him. "I'm well!" he yelled.

The future marquis grinned as he set his horse to a gallop. "Good. Wouldn't want to have to return to rescue you."

Carter knew Crowden meant the flippant remark as a means to break the tension, but his heart stuttered to a halt. How long had the youth waited for Carter's return before the boy had given up hope? *Dear God,* he silently summoned forth the now familiar prayer, *in your eternal goodness, I beg you to protect the boy I have failed.* He had said the prayer when he awoke in the military hospital and every day since, and Carter would repeat it daily until he knew the boy's fate or until he met the youth in Heaven.

Chapter One

"Harumph!" Carter woke with a jerk. He wiped the sweat from along his upper lip and worked hard to steady his breathing. How long had it been since he had slept a full night? How long since the nightmares had not revisited him with a vengeance? *Forever*, he thought. A set of eyes belonging to a boy, likely not yet in his teens, clung to each of his nightmares. He gulped hard to drive the fear and the regret from his chest.

Tossing the counterpane aside, Carter swung his long legs over the edge of the mattress and reached for the water pitcher. Slowly pouring himself a glass, he inhaled deeply, pushing the images away. Allowing the tepid water to flow across his lips, he swallowed the fears, which had gripped him only moments earlier. The haze lifted, and his eyes focused on the dimly lit room: his chambers at Huntingborne Abbey. Reluctantly, he had returned to the Kent estate he had unexpectedly inherited when Prince George had bestowed a newly minted baronetcy upon him.

The reluctance had nothing to do with his dislike for his hard earned estate. Not at all. Carter held great plans to make it a showplace where he might entertain important political guests and build upon his career. No, the reluctance came from the knowledge his parents would arrive at Huntingborne by mid afternoon. Having his father's company for several days while his parents awaited the ship, which would take the Baron and Baroness Blakehell upon an extended tour of the Continent, was not what Carter would term a "pleasure." Reluctance would arrive with his mother's need to organize his house, a place far from being in pristine condition after the former owner's, Sir Louis Levering, life of debauchery, along with his father's expected lecture regarding Carter's determined interference in bringing his older brother Lawrence together with the lovely American heiress, Arabella Tilney. And finally, reluctance at having

1

to leave his fellow Realm members in Paris, to finish the investigation he had begun into a threat on certain members of the Royal family. An investigation, which had grown colder, despite Carter's best efforts.

"Suppose I should ring for Merriweather," he grumbled, but Carter made no move to summon his valet. Instead, he leaned into the loosely stacked pillows to stare upward into the intricate design of the bed drape. He wondered who had chosen the pattern. Certainly, not he. Likely, one of his sisters. When the news of his fortunate rise to the baronetcy had reached Derbyshire, his father and two of his sisters had rushed to Kent to view the property.

"House is sound," Baron Blakehell had declared after a careful inspection of the manor. "The rooms will require repairs, but you can bide your time and complete one room at a time."

His mother, his three married sisters, and even several of his associates had ferried select pieces of furniture to his door, and Carter had held hopes of pleasing his father with the intricate plans he had developed for the property, but as with every other moment of triumph in Carter's life, Baron Niall Blakehell had quickly lost interest.

The baron had arrived with Carter's sisters in tow and had spent a week, meticulously instructing Carter on what to have repaired immediately and what could wait until later, how to organize the estate ledgers, and what livestock to purchase. His father had even invested heavily in the estate to bring it solvency.

"Thought I had finally discovered the door," he murmured in regret. But Law had sent word of trouble with two of the baron's cottagers, and Baron Blakehell had rushed home to Blake's Run, never to rekindle an interest in his youngest child's progress.

Carter had not held his older brother Lawrence to blame: In fact, the baron had crippled Law nearly as effectively as he had Carter. It was only of late the two brothers had banded together to foil Blakehell's manipulations regarding a pledge to marry off Law to Miss Annalee Dryburgh and her connections to Lord Graham, when Lawrence had obviously affected Miss Dryburgh's cousin, Miss Arabella Tilney. "At least, we placed a chink in the baron's armor," Carter told the empty room.

"Perhaps if Law and I were closer in age," he mused. But his brother had been away at his early years of school before Carter had made his familial appearance. Three rambunctious sisters separated them. Three sisters he adored. A brother Carter admired, but he and Lawrence had traveled separate roads to reach their current understanding.

Lawrence Lowery, Blakehell's heir, had been schooled in all facets of the barony. His brother's every waking moment had known the responsibility of his future title. "Never wanted to be Lawrence," Carter declared honestly as he pushed his exhausted frame from the mattress. "Just wanted to be something more than the spare." Carter reached for the bell cord. "Just wished for my share of the recognition," he admitted to the shadows.

"You rang, Sir?" Merriweather breezed into the room. Carter sometimes thought Darek Merriweather slept less than he.

Despite his earlier maudlin, Carter smiled. "Time to face the day."

Merriweather nodded his understanding before reaching for a towel. "I brought up hot water for your morning ablutions, Sir."

When Carter had withdrawn from his official military service to join the Realm, he had left behind his trusted batman, Francis Sanders, and for some time, he had done without the services of a gentleman's gentleman. With the Realm, he was often in dire straits, and Carter had refused to place another in jeopardy; however, at Waterloo, Merriweather had earned his position, along with Carter's gratitude. From that day forward, Merriweather had served him faithfully. Ironically, it was his friend Gabriel Crowden, the Marquis of Godown, who had claimed Sanders as his man of service, and Carter had been glad of the marquis's kindness.

Lazily, he straddled a chair while Merriweather dutifully applied soap to Carter's cheeks to soften his beard. "I will require a second shave before supper," Carter said distractedly. "His Grace has invited my parents to dine at Thorn Hall."

The lack of a smile upon Merriweather's lips was not apparent in his tone. "As you say, Sir."

Carter rolled his eyes good-naturedly. "As if I had a need to instruct you in your duties."

"As you say, Sir." This time the corner of the valet's mouth tugged upward.

Carter ignored Merriweather's jib. He rarely termed the valet as insolent. They had spent the previous two years together. "I wish to confirm the accommodations for the baron and baroness have been prepared to my specifications. How go the preparations below stairs?" Carter had permitted Merriweather a say in the new hires for the estate.

"Cook has seen to hearty meals, which should please the baron and baroness, and the new maids have spent an inordinate amount of time with cleaning and polishing. You will be pleased."

When his man finished, Carter used the small towel to wipe away the remaining soap. "I am easier to please than is the baron," Carter warned.

His man retrieved the mirror. "It will be enough, Sir," Merriweather assured.

Carter said dejectedly, "It is never enough."

"It is most generous, Your Grace, to see to our pleasure this evening," his mother said honestly.

Brantley Fowler set his wine glass to the side. "We are gladdened to serve as your hosts, Baroness. Sir Carter and his family hold a standing invitation at Thorn Hall. It is the least I could do to recognize my venerable allegiance with Sir Carter, as well as the service your eldest, Lord Hellsman, provided me in the pursuit of my duchess." Carter had always admired the way Fowler could easily talk his way through any situation; perhaps, if he could do likewise, he could persuade the committee overseeing replacing Aristotle Pennington as the Realm's leader to choose him. He and Fowler were the two youngest of their "merry band," although they held little in common except their like shortcoming: the desire to please an impossible father.

"Lawrence has spoken to us of the difficulty you encountered with Viscount Averette," the baron confessed. "It was providential Hellsman was in Derbyshire to provide his assistance."

The duke quickly added, "It was also providential Sir Carter reacted to the urgency of recovering my daughter Sonali so I might concentrate on the duchess's rescue. Knowing Sonali would be in your younger son's most capable hands released me to save my wife."

Carter appreciated his friend's efforts, but he knew his father's nature: Much to the detriment of the other four, the baron thought only of Lawrence Lowery's accomplishments. Niall Lowery was not an abusive father; the baron had never raised a hand to any of his children; yet, each of the siblings had instinctively known his or her role in the family unit.

Ignoring the duke's protests, the baron stated, "Carter is built for impossible quests; his accolades are commonplace. It is when a man, who does not know danger every day, takes on the heroic role that a person's character is truly defined."

Carter's ire rose quickly. It was true; Lawrence had thoroughly distracted Viscount Averette, but his brother's actions could never be compared to what Carter, James Kerrington, and Thomas Whittington had faced in their rescue of Sonali Fowler. They had eliminated a dozen hired assailants to save the child. What irritated him more was the baron gave Carter no credit for the good he performed daily in England's name. The whole situation was incogitant. He opened his mouth to express his discontent, but as she had always done, his mother intervened. She effectively squashed the argument before it began. "All my children possess amiable talents," she declared.

The duchess readily agreed, before adding, "You are fortunate, Baroness, to have your daughters so well placed and for both of your sons to hold a title." Carter grumbled under his breath of how Prince George had termed Carter's efforts worth the notice. His mother squeezed his hand in sympathy. Velvet Fowler continued to direct the conversation. "Tell me of your expected journey. I have often wished to travel, but the duke claims he has seen enough of the Continent for one lifetime."

And so the evening had taken on the mundane topics of politics, fashion, and, of course, every Englishman's least favorite subject: the weather. All three played into the Lowerys' travel itinerary. Carter swallowed his growing need to confront the baron. He had held hopes of finally knowing his father's approval when Carter had orchestrated an elaborate plan to save Law's future thorough bred line, but any goodwill the baron had shared had quickly dissipated when Carter had moved Heaven and Earth to bring Lawrence to Arabella Tilney's door. His brother and Lady Hellsman had retreated to the family's Scottish estate to celebrate their joining. Their withdrawal had occurred nearly a month prior.

As part of his mother's "punishment" for the baron's interference in Lawrence's life, the baroness had declared she and Niall Lowery would make an extended tour of the European continent. Therefore, their current residence under Carter's roof. He knew his father held no desire to travel, but the baron would not thwart his wife's desires; and, likewise, Fernalia Lowery would never relent. The baroness meant for each of her children to know the solace of their father's absence, and for that simple gesture, Carter thanked her.

A cold January wind barreled between the closely packed buildings to send the rotted twigs and leaves skipping along the street. Hundreds of feet smashed everything upon which they trod, as the people rushed to work and errands. Lucinda Warren stepped from the boarding house's front door. Despite the chill, she kept her head high. Her father's voice reminded Lucinda how people never accosted a person who appeared in charge. Glancing about the street, she certainly hoped the colonel had known of what he spoke. Her new quarters had been a major step down from what she had left behind, but she had possessed no choice. She must know economy if she were to survive.

She caught the child's hand and started forward. In the week the boy had remained with her, she could count on one hand the number of conversations they had exchanged. It was not as if the child was disrespectful or even withdrawn. Simon said "thank you," "please," "you are welcome," and "pardon me" on a regular basis; yet, Lucinda knew very little of the boy's early years or of his home. It was as if the person who had deposited the child upon Lucinda's doorstep had instructed the boy not to disclose any information.

"Are you warm enough?" Lucinda glanced toward the child beside her. He half hid in her skirt tails as he scrambled to keep up with her pace. Regretting her haste, Lucinda slowed her step.

Dutifully, the boy said, "Yes, Ma'am." The child had carried a small satchel when she had discovered him outside her door. It contained only two shirts, but Lucinda had taken one of her older gowns and made the boy several serviceable shirts of a dark green color. With each, she had created a lining of a sleeveless shirt for Simon to wear beneath his new ones for an extra layer of warmth. London could be quite brutally cold during the winter months, especially for someone unaccustomed to its dampness, and from the way Simon sat close to the hearth for its warmth, she suspected the boy had known kinder weather in his former home.

She tightened her grip on the boy's hand as they reached the cross street. "Today shall be a short jaunt into our new environs," Lucinda said as she leaned down to assure the child. Flat wagons and horses rushed past in a whirlwind of drab colors. With the boy by her side, Lucinda would require a larger opening to cross through the workday traffic. The child's shorter gait would cause her to adjust her step. "Stay close," she said softly to the child's ear, "and be aware of all the moving carts." The boy nodded his understanding as his eyes grew in size. "After the next wagon," Lucinda announced.

As she stepped from the curb—in anticipation of the their sprint, Lucinda tugged gently to nudge the boy into action. When the wagon cleared their position, she set a quick pace. Thankfully, the boy followed her example. Within seconds, they reached the opposing side, and Lucinda released the breath she held. Pausing briefly, she straightened her shoulders before entering the side street sporting several makeshift stalls, which displayed less than fresh vegetables. She sighed with resignation as she inspected the offerings. The life she had known as a child, one of the country gentry, often felt as if she had been another person completely. When Matthew Warren had announced his intention to buy a commission in the British military, Lucinda had not blinked a lash. Instead, she had accepted her duty, first to finish her years in the schoolroom, and then to follow her husband's unit; after all, she was the daughter of Colonel and Mrs. Roderick Rightnour. Her mother, the fourth daughter of Viscount Ross, had taught Lucinda well.

"Four years of playing the fool," she grumbled. Lucinda pinched her upper thigh through the folds of her cloak and skirt to push away the tears, which pricked her lashes. She leaned down to speak to the boy. "We shall purchase a few potatoes and maybe some cabbage. If you see anything else you may desire, tell me." Again, the child nodded obediently.

Lucinda perused each stall before making her choices. When Simon paused to admire a basket of apples, she purchased one as a treat for after their evening meal. No one who ever observed her and Simon together would think the boy hers. The child's hair, dark, nearly black, while hers a golden blonde, with light brown strands. His eyes were dark and his skin the color of those who spent time in the sun. Her pale skin held gold tones: the contrast often shocked her when she touched the child.

Over the previous week, she had often searched for a bit of her late husband in the Simon, but Lucinda was sore to recognize any of Matthew in the boy. In those weak moments, she would convince herself the rolled and beribboned letter delivered within the child's grasp had been some sort of hoax, but immediately, Lucinda would recognize the truth of the letter's assertions. She knew exactly when Matthew practiced his betrayal. When young Simon had likely been conceived. When her husband had lain with another. The knowledge Captain Warren had preferred a woman, so unlike her, ate away at Lucinda's usual genial composure. It was as if one of the French volleys had landed squarely in her chest, burning its way to her heart.

She had added a bit of flour and sugar and salt to her purchases, as well as bacon and a few eggs. Placing everything carefully in the cloth bag she had brought with her, Lucinda caught Simon's hand again. The boy's fingers were cold. She made a mental note to knit the child a pair of mittens; he would require them if they were to remain together during the winter days, and it was her intention to see to the boy's physical growth. There was a small park nearly a mile's walk, but she would find a ball and permit the child to run freely several times per week. Her father had believed in physical activity, as part of a child's education, for both boys and girls. "No child of mine will be cosseted away behind closed doors," the colonel had often asserted.

"Let us find a bit of warmth," she said encouragingly.

The boy fell in step beside her as Lucinda adjusted her reticule and her packages. "Could we borrow another book?" Simon asked as he tugged gently on her cloak.

Lucinda looked left and right before exiting the side street between two families. "We must wait until tomorrow." She looked harriedly about. The street traffic had increased dramatically since they had entered the small market. "We shall set our rooms to right, but tomorrow, we shall walk to the park and stop at the lending library on our return." Distractedly, she tightened her grip on his hand. "Did you finish the book I brought with us?"

"Yes, Ma'am." The child read beyond his young years. Evidently, the child had had a tutor, something she would never be in a place to provide for him. Just as she had promised to see to the child's physical well being, Lucinda was determined to aid in Simon's studies.

"We must cross again." Lucinda rose on her toes for a better view. "After the coal cart," she announced. Keeping her eyes on the cart, she stepped from the curb, and, as before, she tugged on the child's hand.

"I wish for a book on the war," the child declared boldly. "I wish to know more of my father."

The boy's words caught Lucinda by surprise, and her steps faltered just long enough for the horse traffic to change. A mule brayed loudly as a local vendor used a banded stick to slap its hindquarters. Meanwhile, a small pony bucked at its harness and added to the clatter. Lucinda glanced down at the boy and accelerated her pace, but it was too late. She looked up again as several barrels of beer bumped along the uneven stones before and behind her. She caught the boy into her arms and tossed him into the back of a vegetable cart, just as one of the small barrels slammed hard against her legs. Lucinda fought for her balance: finally, one of those rushing to her aid caught her arm.

"Ye be well?" the snaggled-tooth man implored.

Lucinda flushed with embarrassment as a crowd gathered. The street grew eerily quiet. Righting her stance, she nodded her gratitude to the man, but her eyes searched for the child. "Simon! Simon!" she called out, attempting to see beyond the onlookers. "Simon?"

"Here, Ma'am." The boy elbowed his way through the crowd to bury his tearful face in her skirts.

Lucinda instinctively knelt before the child and wrapped the boy in her embrace. "Are you injured?" she whispered.

A loud snort announced young Simon meant to be strong. "My fault," he hiccupped.

Lucinda caressed the boy's cheek. "It is no one's fault." Her ankle throbbed, and she suspected it would be a bright shade of purple tomorrow. "May we go home?" she whispered, and the child nodded.

Straightening, she acknowledged the crowd. "I am gladdened by your concern for the boy and me. I shall likely experience a tender ankle tomorrow, but the child and I shall recover." She wished desperately to remove her boot to examine her injury. With that, Lucinda took a tentative step forward. She kept a brave face and did not wince.

A plump woman handed Simon his lost hat, and Lucinda made a point of extending her gratitude. Mrs. Peterman, her landlady, met them at their door. "I thought I might require a new letter," the woman announced as she hustled them into the dark hallway. "I sees it all from the window," which likely meant the landlady had spied on her comings and goings.

"We are only a bit roughed," Lucinda assured. "Simon and I shall be right as nails in a few days. Shall we not, Simon?"

The boy kept his eyes downcast, but he answered, "Yes, Ma'am."

Lucinda had permitted Mrs. Peterman to believe the boy was hers. The landlady had asked few questions, and Lucinda had gladly kept her own counsel. "If'n ye require anything ye send the boy down to me," Mrs. Peterman called as Lucinda gingerly climbed the stairs.

"I shall, Ma'am." Lucinda leaned heavily against the rail. "Come along, Simon. I shall require your assistance."

Three days. Carter smiled through the personal pain. For three days his father had turned every conversation to Lawrence Lowery's endeavors. *It is a good thing I love and admire my brother*, he thought ironically. *Or else I might wish to strangle Law.*

"I shall attempt to keep your father occupied," the baroness said softly as they strolled along the wharf. Carter enjoyed the comforting feel of her fingers on his arm, an acknowledgement of her love. When he had served in the East, he had actually missed his mother's good sense and her company. Of course, he had never mentioned such longings to the others. They would have teased him as being a "babe in the womb" and it had been difficult enough to prove him worthy of the honor of being chosen to such an elite group. As his unit's youngest, Carter required not another reason for his mates to label him. "Although I spoke of being away for a year, I suspect six months may be more to the baron's limits."

Carter patted the back of her hand. "I understand, Mother. You are placing your happiness on hold to permit Lawrence to redefine his role as Blakehell's heir."

His mother cackled, "Oh, my darling, Carter." She patted his cheek. "You think we all as altruistic as are you." Her gloved hand caressed his chin. "I would love to claim your goodness, but I must confess I have long wished to see part of the world beyond Derbyshire and London, but Niall has always claimed Blake's Run would suffer in our absence. I unapologetically used Lawrence's situation with Arabella to leverage my own desires. Your father experienced regret at your brother's learning of his manipulations. When I spoke on Law's behalf, the baron agreed to withdraw, and I seized the opportunity to advance my wishes. If I could, I would visit all the lands you have known. You have no idea how envious I have been of your youth and your freedom."

Carter thought of the slums and the palaces he had seen. Both held a country's most devious men. He chose to speak more candidly than usual, "Of course, Father would know remorse at losing control of Law's every thought. His remaining children have known no such care."

His mother's expression tightened with disapproval. "Your father cares deeply for each of his children, and Niall Lowery would walk through fire for you and your siblings." Her lips were taut with emotion. "I cannot deny the baron has been singular in his need to direct Lawrence's steps."

"The baron's compulsion to control Lawrence…" he began.

The baroness stopped suddenly. Her eyes darkened in condemnation. "Carter Stephan Lowery," she said in the way of all mothers when they call their children by their full names. "I shall not hear you speak poorly of your father. You hold no knowledge of why the baron acts upon his compunctions, and, therefore, have no right to criticize."

Carter held her hand over his heart. "Then explain it to me," he pleaded. "I am disposed to know the truth of your narrative."

"It is not my tale to share," the baroness said softly. She caressed his cheek. "Why can you not turn your head to the baron's stubbornness? Your sisters have learned to accept your father's ways. Niall's singularity has caused no real harm."

Carter said incredulously. "Father," he hissed, "meant to make a match between Law and Miss Dryburgh! The baron would have *loved* Lawrence enough to see his eldest son miserable."

His mother protested, "I would have put a stop to the baron's maneuverings."

"Possibly. That is if you had returned to Blake Run's in time to know of Lawrence's dilemma," Carter corrected. "If you recall, you were in Staffordshire for Marie's lying in. By the time you had heard of the match, Law would have been pledged to Miss Dryburgh, and Lawrence would not honorably call off the nuptials. Father would never have tolerated such shame on the family name."

11

"Perhaps," the baroness said enigmatically. "I would like to think Lawrence would have stood his ground."

Carter held both his doubts and his words. "I am pleased Lawrence and Arabella have found each other. I pray my new sister gives Law many sons to secure the future baron's peace."

The baroness whispered, "And I pray the present baron sees those children and knows his efforts to assure the barony's future has come to fruition." Carter could not imagine Blake's Run under anyone but Niall Lowery's care; although he knew his father had not assumed his reign until Carter was well into leading strings; there had been great ceremony when Nigel Lowery passed on, and his only son became Baron Blakehell.

They looked up to observe the baron's approach. His father had personally seen to the loading of their luggage aboard ship. "The ship is sound," the baron announced. Carter wished to remind his father, he had already sent men on board to examine the ship's reliability, but he bit back his protest. Despite their often-contentious nature, Carter would never permit his parents to know danger. His position as "Shepherd's" assistant permitted Carter access to the ship and beyond.

"Captain Orson has an excellent record," Carter assured. "Your journey to France will be a short one. I have sent word ahead. Several of my associates will greet you and escort you to the villa I have procured for your use. You will have access to a chaise and four, as well."

His mother squeezed Carter's arm. "Your diligence on our behalf is duly noted, is it not, Niall?"

The baron's cheeks flushed with color. *From anger or embarrassment?* Carter wondered. "Of course, it is noted," his father said brusquely. "Yet, it is no more than what should be expected from a dutiful son."

Dutiful is crossing each "t," Carter considered. *I have known nothing but duty all my life, but never the much-desired praise for a minor son.* He *dutifully* said, "Then I am pleased to have been of service."

"Come along, Fernalia," his father said. "I would prefer to be one of the first aboard. Less riff raff in the small boats." The baron extended his hand to his wife.

She nodded her agreement before turning to Carter. "You will see to your sisters' cares. They have capable husbands, but I trust no one but you to know what is best for the family. You are my rock–my anchor," she said seriously.

It had always been so. He and the baroness had held a relationship different from all the others. "I will make a nuisance with each," he said with an easy grin. "And I will show Baby Harry a sketch of his grandmother so the boy does not forget his 'Nana' in your absence."

Tears misted the baroness's eyes. "Do not say as such, or I shall press the baron into returning to Field Hall to spend more time with Maria and Sheffield."

Carter placed his mother's hand into the baron's. She wrapped her fingers about her husband's arm. "Enjoy your journey, Mother. You have many years to spoil Baby Harry. It is important to hold no regrets. See part of the world beyond England's shores and know your family adores you." He extended his hand to his father. "Be safe, Sir."

The baron reached into his inside pocket. Removing a thick folded document, he handed it to Carter. "Give this to Lawrence, if, Heaven forbid, an accident occurs. My will addresses the estate and its holdings."

Carter placed the paper inside his jacket. "And this?" he asked curiously.

The baron shrugged away the question. "There is no need unless the unspeakable occurs. I trust you to keep the document in a safe place."

Carter nodded his agreement. "Inform me of your return. If it is available, I will send the yacht."

His mother kissed his cheek one last time before walking away with the baron. Carter was tempted to read his father's words. He possessed the skill to remove the sealing wax and later replace it without anyone knowing of his duplicity, but he could not be so callous as to break his father's trust.

He was nearing his waiting coach when he heard his name called. Carter turned to greet Symington Henderson, one of the Realm's post war recruits. "You sought me out?" he asked as the third son of Lord George Henderson, the Earl of Johnseine, approached.

The man bowed in respect. "Shepherd wished me to locate you. I called in at Kent, and the duke spoke of your escorting your family to Dover."

"What is Shepherd's pleasure?" Carter said sarcastically as he accepted the written instructions from Henderson.

"Something of a suspicious Chinese ship in Liverpool. I am to assist you. Monroe has ridden north to retrieve Baron Swenton," Henderson explained as Carter read Shepherd's missive.

He slid the note into his pocket. "Have you secured horses?"

"Aye, Sir."

"Permit me to give my coachman instructions, and then we will depart."

Henderson nodded his agreement before striding away in the direction of the public stables.

Carter secured his father's papers in a large case under the coach's seat. "Tell Merriweather to send clothing on to Liverpool and to secure these papers in my private safe," he told his trusted footman Bines. "I have no idea how long I will be in the port city. I will send word for you and Merriweather to follow when I know the details."

"Aye, Sir."

"Be of good speed," he instructed. "I prefer not to be long without Merriweather's care."

"Mr. Merriweather will not fail you, Sir."

Carter nodded his farewell and quickly followed in Henderson's footsteps. The man was waiting by the gate with two geldings. Carter accepted the reins of the gray and brown one. He hated to know a saddle so soon; in reality, he had another week of his holiday remaining. He had thought to hire a house-keeper for Huntingborne Abbey while time permitted and to set his small staff to several tasks before returning to his position in London. "So much for well placed plans," he grumbled as he adjusted the saddle's stirrups.

"Mr. Shepherd is quite thorough in his instructions," Henderson ventured.

"Shepherd demands no more of me than I do of myself." Carter declared as he set his foot into the stirrup. Catching the horn, Carter lifted his weight to sit upon the seat, but as he shoved off the unfamiliar horse pranced in place; and Carter released the horn as his foot pulled free. At that same moment, a bullet whizzed over his head.

He spun around to find cover behind a large rain barrel. Henderson was pressed close behind him. Carter scanned the area, but saw nothing unusual.

"My God, Sir!" Henderson said on a thready exhale. "If the horse had not pulled free of your grasp, the bullet would have hit you square in the heart."

Chapter Two

Lucinda wiped at the moisture accumulating on the inside of the thin windowpane. For nearly two months, she had explored every resource at her disposal in determining what she might do to survive her nightmare. "It would have proved more profitable if I could have explained why I wished to know more of Mr. Warren's service in Spain," she grumbled under her breath. She wore several layers to keep warm. Coal cost more than Lucinda could afford, and she and the boy had come to wear much of their respective wardrobes to ward off the chill and the dampness. Turning to the child, she announced, "The rain has stopped. We should see to our errands and a bit of air while we might."

"Yes, Ma'am." The boy obediently retrieved his jacket. It was already too small for the lad. She wondered how she was to provide for the child. Of course, Lucinda could always turn Simon over to the authorities, but the thought of the sensitive, frail boy in one of the orphanages fortified her resolve to find a means to save him. She had considered swallowing her pride and begging her uncle for assistance, but Lucinda doubted the Earl of Charleton would take kindly to her asking for funds to raise a Jewish child belonging to her late husband. No, Lucinda would avoid the rumor of ruin awaiting her on the earl's steps for as long as she could.

Thirty minutes saw her approaching the small park she and the boy frequented when the weather permitted. Mrs. Peterman had presented Simon with a small ball, and the boy enjoyed working it up and down a low hill with intricate footwork. Lucinda brushed off a bench with a handkerchief. "You must stay where I may see you," she cautioned. She always worried on how other children might treat the child. "I shall rest here while you enjoy yourself."

Simon smiled largely. The boy's spontaneity surprised her. He was usually so serious-faced. The gesture made him more childlike. "Thank you, Ma'am."

Lucinda watched him go. The well-worn ball twirling through the brown grass. There were days she cursed the boy's appearance in her life, but she had never cursed the child. It was no fault on Simon's part for what had occurred. "Likely someone would have discovered Captain Warren's perfidy before long," she murmured. Lucinda had taken to thinking and speaking of her late husband as either "Mr." or "Captain" Warren. She meant to distance herself from everything for which Matthew Warren stood.

"Mrs. Warren?" Lucinda looked up to see a freckled-faced young man standing before her. Hat in hand, he bowed awkwardly to her.

A familiar face, Lucinda laughed easily. "Lieutenant Worsley? My goodness. To think we have met again after all these years." She patted the bench beside her. "If you have a few moments, please join me." After Matthew's death and that of her father, Lucinda had quickly come to the conclusion she had no true friends, only a string of acquaintances, who had waltzed in and out of her life. The man standing before her was one such acquaintance.

"I would be honored, Ma'am." With a blush of color on his cheeks, the young lieutenant sat stiffly on the other end of the bench. "I could not believe my eyes when I crossed the street and spotted you upon this very bench," he said on a nervous exhalation.

The man was likely several years older than she, but his actions said otherwise. The former lieutenant was quite discomfited. "How long have you been in London?" she asked in politeness.

"We only arrived this week." He nervously ran his finger along the line of his cravat.

Lucinda nearly felt sorry for him. She had not known Lieutenant Worsley well, but she had always noted how he stumbled over his words when he was in the presence of a woman. She assumed him quite naïve, but that had been years prior. Should not the war have given the man more confidence? "We?" she inquired. "With your family or your betrothed perhaps?" She could not erase the teasing tone from her words. Since coming to London, she had known very little company, and it was good to speak to a familiar face.

Worsley fingered his hat. "Oh, no, Ma'am. I am not the one betrothed, but my sister has made a fine match with Sir Robert O'Dell. Mother insisted we come up from Surrey to have a proper dress made for the nuptials. Mama seems to think I should take in some of the entertainments. She believes I require a wife to ease my way into Society." Lucinda doubted a wife would cure the man's bashfulness. He swallowed deeply. "Is Captain Warren in London also? I would enjoy an evening with someone who speaks of all I have seen. It is sometimes difficult for others to accept honesty in my responses."

Lucinda knew immediate regret. Perhaps, more than shyness plagued the man. Those who served had suffered, even if they had survived the devastation. "I fear Captain Warren met his Maker a year before Waterloo. I am alone in the City. I have only recently left behind my mourning weeds for Mr. Warren and for the colonel." In reality, she wished she had never mourned Matthew's passing.

"Your father also?" Worsley said incredulously.

"Yes, at Waterloo." Lucinda would not tell him how foolishly she had responded when the French approached. Sometimes, she wondered if her father would have survived if she had not acted so uncharacteristically.

They sat in companionable silence for several minutes before the lieutenant said, "You must pardon my familiarity, Ma'am, but I do not understand how you could be permitted to live without the guidance of a man."

Lucinda knew many males would not approve of her actions. "As you have said, Lieutenant Worsley, those who were not on the Continent cannot understand the conditions under which we lived. Even the women who followed the drum hold a different perspective of what is important in life. I fear an afternoon tea with companions speaking of frills and lace holds no attraction for me."

"Are you one of those bluestockings?" Worsley snarled with displeasure. The man must learn to curb his tongue if he meant to find a wife. Where had the lieutenant's timidity gone? Had it all been an act? Or was it she who had erred? Her experience with men had always been related to the war. She had no means of knowing when to speak her mind and when to temper her words.

She said calmly, "I have always been a reader, but I am far from advocating universal suffrage. Moreover, I must insist my life is my own concern." Lucinda reached for her gloves.

The lieutenant stood quickly. "Please forgive me, Ma'am. I have spoken out of turn."

Lucinda noted the remorse upon the man's countenance. "I am not annoyed with you, Lieutenant," she said dutifully, although she was embarrassed to admit how she had come to this moment.

Worsley's Adam's apple worked hard. "I truly meant no disrespect, Mrs. Warren. England has changed much in the decade I was away. I am often at sixes and sevens it seems."

"As are we all," she said compliantly.

He shuffled his feet in place. "Would it be?" Tentativeness had returned. "Would it be acceptable for me to call upon you while I am in London?"

Lucinda stood also. "Your offer is greatly appreciated, Lieutenant, but we should each find a means to return to English society. It would be wrong of us to seek comfort in each other." Her words sounded foolish, but Mr. Worsley nodded his agreement.

"You speak with reason, Mrs. Warren. The captain would have been proud to call you his wife," he declared.

Lucinda kept the scorn from her expression, but not totally from her tone. "I am certain Captain Warren rewarded his wife with his devotion," she said enigmatically. She spoke the truth: Mr. Warren had devoted himself to his wife; the only exception was she was not that woman. She extended her hand to the lieutenant. "I wish you well, Mr. Worsley. Find your happiness and seize it tightly to you."

A look of confusion crossed the man's countenance He accepted her hand and bent to kiss her glove. "I pray I know the happiness you did with Captain Warren, Ma'am."

Lucinda withdrew her fingers from the man's grasp. As a squire's son, Mr. Worsley would do well among the genteel sect. "I pray you know happiness beyond what you observed in my stead."

Carter frowned as he read the missive. Much had happened since he had seen his parents aboard *The Northern Star*. First, he had led an operation, which had confiscated a large supply of opium entering England: then he had set about dismantling the vessel to search for clues to the whereabouts of Murhad Jamot, a known enemy of the Realm. Gabriel Crowden had reported seeing Jamot aboard *The Sea Spray* when they had staged their take over, and although Carter had initially declared his disbelief in the marquis's account, he knew the Marquis of Godown would never have said as such if it were not true.

Thinking on the marquis's report brought Carter a moment of regret, and he prayed he had not permanently damaged his relationship with Lord Godown. His actions had been a great mistake. Carter had fished Lady Godown from the water. The woman and the marquis's elderly aunts had been taken captive; when the marquise had escaped, Godown's wife had attempted an impossible swim for shore in the icy waters off England's coast. As he carried Lady Godown to her husband's waiting arms, an unusual loneliness had invaded Carter's heart.

He had lifted the marquise into his arms before light-footing his way from the small boat to the lower planking. "You do that very well, Sir Carter," Lady Godown had murmured from where her head rested below his chin. "I imagine you are an excellent dancer."

The woman's words had brought a smile to Carter's lips. It had felt a lifetime since he had experienced the teasing tone of a handsome woman. He had admitted, if only to himself, to enjoying the warmth of Lady Godown's breath against the base of his neck. At the time, he had wondered how it would feel to carry his own wife into his bedroom and to know the happiness the other of his unit had discovered. Without thinking, he had kissed the soft fuzz at the crown of Lady Godown's head. "I will not fail you," he had whispered hoarsely as he climbed the irregular steps leading to the main docks. "In truth, I will prove myself an excellent partner. Promise you will save me a dance at the first ball of the Season." A gnawing longing had caught in his chest. Carter had looked up from where his lips grazed Lady Godown's hair to see Crowden's approach.

He gave his head a mighty shake. "Almost as great an error as that fiasco at Waterloo," he chastised. The missive he held in his hand would only add to the chaos of late. It was from his assistant at the Home Office: Rumors of "Shepherd's" leaving his post sooner than expected had spread quickly among Lord Sid mouth's staff. Carter frowned. Unlike many of those not of the "inner circle," he was well aware of Shepherd's, whose real name was Aristotle Pennington, interest in the Marquis of Godown's Aunt Bel: Rosabel Murdoch, the Dowager Duchess of Granville. He even held hopes that those in power might consider him for Pennington's replacement. Carter wondered how Pennington's leaving would affect the Realm. If he did not earn the post, he was not certain he wished to follow another's orders. "How would someone else know as much as Shepherd?" he murmured. "Shepherd has knowledge beyond the field. He has defined the Realm's role in the world."

He stared out the window at the harbor. Carter had been in Liverpool since before Twelfth Night, and he was exhausted by the tedium. It was odd: he was the youngest of their band, but it was he who had assumed the duties of King and country. The remainder of his group had sought relief in home and family, while he had looked to his occupation to fill the long hours. "Somehow, Kerrington, Fowler, and Wellston have proved more successful than I," he told the empty room. "I thought I had the right of it…"

The sound of the explosion sent Carter diving for protection. The smell of gunpowder filled the air. Splinters of wood flew past as he instinctively covered the back of his head with his hands. He landed face down on the dirt floor of the warehouse, which the Realm had procured as his headquarters while in Liverpool. A whish of hot air brushed his scalp.

"Sir Carter!" Symington Henderson called as he rushed into the room. Carter did not move, mentally checking each of his limbs for injury. The young lord knelt beside him. "Sir Carter?" Henderson said anxiously. "Are you injured, Sir?"

Carter slowly lowered his hands and pushed upward to sit on his knees. His ears still rang from the impact, and the smell of heated smoke brought back images he had worked hard to squelch. He retrieved his handkerchief to wipe his face and hands. Over his shoulder was a gaping hole in the side of the building, which looked out upon the busy dock. "I appear to be in one piece." Carter's voice trembled, and his breath came in short bursts. A crowd had gathered on the other side of the opening to peer into the small office.

Henderson supported Carter to his feet. He swatted away the dust on Carter's shoulders. "I have sent agents to investigate," Henderson assured.

Carter nodded his gratitude. "Have them ask if anyone saw a stranger in the area." His voice held more authority than he expected.

"I will see to everything, Sir." Henderson began to gather the papers strewn about the room. "Perhaps you should call in at the Golden Apple and refresh your things," Henderson suggested cautiously.

Carter raised an eyebrow in dissatisfaction. "I do not require a nurse," he said adamantly, but a small voice in his head said, *But my mother's presence would be soothing. Why is it*, he thought, *we wish our mother's comfort when the world sends us its worst?* He had heard more than one soldier, while lying wounded upon the battlefield, calling out for his mother.

Henderson halted his efforts. "But, Sir. You must feel the ticking clock," he declared. "After all, this is your third encounter with death in a little more than six weeks. You cannot think to remain invincible forever."

Lucinda had permitted the boy to choose two new books at the makeshift lending library. It was an expense she tolerated. Although but five years of age, Simon devoured books, and they had come to a routine of sorts: she read several chapters of a compelling adventure to the child at night, and the next day, the boy would reread the pages, sounding out the words he did not recognize immediately. Young Simon often carried the book to her and asked Lucinda to pronounce a difficult word. As foolish as it sounded, she believed the child memorized the passages.

She glanced down at the boy. He was an odd one—so mature and yet so innocent. Simon had never questioned why he had been deposited upon her doorstep. He had never complained about the pallet she had made for him before the fire nor of the less than palpable meals she managed to place before him. Lucinda supposed the child's good nature was the reason she tolerated Simon's obsession with books. *Books and the carved wooden horse, which had been among the child's belongings when he had arrived upon her doorstep.*

Early on, she had attempted to question the boy on what he could recall of his previous life, but whoever had sent Simon to her had schooled the child well. Lucinda would not even consider the possibility Simon held no memories of what came before: the child was too intelligent.

Lucinda meant to set her key to the lock of the double rooms she let in the Peterman's household, but the door stood ajar. Instantly, she was on alert. She knew, without a doubt, she had locked the door. She had handed the two books she meant to return to the lending library to Simon to hold while she pulled the door closed and gave the lock a solid shake before releasing it.

"Stay here," she whispered sternly to the boy, who had gone all wide-eyed. "If you hear anything unusual, run for assistance. Do you understand me?"

Simon nodded several times.

Lucinda swallowed hard and stood slowly. She caught the latch in her trembling hand and edged the door open. Through the narrow crack, she could see her few belongings strewn about the room. Her heart clutched in her chest. She wished she had had some sort of weapon.

Glancing back at where the boy clung to the wall opposite, she mouthed, "Be prepared. I mean to check what is inside." Simon appeared less frightened.

Slowly, she turned to face the slender slit. With the palm of her hand, she shoved hard against the flat surface, and the door swung wide to bang against the inside wall. Both she and the child jumped with the sound. Catching at her heart with her hand, Lucinda stepped into the dimly lit space.

Whoever had entered her rooms had pulled the drapes nearly closed to block the view from the buildings across the way. Lucinda edged forward, circling the room, her back to the wall. Carefully, she sidestepped over the blocks scattered upon the floor. Without turning her head from the room, she caught the heavy drape and carried it backward to permit the late afternoon sun to invade the space before tying it off with a ribbon she had found discarded upon the floor.

She looked up to see Simon clinging to the doorframe. Motioning the boy to remain in his place, Lucinda began a more serious search. Even though she thought it foolish to do so, she knelt to peer beneath the bed. Next, she searched the wardrobe and behind the standing screen; finally, Lucinda moved through the small dressing room, which ran the width of her one large room.

Finding nothing unusual, other than the disarray, Lucinda released the pent up breath she had not known she held. "Simon, would you ask Mrs. Peterman to come to our rooms. We should speak to the constable."

His voice wavered, but the child agreed. When the boy disappeared into the house's passageway, Lucinda scrambled to her secret hiding place. She quickly worked the board free under the small side table to retrieve her bag of coins. Peeking inside, she was relieved to find the coins still in the cloth bag.

The sound of approaching footsteps sent her in motion. She would count the coins later, when the boy had gone to sleep. Shoving the bag into the small opening, she slid the board into place just as Simon burst through the open door, followed closely by Mrs. Peterman.

"Oh, my Girl," the matron wailed as she clutched a handkerchief to her lips. "I have never…" The landlady braced her stance by clasping the back of a chair.

Although still shaken, her ever practical self said, "I think it best we contact the authorities."

Mrs. Peterman frowned dramatically. "I am certain this is an anomaly; there is no reason to involve the constable."

"Someone invaded my room," Lucinda said incredulously. "A person climbed two flights of stairs, worked my lock free, and then shuffled through my belongings." Her voice rose quickly as her pulse throbbed in the veins of her neck.

The landlady glanced about the room to the disarray. "Are you certain you locked the door?"

Lucinda swallowed her retort. Despite the disaster of the moment, the rooms were reasonably price. "Ask the boy." She kept her countenance expressionless. "He held my package while I secured the door." She caught her personal wear from a pile on the floor and shoved the items into a now empty drawer. "Someone targeted my room," she insisted.

Mrs. Peterman waved away Lucinda's protest. "I imagine whoever it was simply tried all the doors until he found one he could manipulate. I cannot say I am surprised. I have warned Mr. Peterman we should lock the main door to the house at all times. There are so many men without occupations roaming the streets these days."

Lucinda's shoulders slanted defiantly. "Then you mean to do nothing?"

The landlady pulled herself up to her full height. "I mean to send Mr. Peterman to repair the door. Unless you have lost a fortune, Mrs. Warren," the woman said threateningly, "calling on the authorities would waste their valuable time and show poorly on my household. I shall not have word be known upon the street I do not keep a secure establishment."

Lucinda bit the inside of her jaw to keep from speaking out against the injustice. Instead she said, "If you will ask Mr. Peterman to have a look about the place, I shall be satisfied."

Mrs. Peterman smiled falsely. "Naturally, my Girl." She gestured to the clutter. "When you have set the rooms aright, you and young Simon should join me for tea. I always enjoy your conversation."

"Thank you, Ma'am," Lucinda said respectfully. She had thought she had discovered a place where she and the boy could live out their middling lives. For all she knew, the culprits could easily be the Petermans, rather than an outsider. She must remind her foolish self never to trust anyone. Lucinda had trusted her parents to arrange a comfortable marriage for her, and she had trusted

Matthew Warren to act the role of husband. She would learn her lessons well: No one would know her loyalty ever again.

The nightmare had returned, only this time with a twist. As always, the blood was everywhere, and the acrid smell had filled his lungs. Screams of pain echoed in his ears, but the smoke had parted, and the boy had been there. His cheeks covered with mud, the youth had cringed behind the fallen horse. The French charged their position, and Carter had known real fear. He was not supposed to be at Waterloo; he had sold his commission to join the Realm some fifteen months prior, but when Wellesley had personally asked for his assistance, Carter had readily agreed.

"You men, form a line along the ridge!" he had shouted above the noise of the cannons.

Although he no longer wore a military uniform, the voice of authority had remained. British soldiers scrambled to do his bidding. Men limped and crawled to a defensive position with the hill at their backs. Whoever had been these men's commanding officer had made a strategic error: They were too exposed.

"Come with me," he had commanded as he reached for the lad, who had not moved with the others.

The youth's cinnamon-colored eyes were the most compelling ones Carter had ever seen. "My father?" the boy's voice had squeaked.

Carter had looked about him: Nothing but bodies and destruction everywhere. Why would any father permit his son to view the slaughter that was war? The French advanced with a flourish, and time was of an essence.

"Your father would expect you to live," he had said defiantly. Catching the lad by the arm, he had dragged him along behind him. When they had reached the line, Carter had shoved the boy behind a tree. "Stay hidden!" he had ordered. "I will come for you when this is over." Without looking back, he had stridden away to oversee the rag-tag group of soldiers.

They were outnumbered five to one, but as the French broke into a run, Carter had rallied the men. "No hoity toity Frenchie is to cross the line. Do you hear me? No Frenchies beyond this point. They are soft. They possess half the heart of an Englishman. Now do your duty. For King George and Country and for your loved ones in England! Do it now, or you will see your children speaking French!"

As the squares formed, he had glanced to where he had left the boy. A bit of the youth's shirt had shone behind the tree, and Carter had wondered if either of them would survive the day. "It was the last you saw of the boy," he whispered in bitter regret. Carter had taken a bullet in the leg and had been removed from the field at the battle's end. What with the blood loss and the fever, it had taken him weeks to recover. When learning of Carter's injury, Shepherd had whisked Carter away to a safe house, where he spent countless days and nights reliving each harrowing moment of the battle. By the time he had walked away from the secret facility, he held no idea where to search for the youth.

Somehow, the unit of which he had assumed command had lost only five good Englishmen during the melee, while the French had lost over a hundred before sounding a retreat. Theirs had been but a single skirmish in a chaotic campaign, but Wellesley had proclaimed Carter a hero.

"Never felt the hero," he grumbled as he swung his legs over the bed's edge. "I failed the boy."

Chapter Three

"Why did the viscount not ask for my assistance?" Carter said tersely.

John Swenton smirked, "It was you who sent me to warn Lexford of Jamot's presence in Cheshire."

Carter jammed his fingers into his hair. "That crazy Baloch has caused us enough grief." He stared out the window of his London office. "What did Lexford release you to say?" Swenton had returned to Town with news Aidan Kimbolt had discovered several unsavory truths regarding his family history. Despite being scandalous in nature, the realizations had reportedly discharged Lexford from his past. "I can only say being free of the guilt of his late wife's memory, Lexford has fallen in love with a woman none of us knew existed, and I have promised Lexford I would secure a special license for the viscount's speedy joining."

"Miss Purefoy?" Carter asked, thinking of the woman of whom Lexford spoke so highly when last they had met.

Swenton continued with an ironic chuckle. "Lexford has sworn me to absolute secrecy. The viscount and Hill have ridden to Lancashire to prevent a wedding. If Lexford proves successful in rescuing his ladylove, he is to meet me at Linton Park. I had not thought to involve the others, especially with Pennington's betrothal party this evening; yet, the bishop has denied my request in Lexford's name."

Carter shrugged off the crisis. He would learn the full of it when the time arrived. "Then let us retrieve the others before we speak to the bishop again. If there is any chance Lexford has tasted happiness, then we must have the bishop's approval."

"Viscount Stafford waits below. I asked him to join us. It seemed only appropriate after Stafford walked away from a card game he could have easily won in order to offer me a means of reaching London in a timely manner."

"Lord Godown will not approve." Carter smiled with the possibilities. "Although I enjoy it when the marquis's finely honed composure is ruffled, perhaps we should not inform Godown of what we plan." Swenton shrugged his approval. "I will seek out the earl."

"You mean to call upon the earl for what purpose?" Aristotle Pennington filled the open door with his form.

Carter shot a quick glance to Swenton. A nearly imperceptible nod from the baron spoke his permission for Carter to explain to the Realm leader their mission. "Lexford has set himself the task of rescuing the woman who has captured his heart. The viscount and Lucifer Hill ride to Lancashire. Swenton and I mean to convince the bishop to issue a special license so the pair may marry at Linton Park. Otherwise, Lexford means to race toward the Scottish border."

Swenton explained, "The viscount wished to keep his quest secret, but the bishop turned away my unusual request."

Pennington's mouth twisted into an ironic smile. "Did he now?" He nodded to Carter. "Permit me to retrieve my hat and gloves. As my days as the head of this unit are numbered, I suspect it is time I use my authority more freely."

An hour later, as a unit, they had entered the bishop's office. The elderly cleric's countenance betrayed his surprise at having the Duke of Thornhill, the Earl of Berwick, Viscounts Worthing and Stafford, Baron Swenton, Aristotle Pennington, and Sir Carter Lowery upon his threshold. Needless to say, after viewing the grand audience before him, the bishop's objections faded quickly.

"I will leave you to it," Carter overheard Pennington whisper to Swenton. "Call on me before you depart for Derbyshire. I mean to know the truth of what has occurred at Lexington Arms."

Swenton appeared uncomfortable. "I have sworn an oath of silence to Lexford."

Pennington settled a hard gaze on the baron, and Carter smiled to see the stoical Swenton drop his eyes in submission. The authority displayed by Pennington did not come easily to Carter, and he wondered if he could ever replicate the magnificent line of Pennington's brow in disapproval. "And I have requested the truth of what has occurred in the life of one of my best agents. How may I protect the viscount if I know not the depth of Lexford's agony?"

Swenton said softly, "I will come to you before the ball." Again, Carter questioned his ability to do all Pennington did for the Realm members. "Shepherd," as he and the others fondly called Pennington for his ability to gather "lost souls" and change them into some of the best agents in the world, appeared to recognize what those who served the Realm required most in their lives to know success on missions and happiness at home. For not the first time, Carter wondered if he could accept the life and death decisions Pennington made on a daily basis.

Carter looked on with amusement as Lord Stafford declared, "As I am a viscount, I hold no qualms in signing in Viscount Lexford's stead. After all, I have met his lady and have witnessed his true regard for the woman."

The bishop stammered, "I...I require...the lady's name...for the license."

All eyes fell on Swenton; he said sheepishly, "Mercy Nelson."

While the others gasped, Carter placed the pieces of the puzzle together. "Not Mary Purefoy?" he asked.

"Yes to Mary Purefoy, and yes to Mercy Nelson. One and the same," Swenton admitted.

Worthing questioned, "The missing sister of the marquis's wife?"

The baron confirmed, "By accident, Hill discovered the girl on the road and rescued her. It is a long, complicated story, to which Lexford has demanded my tight lips. The viscount fears failure and does not wish to appear a fool for giving his heart to a woman who does not return his regard. In truth, I believe the viscount fears being duped, as he was with Susan."

Worthing ordered, "Finish the bishop's work, and then we will dine together. We should each own an understanding of the viscount's pain."

In the end, Swenton had confessed more than what the viscount had released him to do. It was decided among them that Swenton would accompany the Worthings to Linton Park on the morrow. Swenton had promised to greet Lexford with the special license in hand.

"I pray the viscount does not experience more failure," Yardley said with real concern. "Lexford appeared quite solemn when he joined Lady Yardley and me at Chesterfield Manor."

Carter suggested, "We will follow, but with a day's delay. If Lexford has not known success, send word, and we will remain from Derbyshire. We will permit the viscount time to grieve and to save countenance."

The others had agreed Carter had chosen wisely. Yardley reasoned, "Worthing and Swenton can tend to Lexford's bruised ego if he does not manage to prevent his lady from marrying another."

Although he had suggested they have an alternative plan, Carter did not like all the long faces. "It appears to me, we have taken the negative slant. Instead of saying 'if,' I suggest we substitute 'when.' We should recall we speak of Aidan Kimbolt, a man who is capable of doing the impossible. I can think of few others I would trust more than Viscount Lexford to play the role of Claudio to claim his Hero."

Worthing nodded his agreement. "Without Lexford's unique ingenuity, I would have lost Lady Worthing. I owe the viscount my devotion." They drank a round in salute to a man they each called "friend." However, Worthing did add one caution. "We should mention none of this to the marquis until we know the outcome. Godown suffers enough with his wife's absence. I would not give him false hopes of finding Grace Crowden. I fear the woman means never to return to her home. When Lexford claims Mercy Nelson as his own, then I will inform Godown of the development."

"What do we tell the marquis of Lexford's absence if he asks?" Yardley inquired.

"I will think of something appropriate. Likely a half-truth, which is much more effective than a prevarication," Worthing assured.

The months had passed quickly, but she was no closer to discovering the truth of Captain Warren's perfidy than she was the day she had opened the door to find the child. Since the invasion of her rooms, Lucinda had taken extra care in securing both the door and the windows. As best she could tell, the only thing missing from the earlier break in had been one of the papers in the small pouch the boy had carried.

Obviously, whoever had intruded upon her quarters had known of the child's existence and the fact she had become Simon's temporary guardian.

Temporary, she thought with an incongruous snigger. "Temporary" would denote a beginning and an end, but no end to her guardianship was in sight. Simon Warren had been with her since shortly after Christmas, and April had arrived in London. "Nearly three months," she murmured. "Not so impermanent, after all."

Each day Lucinda had feared a representative from the British government would appear at her door and demand she repay the widow's allowance provided her as Mr. Warren's wife. She would have no means to support herself or the boy if that scenario occurred.

In addition, she had come to fear someone meant either her or Simon harm. When the barrels had worked loose from the cart and injured her ankle, Lucinda had thought nothing of it–simply an accident. But then came the break in, which was followed by several bricks dislodging from a rooftop and landing at her and Simon's feet, as well as the mysterious man she had observed matching their pace but on the opposing street whenever she and the child went about their daily routines. It was with this realization Lucinda had decided to swallow her pride and seek the assistance of the one person she knew would hold great sway in Society and with the government: Brantley Fowler, the Duke of Thornhill.

"May I visit with Mrs. Peterman?" Lucinda looked up from her stitches to find the boy standing before her. She often wondered in moments such as these if she held no maternal instincts. In the few months of their acquaintance, Lucinda had never once hugged the child nor even ruffled his tightly curled hair. She had never mistreated Simon, and she was certain she would defend the boy with her life; yet, every time she looked upon his countenance a twinge of regret stabbed her heart. Matthew Warren had never thought enough of her to permit Lucinda to know the completeness of holding her own child.

"Have you completed your lessons?" she asked devotedly.

"Yes, Ma'am." He dropped his eyes, a characteristic which irritated her.

"Simon, look at me," she said more tersely than she intended. "Is there something I should know?"

The boy's bottom lip quivered. "It is only…I have never…never read from your Bible."

Lucinda's frown lines met. "I know so little of your religion, and I did not wish to make decisions for you until we know whether a member of your family will return for you." The child nodded his understanding, but Lucinda was certain he held no idea of the quandary in which they found themselves. "If you remain with me, I shall have no choice but to bring you into Christianity. I hold no knowledge of Jewish beliefs, but I do know anything outside the Church of England is frowned upon among the British citizenry. I would not have you know the pain of rejection. If I am to continue as your guardian, I must protect you."

The child's eyes grew in size. "You do not...you do not despise me?"

Lucinda tutted her condemnation. "Of course, I do not abhor you. You are as much a victim in this madness as I." Instinctively, she straightened the child's shirt. "We shall muddle through this together." She gently flicked a single tear from Simon's cheek. It was the first time she had seen him cry. "Now, go off and enjoy the tales Mrs. Peterman spins."

"She is making apple tarts today," he confessed.

Lucinda wondered how her landlady could afford the makings for apple tarts. Evidently, Mr. Peterman managed quite well with his finances. She smiled easily at the boy. She had suspected his possessing an underhanded motive to spending so much time with their landlady. "If Mr. Peterman has finished with his newspaper, ask him if I may borrow it."

Simon declared, "Mrs. Peterman says you are seeking employment."

"Allow Mrs. Peterman her delusions," Lucinda returned to her sewing.

When the boy slipped from the room, she murmured. "I just pray the duke returns to Town soon. I am uncertain I possess the ability to keep the boy safe and to maintain my sanity without a 'knight in shining armor' riding to the rescue."

Lucinda had stood on the busy street corner for a quarter hour, attempting to shore up her nerves. She had carefully read the social register for the past few weeks, waiting for the return of the Duke of Thornhill to his London townhouse. A single line of type had reported Brantley Fowler's presence at Briar House, and Lucinda had wasted no time in sending a note around, requesting an audience with the duke. Thornhill had responded immediately, setting the date and time.

Self-consciously, she checked Captain Warren's pocket watch for the time. She regularly carried her late husband's watch in her reticule. It was one of the few items she had kept to mark her days as Mr. Warren's wife. "Time," she murmured. *Matthew never found the time to speak the truth*, Lucinda thought bitterly. As she set her shoulders to cross the street, she wondered how Thornhill would take to her report of his old friend. *I have no choice*, she assured her rapid pulse.

She sidestepped a fresh pile of horse dung while dodging a young gentleman's poorly driven curricle to step upon the curb before Briar House. It was a magnificent house: plenty of windows to permit the light and warmth of even a weak sun, as well as beautiful columns giving the exterior the look of a Roman theatre. Briar House spoke to the Fowlers' place in Society. Her breath hitched, and Lucinda chastised herself for the very feminine desire to break into tears again. Her eyes swept the townhouse's façade. Splendor she would never know.

With a deep steadying breath, she entered the gate and ascended the few steps to release the knocker. In less than a minute, the door swung wide to reveal the duke's very proper butler. "Yes, Miss?"

Lucinda swallowed hard to clear his throat. "I am Mrs. Warren. His Grace is expecting me."

The butler's eyebrow rose as he peered behind her to search for her maid, but it had been more than a year since Lucinda could afford help of any kind. She supposed she could have borrowed Nancy's services from Mrs. Peterman, but Lucinda did not want her gossipy landlady to know of her destination. Despite feeling very self-conscience, she pretended not to notice the servant's disapproval. "This way, Mrs. Warren," the butler said diplomatically.

Lucinda politely followed the man up the stairs and along an elaborately decorated passage. She had attended the Come Out ball for Thornhill's sister, Lady Eleanor Fowler, and his cousin, Miss Velvet Aldridge, in this house. Now, Miss Aldridge was Brantley Fowler's duchess, and by all accounts the man's one true love. Yet, on that one evening, Lucinda had received the duke's attentions, and although she had been a bit uncomfortable with Thornhill's sudden adoration, the evening remained one of Lucinda's favorite memories. A man of worth had revered her intelligence and her good sense. A well-placed gentleman had found her attractive, something Mr. Warren had never done.

The butler tapped on an already open door. "Your Grace. Mrs. Warren to speak to you." The man stepped aside, and Lucinda entered a very masculine study. Dark wood panels spoke of a strong mind and an unqualified determination, both of which could easily describe the Duke of Thornhill.

The duke rose to greet her. His light brown hair was peppered with strands of gold. It was unstylishly long and tied back with a leather strap. Eyes of darkest chocolate glittered with genuine welcome, and Lucinda breathed a bit easier. "Thank you, Mr. Horace. If you will ask Cook to send in tea."

"Of course, Your Grace."

Brantley Fowler caught Lucinda's hand and brought it to his lips. "I was pleased to hear from you," he said easily, "but I admit you have piqued my interest." Lucinda had always liked Brantley Fowler. The future duke had spent but two months in the same company as had Lucinda's late husband; and during the brief interval, Fowler and Mr. Warren had renewed their university acquaintance. She was proud to say the young lord had always treated her with respect. She was the daughter of the younger son of an earl, and the future duke accepted her as his equal socially. In fact, once when Captain Warren had found fault with the meal she had managed on the few supplies available, it had been Brantley Fowler who had taken up her defense.

"I appreciate your greeting me on such short notice, Your Grace." The duke led her to a nearby settee before assuming the seat across from where Lucinda sat. "I beg your forgiveness for my bold gesture."

The duke frowned. "I would hope you would view me as an ally, Lucinda." His ready familiarity eased her tension.

The butler returned with the tray. "Mrs. Warren will serve, Horace."

"As you wish, Your Grace." The butler closed the door upon his exit.

Lucinda dutifully took up the service. This cup would be a treat for her. Her meager funds did not stretch to expensive tea and what Mrs. Peterman served was less than desirable. The duke must have read her mind for he said, "My sister Eleanor's husband, Lord Worthing, declares he spent seven years of service to his country without a decent cup of tea."

Lucinda nodded her understanding. "Even on English soil," she said as a means to define her purpose in coming to Briar House, "many cannot afford the weak mix with which we suffered on the Continent. The military's idea of tea is less than inspiring, but it would be welcome in many English households."

A long pause kept Thornhill silent. The air was thick with nerves and unspoken truths. Finally, the duke asked, "Are you among those who cannot afford such luxuries?"

Lucinda had always prided herself on her frankness. She had come to beg Thornhill for his support, and the duke deserved the truth, as she knew it. "I am, Your Grace," she said more calmly than she felt.

Setting his cup aside, the duke sat forward bracing his arms along his thighs. He cocked his head as if seeing her for the first time, and Lucinda fought the urge to squirm under the man's close scrutiny. He said with concern, "When last we met, you spoke of a small settlement from your mother and, of course, your widow's pension. Had I known…"

Lucinda cut off the duke's offer. "I am not your responsibility, Your Grace, and a pity call was not my purpose this day."

He jammed his knuckles into the side of his leg. Thornhill held a reputation for rescuing "damsels in distress." It was one of the reasons Lucinda had sought his assistance. "But what of your parents? Or of the Warrens?"

She cleared her throat and hoped her voice did not betray the chaos rushing through her veins. "My mother passed some five months after my marriage to Mr. Warren. The colonel lost his life in Belgium." She could not hide the grief, which tugged heavily at her heart. Losing her father had come close to sending her over the edge, both figuratively and literally. She still blamed herself for not protecting him. "I would prefer not to seek the assistance of the Earl of Charleton. The colonel and Uncle Gerhard were often at odds. I would not wish to claim the role of poor dependent." Lucinda did not think her father's oldest brother would take kindly to the situation in which she now found herself.

"And the Warrens?" the duke prompted. His words caused her heart to stutter. Every time she thought of Matthew Warren's betrayal she wished to curse the heavens.

Lucinda schooled her expression. Her husband's parents had turned from her after their son's death. At the time, she had not understood the reasons the Warrens had placed distance between them. Captain Warren's parents had pledged their only child to Lucinda when they were but babes, and the Rightnours had gloried in the connection. She felt the shame for her parents' hopes. Although she could not say she had loved Matthew Warren, she had always held her husband in great affection; they had been friends for as long as she could recall. "Father Warren has indicated I am no longer welcome at Coltman Hall."

The duke's mouth formed a thin line of disapproval. "I had once thought Warren's parents perfect in every way," he confessed.

Lucinda thought, *Perfect in their outward displays, but greatly lacking in essentials.* "If you hold no objections, Your Grace, I would care to speak to the reasons for my calling upon you."

"By all means." The duke leaned back into the chair's cushions. "I am your servant."

The nerves she had earlier tamped down had roared to life again. A thousand frightening scenarios flitted through her brain. Purposefully, Lucinda took another sip of the tea. It really was quite lovely to taste the bitter leaves. Setting the cup on the tray, she caught Fowler's gaze and held it. "Some five months past, I was presented a most difficult situation. I opened the door to my let rooms to discover a small boy of some five years of age sitting upon the threshold. There were no adults about and upon investigation, no one knew of how the child came to wait outside my quarters."

"Was there no identification?" Thornhill inquired earnestly.

Lucinda set her shoulders in a stiff slant. She dreaded what was to come, but the duke would accept nothing less than the absolute facts. "Only a note pinned to the child's jacket." When the duke did not respond, she continued. "The note announced the child to be Captain Warren's. By his wife, a woman he had married in '09, some two years before he returned to Devon for the pronouncing of our vows." Lucinda kept part of the truth as her own special torment. She did not tell him the complete facts of the child's mother.

"With whom has the child resided over the past five years?" Fresh despair filled Lucinda's heart. It was natural for people to assume Simon's mother had passed before Mr. Warren had taken Lucinda as his wife.

"Simon's mother held the boy's responsibility. The first Mrs. Warren met her end shortly before the child appeared upon my doorstep," she explained with an acerbic smile.

The duke appeared perplexed. "How may that be so? You are telling me, Matthew Warren took another without his parents' knowledge?"

Lucinda had asked herself that very question repeatedly. "I would hope the Warrens did not knowingly foist a sham of a marriage upon me." She forced the tremble from her words.

The duke was up and pacing. "I have heard of such deceit, but I would never place Matthew Warren among those who would practice duplicity. He was my guest several times at Thorn Hall when we were at university. The extent of this falsehood is of the gravest debasement."

Lucinda said softly, "The boy was conceived after our joining." She would not permit the duke to observe how the thought of her husband with another woman had ripped her heart from her chest; yet, she had cried her last tear for the soul of a dishonest man.

Thornhill dejectedly returned to his seat. "This is all too much." With a heavy sigh, he asked, "Where is the child now?"

Lucinda glanced to the sun streaming through one of the windows. There was only one window in her rooms, and she sorely missed fresh air upon her countenance. *Too many years of following the drum,* she thought. "Today, young Simon is with my landlady. The child resides with me." Again, she withheld an important fact from Thornhill, one that would color everything with a black stroke.

The duke set forward again. "You have taken it upon yourself to care for the offspring of your husband's betrayal?" he asked incredulously. "You must realize, Mrs. Warren, your raising this child within your home will bring you ostracism. You are opening yourself to public humiliation when this situation becomes common knowledge."

Lucinda fought back the tears stinging her lashes. "The child has the right to know a touch of love. I could not turn the boy out on the streets nor could I place him in a foundling home; yet, it is Simon's presence, which has brought me to your door. The child has complicated my life in ways I could not anticipate. If Mr. Warren married another before speaking his vows to me, I am not his widow, and my only source of income for the boy and me has vanished into a foggy London sky. I require someone to discover the truth of the note's claim. I can easily voice a myriad of questions, but I possess no resources to discover the answers."

Thornhill caught Carter's arm. "I need to speak to you." Their group had returned to Linton Park for yet another wedding: This time it was for Henry 'Lucifer' Hill, the unofficial eighth man of their group. In the three months since they had last converged upon Worthing's threshold, much had happened. Lexford had known success with Miss Nelson, and the two had not lost the glow of marital bliss. On the evening of Pennington's engagement ball, the marquis's wife had returned to thwart an attack against her husband. Last week, Lady Godown had given birth to the marquis's heir, and all was well in Gabriel Crowden's life. Thornhill awaited the birth of his first child with the former Velvet Aldridge. And Carter? He had continued on as Pennington's assistant and had deftly sidestepped three more attempts on his life.

Once a month, he had noted of late. A pattern had developed before disappearing. The first attack had come on 1 January. The second on 2 February, and so forth. That was until this month. Although he had anticipated another encounter with his own mortality, no attempt had come on 6 June. He still could not understand why the attacks had stopped, and that particular fact frustrated Carter to no end.

"Privately," the duke insisted.

Carter nodded reluctantly and followed Thornhill to Worthing's study. When they were settled, his friend began, "I have a favor to ask." The duke stroked the chair's arm with his fingertip, a nervous habit of which Thornhill had spent many years correcting. In the field, such an insignificant gesture could relay a man's uneasiness or his duplicity. Carter thought of his own bad habits and wondered if he had ever conquered them. He waited in silence for the duke to continue. "Do you recall the lady I invited to Eleanor's and Velvet's Come Out ball?"

Of course, Carter remembered her. He had sat on Mrs. Warren's left during the supper hour, and he was amazed with the lady's ability to make each man at the table easy in his regard for her. Carter had enjoyed the way she met his eyes when she spoke to him of her time following the drum. "Mrs. Warren? I believe you once held a friendly acquaintance with the lady's late husband."

"Matthew Warren and I were mates in the early years at university. We reunited in Portugal for several months, but then Pennington snatched me away from Wellington's army to join Worthing and Wellston. Soon the rest of our group followed. It was the last I saw Mrs. Warren until I met her by chance at a museum gala during Eleanor's Season." The duke's finger returned to the decorative threads on the chair arm, and Carter wondered what Thornhill dreaded to speak.

"Have you renewed your acquaintance with the lady?" Carter asked cautiously. He prayed Brantley Fowler was not considering making Mrs. Warren his mistress. Such a decision would mean the duke had acted impulsively in choosing his cousin as his duchess, but, more importantly, Carter thought the lady deserved a better means in life.

Thornhill must have recognized the question in Carter's response for he said, "It is not as you assume. The duchess holds my heart firmly in her grasp." The duke's mouth tightened into a thin line. "Mrs. Warren made an unexpected call upon me last week at Briar Hall. The lady sought my assistance with a most delicate situation."

Carter encouraged, "Go on." For the next quarter hour, Thornhill apprised Carter of Mrs. Warren's dilemma. "And the lady knows nothing to the child's family?" Carter could not understand how any man could purposely misuse a woman of Mrs. Warren's caliber.

"I believe the lady fears asking too many questions in dread of someone taking notice of her predicament and remove her only source of income."

Carter understood perfectly. Although they stood as strong as did their late husbands, many war widows suffered deprivations. "What do you expect of me? You have as many contacts as do I."

Thornhill smiled sheepishly. "As beautiful as is the duchess, I fear Velvet still doubts her charms. My lady would be most disconcerted by my spending time with Mrs. Warren, and as the duchess carries my child, I would not wish to cause her undue distress."

Carter thought his friend made too much fuss when it came to Velvet Fowler, but, in truth, he had no knowledge of such devotion, unless he considered Ernest Hutton's, the Earl of McLauren, attachment to Carter's sister Louisa or his brother's commitment to Lady Hellsman. In his life, Carter had never experienced an obsession of the heart. Other than his work and his compulsion to rise in the governmental ranks, he had never acted foolishly. "I insist you accompany me when I call upon the lady. Mrs. Warren will be more forthcoming if she recognizes your support."

The duke paused before saying, "I suppose it is best, but I would prefer the others knew nothing of this request. If either Eleanor or Lady Yardley becomes aware of my intervention, the duchess will discover of my actions, and I will have hell to pay."

Carter kept his disapproval from his countenance. "Send word to the lady, I require more details before I can act."

Chapter Four

"Are you certain of the lady's directions?" Carter asked as they looked up at the sandstone building.

Thornhill frowned dramatically. "I held no idea Mrs. Warren had slipped into such distress. The lady is the niece of the Earl of Charleton," he said incredulously.

Two street urchins rushed forward to take their reins as they climbed down. Carter fished a coin from his pocket. "Walk them to keep them fresh," he ordered. "There is another coin for the one who protects my mount."

"Aye, Sir," the oldest of the two replied.

Thornhill slipped another coin in the child's tight fist. "We mean to call in at number twelve. Come for us if there is any sign of trouble."

"We understand," the smaller of the two declared. "They be fine animals, and we be knowin' our duty."

Carter followed Thornhill to the door and waited for his friend to release the knocker. "I have seen worse streets in London," Carter said softly, "But I do not like the idea of Mrs. Warren taking sanctuary among these people."

Thornhill's gaze followed Carter's. "I feel guilty for not keeping in contact with Mrs. Warren. I used her shamelessly at my sister's Come Out to make Velvet jealous."

Carter murmured, "If I recall, the duchess and Godown held similar ideas to entice you to act impulsively."

The duke chuckled. "We were once the destructive ones."

Before Carter could respond, the door swung wide to reveal a matronly woman of a sizeable girth. She eyed Thornhill with awe. "May I be of service, Sir?" she asked with a wobbly curtsy.

41

Thornhill shot Carter a wry glance. "The Duke of Thornhill and Sir Carter for Mrs. Warren." His friend did not bother to present his card. They were obviously not of the neighborhood.

"Yes, Your Grace." The woman bobbed another curtsy. "Mrs. Warren informed me of your call. The lady awaits you in the parlor." She motioned them to follow her along a shadowed hallway. Carter noted a small boy lurking at the bend of the stairs. He involuntarily wondered if the child was the boy in question. If so, the child possessed the features of one who had only of late called England home.

"The Duke of Thornhill and Sir Carter," the woman announced as she opened a door inward on what appeared to be a sitting room and study combined.

Over the duke's shoulder, Carter caught sight of the woman he had spent the previous three days attempting to define beyond the image he held of that long ago evening. Carter had thought he knew what to expect, but his heart slamming into his ribcage announced the error of his earlier musings. Although she was conservatively dressed in a well-worn day dress, his mind and body took exquisite pleasure in gazing upon one of the most handsome women of his acquaintance.

Her hair—golden blond, mixed with darker strands—was pulled back in a tight knot at her nape, but Carter recognized the natural wave as a ring of curls had escaped to frame her face. A long dormant tingle shot through his veins as he raised his eyes to meet her gaze. Large hazel eyes—the type, which would live with a man forever—returned his notice before the lady dropped her gaze and curtsied. "Thank you for the honor you have bestowed upon me, Your Grace," she said sweetly before imparting a brilliant smile upon Thornhill. Immediately, Carter knew real regret. No one, other than his family, had ever looked upon him with such welcome.

Mrs. Warren extended her hands to Thornhill, and the duke readily accepted them before bringing one to his lips. "I am pleased to find you well, my Dear." He motioned toward Carter. "You recall Sir Carter?"

The lady's eyes brightened with an anticipated tease. "I recall a Mr. Lowery, but Sir Carter came into his own several months after our previous meeting."

Carter enjoyed the soft floral fragrance, which wafted over him. *Roses*, he thought. He bowed from long-inbred training as a gentleman, but he would just as soon catch up the woman and keep her by his side. "I will answer to either, Mrs. Warren," he said with an easy smile.

"May I bring tea?" the matron asked from behind them.

Thornhill frowned. "I am content with your company, Mrs. Warren."

Carter noted his friend's sharp glare and followed the duke's lead. "As am I."

Mrs. Warren nodded to the older woman. "Thank you, Mrs. Peterman. I shall come to you if His Grace and Sir Carter change their minds."

The woman, obviously, understood Thornhill's repugnance for alternated tea, often found in poorer homes, but she held her tongue. "Simon shall be with me in the kitchen," she announced before closing the door upon her exit.

Mrs. Warren did a poor job of suppressing her sigh. "Please have a seat." The lady motioned to three chairs gathered closely together.

He and Thornhill waited for the lady to assume her seat before they settled in. They placed their hats and gloves on a nearby table, as the landlady had not thought to accept them on their entrance.

Without preamble, Thornhill declared, "Lucinda, I will not have you spend another day in these conditions." Carter recognized the duke's need to protect "fair damsels," but a woman, such as Mrs. Warren, would not welcome Thornhill's assumption. Perhaps time had dulled Carter's memory of the lady's brilliance, but not of the woman's frank means of speaking.

"Your Grace, I appreciate your concern," she said through tight lips, "but I mean to see to my own future." The lady forced a smile on Thornhill, but Carter suspected it was one firmly planted in agitation.

Carter realized Thornhill would not surrender so quickly, but the duke said, "Then I am pleased I have asked Sir Carter to join us. The baronet and Baron Swenton are the only two of my former mates who have maintained close ties with the government. Nothing moves in England of which Sir Carter is not aware."

Lucinda watched the baronet carefully as the duke praised the man's political ambitions. He was exactly as she remembered him. *Like a Greek god*, she had thought when she had laid eyes upon him. *A God sent protector.* Of course, the baronet would hold no memory of that eventful day on the Continent. He had placed himself between her and danger, and Lucinda had thought him the most magnificent man she had ever seen. She had never felt so safe. Not with her father, who had spent his time with his military maneuverings, much to her neglect, even when she tended the colonel in his tent. And certainly not with her husband, who had treated her as he would the younger sister of a dear friend. No, it was Sir Carter Lowery, who had stirred that foreign need to succumb to a man's protection.

She had met him again purely by accident at Lady Eleanor Fowler's Come Out ball. Lucinda had sat beside Lowery throughout the supper hour, but she had purposely not reminded him of the kindness he had once shown her. She had not been at her best on their previous acquaintance, which could only be described as brief.

Despite the casual slant of his shoulders, Lucinda had no doubt Sir Carter was a man of action. Tall and lean. Muscular. Vivid dark brown eyes. A determined chin. Splendidly thick hair. Dark brown also, with shades of mahogany throughout. A straight, classical nose. Lucinda experienced an unfamiliar flush of heat rush to the core of her femininity.

"Perhaps you might relate the events leading up to the child's appearance on your doorstep, Mrs. Warren," Sir Carter encouraged.

Startled from her reverie, Lucinda flinched in embarrassment. The baronet's eyebrow had risen in wry amusement. Quickly, she diverted her gaze before a blush crept up her neck and cheeks. She swallowed away trepidation and prayed her expression did not betray her irritation with her foolish musings. Lucinda risked a quick glance at the baronet, and his expression spoke of true concern and interest in her dilemma so she shored up her courage and began her tale.

Carter listened to the details the woman provided, but his mind was more agreeably engaged. His strong attraction to Mrs. Warren was so uncharacteristic of him, especially when he was attempting to solve a mystery. Carter had always compartmentalized his life: his objectives were lofty, and he always assumed romantic entanglements would interfere with those aspirations. So he had kept his lust under as much control as he had done his thoughts of advancement.

Yet, a pang of sadness rushed forward. Had he missed out on life? Carter had chastised his older brother for permitting their father to define Lawrence's existence. Ironically, Carter had always thought himself free and independent of his brother's responsibilities, but perhaps he had created his own cage. "And you have discovered nothing of the boy's mother?" he asked instinctively, although his mind had been engaged with the idea of pulling the woman into his embrace, if for no other reason than to observe whether the heat simmering in his groin would spring to life.

Obviously grappling with her response, Mrs. Warren said softly, "There is something regarding Simon I did not initially share with His Grace."

Despite his best efforts, Carter grimaced. Whatever Mrs. Warren had withheld from Thornhill would change everything. "Whenever you are prepared to speak on it, we are prepared to listen," he encouraged. He wished he could comfort her somehow. Swift appreciation registered in her eyes, and Carter was pleased to have said the correct thing.

"Simon," she said with a gentle smile upon her lips, "is a phenomenal child, and I do not regret one minute he has dwelled with me; yet, I fear I shall never be able to give Simon the type of life he deserves."

"Do you mean financially?" the duke asked.

Mrs. Warren chuckled ironically. "Of course, financially, but more than that. The child should have those who understand him in his life. Those who can answer his questions with responses buried deeply in his past."

"I fear I do not understand, Lucinda," the duke said encouragingly. Somehow, the duke's familiarity with the woman rubbed raw against Carter's sensibilities.

She inhaled deeply, and Carter noted the stiffening of her shoulders, as if Mrs. Warren braced for a powerful blow. "The woman Captain Warren took to wife was a Jewess. The boy must be returned to his maternal family. Even then, Simon will know hardship, but not to the extent he will experience if I bring him up as a Christian. How would I educate him, even if could afford to do so?"

For several elongated second, neither Carter nor Thornhill responded. Carter suspected the duke was attempting to stifle the impulse to search out

45

Matthew Warren's grave, dig the captain up, and kill the man all over again. Carter was certainly considering doing just that. "How?" Thornhill growled. "Not only did Warren practice a deception, he did so with a Jew? I have never known prejudice against the race, but this situation is beyond the pale. Such actions taint Society's opinions of all involved. I cannot understand how a man betrothed to you since childhood could take another wife or how the two of them have contrived to foist their child upon your good nature," he said indignantly.

"Thornhill, we must think rationally," Carter cautioned. "Permit Mrs. Warren her explanation."

A sorrowful note laced her words, and tears misted her eyes. Immediately, regret flooded Carter's heart. He recognized the embarrassment and shame Mrs. Warren had suffered. "When I discovered…discovered my husband's treachery," she stammered, "I…I wished…" Carter prayed the lady would not finish her thought, but she did, nonetheless. "I wished to die. Yet, I could not. You see, if something happened to me, Simon would have no one in this world to care for him." Mrs. Warren swallowed hard. Carter ached to comfort her. It was all he could do not to reach for her. The feeling was so strong, and he was not certain he liked it. "I have…it is foolish for me to think so…but I have come to believe Captain Warren arranged to have Simon sent to me. Surely Mr. Warren spoke of me to Simon's mother. My husband knew I would not fail to keep the boy safe."

Carter admired the lady's fortitude. For the child's sake, she had convinced herself to make the benevolent journey. He knew of no one who would open himself to such scrutiny. "Did the child present any papers besides the note you described earlier?" he inquired. Carter quickly reasoned his only means to comfort the woman would be to locate the information she required.

"Simon carried a small bag containing several rolled sheaves," Mrs. Warren explained, "but they are written in Hebrew. I feared bringing notice to the boy if I had someone translate them."

Carter offered, "I could ask one of the recruits we have recently added to our staff to view them, assuming that situation would meet your approval."

"Your offer is one I readily accept." Mrs. Warren smiled sweetly, filling the emptiness Carter experienced earlier. "Yet, I have a confession."

Carter frowned without recognizing he did so. "How so, Mrs. Warren?"

He heard the pause, as if the lady sought the correct words. "Some…some several months back, an intruder entered my rooms while Simon and I returned books to the circulating library." Carter realized the nearest library was well over a mile removed, and he once more admired the strength of the woman before him.

Thornhill swore under his breath, but Carter calmly asked, "Were the child's papers disturbed?"

"Only one," she explained. "One of the three rolled papers has gone missing. I could not understand why that particular item was the source of the invasion; however, Simon explained the paper was a record of his parents' joining."

Carter leaned forward, as if Thornhill's presence no longer existed. "Was the paper also in Hebrew?"

Surprisingly, Mrs. Warren's gaze rested purely upon him, and Carter relished the connection. "Yes, which I found most confusing because the man who follows us when the child and I are about our business appears English…I mean his skin is that of those who call England home." She blushed with the awkwardness of her words.

"Good God!" Thornhill expelled. "Break ins and someone following you!" In frustration, the duke jammed his fingers into his hair. "When had you planned to inform us of all this, Lucinda?" Thornhill was on his feet and pacing. "I had thought your situation one of an administrative nightmare, but this is something much more dangerous."

"Sit, Thornhill," Carter ordered in a voice reminiscent of Aristotle Pennington. "Again. Permit Mrs. Warren time to explain fully, and then we can decide upon a plan of action."

Reluctantly, the duke returned to his seat. Carter thought it ironic that he, a mere baronet, without repercussions, had given orders to a duke. It spoke to his long-standing relationship with Brantley Fowler.

The lady smiled with admiration, and Carter's heart turned a graceful somersault in his chest. He wondered if there might be some means he could employ to keep the smile upon her lips. Yet, as he considered the possibilities, Mrs. Warren's brow tightened in a decided frown. "There have been four questionable incidents," she began. "Shortly after Simon and I moved to these quarters, we nearly met our end when a beer cart lost its load." The lady paused as if choosing the details to share. "The stranger entering our rooms followed that incident. Shortly after the invasion, I began to notice the man who appeared to watch our every move. As my window does not look upon the street, I have no idea whether he is at the same street corner at other times, but he appears to parallel my comings and goings."

Her frown deepened, and Carter wished to smooth away her ills. "Perhaps I have erred. There remains the possibility the man simply pines for a woman in the neighborhood."

Thornhill asked encouragingly, "Could you describe the man?"

She looked off as if conjuring up an image. "Much shorter than either of you or the baronet. The man wears a brown hat—one a man working in the fields might doff. Early on, he sported a fleece lined coat, but he has abandoned its warmth for a plainly cut jacket."

"Which corner?" the duke prompted.

"Across the street. Before the grocer."

Thornhill nodded to Carter. "I have it. I will go out the back and take Murray with me. Finish your conversation with Mrs. Warren. If the man is about, I will find him."

Carter inclined his head in acknowledgement, and the duke disappeared from the room. "Were there other incidents?" He meant to have it all. Carter was suddenly aware of the inappropriateness of being alone with this particular woman; yet, there was no means to correct the situation. They could not permit others to know of what they spoke.

A moment earlier, Lucinda had known nothing but her tale. Now, all upon which her mind could concentrate was the sudden heat shooting through her veins. Instinctively, she glanced at her breasts as they beaded in anticipation. When Lucinda looked up again, she discovered the baronet's eyes rested upon her bust line. Immediately, her heat turned to a flush across her cheeks.

Flustered by the intensity of Sir Carter's eyes, Lucinda could not recall his question. She should be placing her defenses in a row, as she had done with Lieutenant Worsley, but in a perfect world, welcoming the baronet's attentions would be Lucinda's wish. Unfortunately, she recognized her social position as inferior to his. The image of his lips claiming hers played like a beckoning dream, but she managed to shake it off. Without meeting his eyes, she stammered, "Once…bricks fell…bricks fell from a roof top…to land dangerously close to Simon's feet. On another occasion, there was a small fire in the passage leading to our rooms. Fortunately, Mr. Peterman discovered the smoke before the fire spread. It was assumed the maid Nancy had dropped a warm coal on the rug after she cleared the ashes from the fireplace."

"But you hold different thoughts?"

Lucinda uttered a strained laugh. "I have refused to acknowledge my greatest fears until this moment," she rasped through a tight throat.

The baronet moved to sit beside her upon the settee. He did so in natural concern, but Lucinda could not help but to catch her breath. "You must promise me, Mrs. Warren," he said in what sounded of true disposition, "to speak earnestly at all times. If I am to assist you, you must trust me, even with your most private thoughts."

She wondered how the baronet would respond if she had told him she wished to know the warmth of his kiss. Silently, Lucinda laughed at the sheer absurdity of such an idea. "I shall endeavor to do as you ask, Sir Carter."

"May I view the papers of which you spoke earlier?"

Lucinda knew this was a mistake; permitting Sir Carter into her life was a ridiculous scheme. If she had known Thornhill would involve the baronet in the investigation, she would have sought other means before succumbing to her situation. It had not come easy to pretend no knowledge of the man, but to look upon his fine countenance was such a pleasure after so great a time. "Of course," she said stupidly. "If you will excuse me a moment, I shall retrieve them from my quarters."

Carter assisted her to her feet. He had erred when he caught her hand in his. To his regret, she presented him a quick curtsy and moved away. As he watched her go, Carter subconsciously rubbed the zing of recognition, which burned his palm. Some might say, there was nothing uncommon about Lucinda Warren, nothing from the ordinary, but those critics would have erred. Behind those plain threads of a poor war widow stood a remarkable woman. Her exit created a strange sense of loss.

As the lady slipped from the room, Thornhill returned. "Murray escorts Mrs. Warren's spy to the Home Office," the duke said with a bit of bravado.

Carter scowled. "He confessed?" He held no doubt if the man existed, Fowler would apprehend him. The duke was a superb agent. What did not make sense was a ready confession.

"Since I brought him from Cornwall to London, Murray has acquired several convincing methods of discovering information." The duke straightened his waistcoat. "Our culprit did not announce who had hired him, but the man did admit he was to report on Mrs. Warren's presence in Mrs. Peterman's household."

Carter's anxiety spiraled tighter. It was all too easy, and he suspected easy was not how this investigation would go. He stifled a groan of frustration. "We should remove Mrs. Warren and the child to some place safe. What say you to Thorn Hall?"

The duke flinched. "I have spoken previously of the duchess's lack of comfort with Mrs. Warren."

Carter was not impressed by Velvet Fowler's ignorant naiveté. The duchess had a long way to travel to equal the magnanimous nature of her cousin Lady Eleanor Worthing. *Why was it*, he thought, *the more beautiful the woman, the more insecure she became?* "Then do you have another suggestion? The others are farther from London, and our investigation centers about Mrs. Warren's activities since arriving in Town. It would seem best to keep the lady close."

Thornhill said ruefully, "Huntingborne Abbey remains nearly empty."

Carter said incredulously, "I cannot bring the woman to my estate. I have only a minimal staff to attend her. And who would protect Mrs. Warren while I am in London?"

Thornhill reasoned, "I can provide the lady with a maid, as well as men to protect the house." He gestured aristocratically to their surroundings. "It is not as if the lady has been living in austere quarters."

If he were more of a gentleman, Carter might have objected to the absurdity of inviting a woman of Mrs. Warren's station to his home, but his years with the Realm had blurred the lines of propriety. Finally, he said, "I will leave it to you to convince the lady yours is the best plan for her immediate future."

Chapter Five

H e had called on her for three consecutive days. Each time, Carter had
hired a hack, rather than to use his fine coach and to draw attention, actually, more notice than usual, to his presence in the neighborhood. With each
call, he had removed more of her belongings. Daily, Mrs. Warren packed her
personal items in a small valise, and Carter transferred the items to a trunk he
brought with him. In that manner, the lady would appear to return with what
she brought with her. It was an excellent plan if another "spy" had replaced the
one Thornhill had apprehended.

"This one is heavier than the one yesterday," he said with an easy taunt. He
lifted her bag to the carriage bench before he assisted her to the seat.

The lady blushed, and Carter thought the color did wonders for her looks.
"I included my father's papers today. They are in the metal box on the bottom
of the bag."

"I will guard them with my life," he whispered before lifting the boy to the
opening.

As foolish as it seemed, Carter could not recall a time he had been more
excited to spend time with a lady. He had instinctively known from the meeting
three days prior he would enjoy touching her: enjoy lifting her small form from
the carriage and placing her hand upon his arm. The experience was his personal exquisite torture. Yet, he had also discovered she enthralled him with her
intelligent conversation. Mrs. Warren was well versed in the country's politics,
and Carter had delighted in sharing many of the government's not-so-guarded
"secrets" with her. The lady's eyes lit in anticipation, and he relished teasing her
with each new fact.

Just as surprisingly, he had taken pleasure in the boy's antics and the child's
delight at the smallest gesture of kindness. Whether it was an afternoon playing

in Marylebone Park or a gift of a book from one of the many shops or an ice from Gunthers, Simon Warren freely expressed his gratitude. He thought the child and the lady were well matched in temperament.

Only yesterday, she had confided something he had never considered. "If what we suspect holds true, I must decide whether to announce to the world my imprudence by resuming my former name or falsely claim the name of a man I have learned to despise." The boy chased a ball Carter had found in his suite of offices, while Carter and the lady shared a park bench.

Carter paused before responding. "If you choose to raise the boy as your ward, it would prove well to keep Captain Warren's name."

Her lip took a bitter curl. "Yet, in their grief, my husband's parents have rejected me. I am certain they would not have a care if I kept their son's name alive," she protested.

The sun hid behind a cloud, and the shadows blurred his view of her countenance. Wishing to understand her better, he said, "Perhaps you could tell me a bit more of your marriage. Even the most miniscule fact could be the one to solve this mystery."

She turned her chin to watch the boy at play, and Carter recognized the pain, which crossed her brow. Brutal self-appraisal crossed her countenance. "Our parents' estates ran along side each other, and the Warrens and the Rightnours were great friends. With my birth, the colonel and Father Warren drew up an agreement. From my earliest memory, I knew I was to be Matthew Warren's wife. We never discussed the arrangement, and I had thought Captain Warren had accepted our parents' wishes."

Mrs. Warren caught the ball as it rolled toward her feet before returning it to the boy with an encouraging smile. "Mr. Warren departed for the war in the later part of '07, but I did not follow as I was still in the schoolroom. At the time, the colonel had accepted half pay, and we were in Devon until he was recalled into service in early 1811. My father's return to the war was the reason for Mr. Warren's homecoming to exchange our vows. Little did I know he had kept the secret of another wife." The lady's former conceit obviously gulled her.

Her gaze veered skyward, and she muttered something, which sounded of a curse. The fact the lady held a spark of defiance pleased Carter immensely. Resilience would serve her well in overcoming the evils surrounding her. "I lost Captain Warren to a fever after we had spent a fortnight in the cold and rain. I could not return to Devon for the colonel had let the estate, and Uncle Gerhard had parted ways with our family long before I was born. My mother had passed shortly after I married, and all I had remaining in the world was my father. There was no time to grieve for my husband's passing. My father was alone, so I joined the colonel. Beyond my early years in Devon, following the drum is all I have ever known." A single tear crept down her cheek, and Carter resisted the urge to flick it away. "I lost the colonel at Waterloo. I have no family remaining, which makes Captain Warren's betrayal even more painful."

Hers was a twisted tale of woe, and Carter had difficulty believing Warren had not given some indication of the duplicity he practiced. Likely, Mrs. Warren had chosen to ignore her husband's dual life, telling herself his absence from her bed was a result of the war. For Carter, perhaps this was the hardest part of her story to believe: What he knew of the lady would not speak of unwariness, but she had turned her vision from what was evidently her husband's unfaithfulness. It was only with her retelling that he realized who her father had been. "Colonel Roderick Rightnour was your father?" Her casual mention of the colonel and Waterloo meant Mrs. Warren was not aware of his connection. He wondered what she would think of him if Carter spoke his heart regarding Rightnour's grievous mistakes during the battle.

The lady looked at him in dismay. "Were you unaware of my parentage?"

Experiencing a touch of guilt, Carter attempted to conceal his knowledge of Rightnour's ability to lead his men in battle. "I had only known you by your husband's name," he explained. "From Thornhill, I recently learned your father served England, but I had not placed the connection until I heard you speak of the colonel's demise."

A suspicious frown crossed her countenance. "Did you know my father?"

Carter again withheld his true thought regarding the man. "I served Wellington for only a short time. When the opportunity arrived to make a more personal difference in our country's struggle, I seized it. I had only briefly known private service when Wellington pressed me into action at Waterloo. Otherwise, I would not have been involved. I was aware of Colonel Rightnour's service. It was I who assumed the command of the colonel's regiment after his fall."

"So it was you who was credited with saving the lives of his men," she countered.

All emotions faded from his eyes. Carter shrugged away the accolades. "I did what any good Englishman would have done."

"And knew a severe injury for it."

"How did you know I was wounded?" His eyebrow rose in curiosity. "Those in charge removed me from the field."

Mrs. Warren blushed thoroughly, but her voice remained steady. "I am a colonel's daughter, and I volunteered in the records' office. When the Duke of Wellington requested a special transfer for a wounded soldier, I took notice. Then I saw who you were and what you did. I was indebted to you for saving my father's reputation, and I meant to express my gratitude, but you were gone. Like you, I thought no more of the name I had discovered."

Carter was not certain he liked the idea of the lady being privy to the Realm's secret maneuverings in his behalf. "As I was intended to be nothing more than a messenger on that day, the Duke assumed responsibility for my condition," he explained.

"I thought it a wonderful gesture on His Grace's part," she admitted. "Unfortunately, with the loss of my father, my world shifted under me. I had no time to know more of your recovery."

Arrangements had been made for what appeared to be a fourth outing on their part. Carter arrived in the hired hack, but this time he sent the driver toward the city's outskirts. Through one of his agents posing as Mrs. Warren's cousin and claiming to have invited her and the boy for a holiday to Warwickshire, Carter had paid the lady's rent in advance to keep Mr. and Mrs. Peterman's silence. Questioning the man Thornhill had captured had proved fruitless. All they had discovered was the man who had hired her culprit was an older gentleman of some wealth for Mrs. Warren's enemy had paid the man well to spy upon her. The hireling, who gave his name as Jacob Parker, had sworn no knowledge of the attempts to harm the lady.

When they reached the country roads, Carter transferred the last of her belongings to his personal coach. "Where are we going?" Simon asked as he lifted the boy into the coach. Purposely, they had not told the child of their plans. Mrs. Warren feared Simon might accidentally inform Mrs. Peterman of their whereabouts.

"Sir Carter has suggested we might partake of a short holiday in the country," she explained as she followed the child into the coach's interior. "He is escorting us to his estate."

"You will enjoy the opportunity to ride and to play with the other children, will you not?" Carter added in encouragement.

The boy's eyes grew wide with anticipation. "Oh, yes, Sir Carter. That would be most excellent."

Mrs. Warren breathed easier. Carter whispered in her ear. "His Grace has sent a maid to chaperone us. The duke thought it best if you did not arrive in Kent with a spoiled reputation."

She glanced up at him, and Carter's heart flipped in his chest when their eyes met. Whenever the lady was close, he fought the urge to touch her. "I appreciate the duke's forethought, but I fear my husband's reputation has doomed mine."

Carter stood in the carriage's opening while she crouched in the doorway. "Thornhill means well." He was not certain how the *ton* might react to what she had suffered. Some might celebrate her determination, while others would shun her. "I will see you safely settled at Huntingborne, and tomorrow, I will return to London and the investigation," he confided.

Mrs. Warren frowned deeply. "So soon?" she whispered.

Carter leaned closer. Close enough to claim her lips if he did not restrain his desires. "I fear so."

Her cheeks flushed with color before she blew out a sigh. "It is just that I have enjoyed our conversations…" The red upon her cheeks deepened. "It has been so long since I have known a person who takes interest in what brings me pleasure."

Carter's lust raced to notice. He could think of several "interesting" means to bring her pleasure. Yet, before he could respond, his coachman announced, "The lady's belongings are secured, Sir."

Carter released her hand—a hand he did not even realize he still held. "Excellent." He cleared the rasp from his throat. "Set a course for Kent, Watkins."

Simon had asked what seemed a hundred questions upon the journey, but Carter had enjoyed explaining to the boy about the different terrain and vegetation. He even answered a few of the child's questions regarding the war. "Did you know my father?"

"I fear not," he had said honestly, "but perhaps you could direct your questions to the Duke of Thornhill. His Grace is my nearest neighbor, and it is my understanding your father and the duke were at university together."

The boy looked pleadingly at Mrs. Warren. "Would it be acceptable, Ma'am, if I speak to His Grace?"

The lady smiled indulgently at the child. "You did not seek my permission to question Sir Carter," she teased.

"Sir Carter is not so grand as a duke," Simon reasoned aloud.

Carter barked out a robust laugh. "I must remember to convey your opinion to Thornhill," he said good-naturedly. "I am certain the duke will be pleased to know someone views him as grand."

Mrs. Warren suggested, "Permit me to speak to His Grace first. If the duke agrees, then you may ask of Mr. Warren." Her words had satisfied the child.

That had been several hours prior. They had spent the afternoon settling in. Carter had felt the shame of having his renovations incomplete. He would have preferred to introduce the lady to a showcase manor.

"I am often in London, and the former owner left the estate in a deplorable condition," he offered in explanation for several of the still empty rooms.

However, rather than to snarl her nose in disgust, the lady appeared delighted with the size of the rooms and the prospect. "It is beautiful, Sir Carter," she freely declared, and he experienced pride for the first time in the manor house he had received as a presentation from the Prince Regent. "The rooms are neither too large or too small. Each has plenty of natural light."

"I hope to improve the vista," he said lamely to impress her.

She drew back the drapes. "In time, it will be a very inviting house, one any family would welcome as its home."

"Supper is served, Sir Carter," Mr. Vance announced. The butler held the door for them. Mrs. Warren had seen the child to his bed, and one of the new maids tended the boy.

"Shall we go in?" Carter offered his arm to the lady. He enjoyed the idea of their extending their time together. Like her, he had found their conversations stimulating. In the small dining room, Carter seated her on his right. "As I said previously, I am rarely in attendance at Huntingborne Abbey, but while you are here, I wish you to treat the house as your own. I hold no objections to your setting your own rules in my absence." He had purposely said the words before his servants so they would know his wishes.

"You are most generous, Sir Carter," Mrs. Warren murmured as the footman served the first course. "But I am certain Simon and I shall require nothing special of note."

"Nevertheless, I have left specific orders for someone to escort you and the boy when you are outside the house, and Thornhill has placed additional men to guard the immediate estate."

Mrs. Warren responded with weariness. "You and His Grace have acted with such honor. I despise the fact Simon and I have brought distress to your doorstep." Pride and stubbornness laced her tone. They were excellent defenses, means for the lady to hide from the world.

"Thornhill and I will have no words of gratitude, Mrs. Warren. We have chosen to serve English citizens on British soil or elsewhere."

"As you wish, Sir Carter," she said softly, "but I cannot imagine my dilemma being of any significance in comparison to England's diplomatic and political issues." A hint of disapproval marred her all too handsome features.

His lips twisted with sardonic amusement. "Humor me, Mrs. Warren. With fortune's freewill, we will discover the truth of your situation in a timely manner, and then you may return to your life."

A flare of heat colored her skin before she tamped down her emotions. "I am in no hurry to return to London's summer," she admitted with a small smile, and Carter returned a sympathetic one. The lady reached for her soupspoon. "While I enjoy your cook's talents, I mean to learn more of your relations, Sir Carter."

With a choked burst of surprise, Carter remarked, "You may be sorry you asked, Mrs. Warren. I come from a hearty family." What was it about this woman, he wondered, that set his heart reeling whenever he looked upon her countenance? When she did not respond immediately, Carter began ticking off his siblings upon his fingers.

"I am the youngest of the Lowery brood," he confessed. "My father's spare. My brother Lawrence is the heir, and the oldest among the Lowery offspring. He has recently married an American, Miss Arabella Tilney, who is the granddaughter of the Earl of Vaughn. Law and Arabella have spent the winter months at one of the minor estates in Scotland, but I have had a recent letter from Bella announcing their plans to return to Derbyshire."

"Your family seat is in Derbyshire?" she inquired.

Carter nodded his acknowledgement. "In the northern section, near the Dark Peaks. Ironically, my friend James Kerrington's estate is the largest in Derbyshire. You likely recall Lord Worthing from Lady Eleanor's ball. The viscount pursued Thornhill's sister with a singularity. They recently welcomed their first child, a girl."

"And your brother?" she asked. "Has he his own estate?"

Carter laughed ironically. "Father would never have tolerated Lawrence so far from his control. My older brother was known to toe the line, that is, until he chose Miss Tilney as his bride. My brother's joining has forced the baron to relinquish his hold on Law's life. The next few months will determine how Law weathers this change. He and Lady Hellsman have chosen to reside in the dowager house rather than to share Blake's Run with our parents."

Her lashes elegantly swept downward, as if she chose her words carefully. "Then perhaps it is best you are situated in Kent."

"Trust me," Carter said bitterly. "Baron Blakehell holds no interest in anything or anyone beyond his estate."

Mrs. Warren's lips tightened in condemnation, but the lady judiciously chose not to comment on Carter's admission. Instead, she asked, "How many years are there between you and your brother?"

Carter swallowed the anger, which always flooded his chest when frustrations ruled his tongue. "Over eight. Law saw his birthday before he claimed Miss Tilney's hand. He is three and thirty."

"Eight years?" Her eyebrow rose in curiosity. "A long time between sons..."

Carter laughed easily. "Three daughters filled the void. My sisters adore me, as they should," he said teasingly.

Despite the lady's best efforts, her lips twitched with a growing smile. "Sisters always adore the baby in the family," she mocked. After a sip of her wine, she asked, "Have they each married?"

"I fear I am the only one remaining upon whom my mother may ply her matchmaking skills." He smiled easily with the memory of his dear mother. "The baroness is quite tenacious in her efforts. She easily maneuvered Louisa into Ernest Hutton's path. Lord McLauren is the eldest son of mother's dearest friend, Lady Edna McLauren. Louisa and McLauren live in Lincolnshire; they married some years prior and have presented my mother with two grandchildren, Ethan and Lisette."

Without waiting for her response, Carter continued his recitation. "Mother had more difficulty bringing Delia to heel. My youngest sister is a bit of a hoyden." He offered her a silly grin. "If one saw her now, he would not believe Viscountess Duff could be the same cheeky minx. Delia had always declared never to marry, not because she objected to men's attentions, but because she refused to relinquish her independence to any man; however, when my sister met Stewart Roxbury during her first Season, Mama had to reel in her youngest daughter's enthusiasm for the man."

"Does Miss Delia claim a family?" Mrs. Warren asked in earnest. Carter liked the idea of another person holding interest in his family. He held great pride and respect for each of his siblings.

"Delia and Roxbury have a daughter Catherine. When I was last in Warwickhshire, she confided there will be another addition to Viscount Duff's brood shortly before Christmastide."

Mrs. Warren sighed heavily. "Such a large family. How wonderfully delicious! I have no siblings. It would have been heavenly to squabble over dresses and beaus with a sister or to challenge a brother's stubbornness." A second sigh slipped her lips, and Carter considered how alone in the world she must feel. "And what of the middle sister?"

"Marie is the one most like me in personality. She resisted the idea of marriage even after she had accepted Jonathon Laroche's proposal. If possible, Marie would have ridden off to war with me; yet, finally, she succumbed to Viscount Sheffield's charms. She welcomed her first son in late November. My darling sister glows with love for her family."

Mrs. Warren leaned closer. A flicker of candlelight illuminated the golden highlights of her hair. The light framed her in softness, and Carter fought the desire to touch her. "It is as it should be, Sir Carter. You possess the best gift God can bestow upon a man."

Carter could not deny the Lord had extolled upon him a loving mother and siblings. It was only his father who had denied Carter recognition. However, when he compared his blessings with Mrs. Warren's bleakness, he felt petty for wanting more than he deserved.

"I will send word or return for you when I have news of import regarding your situation," Carter had told her while he waited for the groom to bring his horse about. Mrs. Warren had insisted on seeing him off, and Carter was aware of how intimate the moment felt. The lady never seemed conscious of how their relationship crossed the lines. "You and the boy should enjoy the country air and the estate."

Mrs. Warren sighed deeply. "It has been since before my marriage that I spent time in the English countryside. The landscape is quite different," she swept her hand in all-encompassing gesture toward the groomed lawns, "from what I knew in Devon, but I shall cherish each minute."

Carter thought the change in location had already brought a kiss of freshness to her countenance. Mrs. Warren's posture had lost the stress in her shoulders. He hated to issue his warning for it would bring her more worry, but Carter would be remiss if he did not. "I must add a caution. Although we have executed diversions, if someone wishes to follow you, our trail is not invisible. The duke and I mean to exercise vigilance, but it would make our task easier if we could capture the perpetrator in the act."

Her eyes and mouth scrunched in disapproval. "Is my stay at Huntingborne Abbey meant to be a designed trap, Sir Carter?"

He confessed, "Not intentionally so. Thornhill and I believe the country would make it more difficult for a stranger to hide than upon a busy city street. It is simply more practical."

She nodded thoughtfully. "As I am known for my practicality, I shall acquiesce to your experience."

Carter had the urge to chuck her chin good-naturedly and then kiss her lovely mouth before departing. Instead, he accepted Prime's reins from his groom. "I will contact you whenever I have anything to share." He touched his hat with his crop. "Farewell, Mrs. Warren."

She stepped back as he mounted, and Carter felt bereft of her closeness. He stared down upon her, memorizing each line of her countenance, before he touched his heels to Prime's flanks. Her voice followed him across the circle. "Safe journey, Sir Carter."

"Mrs. Warren?" Sir Carter's butler appeared in the library's doorway. Lucinda had permitted Simon to choose among the baronet's books, and she and the child now shared a volume with fabulous etchings of butterflies and birds and dragonflies.

Lucinda glanced at the man. "Yes, Mr. Vance."

"The Duke and Duchess of Thornhill have asked to speak to you, Ma'am."

Lucinda sprang to her feet and tucked a strand of loose hair into her chignon. The butler's face spoke of his surprise to have the pair upon the Huntingborne threshold. "The duke…" She caught her breath and swallowed slowly. "Please show His Grace and the duchess in, Mr. Vance, and then bring tea and refreshments."

"Yes, Ma'am." When Mr. Vance exited, she reached for the boy to straighten his clothes and wipe a smudge of jam from Simon's cheek. "Mind your manners," she said through trembling lips.

The child nodded nervously. "Why has the duke come?" he whispered.

Lucinda smoothed the wrinkles from her day dress. "A duty call," she murmured. She wished she had something new to wear before the beautiful duchess. She could barely breath by the time Mr. Vance ushered the Duke and Duchess of Thornhill into the room. Lucinda curtsied while bracing Simon's awkward bow. "Your Grace," she murmured, and then offered a second curtsy to the duchess.

"None of that," Thornhill declared and caught Lucinda's fingers to assist her to stand. "We are friends of long-standing, Mrs. Warren."

Lucinda shot a quick glance at the duchess to discover a look of dissatisfaction upon the woman's countenance. The duke may consider her a "friend," but his wife held a different opinion.

Judiciously, Lucinda said, "'Tis true, Your Grace, but I have only a brief acquaintance with your duchess, and I owe her my respect." The girl's countenance softened when she looked upon her husband, but Lucinda recognized the frown, which tugged gently at the duchess's mouth. "Please join me." She gestured to the chairs. "I have asked Mr. Vance to bring tea." It was very odd to be acting as hostess in Sir Carter's house.

The duke paused to assist his wife to her seat. The duchess was heavy with child, but even so, Velvet Fowler was magnificently beautiful. Hair the color of midnight and violet eyes, which spoke of spring. It was a breath taking combination. Lucinda motioned Simon forward to make his addresses to the couple. Catching the child's small hand in her damp one, she said, "Your Grace, please permit me to introduce my late husband's son, Simon." The boy executed another awkward bow.

Thornhill studied the child before saying, "Your father was a fine soldier, Boy."

Lucinda thought Thornhill had spoken the only truth they shared about Matthew Warren: the captain had served his country honorably; it was only her he had betrayed.

"Thank you, Your Grace," Simon said maturely, and Lucinda knew a moment of pride.

She explained, "Simon would wish to know more of his father. Mayhap before we leave Kent, you might indulge the child with tales of your university days, Your Grace."

Unsurprisingly, Thornhill readily agreed. "What say you, if you spend the day at Thorn Hall with my daughter Sonali and me. I have promised the duchess to spend the entire day with the child on Friday." Again, Lucinda cautiously glanced to the duchess to determine whether the woman would approve of her husband's easy nature. The duchess delivered a hard stare, her eyes hooded. Again, the tension in the lady's shoulders said her endorsement was not forthcoming. Purposely, Lucinda returned the duchess's gaze with a noncommittal one. "It will be Sonali's seventh birthday, and I am certain my daughter would enjoy a playmate with which to share the day. Of course, you would be forced to eat your share of apple tarts, if you attend."

Simon's eyes grew in disbelief. "I am very fond of apple tarts, Your Grace." Remembering himself, he added quickly, "I would be honored."

"How gracious!" Lucinda gushed. The duke's generosity had always been a great kindness. She had begun to question her ability to see this situation to its end, but Thornhill's actions bolstered her resolve. "Simon, perhaps you should take the book we shared to your room. We shall enjoy it together a bit later. Mr. Vance will send up refreshments."

"Yes, Ma'am."

As he caught the book and executed another bow, Lucinda cautioned, "Permit the maid to prepare the tea."

The boy understood immediately, and he smiled largely. "Yes, Ma'am. I will protect Sir Carter's tea service." With a joyful skip, the boy hustled from the room.

Lucinda returned her attention to the baronet's guests. "How may I serve you, Your Grace?"

Thornhill leaned easily into the chair. "I am merely an escort, Mrs. Warren. It was the duchess's idea to pay a obligation call." His pronouncement did not bode well for Lucinda. The only other time she had met the duchess had been the evening His Grace used her to make his lady jealous.

"We promised Sir Carter the wardrobe from your father's chambers for the one he has deemed for Baron Blakehell's exclusive use. Little did I know, the baronet would spend but one night under his own roof," the duchess protested with a tone of falsehood. Lucinda knew for certain the woman had an ulterior motive, but she could not name the duchess's duplicity.

The duke smiled lovingly at his wife. He was blind to her manipulation. Thornhill mildly chastised. "Sir Carter has assumed many of Pennington's former duties. If you expected the baronet to participate in the refurbishing of his home, I fear you will be sadly disenchanted, my Dear."

The duchess pouted in the way of women who knew the effect puffing lips had over a man. "I simply wished to know the baronet's pleasure with the piece."

Lucinda ventured, "In my experience with the military, few men take note of such finery unless a woman points out the perfection."

The duke chuckled. "Point made, Mrs. Warren."

The duchess scowled, and Lucinda suspected her remarks had displeased the woman further. However, the lady said sweetly, "Perhaps, Bran, you would oversee the unloading of the piece."

"I am certain Mr. Vance…" Thornhill began, but he readily curtailed his response when his wife sent the duke a deathly glare. "It appears, Mrs. Warren, my duchess wishes a private word with you." He rose easily from the chair. "Do not be afeared, Ma'am. My wife only torments me," he teased.

"Do not give Mrs. Warren a predisposed opinion of me, Your Grace," the duchess warned sweetly.

The duke presented his wife a proper bow. "I hold no delusions you have not completed the task previously, my Dear." With a wink in Lucinda's direction, Thornhill exited the room, pointedly closing the door behind him.

Lucinda wished to call him back, but she set her shoulders to meet the duchess's poorly disguised plan. Lucinda repeated her earlier query, "How may I serve you, Your Grace?"

The woman drew herself up in an air of self-importance. "You may begin by explaining your true connection to my husband."

Chapter Six

Lucinda had expected a fit of jealousy. Thornhill's bride was quite young and likely uncertain of her position in the duke's life. After all, it was not uncommon among the *ton* for a man in Thornhill's position to have several liaisons, but the girl's tone set Lucinda's teeth on edge. Instead of responding in a manner to ease Velvet Fowler's mind, Lucinda's pride raised its ugly head, and she said snidely, "Perhaps you should direct your question to His Grace."

The girl's eyes widened in disbelief. "I am not accustomed to brooking disappointment, Mrs. Warren. Your own conscience, must tell you what I most desire to know."

Lucinda looked on with unaffected astonishment. "Indeed, you are mistaken, Your Grace. I cannot account as to why you assume something amiss." She knew better, but it was quite gratifying to have such a beautiful woman think her a threat. Deliciously, she insinuated, "Does your question rest in something His Grace has done to bring you anguish or in your own insecurities regarding your husband's love for you?"

"Mrs. Warren," the duchess replied in an angry tone, "you ought to know as Thornhill's wife, I wield great power, and however insincere you may choose to be, you shall not find me so. I shall certainly not depart from that commemoration of my character."

Lucinda countered, "And mine is known for both its frankness and its resolve."

"Though I know it a disgraceful fabrication, I have heard of an alliance between you and the duke," her companion accused.

"From the duke?" Lucinda demanded. When would she learn? She had heard such accusations previously. Only then the words had come from Matthew Warren. As foolish as it may seem, at the time, Lucinda had secretly celebrated her husband's hurtful words because they had proved Captain Warren had cared for her.

The duchess declared, "I would not injure His Grace so by demanding the truth from him. However, upon learning of your relocation to Huntingborne Abbey, I instantly resolved on calling upon the household to make my sentiments known to you."

"If you truly believed such an involvement impossible," Lucinda said, coloring with astonishment and disdain, "I wonder you took the trouble of bringing the furniture as part of your ruse." She knew it would be best if she countered the duchess's insults with an assumed graciousness, but her temper had brought heat to Lucinda's cheeks. "Do you mistrust all of the duke's associates or is only Sir Carter who you believe would foster a tryst with a war widow?" Lucinda asked incredulously, "What could Your Grace propose by it?"

The duchess ignored Lucinda's dismissal. "As to Sir Carter, the baronet has sworn an allegiance to the duke, and likewise the duke reciprocates; and as to why I chose to come to Huntingborne Abbey, it was to insist upon having such a report contradicted."

"Your early attendance upon the baronet's estate," said Lucinda through tight lips, "will be an authentication of whatever fantasy your mind has conjured."

"Then deny the report by explaining why His Grace has taken an active interest in your concerns. Deny you have not maintained a relationship with my husband. I know you called upon Briar House in my absence. Can you declare there is no foundation for the rumors?"

Lucinda instantly regretted not having hired Nancy for the day, but she had not wanted the Petermans to know of her destination. She was certain Brantley Fowler held no knowledge of such declarations; the duke would not have taken kindly to his servants speaking openly of his personal business. Neither did Lucinda. She did not fault the young duchess for her confusion, but neither could Lucinda tolerate the girl's censorious attitude. So, although she wished the ground to open and swallow her whole, she said, "If I were involved with the duke, I would be the last person to confess it." She stood quickly and dropped a curtsy. "Please excuse me, Your Grace. I promised the boy I would assist him in reading his chosen book. I shall ask Mr. Vance to send in His Grace. Good day, Duchess." With that, Lucinda strode from the room. *So much for your chances of ever returning to Society,* she thought as she rushed toward her room. Lucinda's legs were shaking, and tears misted her eyes. "The duke's mistress," she growled as she slammed the outer door. "All my life I have done the correct thing, and what have I to show for it? No one to love me. A husband who preferred another. A father who placed me in danger in Brussels. An uncle who would deny me because of the scandal I would bring to his door. A child I can never love because he reminds me of Captain Warren's betrayal. And now the reputation of a wanton."

Carter had reported directly to his office upon his return to London, but his devotion to his position had not driven the image of Mrs. Warren's countenance from his mind. "Damn!" he growled under his breath as he read the report before him for the third time. "Not like me."

"What is not like you?" Pennington asked from the open doorway.

Carter was not in a secure enough position to inform his superior of how an unorthodox female had distracted him. "I thought you at your estate," he said as a diversion.

"The duchess…" Pennington began before correcting himself with a chuckle. "I mean to say Mrs. Pennington means to order new items for several of the rooms at Fox Run Manor."

Carter motioned the man into the room. "Are your pockets deep enough to support your lady's tastes?" he teased.

"To view the smile upon Bel's lips, I would risk it all," Pennington confessed.

Unlike his friends, Carter had never entertained the idea of setting up his nursery and knowing love. After all, he was the youngest of their band, and at age four and twenty, he meant to build a successful career before stepping into the Marriage Mart. However, he felt the twinge of regret at not knowing the same type of contentment he observed on the elder man's countenance. "If Mrs. Pennington's smile mimics the one displayed upon your lips, then I must admit to knowing jealousy." Carter reached for the decanter to pour them each a drink. "Godown's Aunt Bel has been good for your disposition," he teased.

"I cannot argue with that statement." Pennington accepted the glass and sipped the brandy. Then in his typical all-business tone, Pennington said, "I have news of Jamot's whereabouts."

Carter set forward with interest. He had hoped to capture the Baloch in order to solidify his position in his section of the Home Office. When his unit of the Realm had returned from their service, Murhad Jamot and Rahmat Talpur had followed to search for the elusive emerald. Talpur had lost his life in Cornwall at James Kerrington's hands when Carter and Viscount Worthing had staged the rescue of Thornhill's daughter Sonali. Jamot had managed to escape from the fiasco of Sir Louis Levering's transportation, from the warehouse in which the Baloch had held Velvet Aldridge, and from the glass cone in Scotland while Marcus Wellston had saved his ladylove, Cashémere Aldridge, from certain death.

With each of those attempts to recover the emerald, Jamot had acted predictably. The Baloch had used an innocent to coerce information regarding the missing emerald from one of Carter's associates. The fact none of the Realm held knowledge of the gem had not deterred Jamot's efforts. During those first three attempts at capturing the Baloch, Carter had learned all he could of the man. He knew Jamot to be cagey and clever and lethal–a man without a conscious.

However, since the Baloch had become more involved in the opium trade, or perhaps, because Jamot had become more knowledgeable of English life, their enemy had softened. Of late, the man who had followed them from the mountains overlooking the Persian-Indian border had acted uncharacteristically, and Carter had known the frustration of their enemy's unpredictable actions.

The Baloch had assisted Lady Godown from her captivity aboard the Chinese ship, and although he had reportedly informed Mathias Trent of Mercy Nelson's existence under Lord Lexford's roof, Jamot had risked knowing the future baronet's displeasure by protecting the girl until Lexford arrived to rescue his future viscountess.

It took a moment for his scattered thoughts to form a question. "And that would be?" Carter asked cautiously.

Pennington sat his glass upon the desk before lacing his fingers across his abdomen. Although the Realm's leader was of the age to be Carter's father, he certainly did not look the part. Aristotle Pennington prided himself on staying fit.

"The Baloch spends his time among a group of smugglers along the Suffolk coast. Jamot has been calling himself 'Black Bounty.' It appears he has steered cleared of the illegal drug trade."

Carter remarked, "Whatever Jamot does is immersed in evil."

Pennington observed, "The war has driven up the cost of fine lace, art-work, and brandy from the Continent." He lifted his glass in a silent reminder of how they each contributed to the trade. "With the poor crops on both the European front and at home, men have turned to extreme measures to feed and to clothe their families."

"Jamot has no family," Carter argued.

"No. The Baloch lost his family when Shaheed Mir declared Ashmita a whore and then turned the girl into one," Pennington reasoned.

Carter countered, "Jamot should have fought for the woman he affected. It should never have been Thornhill's place to save the girl."

"Mayhap." Pennington finished his drink. "Yet, we both know Thornhill's decision to save Ashmita also saved the duke's life. Without his need to give Sonali a decent life, Thornhill might have known an early death due to his immature impetuousness. That incident provided Thornhill a reason to return to Kent and reclaim his title."

"What do you wish me to do about Jamot?"

Pennington rose easily and turned toward the door. "Send Clayton Bradwick and Swonton Van Dyke to investigate while you resolve Mrs. Warren's dilemma."

Privately alarmed, Carter called after him. "How did you know of Mrs. Warren?"

Pennington paused to level a steady gaze upon Carter, and Carter felt he had been called before the schoolmaster. "I have known from the beginning of your recruitment to our cause you would be an asset to this organization, Lowery. The same as I know James Kerrington will make an excellent diplomat and Crowden a superior future ambassador, I know your place is here in this office. You have the drive to succeed, but you will fall short of your expecta-tions if you do not extend your lines of information. Entertain politicians and the common folks. Learn whom you can trust and whom to watch. Develop a cache of solid informants. Otherwise, the powers at be will deny you what should rightly be yours." As he turned away, Pennington added, "I know of Mrs. Warren because as your leader, I am expected to be aware of every facet of your life."

The duke had sent a note of apology for his wife's actions, citing the duchess's emotional state with her impending lying in. He then begged Lucinda's forgiveness for the misunderstanding, as well as her continued permission for the boy to come to Thorn Hall on Friday. Lucinda wished to hide herself away from the potential scandal, but she had weathered her early exit among Sir Carter's staff by explaining how the duchess had excused her as Lucinda claimed a megrim. Her taking to her room for some thirty hours following the incident had served as proof of her excuses.

"His Grace will send one of his men to escort you to Thorn Hall," she explained to Simon on Thursday evening. They had been at Huntingborne Abbey since the early afternoon on Monday, but it had seemed much longer. "I found a box of scraps of material in the attic. Mrs. Shelton assured me I could have free use of them so I have made a gift for you to present to the duke's daughter." Lucinda produced a small rag doll from her sewing basket. "I am certain Miss Sonali has those which are finer, but it is all I have which you might share with the duke's daughter."

The boy fingered the lace and gold buttons Lucinda had added in hopes of pleasing a child she had yet to meet. "I would suppose any girl would think this a fine gift, Ma'am."

Lucinda had to remind herself the child had not been with her for longer than a half year. He was so wise for one so young, and she had come to admire Simon's sweet nature. "Mrs. Shelton says she will assist you in wrapping the package."

"May I be excused?" Simon asked hopefully.

Lucinda smiled easily. The boy had had a disrupted life, and she wished to provide him a taste of normalcy. "Of course. And do not forget to tend carefully to your ablutions. I would not have the duchess think poorly of you." *Not the way Velvet Fowler disapproves of me*, Lucinda thought. She caressed his cheek. "Now, be off with you. You have an important engagement tomorrow."

She watched him skip happily from the room. The boy clutched the doll as if it were a pot of gold. She prayed Thornhill's child knew better manners than did the duchess, and that Miss Sonali would not openly mock Simon's gift. It made her sad to think of the possibility that someone would rebuke Simon, and the boy would know pain.

She would never wish the boy to think upon himself as less than desirable. There was so much more for Simon to learn than the crucial boundaries in which Society defined a soul. Family, whether immediate or extended, should never turn its back upon a child. Should never suffocate a child's hopes and dreams. It was fair for a child not to know approval of his every thought and action, but never fair for a child not to know love.

Since the day the boy had arrived in her life, Lucinda had questioned every decision she had made in his behalf. Some days she would just be satisfied to hear the boy laugh. Like her, the child had suffered a devastating loss. From what little the boy had revealed, Simon had last seen his father when he was two. Lucinda wondered if the boy's memory was a true one or one borrowed from the adults in his life. She suspected it a "'borrowed" one, the same as the child meant to borrow the duke's remembrances and adopt them as his own.

The boy had reminded Lucinda of her own upbringing. When she was younger, she had thought of her life as one like most in the English countryside. Her parents were minor aristocrats, each with strong pedigrees, and although they were not, obviously, in love, she knew her parents had held the highest respect for each other. She had noted a decided expression of longing on her father's countenance when he looked upon his wife. As a young girl full of fanciful dreams, she had thought it the look of love. However, after her many years of following first her father and then Matthew, she had learned it the look of lust. She knew herself excruciatingly proper at times, but if someone would simply look upon her—to see the real Lucinda Elaine Rightnour Warren... If someone would look, he would find beneath the quiet reserve, she hid a ready smile, an insatiable curiosity, and unregulated dreams—enough so to find her fascinating—something Matthew Warren had never bothered doing.

"Mrs. Warren?" she looked up to see Sir Carter's housekeeper. Mrs. Shelton had held her position for less than a month, but from what Lucinda had observed the woman had taken the staff well in hand. "Might I presume upon your time, Ma'am?"

Lucinda hated being referred to as "Ma'am." She thought it made her sound terribly old. "Certainly, Mrs. Shelton." She offered the woman a welcoming smile. "How may I serve you?"

The woman, a lady of forty plus years, stepped further into the room. The housekeeper's strict posture and well-rehearsed facial expressions hid an attractive woman who likely had experienced the world's sour side. "Sir Carter, Ma'am. The baronet asked that I oversee the renovations of the rooms in the

71

east wing. The men have completed the changes Baroness Blakehell left with her son, but the décor is lacking something, which I possess no experience in defining. I wondered if you might have a look." The woman appeared nervous, and Lucinda realized the impropriety Mrs. Shelton ventured. "It is just that Sir Carter speaks so highly of you, and I thought a fresh set of eyes might recognize what is missing."

Lucinda thought to refuse. What right did she have to offer an opinion in Sir Carter's house? After all, she was a mere guest, but the housekeeper's words of the baronet's praise had warmed her after three days of desolation. "I am not certain I shall have much to add. My life has been one of military tents and small cottages," she confessed. "But I would be pleased to view the progress in the east wing. Do you mean to do so now, Mrs. Shelton?"

"If you can spare the time, Ma'am."

There was that detestable word again, the one which labeled her as a widow, as a woman who had known her husband's every thought. Such a foul word! Swallowing the bile rising in her throat, Lucinda said evenly, "Certainly. Please lead the way, Mrs. Shelton."

Carter had received the initial reports on Jamot's presence in Suffolk and on the largest of the Jewish populations spread throughout England. Since meeting Mrs. Warren, he had spent more than a few hours immersing himself in the history of the Jews in England since the accession of George III to the throne. He was convinced Simon Warren's mother had dwelt with one of the pockets of Jews congregating in England.

He had made several calculated assumptions. First, despite Captain Warren having met, wooed, and married Simon's mother in Spain, or possibly Portugal, no one could say whether he had sent the woman and the boy to England. Warren's military records showed from the time of his joining the service, the man had made but one journey to his home in Devon, the one where he had exchanged vows with Lucinda Rightnour.

Carter had assigned a man to search ship records to learn whether Warren had traveled alone. Perhaps, Matthew Warren had settled his "wife" before claiming Miss Rightnour. He shook his head in disbelief. It was against Carter's nature to permit a woman to know the evils of war. In contrast to what Mrs. Warren believed, he was of the persuasion to think Simon the product of an illicit love encounter, rather than to be Captain Warren's heir for he doubted any man of a right mind could ignore Lucinda Warren's charms.

Although Carter worked daily with people of the Jewish persuasion, he had never really thought about the impact of the Jewish religion on the daily life of those in London and the English countryside. From his governmental studies, he was aware that with King George's rise to the throne, two standing committees had formed to address urgent political developments, which might affect the Ashkenazi and the Sephardic sects. The appointed *Deputados* would approach the government on their behalves. The two "Nations" had been forced to communicate and to meet jointly and to receive a degree of statutory recognition.

Numbering in the thousands, there were distinct economic differences between the two assemblages. The more anglicized and wealthier of the two were those from Spain and Portugal; the lower social strata were those from Eastern Europe, predominantly from Germany. Carter prayed progress had been made between the "Nations." He was ashamed to admit he knew little of the Jewish faith and had few social contacts of a Jewish affiliation.

"Perhaps you know more of the people than you think," John Swenton had declared when they met over a drink at White's. The baron had arrived in London to conduct estate business and to call upon Pennington before retreating to York for the summer months. "After all, there has been a steady, though narrow, stream of reformation. Conversionistic hopes were not stymied by Lord George Gordon's switch from Protestantism to Judaism." Swenton smiled wryly.

Carter said dryly, "I know you correct." It was the second time in a day he had recognized one of his shortcomings. First, Pennington had pointed out how Carter had not developed a deep reservoir of contacts, and now he gave credence to the idea of his weak education, especially in history. How could he ever hope to succeed Aristotle Pennington in the role of the Realm's leader if he was constantly found wanting.

As if Swenton read Carter's thoughts, the baron suggested, "Surely you have encountered the Rag Fair, and I know you have bought items from the Jewish peddlers who roam the countryside. Hell, Lowery, we have encountered more than one wealthy Jew serving as a ship's agent, and it is easy to note every official list of the Navy's agents holds a directory of the Jewish communities supporting the war and England." Swenton scowled. "What does this involve? Is it an investigation with which I may assist you?"

It was Carter's turn to frown. He had spoken too freely. "Nothing of import," he added quickly. "Just an encounter, which has sprung my curiosity." He motioned the server to bring them another drink. "Instead, permit me to apprise you of Jamot's latest dealings."

Lucinda looked about the guest bedchamber. Based upon her limited experience with British country manor houses, it was quite typical. She held images of her life at Merritt House, her parents' modest estate in Devon, but she possessed little knowledge beyond those idyllic years spent with her vivacious mother.

Mahogany pillars supported linen bed draperies, gathered in folds and tied about the posts, which matched the draperies hung at the tall, thin windows. Mrs. Shelton and her staff had scrubbed away the filth reportedly left behind by the previous owner, but in its simplicity, the room lacked appeal. Wool blankets displayed upon a chest were a pale brown, as were the sheets. The counterpane was of white cotton with cotton knots. A mahogany press. An oval mirror. A small table holding a basin and pitcher. Another table beside the bed. "Quite efficient," she murmured softly, "but it has the feel of a let room." She should know; Lucinda had spent many days in rooms not her own.

"Exactly," Mrs. Shelton said in exasperation. "I have never held the responsibility of refurbishing the master's rooms, only with cleaning them."

Lucinda glanced to the woman. "Obviously, Sir Carter trusts your opinions."

"I do not think so, Mrs. Warren." The housekeeper gestured to the room's furnishings. "It is my opinion Sir Carter does not know where to begin. The baronet realizes he requires a home, which will impress those he entertains, but Sir Carter does not see beyond the basics. It is as if he expects a fairy's magic wand to make everything as he envisioned it; yet had no concept beyond these simple items."

"Has the baronet forbidden additional expenses?"

"Oh, no, Ma'am. The baronet established an account for whatever I saw fit," the housekeeper protested.

"Then I do not see the concern," Lucinda declared.

The housekeeper shook her head in strict denial. "I could not think to place my taste in the baronet's home. I was not raised to know the differences in lace, only which soap to use to wash it."

Lucinda wanted to scream, neither had she, but that pronouncement would be an untruth: Her dear mother, Sophia Rightnour, had overseen all Lucinda's lessons upon being a fine lady. It had been Sophia's wish when both the Rightnours and the Warrens passed, she and Captain Warren would combine the estates and live grandly as husband and wife. "It shall be a fine legacy for my grandchildren," her mother had said upon more than one occasion. *So much for your distinguished dreams, Mother,* Lucinda murmured beneath her breath. "I am a guest in the baronet's house," she pleaded. "I do not believe it fit I should interfere."

"*Interference* is hardly the word," Mrs. Shelton reasoned. "From what the others have said, you are the only guest other than the baronet's family who have dined and rested below Sir Carter's roof for more than one evening. In my humble opinion, the baronet holds you in highest regard. He instructed the staff to accept your orders in his stead. To me, it sounds as if he would gladly respect whatever choices you made. In fact, your opinions and insights would be a means to repay Sir Carter for his generosity."

Lucinda immediately wondered how much the baronet's staff knew of the real reason for her stay at Huntingborne Abbey. Despite her desire to remain removed from the chaos surrounding her arrival in Kent, she conceded Mrs. Shelton stated the obvious: Lucinda owed Sir Carter Lowery. Pausing to choose her words carefully, she said, "I shall write the baronet to seek Sir Carter's permission to assist you." She would feel better knowing she had not offended the baronet by being so bold. "Meanwhile, perhaps we might inventory what is available in the house we might use to decorate the various chambers."

Carter had ridden to Oxfordshire to meet with an informant regarding another recent investigation in which he was involved: This time with a PM who had proved a traitor during the war. Mr. Cyrus Woodstone had traded information, which he had accessed as a member of the War Board, for expensive pieces of European art. The man had erred by showing Lord Witmore a painted tapestry by José del Castillo. Witmore had immediately recognized the artist and had reported his suspicions to Pennington.

Under Carter's direction, one of the Realm's elite units had spent the past year gathering information against Woodstone; but the gentleman had correctly made adjustments and had hidden away the items, sending Carter's men on a fox run: chasing after each scent. The Realm could not move against Woodstone until they recovered the artwork. The British government wished to return the pieces to the respective courts as a symbol of goodwill.

His meeting with Ward Dartmour had proved very productive, and Carter's demeanor had lightened. Even if he could not capture Murhad Jamot, sealing Woodstone's fate would bring him positive note among those debating who should replace Pennington. He rode comfortably, feeling the warmth of the day upon his cheeks.

Last night, he had dreamed again of the boy—the one he had left upon the fields outside Bousval, but before he had awakened in a cold sweat to the horror of death all around him, a light had opened, and the boy had stepped through. He had awakened with a jerk, but dread had not filled his chest. Instead, a flicker of hope had taken root. It was possible the boy had not died a horrendous death. Until he had awakened from the familiar nightmare, Carter had held no delusion the youth had survived, and he had prayed some crazed Frenchman had not taken the lad prisoner and had ill-abused him. If the youth had lost his life that terrible day, Carter prayed the deed had been swift. However, the light's shaft in the midst of his bloody nightmare had given Carter hope for the first time since the day he awoke in a Realm-controlled hospital. "Perhaps…" he had announced to the day.

The word had barely escaped his lips when the shot rang out, and Carter felt the graze of hot metal across his thigh as he reined in his horse. Leaping from the saddle, he ran toward a nearby hedgerow. A second shot whizzed over his head. He threw his hat upon the ground and dove behind the thick greenery. His horse skittered away, but Carter gave it little thought. Instead, his eyes searched for movement in the clump of woodland on the other side of the road.

The shooter likely used an infantry rifle. The Baker rifle was known for its accuracy, but only the rifle regiments used them during the war. Average soldiers used the issued Brown Bess. "An expert shot. Likely the same person who found me in Dover," he reasoned aloud. His eyes swept the opposing cover again. Nothing moved, which told Carter someone had been there–likely still there. *Nature always goes silent when men invade its territory*, he thought.

Finally, a flash of sun upon metal caught his eyes, and Carter was on the move, paralleling his attacker's retreat. He ran bent over, keeping his eyes peeled upon the spot where he had seen the split of color.

When his assailant broke into a run, Carter burst through the hedgerow to give pursuit. The man was heavier than he and struggled with the rugged terrain. When his attacker stumbled, Carter overtook him. A diving lunge brought him crashing down upon the man's broad back, but Carter had misjudged the distance enough to where he brought his assailant only to his knees, rather than flat. The man turned quickly to land a blow to Carter's chin. Swinging wildly, the shooter scrambled to his feet as Carter, still reeling from the man's fist, struggled to reach his own.

As the stranger set off again through the brambles, Carter swayed in place for a second before following. His senses rattled, his reflexes had slowed, and he had not anticipated the blow across his upper back, which drove him to his knees. Carter's eyes caught the image of a highly polished boot before the world went black.

Chapter Seven

"Is Mrs. Warren your mother?" the girl asked as Simon built a castle for her dolls from the wooden blocks scattered upon the nursery room floor. He had spent several hours at the Duke of Thornhill's manor and had attempted to imagine his father walking through these very halls. He held no true memory of his father other than a voice he heard sometimes in his dreams. Mrs. Warren had given him a sketch of Captain Warren she had made. "Although I am not much of an artist, it favors Mr. Warren," she had said as she handed over the folded paper, holding a pencil drawing of a man in a uniform.

He did not look at the girl. She was dressed in frills and lace, much as he expected fitting a duke's daughter, but to Simon's surprise she had freely shared her toys and books with him. "No. Mrs. Warren was once married to my father," he explained. "My mother was sick. She paid a man to escort me to England. I imagine she has died." The realization made him duck his head to hide the tears teasing his eyes.

The girl sprawled beside him on the floor, and Simon shot a glance to the disapproving look upon her nurse's countenance. Sonali Fowler was two years older than he, but they were about the same size. Simon had had only two friends with whom his mother had permitted him to play, and neither had been a girl. "My mother died also," she announced. "She was very sick and a long time in her bed. Papa says Mama fought to live long enough for me to be born."

"I thought the duchess your mother," he said.

The girl traced the line of the wooden floor with her finger. "The duchess is my mama because she and I wanted it to be so." She said brightly, "Maybe Mrs. Warren can be your mama. Would you wish for her to become your new mama?"

Simon thought upon what the girl asked. "Mrs. Warren treats me kindly."

"That is something," she declared. "Papa says many children have no one to care for them, and I am fortunate to have both him and my new mama, as well as his friends. I call Sir Carter 'Uncle Carter.' There is also Uncle James, Uncle Marcus, Uncle Aidan, Uncle Gabriel, and Uncle John. They are not my real uncles, but they assisted Papa with me when he had business from home."

"I suppose you are correct: Having Mrs. Warren as a my mama and Sir Carter as an uncle would be very fine." He placed a sheet of brown paper on the floor beside the make believe castle. "This will be the drawbridge."

"It is an excellent castle!" she exclaimed as she clapped her hands together. "Your castle is nearly as well done as Papa's." Simon liked that particular idea. From what he had seen of the duke, he thought the man quite brave. Earlier, Thornhill had spoken to Simon of how he and Simon's father had attended university together. The duke shared tales of boyhood pranks and studies. Then he spoke of spending several months in the same military unit as Captain Warren.

"Your Papa and I were both captains," the duke explained, "which meant we held great responsibility for the men under us. Your father was a great one for responsibility, Boy. You should be very proud of his service to England."

The girl, who had sat upon her father's lap throughout the duke's tales, had said, "Mama says you met Mrs. Warren when you were with Simon's papa during the war."

The duke had appeared uncomfortable, as if there was a secret he would not share, and Simon had wondered what if might be. Adults always kept secrets from their children. His mama had kept the secret of his birth from everyone, and she had also not told Simon she might be dying until it was too late for him to seek out assistance for her. "Yes, Mrs. Warren followed the drum; that means she and the women like her traveled with their husbands during the war."

"Would my real mama have followed you, Papa?"

The duke caressed his daughter's cheek, and Simon was a bit jealous. He would never have a 'papa' to offer him such a gesture. "Ashmita was very brave," Thornhill assured his child. "I hold no doubt, had she lived and had I remained under the Duke of Wellington's command the two of us would have been among those surviving the war together." Simon wondered why his own mother had not followed Captain Warren. Was it because she was a Jewess? Mrs. Warren had said others did not care for those who followed the Jewish ways.

From beside him, the girl scrambled to catch up the doll Mrs. Warren had made for her. "I plan to call this one Chenille; it is the name of my new mama's mother. She will go well with Isana." From a drawer, the girl produced an unusual rag doll with a porcelain head. The doll's painted face held a small crescent moon painted on its forehead, along with a blue throat and a stringy braid of matted black hair. "This is a special doll. My real mama made it for me." Sonali placed the doll reverently upon a miniature bed. "Now I have an English doll and an Indian one. They are like me, a little of each."

"Do people say bad things to you?" he asked. "Because your skin is darker than theirs. As dark as mine."

She reasoned, "I am a duke's daughter, so no one says bad things anymore, but when we lived in Cornwall…" Simon cringed. He suspected several adults must have spoken unkindly of the girl. Perhaps, Mrs. Warren had spoken the truth of others not treating everyone fairly. This was a strange idea for a child accustomed to living among his family and church. The girl did not finish her thought. Instead, she reached for a small box. "These were my mother's belongings," she explained. "This was her favorite dress and shoes and the cloth for a sari. When I am older, I plan to wear these, and I shall not care if anyone thinks them odd. My papa says I cannot live for others." Simon wondered again if others would accept him. In England, it seemed no one looked liked him, and if Mrs. Warren's drawing held any truth, he held no resemblance to the late Captain Warren.

He had returned to London but three days prior. A farmer transporting sheep pelts to Oxford had discovered Carter's untethered mount and had come searching for the animal's owner. Carter had begged for a ride, even upon the smelly sheepskins, so he might seek out the talents of a gifted surgeon in Oxford of whom he was acquainted. The surgeon had stitched up the deep cut across his shoulder and had bandaged the wound on the back of Carter's head, but, thankfully, he had pronounced Carter well enough to travel. His arm remained stiff, but Carter had attempted to ignore it. "What did we learn of my attacker?" he asked Van Dyke, the Realm recruit assigned to assist him with the investigation.

"We recovered the shrapnel; and you were correct. It was of the type used by the infantry units during the war. Whoever struck you broke the stock across your upper back." Van Dyke ticked off the facts on his fingers.

Carter frowned. "Was there evidence of more than one attacker?"

"Two days of rain had muddied the area…"

It was as Carter feared: no evidence other than the vague image of the toe of a polished boot. "I want one more sweep of the area. Take fresh eyes with you. Ask more questions. Hopefully, someone took note of strangers."

Lucinda had received a short, succinct note from Sir Carter giving her permission to proceed with whatever decorating in which she chose to participate. The note's brevity had disappointed her. She had held some girlish fantasy the baronet might ask of her wellbeing or inquire of Simon's taking to the country. "You are being the world's worst fool," she had chastised her reflection in the mirror as she brushed her hair. Lucinda had refused the maid Sir Carter had assigned to her: She would not permit herself a luxury she would be later be denied. "The viscount does not wish your friendship."

When she had written to ask his permission to purchase several items for the estate, Lucinda had carefully described what she had planned. She had expected the baronet's response to include his opinion of her suggestions, and from there they could regularly correspond. Lucinda was quite lonely in the baronet's household. Only she, Simon, and the servants occupied the manor. No one had made neighborly calls beyond the Duke and Duchess of Thornhill; no one knew of her residency. It made sense for the baronet to avoid explaining turning over his home to a stranger. The local gentry would think her Sir Carter's mistress, or worse, as the duchess had explained, think her Thornhill's mistress. Even Simon had deserted daily her for the pleasures of Thorn Hall's library.

However, Sir Carter's note had dashed all her hopes of anticipating a letter from him. Try as she might, she did not understand what drove the baronet. Her failings were quite obvious, but what of his aloofness? Ironically, even in its conciseness, the note was more than she had ever received from Matthew Warren. In fact, she had never received a letter, all her own, from anyone. True, her father had included her in his, but they were truly meant for her mother.

Unfortunately for Lucinda "You have my permission to make necessary changes. SCL" did not provide her the basis for an epistolary relationship. "Just set the changes in motion," Lucinda warned her heart, "and cease your pining for something never to be." Lacing the ribbon about the end of her plait, she wrapped the long braid into a severe bun. It would likely give her a megrim, but Lucinda thought it justice for her fanciful musings. She was not meant for a life of normalcy.

"What do you think?" she nervously asked Mrs. Shelton. While they had awaited Sir Carter's permission, she and the housekeeper had made detailed lists of the items once belonging to Sir Louis Levering, as well as the items sent to Sir Carter from the various members of his immediate family. From these, they had chosen several to decorate the rooms in question. Mrs. Shelton had suggested they separate the items according to color. "A palette of complementary shades," Lucinda had agreed. "We will choose a color scheme for each chamber. Purchase small items—trays for soap and towels. Those sorts of necessities. Ribbon to trim drapes and pillows. Then we will add a vase of similar shade for fresh flowers. Nothing ostentatious. That would not be to Sir Carter's tastes."

"Classic lines," Mrs. Shelton agreed. "Perfect."

Lucinda had enjoyed the lady's praise. She had never had the opportunity to express her eye for décor previously. It was a heady sensation to do so in Sir Carter's name. "We should finish the rose chamber first. If all goes well, then we will have a pattern for the others."

"Jamot has resurfaced," Pennington announced as he entered Carter's office. The Realm's leader rubbed his hands together in anticipation. Carter had been daydreaming; he had read Thornhill's latest report on Mrs. Warren and had thought to return to Huntingborne to observe for himself how the lady got on.

His face lit with the shared expectancy. "Is the Baloch still in Suffolk?"

"Yes, Mir's man has pledged his larcenous efforts with those of a rag tag group of former soldiers. Our informants say the band is responsible for much of the smuggled goods in the area. Part of the group serves upon a recently repaired Indian vessel believed to have been financed by Mir himself."

Carter scowled. "That fact does not ring true. Mir is singular in his insistence that one of us has his emerald. For him to finance a scheme, which does little more than to ruffle the feathers of local authorities is not in the Baloch lord's scope. He is a ruthless warlord, as well as an intelligent strategist. It is how he has eluded the numerous attempts by the British government to capture him for so long. Mir engages only in 'wars' he can win. Fighting the British government on British soil would be a losing endeavor, one the Baloch chief would never choose. It would cost him dearly to lose face among his people. It is why Mir sent Jamot and Talpur, rather than to seek out the Realm himself. If his emissaries are unsuccessful, Mir may blame his servants."

Pennington nodded approvingly. "You have found the weakness in the report. It is always to your benefit to know your enemy better than he knows you. So, what say you is the truth?"

Carter wondered if this was some sort of test of his ability to lead or perhaps Pennington meant to tutor him in his responsibilities. If those were the two choices for this encounter, he would choose the latter. Learning everything Pennington knew of threats to England's safety had been Carter's desire since he joined the Realm. "More than likely, Jamot has used Mir's name, as he has done in the past with Talpur. Jamot is lethal, but he thinks small, while Mir dwells on grand schemes. Murhad Jamot is the perfect henchman: He blames others for his shortcomings and uses his guilt to punish those he deems his enemies."

"Interesting," Pennington said pensively. Carter worried whether his superior meant "interesting," as if Pennington had never considered Carter's summation or "interesting," as if Carter had missed the obvious. It would be another moment to replay over his evening meal, but Carter knew after four years of service under Pennington, the Realm's leader would say little else on the matter. "I assume you will be to Suffolk within the hour."

Carter reached for his jacket, which he had hung on the back of his chair. "I will send Monroe to the mews to saddle my horse. A Realm courier will bring you news of my progress." As he slid his arms into the sleeves, he regretted the interruption, which would keep him from Mrs. Warren's company. It was foolish to miss those few moments they had shared. After all, he was only her... Her what? Her savior? Not likely. He had learned little of her circumstances. In fact, since returning to London, he had spent his time chasing after information on Cyrus Woodstone, on his attacker, and on Jamot, but not on the lady's dilemma. He had safely absconded her away, but he could not keep her there… in the country…in his home forever. She belonged with her family, not with him. Shaking off his rampant musings of blonde curls wrapped about his fist, Carter said, "Hopefully, this time Jamot will not slip away before I arrive."

Lucinda looked up in surprise when Mr. Vance presented her a silver salver with a letter resting upon its surface. She had been at Huntingborne Abbey a fortnight, but other than the one note from the baronet, she had corresponded with no one beyond the servants and the Duke of Thornhill. She frowned as she accepted the letter from Sir Carter's butler. "Is something amiss, Mrs. Warren?"

She blushed thoroughly. "Certainly not, Mr. Vance. I was simply considering who might know of my residence in Kent."

"I could not say, Ma'am."

With his exit, Lucinda broke the wax seal to unfold the page. If the message was from Sir Carter, the baronet had not bothered to use his seal upon the wax. Anxiously, she opened the page to read another brief message: "Bring the boy to the Rising Son Inn on Friday. I have information regarding the child's parents." Lucinda frowned. The message left much to be explained.

"That is all?" she mumbled as she turned the paper over several times as if something had been omitted. "Nothing regarding how I might travel so far nor the nature of the information the baronet has discovered. Has Sir Carter found Simon's missing mother? Am I to turn over the child to a stranger?" The thought of parting with the boy squeezed her heart in anguish. She would not wish to place Simon in a home where he was not fully welcomed. "And where is the Rising Son Inn? It is not as if I am aware of each hostelry in England." Lucinda read the note a second time. She snorted her disapproval. "The baronet did not even include a salutation or a closing signature. I never thought of him as a man of so few words."

Lucinda sat heavily against the hard leather seat. The duke had hired a hack to transport her and the child to an inn somewhere north of the Essex border. Thornhill had wanted her to use either Sir Carter's coach or one of his smaller ones, but Lucinda had adamantly refused. She had also declined his offer to escort her. "I shall have none of it. Your kindness has already created a riff between you and the duchess. I would not add flames to the fire."

Of course, Thornhill had declared he would not permit his duchess to speak for him, but Lucinda was certain he would be satisfied not to witness his wife's displeasure. She did graciously accept the services of Sir Carter's coachman, Mr. Watkins.

The boy had not been happy to leave the comfort of Huntingborne Abbey nor his new friendship with Sonali Fowler. She suspected Simon as lonely as she. "Perhaps, Sir Carter has found your mother," she encouraged, but Simon had turned his head away. In silence, the boy wiped at a tear rolling slowly over his cheekbone. Lucinda wished he would share with her what little he knew of his parents. Any bit of information might prove the difference. As the shadows gathered, they rolled on. Mr. Watkins declared they would arrive in time for a late meal.

The duke had provided her with enough coinage to purchase a room for her and the boy. "For a man known to tend strictly to details, Sir Carter is sorely lacking in this matter," Thornhill had proclaimed, and Lucinda was very much in agreement.

A sharp whistle announced their arrival. Mr. Watkins slowed the coach and reined in before a well-lit inn. She heard the scurry of feet as men rushed to secure the coach. Within a minute, Mr. Watkins opened the door to assist them down. "We've arrived, Ma'am." He set the steps and reached for Lucinda's hand. "I don't see the baronet's horse, but it may already be in the stable. I'll look for Prime. If'n he not be within, I'll come to watch over ye and the boy."

"Thank you, Mr. Watkins." She did not like the looks of the inn. It was not a place for a woman alone. A shiver of dread ran down her spine. "Stay close, Simon." Lucinda caught the boy's hand. It felt so familiar in her grasp.

A rotund man with a jovial countenance rushed forward to greet them. "I am Mrs. Warren. The boy and I require a room for the evening." Her gaze slid across the common room, searching for Sir Carter's familiar countenance. She realized belatedly she knew nothing of how they were to make contact. Lucinda had assumed the baronet would greet her upon her arrival.

"I have a small room facing the back of the inn, if that would meet your requirements, Ma'am."

Lucinda's eyes made another sweep of the main room. Should she instruct the innkeeper to direct Sir Carter to her upon his arrival? She certainly would not wish to appear to be expecting an assignation. "The room shall be acceptable. Please have someone bring a meal for the boy and me, as well as provide one for my driver." She hoped Mr. Watkins would inform the baronet of her presence.

A few minutes later, she had paid the innkeeper and stood in the middle of a starkly simple room. "It is not much," Simon said with disapproval.

Lucinda's opinion mirrored the child's, but she held her tongue. She thought of the simple touches she and Mrs. Shelton had added to the rooms at Huntingborne. They had enlivened the rooms without making them overly ornate. *This room could use some of what she had left behind.* "We have been spoiled by the baronet's generosity," she declared. "Unfortunately, this is our reality." She gestured to the plain furnishings.

He had followed Jamot's trail for three days, and with each frustrating dead end, his temper had grown tighter. An informant had claimed Jamot frequented an inn on Surrey's southern border, and so Carter and Monroe had donned their working clothes to assume a familiar role as ex-soldiers searching for gainful employment. Carter had tethered their horses in the woods behind the inn, and they had approached on foot. He feigned a limp as they entered the open room. The movement was not so foreign a feeling. After Waterloo, it had taken him several months to walk normally after a surgeon had dug a French bullet from his thigh.

He and Monroe pushed past the hovering innkeeper and sought a table in a dark corner. When the busty barmaid arrived with two beers for which neither he nor Monroe had placed an order, Carter slid a coin across the table. "What if we wished yer best brandy?" he asked caustically.

"You, Gents, kant 'ford no brandy," she said saucily. "Besides, the brandy be watered down." She smiled a toothy grin at Monroe. "Ye be requirin' anything else, ye ask fer Nell."

When she strolled away, purposely twitching her hips, Monroe leaned Carter's way. "I would be afeared of what I might take with me from the fair Nell's bed."

Carter chuckled. "Aye, a man must be careful with whom he shares his time." Immediately, he thought of the "fair Lucinda Warren" and knew he would gladly share whatever she offered.

Monroe jabbed Carter in the side with his elbow. "Is that Jamot at the bar's end? Beside the man with the gray hair."

Carter's heart rate jumped: Monroe's keen eyes had cut through the shadows and the tobacco smoke to discover their man across a crowded room. It was the closest Carter had been to Jamot in over the year. Unfortunately, there were some two-dozen people between him and the Baloch. His eyes searched the room for possible escape routes, as well as for accomplices. For a year, he had investigated Jamot's associates in the opium ring, but this was a new group of compatriots. The majority of England's smugglers were villagers and farmers. Few were harden criminals: Most wished only to supplement their meager incomes. Some thought they had a right to the goods denied them by embargos and treaties and political maneuverings. Despite their lack of training and motivation, Carter held no doubt Jamot's latest companions would fight to protect the Baloch.

"I will attempt to move closer," he said under his breath. "There are too many innocents between Jamot and us, and the Baloch has never been ashamed of placing others between him and a bullet. Stay alert and watch for my signal." Monroe nodded. Carter rose slowly, giving any watchful eyes the impression he had had too much to drink. Keeping his back to the room, he staggered between the tables, pausing occasionally to slap one of the locals on the back in a friendly manner and to motion to Nell to bring a round of drink for a table he had jostled.

Throughout his antics, he kept one eye on the Baloch. Jamot had yet to look up at him. The Realm's enemy appeared deep in conversation with a man who was dressed a bit too finely for those who regularly patronized the Rising Son. Within fifteen feet of a man he had sought for more than two years, Carter leaned heavily on the lip of the bar. With his head down, he reached into an inside pocket to ease a specially crafted pistol into his palm. Now, it was a matter of waiting. He would wait until the three men arguing over the price of grain shifted from the line of fire, and then he would make his move.

However, the farmers tarried, and Jamot had become irritated with his companion, and before Carter could react Jamot sat his mug heavily upon the bar's marred surface and turned toward the exit.

Carter snapped into action a second behind the Baloch. "Jamot!" he called over the din of voices as he lifted the gun for a safe shot. Shouts of dismay filled the air while people scrambled from the way, but Carter's focus remained on the Realm's long-time enemy.

The Baloch froze and lifted his hands in the air in casual surrender. Too casual for Carter's liking. "Monroe?" he called without turning his head.

"Aye, Sir."

"Search Jamot, but be wary. Our friend is known for his caginess." Monroe cautiously knelt behind the Baloch and bent to run his hands over Jamot's person. To the room, Carter announced, "I am an agent of the King, and I mean no one harm. I have searched for this man for more than two years. He is charged with murder and kidnapping." Carter would not mention Jamot's dealing in illegal goods. Those who crouched in anticipation of what would occur next could construe his words to mean the unlawful brandy easily found in eastern English homes.

Jamot flinched when Monroe fished a pistol from his jacket pocket, but, otherwise, the Baloch did not move, and neither did anyone else in the room. The tension clung to Carter's shoulders, and he was glad when Jamot spoke. It brought life to a terrible tableau.

"Your disguise was most effective, Sir Carter," the Baloch said with an ironic sneer. "I must remember your ability to assimilate for when next we meet."

Carter said defiantly, "There will be no next time, Jamot. Your mission for Shaheed Mir has reached its end."

Jamot snorted his contempt. "It is only over when I discover Mir's prize."

"Each of your previous attempts have proved futile," Carter countered, choking back his anger.

The Baloch smiled wryly. "But there are two remaining who could prove guilty."

Carter would not argue with his enemy. "Step away, Monroe." He gestured with the gun he still held upon the Baloch. "Everyone remain where you are, and we will trouble you no further." He stepped around the men hunkered down before the bar to approach Jamot. "No impulsive moves," he warned. "I would prefer to escort you to London alive, but I would hold no qualms in seeing your body slung over a saddle."

Jamot smirked, "And here I had come to think you held a fondness for the likes of me."

"Monroe, you are to provide cover," Carter ordered as he gestured Jamot toward the door.

Lucinda had finally convinced the boy to sleep. "He be a good lad, Mrs. Warren," Mr. Watkins assured. "All at the estate say so. Ye shud be proud of him, Ma'am."

She would not abuse the coachman for his error. "If Sir Carter does not arrive this evening, I suppose we should return to Kent tomorrow. I cannot imagine the reason for the baronet's delay, but we cannot remain in these quarters. If it were not so late, I would press you to return tonight."

"It is not like Sir Carter to mislead a person, but I agree, Ma'am. This not be fit quarters for a lady." He reached for the door's handle. "I'll check the room below for the baronet, and then I be retrieving my roll from the coach. I make me bed outside yer door."

Lucinda caught the man's rough hand. "I do not know how to thank you for your kindness. Simon and I are in your debt."

"It be likely the baronet come lookin' fer ye when he arrives," Watkins declared in all earnestness. "Sir Carter would have me hide if'n I not see to yer safety."

Lucinda thought the baronet sorely lacking in his concern for her, but she kept her thoughts to herself. "I hope you correct, Mr. Watkins. If not, Simon and I shall be prepared to depart early." She swung the door wide.

He had prodded Jamot with a nudge of the Baloch's shoulder, but just as Carter fell into step behind the man, a shot rang out, and from his eye's corner, he saw Monroe spin away from the room before clawing at the wall behind him. Carter's natural reflexes reached for the young recruit, permitting Jamot his opportunity. The Baloch bolted for the stairs.

Carter caught Monroe and braced the young man's slide to a seated position before following Jamot. He fished a handkerchief from an inside pocket and shoved it into Monroe's hand. "Hold tight," he ordered before he cautiously climbed the steps, his gun hand leading the way and at the ready. As he passed each closed door, he caught the handle to swing it wide. Yet, the Baloch had disappeared. Carter was near to abandoning his search when he turned a corner to discover his worst nightmare.

She certainly had not expected a stranger upon her portal when she had opened the door for Mr. Watkins, and she had not reacted quickly enough to prevent the intruder from capturing her about the neck and dragging her toward an open draft window.

Lucinda fought for her life. She dug her nails into the man's meaty hands, but her efforts were of little note. The man was too tall and too strong for her to prevent him from executing whatever mischief he chose. He tugged her along, half carrying her, and Lucinda fully expected to be tossed out the open window. She heard Mr. Watkins scramble to recover from the blow her captor had placed across the coachman's chest, but Lucinda knew the elderly driver no match for the man who held her pressed tight to his chest.

"Release her!" a familiar voice growled lethally. His cold tone sucked the air from the passageway. If she could have uttered a sound, Lucinda would have cheered Sir Carter's arrival. She squirmed to throw her attacker off balance, but a steady gaze from the baronet stilled her efforts. He said with hesitation, "I repeat, Jamot: Release the lady."

"And why would I do as you ask?" the Baloch taunted.

Lucinda's heart clenched with dread as she looked upon Sir Carter's countenance. It physically pained the baronet to speak his offer. "Permit the lady her freedom, and I will not give chase. You will live to fight the next battle. What say you, Jamot?"

Chapter Eight

Silently, he counted to five. It was one of the best means for him to control the anger coursing through him. With the arrest of Murhad Jamot, he could have easily claimed the title of the Realm's leader, but those hopes would go out the window with the Baloch's escape. And Carter held no doubt Jamot would accept his offer. The Baloch was all things vile, but he was not a foolish man. Jamot possessed a strong sense of survival.

When Carter had discovered Mrs. Warren in Jamot's grasp, his heart had stumbled to a halt. His first thoughts had been those of elation in knowing she was here; after all, over the past fortnight, her essence had clung to him like a wet jacket. Yet, reality had quickly intruded. She was in residence at a disreputable inn—without his knowledge of her traveling alone. *Was she alone? Or had the lady chosen an assignation? Perhaps, even with Jamot.*

The errant possibility rocked Carter's composure. However, he held no choice but to negotiate for her release. Biting his tongue in frustration, he said sternly, "Permit the lady her freedom, and I will not give chase." He swallowed the bile rising in his throat. "You will live to fight the next battle. What say you, Jamot?" Something dangerous coiled and twisted within his gut.

The Baloch glanced to the open door leading to what Carter assumed was Mrs. Warren's room, and again the idea the Baloch had rushed toward the sleeping quarters rather than the main entrance because of her gnawed at the edges of Carter's mind. "You are known to be an honorable man," Jamot said with confidence. "That particular trait will be your downfall, Sir Carter."

Carter was well aware of how his actions would appear in his report to Pennington. He had underestimated Jamot's influence on those below. He had permitted Monroe to suffer an attack and had negotiated the release of a woman known to him. A woman who should be enjoying herself at *his* estate.

Pennington would express his continued disappointment with Carter's handling of the situation, as would the committee overseeing the search for a new director. "Time will tell the tale." He edged further to the left, seeking a clear shot in case the Baloch thought to do something ill advised.

Jamot's finger caressed the underside of Mrs. Warren's chin, and Carter noted how she had stiffened with the Baloch's touch. "Do you fancy the lady, Sir Carter?" Jamot said on a taunt.

"I fancy the lady's safety," Carter said noncommittally.

With a nod of acceptance, Jamot wasted no time in shoving Mrs. Warren's into Carter's waiting arms. As he had promised, Carter made no move to follow. Instead, he wrapped his arms about the lady's trembling body and buried his face in her rumpled hair. "I have you, Lucinda," he whispered. It felt natural to use her Christian name, and Carter instinctively tightened his embrace. He lifted her chin where he might look upon her countenance. "Did he injure you?" Carter ran his finger lightly along the red line left by Jamot's grasp.

Tears streamed down her cheeks, and her shoulders quaked with silent sobs, but she shook her head in the negative. "Nothing…nothing of import," she said on a harsh rasp.

Carter loosened his grip. Although obviously upset, she would recover quickly. Perhaps more quickly than he. Her nearness had warmed his blood dramatically. She was petite in comparison to his height, and her bust line sported full globes to enflame his desire. Strands of chocolate and of strawberry peppered her blonde hair, which tumbled over his fist. He would love to splay his fingers through it, to send the pins, which once tugged it into place, flying.

"You were terribly late," she accused, and any images of naked bodies, which Carter had conjured up, quickly dissipated.

He set her from him. "I assure you, Mrs. Warren, had I known you required my rescue, I would have arrived more speedily. As you have been so gracious in your expression of gratitude," he said testily, "how could I not respond happily?"

The lady's forehead crunched in lines of disapproval. "As you placed me in danger, Sir," she countered, "it seemed only appropriate for you to save me."

Carter leaned over her, using his height as an advantage. "You are delusional, Madam. Until I tracked Jamot to your open door, I held no knowledge of your presence under The Rising Son's roof. Instead of making accusations, perhaps you might explain why one of my most constant enemies chose you as his shield of protection. Are you among the Baloch's admirers?" He was acting unreasonably, but he could not control his ire when he thought she had betrayed him.

The lady looked to the still open window. Her gaze was furious. "You think I would align myself with the likes of that...of that..." Mrs. Warren gestured wildly to the gaping darkness. "Of that *man!*" she said vehemently. "Thank you for your lack of confidence in my character." She caught her skirt tail to step around him. "The boy and I will return to London on the morrow, and we shall bother you no further. Good evening, Sir Carter."

"Wait!" His voice was both harsh and urgent. In annoyance, he caught her arm, but before he could sort out her complaint, he heard Monroe groan with pain. Looking over his shoulder, Carter saw four men carrying Monroe to an empty room. To Mrs. Warren, Carter said, "You are to go nowhere until we settle this, but first I must tend to my companion. Mr. Monroe was shot in the madness of apprehending Jamot." He gave her arm a good shake to stress the urgency of what he required.

Her chin bumped higher: her gaze glacial. "Do you expect a salute of obedience, Lieutenant Lowery?" No one ever dared to speak to him in that tone of contempt, and in many ways, Carter admired the lady's bravado.

"I would simply prefer the obedience without either the salute or the posturing," he hissed. Uncertain if she would demand an immediate withdrawal and how he might convince her to stay until he could decipher the events leading to the current chaos, he cautiously stepped away from her. Carter expected her to bolt toward her room, but nothing of the woman was predictable. Instead, she pushed past him to follow the men carrying Monroe's limp body into the adjoining room. She presented Carter a deathly glare, and he did not know whether to look offended or to laugh. He heard Law's voice warning: *Definitely do not laugh, Carter. Never laugh at a lady in discord.*

"Damnable woman!" he murmured as he fell into step behind her.

On shaky legs, just to be away from the infuriating baronet, Lucinda rushed to the side of a man she had never met. His accusations stung in the manner of her late husband's insinuations regarding her actions toward the other officers. At the time, Lucinda had seen Captain Warren's biting words as a sign he truly cared for her, and they would have a normal marriage after the war ended. Only in the last six months had she realized Mr. Warren's words had hid his guilt, rather than to define his unspoken love for her.

"Permit me to see to the gentleman's wound," she said as she shoved one of the bar patrons from her way. "I shall require clean water and rags to wash away the possible infection. Is there a surgeon available?"

The innkeeper, Mr. Blackston, replied, "Only a midwife. We could send someone to the next village if'n ye think it best, Ma'am."

Lucinda wrestled with Monroe's jacket before tearing away the cloth of the man's shirt to better view the wound. Her fingers probed the opening. From behind her, she could feel the baronet's eyes upon her back, but Lucinda did not turn to see whether those dark eyes held disdain or approval. If the former, she would likely lose her nerve and abandon Mr. Monroe to the likes of a midwife. "The bullet went through the fleshy part of the shoulder. Permit me to clean the wound, and then we will determine whether to send someone for a surgeon."

"Thank you, Ma'am," Monroe said in some discomfort.

"Mrs. Warren," she said. A bit of mischief made her want to tell the man to call her "Lucinda," just to view Sir Carter's reaction to her daring. Before the moment passed, she added, "Lucinda Warren."

Before she could rise from where she sat upon the bed beside Mr. Monroe, the baronet joined them, possessively placing his hand on her shoulder, as if he claimed her, an action again reminiscent of Matthew Warren. "Mrs. Warren followed the drum, Mr. Monroe," she heard a bit of pride in the baronet's voice. "I would trust her judgment over a country doctor, who has seen few wounds."

Despite his words of trust, Lucinda did not like the feel of his hand upon his shoulder. It weighed her down, holding Lucinda in place, making her feel helpless. But worse, it spread warmth through her veins—an uncomfortable feeling after her earlier anger. She glanced up at Sir Carter. "Perhaps, you could see to Simon while I tend your associate."

"The boy is here?" he asked suspiciously.

"Of course," she said sweetly. "Your note asked me to bring the boy to The Rising Son." She watched with satisfaction as he fought the urge to refute her words, but he would not argue with her before the others.

Sir Carter bowed. "I will leave you to your ministrations. Monroe, you are in excellent hands."

Carter schooled his countenance and strode from the room. He turned to the still open door to find his coachman lingering in the opening. He had a thousand questions for Mr. Watkins, but first he would care for the child. "The boy?" he asked as he nodded at Watkins.

"Within, Sir, and worried for Mrs. Warren's safety."

Carter squeezed Watkins' shoulder as he entered the room. His eyes immediately fell on Simon. The boy, in a too large shirt, stood barefoot in the room's middle. "You came, at last," he accused.

Carter still was not certain how the lady had thought to be at this particular inn, but he would not upset the child further. "I have, and everything is safe. You have nothing of which to worry."

As was typical for the boy, Simon would not relent until he knew all the facts. "Who was injured? Is Mrs. Warren well?" The child's voice rose with anxiousness.

"Mrs. Warren has not suffered from the ordeal. In fact, she tends one of my associates, who was injured in the skirmish below. The lady will return as soon as she finishes with Mr. Monroe." Belatedly, he wondered if he should have spoken so honestly. With his young nieces and nephews, he generally spoke of fairy tales and butterflies, certainly not of bullets and raging Balochs. "I will leave Mr. Watkins with you until Mrs. Warren returns. I must assist the innkeeper and the local magistrate in discovering the culprit." He walked purposely toward the bed and straightened the counterpane. "Now, return to bed," he encouraged without looking at the boy. "You have nothing to fear."

Reluctantly, the boy climbed into bed, but Carter doubted the child would sleep. "You will protect Mrs. Warren?" Simon whispered. "She is a good person."

Carter ruffled the boy's wiry hair. "With my life." He blew out the candle and exited the room. The child was correct: The lady was exceptional. From the hall, he motioned Watkins to step into the passageway. "Tell me what you know of Mrs. Warren's presence at The Rising Son."

Watkins leaned closer as if in secret. "According to Mr. Vance, Mrs. Warren received a letter two days prior. Mr. Vance delivered it hisself and says the lady claimed the message be from you, Sir. The duke meant to send her on her journey, but she refused both the duke's small coach, as well as yers. The Duke of Thornhill let a hack, and I's volunteered to drive the lady." Carter relived his earlier accusations with regret. Instantly, he wished to read the note Mrs. Warren had thought to be from him. He felt compelled to discover who practiced deception in his name. However, first he must learn what he could of what had occurred below, and then he must apologize to Mrs. Warren.

Lucinda had cleaned and dressed Mr. Monroe's wound before assisting the man to know restorative sleep by adding a few drops of laudanum to the man's ale. Mrs. Blackston kept the drug in storage "for those who be causin' trouble in me inn." She was just gathering her things when Sir Carter slipped into the room. Still angry from his earlier attitude, Lucinda purposely ignored him. She placed the bloody rags in a bow before brushing a strand of straw blonde hair from Mr. Monroe's forehead.

Finally, unable to avoid Sir Carter any longer, she stood and straightened her shoulders before turning to face him. In the soft candlelight, he was even more appealing than before. The baronet leaned casually against the door. "Has Simon found his bed?" she asked for she could think of nothing intelligent to say.

"Watkins is with the boy," he said softly so as not to wake his friend. "The child worries for your safety."

She found herself frowning. "I can be nothing to the boy," she said in protest.

"Those are the most foolish words I have ever heard cross your lips," he protested. The baronet watched her intently. His broad shoulders spoke of strength, and Lucinda would love to give over to the illusion of his protection, but his earlier actions had cut her to the bone.

She swallowed hard to find a bit more resolve and set her feet in action. "Then I should tend to the child's anxiousness. If you will excuse me, Sir Carter, I shall seek my bed. In the morning, I must make arrangements for Simon and me to return to London. I assume you will send my belongings on once when the child and I are settled." The thought of the unknown future frightened her more than had the Baloch's assault.

The baronet did not step aside as she had anticipated. Instead, he blocked her exit. "Mrs. Warren," he said so close to her ear that Lucinda felt the warmth of his breath against the shorter hair tickling her nape. "I am truly aggrieved for my earlier response. I acted unreasonably and placed my frustrations upon your shoulders. I beg your forgiveness." He caught her hand and held it firmly in his grip.

Lucinda heard the hitch of her breath, but she had yet to forget his offense. "It is my experience, Sir Carter, words spoken in anger are what a person wished he could say if Society did not forbid it. You thought me the world's worst wanton. When you made your accusations, you believed every word you spoke."

"And what of you? Was your characterization of me as a tyrant said in frustration or in truth?"

Lucinda enjoyed keeping the baronet off balance. "You may decide for yourself, Sir."

He caught the bowl she carried and set it on a small table. Her defiance enflamed him as no woman ever had, and Carter was not certain if his heated blood came from his ire or his desire. Either way, he was lost to her closeness. She was not the sort of woman to whom he was normally attracted. With the golden highlights framing her face and the changing color of her eyes, she reminded him of a pixie set upon mischief. The thought brought a wry smile to his lips, but he swallowed his thoughts when a flash of irritation crossed her countenance.

He watched with interest as the lady pushed a stray curl behind her ear. Carter murmured, "Perhaps we should start again." Despite knowing her mere touch would send his blood reeling, he gently brushed her hand away before catching the loose strand between his fingers. Slowly, he wrapped the hair about his finger. "There is no need for us to be ill friends." He leaned closer, where his lips might graze her temple. His was a primal need. A slow, easy smile tugged at his lips' corners when he heard the delay in her breathing. It was satisfying to know his presence disturbed her as much as hers did his.

"I should go," she said on a rasp, but rather than reaching for the door's handle, the palm of her hand slid up the front of his jacket. He wondered whether she planned to push him away, but she fingered the thread of his badly worn costume.

Carter turned his head to slide his lips along her cheek. "Must you?" he said huskily. "You have yet to forgive me."

Her eyes closed in anticipation. "Forgive?" she whispered, as if she held no knowledge of the word.

Carter used his fingertips to raise her chin. "You are so beautiful." Her eyes blinked several times in an unknowing response, and he used the moment to claim her mouth. Gently. Encouragingly. Testing. A soft sigh of expectation.

When she leaned toward him, Carter slid his arms about the lady's waist. The taste of her lips brought the blood to his erection. Although she was tentative, Carter recognized the signs of her desire.

However, before the kiss could progress to something more pleasurable, Mrs. Warren jumped, in what could only be termed surprise.

The movement had broken the connection, but not Carter's desire for her. Instinctively, he tightened his hold. "What is amiss?" he asked with a bit more irritation than he intended.

The heels of her hands pressed against his chest. "Release me, Sir."

Carter relaxed his grip, but he did not set her from him. He repeated, "What is amiss?" He suspected her request had nothing to do with actions. His kiss held no demands, and surely as a widow, she had known passion previously.

She looked down with a frown. "Something bumped against my foot."

Reluctantly, Carter opened his embrace so they both might determine the culprit. She stepped back to reveal a torn piece of foolscap. Her heel caught the sheet, and it crinkled under the pressure. "Stand still," he ordered as he bent to retrieve the folded sheet.

"What is it?"

Carter opened the sheet. "Appears to be some sort of note," he said as his eyes scanned the page.

Rising up on her toes, Mrs. Warren peered over his forearm. "What does it say?"

Carter's uneasiness rose. "Read it for yourself." He shoved the note into her grasp before striding away to gather his thoughts. He watched as she smoothed the page against the side of her dress. "Read it aloud," he encouraged. He hoped his eyes had failed him.

She lifted the page closer where she might read accurately. "Heard the man who shot yer frind say he ment tu kill the weman. Thought ye shud no." Her hand trembled, and her eyes never left the page.

Carter whirled to face her. Hauling her to him, he wrapped his arms tightly to him. "I will never permit anyone to harm you."

"What if you are not near?" she asked in a dispassionate voice.

He cupped her cheek in his large palm, staring deeply into her eyes. His heart thundered with the possibility she could know danger. "We have no basis to believe the note to be true. It is likely a poor attempt of one of Jamot's smuggler friends to drive me from the area. Those below know me to be an agent of the Crown. I am certain my presence at this inn affects their ability to move their goods. It is a farce: Our author recognizes how a man would always remove a woman from danger." The frown, which crossed her countenance, said the lady did not necessarily agree.

However, she snuggled closer, wrapping her arms about his waist. It was as if the lady craved his protection. For several minutes, she remained as such, and Carter enjoyed the feeling of being of use to her. Finally, she said, "When we were arguing earlier, you spoke of possessing no knowledge of the letter I received asking me to come to Suffolk."

Carter caressed her back. She fit perfectly under his chin. It was a heady situation to surround her with his body. "Mr. Watkins explained the truth of your accusations," he said, but his mind had returned to the sensation of her body rubbing softly against his.

Her body arched, but instead of seeking more of his attentions, for a second time, the lady pushed away from him. This time, he permitted her release. "I am pleased you believe someone," she said smartly. "And to clarify, I received a letter stating you wished for Simon and me to meet you at this particular inn." Her voice cracked as she said, "If the letter was not of your making, Sir Carter, it means someone knew of my residence at Huntingborne Abbey and of your presence in London. The letter was franked in the capital."

Without her in his embrace, Carter's reasoning returned. Solemnly, he responded, "Whomever our shooter may be, you were his true target. Someone lured you to this inn with the intent of killing you."

Chapter Nine

It had taken longer than Carter expected to calm her misgivings. He finally agreed to make his bed in the hall outside her door. He had sent Watkins to guard Monroe. It had been a miserable night with the sound of raucous patrons below, plus the memory of Mrs. Warren's lips pressed to his clung to him. He had no excuse for acting upon his desires, but, thankfully, Mrs. Warren had proved the insignificance of the moment: The lady had ignored his impulsiveness, as if nothing had occurred. Carter was not certain he approved of her indifference. After all, he rarely acted without a logical end. Obviously, kissing Lucinda Warren had been the most unsound act of recent history. That is next to assuming Colonel Rightnour's command on the battlefield. What was it about the Rightnour family, which robbed him of his good sense?

Mrs. Warren had thought it best if they returned to London, but Carter had had second thoughts once he had had time alone to consider what had occurred. The lady had retrieved the letter for him to study, but he took no note of anything unusual. Whoever had written the message had been literate, which eliminated many of those below. It was written on good quality paper, indicating someone with money. The letter held only "London" as its return direction, and the handwriting resembled his slant.

After he had convinced Mrs. Warren to retire, Carter had returned below, where he nursed two drinks. He had hoped against hope someone would approach him with more information, but even Nell had avoided him. Mr. Blackston had been the only one to offer him any conversation; therefore, Carter had spent his time learning what he could of those gathered in the common room. He had watched the gathering's interactions previously, but now there was someone missing: the man with whom Jamot had conversed. The older gentleman who dressed beyond those who called The Rising Son home, but who had been accepted as one of its favorites. The one with whom Jamot had disagreed.

Had the Baloch refused to do the man's bidding? Carter easily recalled the man Thornhill had captured in London had spoken of an older, well-dressed gentleman, who had hired him. "Whom has Mrs. Warren offended?" he wondered as he stretched out on the floor before her room. The unforgiving hardness reminded him of the years of sleeping on rock surfaces and forest floors; ironically, the familiarity soon lulled Carter to sleep.

Lucinda had shared the small bed with Simon, but sleep did not come. Someone had threatened to kill her. Her! A woman who had never known an enemy! Even her late husband had not been her enemy until after his death. Only then had she indelicately uttered the oaths she had learned from the soldiers, and even then, in the privacy of her quarters. Never to another person.

"The threat must have some connection to Simon's appearance," she whispered to the room. "But why would anyone wish to hurt the boy? Could someone believe she had stolen Simon from his family?"

She stared at the poorly draped frame of the four-poster. "The only other person who might wish me ill is Uncle Gerhard. Could the earl's animosity toward my father be transferred to me?" Lucinda shook off the notion. "How could that possibility exist?" Despite her father's stubborn aversion for the present earl, Sophia Rightnour had often spoken kindly of the man. Surely, her mother could not have erred so drastically.

She would love to discuss her suppositions with someone. Naturally, she looked to the door where the baronet meant to sleep. "Oh, how shall I face him in the light of a new morning?" she chastised as she rolled to her side. No shadow of light showed beneath the door. Did that mean the baronet had made his bed in the inn's hallway, as he had promised, or had Mr. Blackston shuttered the candles in the wall sconces? Without opening the door to look, Lucinda knew the answer. Sir Carter was built for protection: His unselfish need to see to the safety of others was why she had clung to him—why she wished to return to his embrace—why she had permitted his kiss.

Her first kiss. Matthew Warren had always claimed a kiss would lead to other complications in their marriage. He had claimed it too dangerous for her to be with child with the war exploding all around them. "My husband did not practice such tender care with his first wife," she said bitterly. "Matthew robbed me of an opportunity for a family. Robbed me of knowing the depth of a child's love. Robbed me of my identity. Gave me his name, but not his devotion."

Her eyes instinctively rested upon the door. Oh, how she longed to open it and to throw herself into the baronet's arms. To take up where they had left off. To feel his warmth along her body. To listen to the steady beat of his heart. To finally discover the intimacy between a man and a woman. To feel his sensual caresses streaming fire through her veins. Her cheeks heated with the possibility. It was wanton of her to think so, but as a soldier's widow, she would hold few opportunities to discover a husband's tender care. In fact, with her unfavorable financial straits, finding a husband of any age and status would be difficult.

"Would Sir Carter turn away?" she wondered. Somehow, she did not think so. Lucinda closed her eyes to imagine herself brave enough to act upon her impulses. "If only..." she whispered. "If only I were a different woman."

After an early breakfast, Carter had hustled his rag-tag group into the let coach. He placed Monroe in the carriage with Mrs. Warren and the boy. His associate had gathered his wits enough to stumble to the carriage. He had tied Monroe's horse to the coach's boot and recovered Prime from where they had hidden the animals.

"Where to?" Mr. Watkins asked as he took up the reins.

"The Earl of McLauren's estate in Lincolnshire," he announced. He had made his decision while he lay awake upon the inn's well-worn floor.

"Why not London?" Mrs. Warren asked from the coach's open window.

Carter spoke for her ears only. He had not shared the suspicious note with either Watkins or Monroe. It did not seem appropriate to do so, and he relished their confidences, which created the illusion of intimacy. "In London, with its congestion, I cannot adequately protect you. My oldest sister, the Countess McLauren, resides at Maryborne Park in Lincolnshire. As the duke and I did in Kent, I can set up a perimeter about the estate. No one will access the earl's home."

Mrs. Warren frowned in disapproval. "I would not wish to place Lady McLauren's family in any danger."

Carter smiled easily. "Have no care for Louisa's safety. McLauren guards her and the children from all possibilities. Little does the earl know Louisa can hold her place with any man. I have seen her ring my brother's ears on more than one occasion. Lawrence dances to her tune. I suspect you will enjoy her company." So as not to argue, he left her before the lady could object. "Lead on, Mr. Watkins," he called as he mounted. Kicking Prime's flanks, he thought, "Mrs. Warren and Louisa will get on famously, or they will butt heads repeatedly. They both possess a bit of the shrew in their personalities. Either way, the encounter will be interesting."

It was near dusk when the carriage rolled into Maryborne's parkland. They had stopped twice for meals and a third time to change horses. Mr. Watkins knew when to push the animals and when to slack off to get the most from the team. "Is that the house?" Simon called excitedly from the coach as the manor had come into view. Over the evening meal, Carter had disclosed the fact his sister and the earl had a six-year-old son named *Ethan* and a four-year-old daughter called *Lisette*. The boy anticipated having new playmates.

Carter brought Prime along side the coach. "Yes. We will be there within minutes." When the boy's head disappeared inside the coach, Carter had imagined Mrs. Warren straightening the child's clothing before they disembarked. It was a very maternal picture, and he found it brought an easy smile to his lips.

Carter rode ahead and dismounted as the manor's door swung wide to reveal his sister. He had promised the baroness he would call regularly upon his siblings, but he had only traveled to Lincolnshire once in the past six months. He knew instant regret at having failed his mother. However, in his defense, he had visited with Maria and the new grandchild in Staffordshire three times. Harry was a delightful child, and Carter loved the role of adoring uncle. He had also joined Delia and Viscount Duff in Warwickshire twice. Their daughter Catherine was two and her father's "princess."

With Maria and Delia, Carter could spend an evening or a week. Neither chastised him for always being in a rush to return to his governmental obligations. Louisa, on the other hand, rarely accepted his responsibilities as reason for his absence. Her insistence upon his tarrying with her kept Carter from calling more often.

"Carter!" she called as she rushed to embrace him. Although Louisa was his oldest sister, she was petite, like their mother and Delia. Maria was tall for a woman, but Viscount Sheffield had not minded. "Harry will be a tall, strapping youth," the viscount had declared lovingly when the brothers had teased their middle sister.

He caught Louisa up in his arms, lifting her feet from the ground and spinning her the way he had done since he had grown six inches in one year in his early teens. "You always smell of lemons, Louisa," he said jovially.

His sister slapped at his chest. "Put me down," she protested, but girlish giggles filled the air.

"Easy with how you handle my wife," Ernest Hutton, the Earl of McLauren, warned from where he waited his turn to greet Carter. "Those are fragile goods."

Carter placed his sister down gently. "Fragile, are we?" he said with a smile. "Does that mean the baroness will return early for another lying in?"

His sister blushed, but nodded as Carter extended his hand to Hutton. "Congratulations. When might you call me 'Uncle' again?"

The earl claimed Carter's hand. "Early November." Hutton looked up as the coach rolled into the circle. "Surely that is not your carriage, Lowery?"

"No," Carter said softly. "It is let. I will explain all much later, but please accept those within as your house guests."

"Of course," Hutton assured. The earl reached for Louisa's hand. "Come, Countess, your brother has brought guests to brighten our day."

Cater could observe the manipulation forming in Louisa's mind the moment his sister drew Mrs. Warren's acquaintance. His oldest sister meant to play matchmaker, but not for him. She meant to place the lady in Mr. Monroe's way. Carter was certainly not seeking a connection, but could not Louisa plainly observe the woman held too much worldly experience for a man of Monroe's limited insights? His assistant had not served in the war nor had Monroe traveled abroad. He had no commonality with Mrs. Warren.

"This is wonderful," Louisa gushed. They had enjoyed light refreshments in the yellow drawing room after Monroe had excused himself for the evening. "We received news yesterday that Lawrence and Arabella will join us for a few days on their return to Blake's Run. I expect them some time tomorrow. It will be pleasant to have both my brothers together under my roof."

Carter glanced to Mrs. Warren. He had not wished to expose her to too many strangers in one sitting, but thoughts of his brother's wife having the measure of Mrs. Warren pleased him. Although she was the granddaughter of the Earl of Vaughn, the former Arabella Tilney had been reared in America and was a bit hoydenish in an adorably adventurous manner. He thought Mrs. Warren could benefit from Arabella's confidence and from his sister in marriage's acknowledgement. "I was unaware Lord and Lady Hellsman had departed Scotland."

"Our brother reports of an outbreak of typhus in both Glasgow and Edinburgh. He removed his wife from danger," Louisa shared. Law's news had put one of Carter's escape routes on hold. If someone continued to pursue her, he had thought he might send Mrs. Warren and the boy to his family's Scottish estate.

Hutton shared, "My countess is hoping the future baron's actions prove an heir is anticipated on Lawrence's part."

Carter teased, "Not every couple is so anxious to set up their nursery as were you and Hutton, Louisa."

His sister flicked his taunt away with a brush of her wrist. "It is a woman's providence to bear children. It is how England will survive," she declared. "Would you not agree, Mrs. Warren?"

Carter saw Lucinda flinch. "I have no family, Lady McLauren, and I have been a widow for over three years. I lost Captain Warren after the Battle of Vitoria during the Peninsular campaign."

"But I thought…" Louisa began.

As if recognizing her discomfort, Carter explained, "Captain Warren had married prior to speaking his vows to Mrs. Warren. The boy's mother is deceased. With the captain's demise, Mrs. Warren serves as Simon's guardian."

Hutton asked, "Captain Matthew Warren?"

"Yes, Sir," Lucinda said softly. It bothered Carter she had lowered her eyes. He was beginning to believe someone had abused her emotionally. *Captain Warren or Colonel Rightnour? Or both?*

"I recall Warren from my university days. He was younger than I, but I knew the man in passing." Carter noted Hutton's raised eyebrow, and he realized the earl had something private to share with him.

"Yes, Thornhill and Warren were familiar acquaintances. The duke requested my assistance in aiding Mrs. Warren in locating the child's maternal relatives. Mrs. Warren believes it important for the boy to know family." It was a stretch of the truth for Louisa's sake and to protect Mrs. Warren's reputation.

"Well, whatever the reason, you are welcome in Lincolnshire," Louisa professed. "I am thrilled to have your company."

At mid afternoon the following day, Carter joined Louisa and McLauren on the estate's main steps to greet his brother's coach. He had not seen Lawrence since Carter had orchestrated his brother's marriage proposal and wedding shortly before Christmastide. Watching the coach roll to a stop before the manor, he quickly realized how much he had missed Law. Immediately, he was assisting his brother's footman with the steps.

A squeal and a shout of "Carter" was all the warning he had before his brother's wife launched herself into his arms. Marriage had, obviously, not stifled Arabella Lowery's spontaneity. He caught her and spun her around as he had done with Louisa only the day prior. Arabella laughed heartily. "What fun!" she announced as he sat her upon the ground. "Lawrence never mentioned you were at Maryborne. My, how I have missed you."

"And I you, Bella," he said genuinely.

His brother caught Carter up in a familiar man hug. "It is good to find you here," Law said in that baritone timbre Carter had always associated with strength. Although they were relatively equal in height and weight, Carter had always thought at eight years his senior Lawrence outshone him in many ways.

Carter patted his brother's back as they parted. "Has the glow decreased?" he asked softly. Although their father had disagreed, Carter had recognized

Law's obsession with Miss Arabella Tilney the first time he had observed the two together.

Law glanced to where his wife greeted Louisa and the earl. "Lord, no." Lawrence's smile widened. "I have never been so content. You should make the effort, Carter. Marriage would be good for you."

Carter immediately thought of the lady awaiting their appearance in the drawing room, but quickly placed the thought from his mind. Their connection was nothing more than pure fancy. Marriage was not for him in the near future. He had a position to win and several investigations to solve before he seriously considered searching for a wife among the *ton's* newest crop of ingénues. "I am but four and twenty. There is time for such thoughts as I approach thirty. You waited until three and thirty."

"If Bella had made her arrival earlier, I would have been just as ready to claim her," Lawrence confessed.

Arabella rejoined them. "Louisa and I have decided our husbands must emulate Carter's greeting. I find I quite like being lifted high in the air," she teased as she laced her arm through her husband's.

Law laughed easily, and it was a comforting sound. Carter realized it had been many years since Lawrence had been so carefree. "And what if I am not as able bodied as my younger brother?" Law taunted as he playfully tweaked his wife's nose.

Bella offered a pretend pout as they followed Louisa and McLauren inside. "Have I chosen the wrong brother?"

Law gave Carter's shoulder a hearty shove. "I assure you Lady Hellsman, I have no brother."

Carter joined their playful laugher, and they entered the drawing room as a trio. However, noting Monroe's presence on the settee beside Mrs. Warren brought him to a stumbling halt.

"Oh, my!" Arabella gasped. "I had no idea Lady McLauren had company."

Louisa looked pleased at the domestic setting upon which they had come. His sister said sweetly, "Carter brought guests with him." She gave him an expectant look.

Leaving Bella's side he joined the couple. "Lord and Lady Hellsman," he said formally, "may I present one of my colleagues from the Home Office, Mr. Dylan Monroe, and an acquaintance of some duration, Mrs. Warren." He shot a quick glance to McLauren; Carter had spent over an hour this morning apprising the earl of the true reasons for his seeking refuge at Maryborne. His brother in marriage had immediately placed orders for additional men to guard the estate's perimeter. There was much unrest in the Northern shires, and many wealthy landowners hired armed men to protect land and property.

During the conversation, Hutton had expressed his earlier reservations regarding Matthew Warren. "There were rumors of young Warren being involved in some sort of minor theft. Some said he was the one who sold what was stolen to those within the village and the surrounding countryside. He was never brought up on charges, but it was common knowledge if one required a new shirt, a pen, potent drinks, or a dozen other such items, Warren was the man to see. I hold no proof of Warren's involvement, but I thought you should know. Likely, he did not have the funds for his education. Many turned to outside means to support their schooling. I suppose Mrs. Warren held no knowledge of her husband's propensity to handle stolen goods."

Carter scowled. "I cannot imagine Lucinda Warren would tolerate her fiancé making his way in school in such a manner. They were betrothed from birth, and Warren was several years her senior. I hold a strong suspicion the lady learned of Captain Warren's nature after their vows were pronounced, but she has shared nothing of his continuing his thieving ways after joining the military. The captain served under her father during the Peninsular campaign. If Colonel Rightnour had known of such actions from one of his officers, I am certain the colonel would have called his son in marriage up on charges. Rightnour was known to be a stickler for protocol. From what I know of Warren, he was very possessive of his wife, and she suffered from the lack of freedom."

"Was not Rightnour the man you replaced at Waterloo? Does Mrs. Warren know what happened in Belgium?"

Carter's frown lines deepened. "I do not think the lady is aware of my disapproval of what occurred on the battlefield. She was in Brussels with Rightnour, but I assume she was too distraught to recognize her father's error during that last siege from the French."

Hutton added, "Do you not find it ironic that years later, you meet the daughter of the man who made such a blunder in England's most important battle to date?"

Carter gave himself a mental shake before continuing the introductions. "Monroe. Mrs. Warren. It is with the greatest pleasure I offer you the acquaintance of my brother, Lawrence Lowery, Lord Hellsman, and future Baron Blakehell, and his wife Lady Hellsman."

Courtesies followed. For the next hour, he enjoyed how Bella easily maneuvered Lucinda from Monroe's notice. With amusement, he thought it would be interesting to watch Louisa's manipulations thwarted by Bella. "And how long have you known Mrs. Warren?" Law asked suspiciously as they stood together upon the balcony. Louisa had ushered Bella to her quarters, and Monroe had joined McLauren at the stables, while Mrs. Warren had called upon Simon in the nursery.

"Some fifteen months," he admitted. "I took her acquaintance at the Come Out for Lady Worthing. Thornhill had known her late husband, Captain Warren, and the duke shamelessly used the lady to make Miss Aldridge jealous."

"Oh, yes. I recall when we attended Thornhill's wedding breakfast, Lady Worthing made reference to another woman." Law said cautiously, "Mrs. Warren certainly has not the look of the duchess."

Carter knew he had said too much as soon as the words left his lips. "The lady is more beautiful than the duchess. Mrs. Warren has a kind heart and a quick mind to support her handsome countenance."

His brother, thankfully, made no comment, but he did ask, "And why is the lady now your responsibility?"

Carter had shared bits of Mrs. Warren's life with McLauren, but he judged it best to speak only to the urgency of protecting the woman. "Someone has made several attempts to harm the lady. Without family as protection, Mrs. Warren sought Thornhill's assistance."

"And the duke, naturally, placed the woman into your most capable hands for Thornhill fears his wife's sharp tongue." Law drew his own conclusions.

Carter chuckled lightly. "That is your summation, dear Brother. I would not venture such an opinion about Thornhill. The man's pride might result in our meeting at Putney Heath at dawn."

"Come," Law directed Carter's steps toward the drawing room. "Over supper, I mean to learn more of *your* Mrs. Warren."

Everything had gone well over the casually constructed meal until Louisa announced, "I have spoken to Lord McLauren and have obtained my husband's permission to host a small supper party at week's end. It is not often both my brothers are in residence at Maryborne at the same time, and I mean to take advantage. I am quite proud of the Lowery men."

Law ventured, "Lady Hellsman and I planned to travel to Blake's Run before that time."

Louisa dismissed his objection with a fluttering wrist. "Then why bother to tarry in Lincolnshire at all?" she argued. "No one of polite Society would spend less than a week at a relative's home."

McLauren chuckled. "Surrender, Hellsman. You lived with Louisa some twenty years, and you should know, as well as the next man, when your sister sets her mind to a plan, we all stand aside to permit Louisa her head."

Lawrence asked, "What say you, Bella?"

"Monday shall be soon enough to return to Derbyshire, but no more, Lawrence. I sorely miss my father, and I mean to call upon my grandfather before the weather turns foul again."

Carter enjoyed how Arabella had accepted Louisa's maneuverings, but had also placed limitations on how much she would tolerate. He suspected his "sisters" would have multiple disagreements over the coming years. He liked the idea. Louisa had had her way too often, and she required a good set down from time to time.

"And what of you, Mrs. Warren?" Louisa asked pointedly. His eldest sister meant to circumvent any objections Carter might hold to her plan by placing the lady upon a pincushion.

"I am at Sir Carter's disposal," Mrs. Warren murmured, but Carter noted the panic in her eyes. "But I would ask your permission, Lady McLauren, to remain with the children that evening."

"Nonsense," Louisa declared. "A hostess must maintain an equal number of males and females for a successful service."

Mrs. Warren pleaded, "Surely there is another female in the neighborhood…"

Carter leaned closer. "I will send a rider to Huntingborne for appropriate clothing," he whispered.

She hissed, "I own nothing grand enough."

He nodded his understanding, but he said, "We would be pleased for the company, Louisa." Beneath the table's cloth, he caught Lucinda's hand to give it a gentle squeeze.

When the men joined the ladies in the drawing room, Carter motioned Bella to the side. "Mrs. Warren is in need of your assistance," he said softly. "She requires a gown for Louisa's supper."

Bella nodded her agreement. "I recall how thankful I was to discover Delia's lovely gowns fit me after my unexpected dip in Blake Run's tarn." Bella glanced to where Mr. Monroe entertained the lady with tales of the Chinese ship they had overtaken. Carter would again emphasize to the man the necessity for secrecy. "The lady is a bit taller than I, but I have a lovely gown I think would do her well."

Carter smiled easily. "I knew you would save the evening. Thank you, Bella."

She laid her hand on his arm. "Permit me to make the offer rather than have the lady assume you have assumed pity for her."

He shot a quick glance to where Mrs. Warren sank quietly into the cushions. "I admit I am at sixes and sevens." Carter had taken an immediate liking to Arabella Tilney; they had known a comfortable familiarity from the beginning of their acquaintance. "At Lady Worthing's Come Out ball, Mrs. Warren outshone many of Society's finest, but since our reacquaintance, I have noted how the lady's confidence has waned. Do you suppose Captain Warren dealt his wife a disservice? One in which she never knew how to respond? Thornhill mentioned an incident when he had served along side Warren several years back, but the duke assumed the situation had been an aberration. I am no longer so certain."

Bella squeezed his arm. "I shall attempt to become the lady's confidant, but I shall only share her thoughts if you mean to be Mrs. Warren's champion."

Carter considered the concept and found no apparent misgivings. "If the lady requires a champion, I would offer my services."

For two days, Carter had observed Louisa's elaborate manipulations. His sister placed Mrs. Warren beside Monroe during meals, had asked the gentleman to escort Mrs. Warren and Bella into the village, and had arranged an impromptu picnic for her, the couple, and the children upon the front lawns. With each event, Carter had searched the lady's countenance for evidence of Mrs. Warren's pleasure in the acquaintance. What he discovered disturbed him greatly. Mrs. Warren had smiled at all the appropriate times, but other than the lady's interactions with Simon, her countenance spoke of despair. The knowledge of her pain ripped at his heart. He wished to find a means to change her steps—to set them aright.

"Law has volunteered you to serve as my and Mrs. Warren's escort this afternoon," Arabella announced over breakfast on Thursday.

Carter spoke over his shoulder as he filled a second plate with toast, bacon, and kippers, one of his favorite foods. Louisa had made a point of serving them just for him. "And where are we off to today, Ladies?"

Bella kept the floor. "We are in need of a bit more lace for Mrs. Warren's gown for Louisa's supper."

Carter noted how the lady blushed, but he pretended not to see. "A very worthy cause," he said in a good-natured taunt. "It has been too long since I have been on a lace hunt. Should I bring out the hounds?"

Bella struck his shoulder with her folded serviette. "As I ride to the hounds as well as you, Sir, you shall regret your levity."

Carter laughed lightly. He leaned down to place a kiss on Bella's forehead. "That you do, my Dear. I must choose my taunts more carefully."

Bella smiled easily, "You are a gracious loser, Carter. So, we may depend upon your goodwill?"

"It will be my pleasure, but why has my brother bowed from the task?"

Bella rolled her eyes. "Some pressing estate business. I swear, Carter, I will not have my husband return to the man he was prior to our joining."

"Stand your ground, Bella. Law deserves success, but not to the point it robs him of the first happiness he has ever known."

Lucinda listened to the easy exchange between Sir Carter and his brother's wife. She wondered what it would be to have a large family, one where all the others made her business theirs. She could not quite stifle her sigh of envy.

Because she had arrived with the baronet, his family had opened their arms to her. It was an invigorating feeling to have others interested in her opinions and her happiness, and Lucinda fought hard not to become too comfortable with the baronet's family. Their acceptance of her was an illusion, one to be snatched away when he had discovered the truths of Simon's parenthood and of her marriage.

However, Lucinda would easily admit she thoroughly enjoyed her time with Arabella Lowery. Sometimes she felt they could be life-long friends. In three short days, they had taken to finishing each other's sentences. Their tastes in clothes and foods were so similar Lucinda knew true amazement. Lady Hellsman was the sister she had never known—that special friend of which her life as the only child of a famous military leader and later of a soldier's wife had robbed her.

"Bella tells me you have chosen a gown for Louisa's party," Sir Carter said softly as he seated himself beside her.

Lucinda glanced to where Lady Hellsman gave the footman specific instructions on how she wished her eggs prepared. She suspected the lady was with child, but Bella had yet to share her news, and so Lucinda had kept her own counsel. "Your brother's wife is wonderfully gracious. She has offered me the use of one of her gowns, and her maid Lizzie has made the necessary adjustments. I cannot thank her or you enough."

"Me?" Sir Carter protested. Lucinda enjoyed the baronet's antics when he feigned obtuseness. He appeared so much more approachable in those rare moments.

"I am not a woman without intelligence, Sir Carter," she said softly. "You shushed my objections to your sister's party, and then Lady Hellsman appears with an offer of a magnificent gown. I do not believe in coincidence. It was of your doing." She presented him a calm, direct look.

"I did nothing special. Arabella would have come to the same conclusion upon her own. She is quite generous by nature, very much like my sister Delia. All I shall claim is the desire to expedite the process."

Before she could reply, Bella returned to the table. "Has Carter told you of how he brought his brother to his knees before all the *ton* and then the two of them made a fool of my Cousin Annalee's husband?"

"I fear Sir Carter has shared few amusing tales," Lucinda said playfully. "I have sadly come to the opinion the man is meant only for governmental business."

He regarded her in surprise. "I never thought my family's antics would be of interest to you." Although his tone was light, there was a philosophical grimace lurking behind his smile. He carried his pain better than did she; yet, nevertheless, it was there. The possibility wiped every other thought from her mind. Lucinda closed her eyes, desperately fighting to shore up her defenses, but she feared her efforts too late. This man had opened her heart to more pain.

"That is where you erred, Sir Carter. I am a woman who enjoys an amusing anecdote, and Lady Hellsman has extolled your storytelling abilities. My interests are decidedly piqued."

Chapter Ten

The mercantile was as Carter remembered it, stocked with everything a villager might desire. He had left the ladies within and had called at the smith's for McLauren had asked Carter to retrieve a new saddle for Louisa. "Your sister will have little use for it in her condition, but Louisa insists she requires a new one." Carter had chuckled. The earl spoiled Louisa in the manner her parents never had. His eldest sister relished the role as "pampered countess," and "God knows she deserves it," he told the horse he stroked while he waited for the smith to return with the saddle. "Louisa had had her hands full being mistress of the nursery. We did not give her an easy time."

"Have we made our decisions?" he asked as he approached Bella and Mrs. Warren in the draperies section of the store.

Bella looked up with a smile. "You will learn, dear brother of mine, women never tire of such fripperies. Come give us your opinion."

He stepped between them to examine the three samples they had chosen. "I had thought Lady Hellsman, you left the lace and satin to your sister Abigail," he teased. "I recall your cousin, Viscountess Ransing, accusing you of having a saucy nature."

"A bird may change its feathers," Bella argued good-naturedly.

Carter could not prevent a light laugh. "That it can, Sweetling." He picked up the first piece of lace. "Now, explain for what I am looking."

Bella, with her normal exuberance, wove a tale of the need for the proper piece of lace to give the appearance of length on Mrs. Warren's gown. Carter smiled knowingly throughout. Little did they know he had spent part of his training in the shops along the wharfs of Bombay. Carter had learned more than he had ever hoped to know of silks and linens and satins. Today, he ignored the ladies' choices and reached instead for a finely made cream lace.

"I prefer this one," he announced baldly. "See how the artisan has used a gold thread that appears in alternating loops. This piece is hand woven, likely by an advocate of St. John Francis Regis." Both women stood with mouths agape; he smiled kindly before walking casually away. It was quite satisfying to leave them speechless.

He waited by the main counter while Bella led Mrs. Warren through the display tables. "I insist," she was saying.

"I cannot permit you to purchase them on by behalf," Mrs. Warren argued.

"Purchase what?" he asked as they approached.

Bella shot a disapproving glance to Mrs. Warren. "Lucinda has nothing but her half boots with her. She cannot wear her every day footwear with her new gown."

Mrs. Warren's lips thinned in a tight line. "Yet, it would be inappropriate for me to assume the role of borrower. You have been more than generous, Lady Hellsman."

Carter knew Mrs. Warren's pride would prevent her from accepting the gift graciously. "Then I will stand you a loan until we return to Town. Whereas, it would be cumbersome to contact Arabella, I will be near, and you can see me repaid to ease your conscience."

A myriad of emotions crossed the lady's countenance: desire, worry, indecision. Finally, she said, "It will be a loan, Sir Carter. I pay my debts."

"I hold no doubts, Mrs. Warren. You are one of the most honorable personages of my acquaintances."

His words snatched her objections from her lips. With a curt nod, the lady accepted his offer. "As you wish, Sir Carter."

Carter motioned the footman forward. "Escort the ladies to the carriage while I see to Mr. Edmunds' fees."

"Yes, Sir."

While the shopkeeper tallied the charges, Carter chose a small toy for his niece, another for his nephew, and yet a third for Simon, along with a measure of sugar candy. He suspected the boy had never known such pleasure. "Will these items be all, Sir?" Mr. Edmunds asked with a well-developed smile.

Carter glanced about the store. No other patrons were in attendance. Earlier, his eyes had fallen upon an attractive display, and his lips had turned upward in delight. He could easily imagine Mrs. Warren, in all her glory, and wearing the items. He still could not explain his fascination with the woman, but Carter accepted his raptness with as much aplomb as he could muster. "Just one more purchase, Mr. Edmunds. Or maybe two." He whisked the items from the store's timely display.

The shopkeeper wrapped Carter's impulsive purchases. "The lady will be pleased by your kindness, Sir Carter."

Carter doubted "pleased" was the correct word to describe Mrs. Warren's eventual reaction, but he was satisfied with the gesture; for he knew the gloves and the fan would complement the gown Bella had described for him.

Within minutes, he had placed his treasures in the carriage's boot and had joined the ladies. As they departed the village, he remarked, "After such a fine afternoon, I am anticipating Louisa's gathering even more than before."

"Lady McLauren takes her position in the neighborhood seriously," Arabella said with a stifled giggle.

Carter did not take offense. Even with her obvious manipulations, Louisa had a kind heart, and he cherished her completely. "It is not often Louisa has so many guests to claim before her usual companions. I fear we Lowerys are scattered over England's best shires."

However, before either lady could respond, a shot rang out, and Carter was shoving them to the floor, covering them with his body. When he raised his head to examine the scene, a second shot less than a half minute after the first sent Law's footman pitching rearward to tumble from his place on the coach's back hitch. Mr. Croft, Hellsman's coachman, slapped the reins across the horses' backs, and the coach lurched forward.

Carter fought for his balance. "Stay down," he hissed in Mrs. Warren's ear as he straddled the women to right his position. Tearing the window's drape away, he examined the passing scenery. Unable to observe their attacker, he pounded on the coach's roof to signal the driver to slow his pace before the coach pitched to the side on the curvy road. He yelled, "We're clear!' thorough the trap, and Mr. Croft slowed the animals.

Meanwhile, Carter reached for Mrs. Warren. She cupped Arabella beneath her, as she looked about frantically. "I have you," he said out of breath as he lifted the woman to a seat. He had but seconds to realize his hands spanned the lady's small waist. "Are you injured?" A bit of blood showed upon her lip, and he handed her his handkerchief.

"No…" she said a bit uncertainly.

Carter turned his attention to his brother's wife. "Bella?" he said as he draped himself about her. "Bella? Are you injured?" He lifted her gently from where she laid sprawled on the coach's floor. "Bella? Please answer me."

He sat her on the seat beside Mrs. Warren, but Bella's eyes were closed. Carter immediately set about checking his sister's breathing. "Her pulse is a bit weak, but she is breathing evenly."

"Here!" Mrs. Warren shoved a small bottle of smelling salts into his hand.

Carter raised his eyebrow in curiosity; she did not appear the type to carry the sour mixture with her. With a shrug, she said, "Because of the boy. Simon coughed hardily until he became accustomed to London's yellow smoke. I always thought it a clue to the boy's origins."

He nodded his gratitude and uncorked the vial. Moving it forth and back under Bella's nose, he was rewarded by a gasp and a cough before Bella's eyes flickered open and closed. "Come, Arabella," he said gently as he eased her higher in the seat.

"Where?" Bella said on a rasp, and then realization arrived. "Is everyone well?" She caught Mrs. Warren's hand.

Carter would prefer to tend to *his* women, but it was necessary for him to investigate what had occurred. He slid a pocket pistol into Mrs. Warren's palm. "Do you know how to use one of these?" he said as he grabbed his other gun from the bench seat.

"I was raised by a career military man," she said with a serious scowl.

The corners of Carter's lips tugged upward. "It was as I assumed." Even in the midst of this chaos, Carter's intense attraction to Lucinda Warren sprung to life. He glanced to the coach's door as the carriage shifted. Mr. Croft climbed down from his seat. "If anyone other than Croft or I appear in the opening, do not hesitate to shoot."

"What happened?" Bella asked, still a bit incoherent.

Carter shifted his position to catch up the door's handle. "We lost Hamby some ways back. I must determine if he is injured." He held no doubt the foot-man had been hit, but he would not frighten the women further.

Mrs. Warren caught his hand. "Please be cautious."

He nodded his understanding before climbing from the coach. "Croft, stay with the ladies. If anything more than a bird moves in this area, you are to remove this coach immediately to Maryborne. Send my brother and the earl to assist me and Hamby."

"Aye, Sir."

Lucinda watched him dart away into the underbrush. He was so masculine. So in control. But he was not God; he could be injured, and her heart would know real regret. Moreover, who would protect her if something amiss occurred with Sir Carter? "Then what shall you do?" she asked silently. "Die also?" The possibility shook her to the core, and she openly shivered.

"He will be well," Lady Hellsman said from somewhere behind her, but Lucinda did not turn her head. Instead, she studied the patch of road she could see in the opening. With every ounce of energy she could muster, Lucinda willed his return.

Carter searched the woodland paralleling the village road. He did not walk in the open, nor did he make himself a larger target. As an alternative, he moved quickly between and around trees and bushes. There was no clear-cut path, but Carter had no problem pushing his way through the bramble. Ignoring the scratches on his face and hands, he burst through the heavy undergrowth.

On the road, Hamby wreathed in pain. Cautiously, Carter approached the footman, but his eyes scanned the forest line. "Were you shot?" he asked the servant.

"In the leg, Sir," Hamby groaned.

Carter cracked a glance to the man. "You must be brave," he ordered. "I must search the area to make certain no one lies in wait before I can move you."

Hamby bit his bottom lip. "Do what is required, Sir."

Carter nodded, "I will return for you." With that, he darted toward the ditch line. A grated road–higher in the middle to permit the rain to drain into the cut ditches–it was a masterly designed roadway. If Hamby had been hit, while riding on the back of the coach, the bullet had to come from a higher point; therefore, he made his way to the low rise overlooking the road. His shooter had obviously lain in wait upon the ridge.

Within minutes, Carter stood upon the uplands highest point. He had discovered hoof prints leading to this position, as well as several fragments of the ammunition used. From where he stood, the road was as clear as the sky above him. There was nothing to block his view. "Damn!" he kicked at the dirt. "Who was the target?" he wondered. He squatted to run a bit of the dust through his fingers. "The note from the inn indicated Mrs. Warren was marked. Could someone have followed us to Lincolnshire? After all, I could not misdirect the lady's pursuer forever."

He stood again and turned slowly in a circle. "Or perhaps I was the target. From this distance, the shooter must have used a rifleman's talents. The second shot came too quickly after the first. Someone possesses exceptional training. Exceptional *military* training." He paused to examine the open road. "Easy enough to see one's victim. Just as it was when I was returning from Oxford." He glanced to the shrapnel he had recovered. "The same type of ammunition as what I discovered earlier. So, who is in danger? The lady or me?" With a shrug of defeat, he set his feet to the task of recovering Hamby. "Two shooters or one? Could someone know of my aiding Mrs. Warren? But that possibility makes little sense. Someone sought me out on Dover's docks, long before I knew of Mrs. Warren's plight. Yet…"

A third shot sent a bullet whistling over his shoulder as Carter dove for protection.

The sound echoed through her body, and Lucinda flinched. "What was that?" she squealed as Lady Hellsman clawed at her arm.

"I do not know."

Mr. Croft turned to the coach. "We be removin' from here!" he declared as he climbed to the seat.

"No!" Lucinda yelled about the fracas. "You cannot leave Sir Carter!"

"I have me orders!"

She heard Croft's low whistle and a click of the man's tongue before the coach rolled slowly forward. Without thinking of the consequences, Lucinda scrambled to the unlatched door and launched herself through the opening. Her body vibrated both with excitement and the jolt of landing unceremoniously on the hard dirt. As the carriage raced from sight, she could hear Lady Hellsman screaming for Mr. Croft to stop the coach, but neither the horses nor the man responded. With no time to consider her choices, Lucinda rolled to her knees to stand. Hiking her skirts, she ran toward the unknown. With each step, she prayed Carter Lowery had not known harm.

Before Carter could react, his assailant had straddled his back and had pointed a pistol at the base of Carter's skull. "Move and I will kill you."

Carter lay face down in the patchy grass. His gun rested on the ground just from reach, while the stranger's knee burrowed into Carter's shoulder blade, and he could not turn his head far enough to the side for a closer look at his attacker. Therefore, he used his other senses to learn what he could of the man. The smell of boot polish. A clean scent of soap and sandalwood. The man was likely of the gentry. "You are a smart one, Lowery, but not smart enough." A subtle accent spoke of French descent. Carter had heard such refinement in Gabriel Crowden's speech, as if the listener expected Crowden easily to switch to French in mid sentence. So it was with this stranger.

"What do you want from me?" he asked, his voice muffled by the clump of grass in which his nose had been shoved. He felt the panic rise in his chest. The smell of fresh earth brought back the nightmare of being driven to his knees as French soldiers rushed the English lines. He bit his lower lip to drive the images to his mind's recesses.

His assailant pressed the gun to the back of Carter's head, and Carter could barely breathe, his nose smashed against the rich soil. Each inhalation sucked in God's footprint. "I want you to die," the stranger declared boldly before pressing his weight into Carter's back.

Carter heard the cock of the man's gun and felt the cold tip at the nape of his neck. He squeezed his eyes shut and said a quick prayer for his family and another for Mrs. Warren. The thought of never seeing her again brought a severe pain to his heart.

Lucinda clutched at her side. When she was on the Continent, she often walked miles on end, surrendering her place on the wagon to one of the older women;

but she had lost her stamina. Living in London's cramped quarters had made her weak. "Made you more than useless," she gasped as she stumbled to a halt. She bent over and slurped in air to refill her lungs.

How much further? she wondered, but before she could discover an answer, the sound of an angry voice warned her that danger was near. Reaching in her pocket for the pistol Sir Carter had given her, Lucinda stepped softly into the underbrush. When she was but a child, her father had taught her how to walk quietly. "Never know when the enemy is near," the colonel had warned. Now, she stepped lightly over fallen tree trunks and around patches of dried grass and twigs.

The significance of the voices grew louder. One was muffled, but the other spoke with such ferocity, Lucinda thought to turn back; however, she pressed on. The footman and Sir Carter were close, and she meant to find them. She released the knot from her bonnet and permitted the headwear to fall to the ground behind her.

Stepping past a wild rosebush, whose brambles pulled at her gown, Lucinda circled the base of a rolling hill to come upon a sight she had hoped never to witness again. Sir Carter lay upon the ground, and a masked man held a gun to the baronet's head. "I want you to die," the man hissed.

The gun cocked, and she held her breath. Lucinda knew she should look away, but she could not. With an unsteady breath, she stepped into a perilous clearing. "Toss your gun away," she said with more bravado than she actually felt.

Carter's heart stuttered, not from the possibility he might die in the next few seconds, but that she—Lucinda Warren—might meet her end, as well. From where had she come? He had left instructions for Croft to remove her and Arabella from danger. Had he not just considered the pain of never seeing her again? Had he conjured her up somehow? He could not permit the stranger to hurt her.

When his assailant had turned his head toward where Mrs. Warren stood, the pressure he had placed on Carter's back lessened ever so slightly, but enough to shift the advantage to Carter. He bucked like the wildest horse in Lawrence's stables, sending his attacker tumbling backward. Carter scrambled to catch hold of the man. They were rolling. Kicking. Punching. A jab in his kidneys stung, but Carter ignored the impulse to reach for the point of contact.

Instead, he brought his knees up to wedge them against the man's chest and to flip his assailant over Carter's head to sprawl upon his back. Rolling to his feet, he stomped hard upon his attacker's chest. The sound of ribs cracking brought a quick end to the fight. The masked man clutched at the pain.

He watched warily, but Carter stepped from the stranger's reach and opened his arms to the woman who had saved him. Instantly, she was in his embrace, and his world righted. "I thought he would kill you," she sobbed against his chest. She possessed daring and cleverness, and the woman stirred his protective instincts.

Carter nestled her beneath his chin and carefully eased the pocket pistol from her trembling fingers. "Your appearance saved the day," he whispered as he kissed her forehead. The gesture reminded him of another kiss—just a brush of his lips across Grace Crowden's cheek. It had spoken to him of the missing parts in his life, and suddenly his world tilted closer to Mrs. Warren.

She continued to cling tightly to his lapels, but Mrs. Warren's practical side had returned. "Who is he? Is he the one who threatened me?"

Carter kept the pistol pointed at the man. "I am uncertain." He nodded toward where his gun rested on the ground. "Could you retrieve my gun and bring it here?"

She dashed away her tears with her knuckles before turning to do as he had asked. If he had had his choice, Carter would have caught her tightly to him to kiss the lady senseless, but danger had not receded. It had only taken a step back. The situation required he remain alert.

When she returned to his side, she also held his assailant's gun. He smiled at her ingenuity. Mrs. Warren was one of a kind. He regretted she had given her heart and her loyalty to a man of Captain Warren's caliber. She deserved better. The lady deserved a man who would worship her bravery, her good sense, and her beauty.

He accepted his gun and set it for firing before returning it to her hands. "I plan to remove our attacker's mask," he said softly. "If he makes any unnecessary moves, shoot him." It was an unusual request; a gentleman never exposed a woman to danger, but their relationship had never been one to follow propriety's standards. Carter trusted her to protect him, as she trusted him to do the same for her.

She nodded her agreement. "I shall do my utmost to prove myself worthy." Mrs. Warren handed him the stranger's gun before adjusting her grip upon his weapon.

Carter leaned closer to say, "You are the most incomparable woman of my acquaintance. I am blessed you have chosen me as one of those you safeguard." He smiled to ease her nervousness. "Remember," he said with a tease, "When pointing your weapon, I am the handsome one."

The lady presented him a serious scowl, but her countenance quickly recognized the mirth in his words. With a very feminine giggle, she countered, "We shall see if that assumption holds true. Perhaps, Sir Carter, the man bears the countenance of Apollo."

He tapped her upturned nose with a gentle stroke of his finger. "I cannot have my Lady Fair preferring another. If yon stranger is fair of face, I will be forced to rearrange the man's generous features."

Mrs. Warren smiled, and Carter's heart did a double flip. He wondered what it would be to start each of his days with that smile. "I shall endeavor to disguise my reaction to my masked dark knight."

Pleased that her good nature had returned, Carter left her where she stood some six feet from the man, who had rolled to his side. Glancing to her again, he leaned over his assailant. He caught the man's mask and jerked it upward. What he found was a man of some five and thirty years with dark brown hair and matching eyes. He had the look of those of Western Europe, with skin pale and pasty, but features finely chiseled. "Who are you?" Carter demanded. "Why have you chosen to make my family your target?"

Although he clutched at his chest, the man defiantly spat in Carter's face. "I will...tell you nothing," he growled.

Carter said viciously, "We will see how brave you are when my friends and I have a session with you." He carefully searched the man's pockets for additional weapons before standing slowly to survey the situation. Carter would never permit a woman to witness the Realm's techniques for securing information. He wished for Brantley Fowler's assistance; Thornhill had a knack for the unusual when it came to questioning prisoners. The scene told him he required a means to transport both Hamby and the stranger to Maryborne.

"What of Mr. Croft?" he asked casually, although he was well aware Mrs. Warren's gaze had not varied from where the man rested upon the ground. For a brief second, he wondered if she possessed some knowledge of the stranger. In reality, her intensity was more frightening than was their captive's.

She did not move a muscle, but she said, "The coachman followed your orders to protect Lady Hellsman."

He slowly circled the man's body. Carter held no doubt she would empty the gun into the stranger if the man made a move to escape. Carter preferred not to be in the lady's sight lines if that particular scenario occurred. "My orders said Mr. Croft was to protect you, as well as the future baroness." He moved behind her and reached around her to take possession of the gun. It was a brilliant idea to secure the weapon, but it was a terrible one for his body to spoon hers. The intimacy called for him to linger. He nuzzled Mrs. Warren's neck, leaving a brush of his lips on her skin to be rewarded with a quick hitch of her breath. It was a stimulating reality that his presence affected her. He felt an inexplicable rush to stake his claim to her.

He thought he could remain as such forever, but the sound of advancing hoof beats brought him to alert. He shoved her behind a twisted bush. "Perhaps our attacker has reinforcements," he warned.

Surprisingly, Mrs. Warren did not panic. *Bloody hell! She was magnificent!* Instead, she whispered, "Tell me what you wish me to do."

Spend the night in my bed, his body screamed, but Carter's Realm training spoke with more sensibility. "Stay here, while I have a look." He started away, but paused. "This time, if something happens to me, you are not to interfere. You must save yourself. The boy's future depends on it."

Lucinda stared into the intenseness found in his eyes. They were the eyes, which had haunted her dreams. Since they had shared their kiss, Lucinda had wondered whether he was truly attracted to her. More than once, Sir Carter had called her "beautiful," but she was certain that many times he found her extremely annoying. Yet, he had kissed the back of her neck, as if he had found her alluring. *Alluring?* she thought. Since her schoolroom days, she had never considered herself more than plainly acceptable, certainly not *beautiful*

and definitely never approaching *alluring*. What confused her most was if the baronet truly found her handsome, why did Sir Carter accept his sister's match-making schemes. Lady McLauren had thought Mr. Monroe a good prospect for a war widow, and Sir Carter had made no effort to turn Louisa Hutton's head.

Little did the countess know of the thoughts and dreams, which flooded Lucinda's mind, nor did Lady McLauren hold knowledge of the experiences, which had defined Lucinda as a woman. Had she known war's hardships? Most definitely. Yet, was she a widow? Most assuredly not. She was a woman who understood the ferocity practiced by men, but had never known a man's passion. To be a widow, a woman must have known her husband in the Biblical sense. No, Lucinda was a not the type of woman to know a man such as Dylan Monroe. Mr. Monroe was too "green." He thought of her as something fragile and breakable, but "breakable" was not a word Lucinda associated with herself.

Neither was she the woman for Carter Lowery, at least, not in Lady McLauren's opinion. Lucinda had overheard Lady McLauren and Arabella Lowery discussing Sir Carter's aspirations. "Our Carter hopes to replace Aristotle Pennington," Louisa Hutton had explained as the pair oversaw Lucinda's fitting for the gown she would wear at Lady McLauren's upcoming evening of entertainment.

"Lawrence believes Sir Carter's youth could be detrimental. Although our brother has the most experience, the committee may pass him over for a man less worthy."

Lady McLauren shook off the idea. "Ernest assures me for Carter to know success, our brother must choose a Society catch with deep connections. If he could court and win either Lady Cecilia Pickford or Lady Marquerite Nichols-David, his nomination would be easily confirmed. Both women hold multiple connections to those within the Home Office."

Hearing so, Lucinda's hopes had skittered to a stumbling halt. She held only a thin connection to the Earl of Charleton, and scandal covered every facet of her life. No, Sir Carter would never consider her a proper choice. He might dally with her, but she would never know him as her husband. The idea was too bizarre.

Lucinda forced herself to listen for any sign of danger. She had watched Sir Carter make his way silently toward where the coach had first met with disaster, and she had filled her mind with the fluidity of the baronet's movements. Of how he was designed to defend others. Of the perfect protection of his soul.

Staring intently at the opening in the shrubbery into which Sir Carter had disappeared, she waited impatiently for any sign of danger, but when a broken twig sounded behind her, Lucinda swung around to meet the intruder. With trembling hands, she raised the gun to greet the unknown. "Show yourself, or I shall shoot," she threatened with the appearance of more confidence than she possessed.

Chapter Eleven

"Easy, Mrs. Warren," a familiar voice called. "It is I, Lord Hellsman." The future baron stepped into the opening.

Lucinda released the breath she held. "Thank Goodness!" She felt her knees buckle just as Lord Hellsman's hand caught her arm.

"Are you unwell?" he said with concern.

Lucinda shook her head in denial. "Just relieved," she admitted. She glanced to Sir Carter's brother–so alike, but so different. She pleaded, "Please tell me Lady Hellsman did not suffer from the return to Maryborne Park."

Hellsman scowled. "No thanks to Mr. Croft's actions. Arabella was thrown quite violently about the coach."

"Was your lady injured?" She wondered whether to ask of the child she suspected Lady Hellsman carried, but no one had made an official announcement so Lucinda swallowed her words.

"Arabella is distraught over the fact you were left behind, and she worries for your safety." He studied her carefully, and Lucinda fought the urge to fidget.

"I acted impulsively," she admitted. "I simply could not fathom the possibility of Sir Carter knowing danger."

Hellsman grinned widely. "In reality, I suspect Lady Hellsman is most upset because she did not react with equal resolve and equal timing. My wife is more than a bit adventurous."

Lucinda chuckled lightly. "Yes, Lady Hellsman has shared the tale of her ride to save your favorite thoroughbred." Hellsman rolled his eyes good-naturedly, and Lucinda quickly added, "And you admire Lady Arabella for bringing her light to your life."

"I could not survive without it," he said as he led Lucinda toward the opening in the hedges. "Now, permit me to see to your and my brother's safety."

Carter had sent Lawrence to retrieve Mrs. Warren and his attacker while he tended to Hamby. In reality, he was not certain it was a good idea for him to be close to the lady again. Every time she was near, he had the desire to touch her— to feel her respond to his touch, which was most definitely a mistake. There was no future for them, and playing with her affections was not in Carter's nature. She remained a temptation he did not require in his life. His world was crowded enough with duties and responsibilities. If Lucinda Warren had been an innocent debutant, Carter would be speaking his proposals.

As he bent to examine the footman's injury, his mind and his body remained with the lady. Her scent clung to him, and the taste of her skin tantalized his memory. Forcing his concentration on the task at hand, Carter announced, "You are a fortunate man. The bullet went through the flesh just above your boots. I suspect the metal button deflected the impact. You must be aware of infection, but you will heal quickly."

"Thank you, Sir." Several of the servants lifted Hamby to the waiting wagon. Lawrence and McLauren had arrived first, followed by several grooms-men and a flat wagon. "McLauren, would you see to the loading of our pris-oner. Remind your men our attacker has several broken ribs."

The earl nodded his agreement. McLauren was the highest-ranking aristo-crat in the area, and Ernest Hutton took his responsibilities seriously. "I have sent young Jemy for the surgeon."

Carter looked up to see his brother escorting Mrs. Warren toward the wagon. Impulsively, Carter said, "I will take the lady up with me." If he had possession of a thick stick, he would have smacked himself upon the head: He played with fire, and he was likely to see his fingers burned. But the pleas-ant tingling sensation from where his lips had skimmed her skin remained. He explained, "I would prefer not to expose Mrs. Warren to the likes of our stranger."

"I could carry Mrs. Warren to the estate," his brother offered, but Carter disliked the idea of the woman being from his sight.

"I believe you and McLauren can handle this situation. Suddenly, I am quite exhausted, and I wish to tend my wounds before the magistrate arrives with his questions." He accepted a horse from one of the earl's grooms.

Lawrence's eyebrow rose skeptically, but he said, "As you wish. Please assure Arabella and Louisa that McLauren and I met no armed force."

Carter grinned. "You were too late to play the hero, Law." It felt good to taunt his older brother. It brought a sense of normalcy, something Carter had not experienced since the onset of his acquaintance with Mrs. Warren.

Lawrence scowled. "It is hard to achieve such recognition as younger brothers rarely learn to share."

Carter easily swung up into the saddle before accepting Mrs. Warren from the waiting groom's boost. He settled her upon his lap. "Next time, Law, you are to escort the ladies about the village." With that, he dug his heels into the horse's sides.

He had met with the local sheriff regarding the attack. With McLauren's assistance, he had convinced Mr. Wendel to leave the stranger in his custody overnight, but the effort had proved fruitless. His assailant refused to provide his name or the reasons for the attack. What troubled Carter the most was he still held no idea whether he or Mrs. Warren had been the shooter's target.

Actually, the lack of information was not his greatest worry: The remembrance of his stilted conversation with the lady upon their return to the estate peppered his conscience with regret. Evidently, his more recent liberties had offended Mrs. Warren. Although she had clung to him as he set the horse in motion, the woman had refused to meet his eyes. She asked of his injuries, of what he would do with the man he had caught, and if she was to guard her tongue before the sheriff and with his family.

"Obviously, we should not raise my sister's expectations with news of our seeking comfort in each other." The words had been difficult to pronounce when he wished the contrary.

She blushed, and Carter was aware of the heat rushing through her veins. "Of course," she murmured. "Lady McLauren has spoken of your need for a wife who would advance your career."

Carter had not known how to reply and had, therefore, remained silent, which had solidified his sister's assertions in Mrs. Warren's mind. If he now refuted Louisa's predictions, Mrs. Warren would likely interpret his denial as a seduction, and despite Carter's desire to know more of Lucinda Warren's sweetness, he was not prepared to lead the woman through a "merry dance." When he considered all involved, he knew it best to keep his desires on the shelf.

"What would you have me do?" McLauren asked cautiously. Carter, Law, and the earl remained longer than usual over their port. So long, in fact, Louisa, Arabella, and Mrs. Warren had decided to retire early.

"I have sent word to London for the Home Office to send agents to Lincolnshire to place our shooter in custody."

The earl pressed, "Do you suspect the man an enemy of Mrs. Warren?"

Carter noted Lawrence's raised eyebrow, but his brother held his tongue. "I hold no reason to suspect Mrs. Warren was the man's target."

McLauren scowled. "Then who? I thought you said someone had threatened the lady."

"True. There was an anonymous note, which indicated Mrs. Warren had been singled out. Previously, she has experienced a break in, a bizarre accident while crossing a busy street, and a mysterious fire," he confided. "But I could just as easily be the target. My position creates innumerable enemies." Carter paused for emphasis. "Or the man could have been an inept highwayman. He wore a mask."

Law chastised, "No one would believe our culprit to be inept. His aim was quite accurate. And what respectable highwayman robs a coach in mid afternoon on a busy village road?"

Carter had simply placed the possibility of the shooter's nefarious ways into the conversation to distract his brother and McLauren. "Then no highwayman," he said ruefully. "But as the stranger is refusing to divulge any information, either Mrs. Warren or I could be the intended victim."

His brother's voice was ragged. "When Arabella and I return to Blake's Run on Monday, I expect you and Mrs. Warren to accompany us."

"Yours could be a dangerous move," Carter warned. He did not like the idea of placing his family in danger. In fact, if he could discover a means of leaving Lincolnshire before Louisa's planned supper, Carter would do so. He preferred to keep his personal life and his work separate.

A muscle ticked in Lawrence's jaw, and Carter noted his brother's disapproval. He said slowly and deliberately, "If you think I would turn you aside because of the complications involved in Mrs. Warren's situation, I have greatly failed you as a brother. My God, Carter! Do you not realize how far each of your siblings would go to protect you? I may not have your training, but I will stand beside you throughout whatever danger you face. Blake's Run is your home. If trouble arrives, we will defend it together."

Carter felt the sting of having his integrity called into question, but he supposed he had deserved Law's chastisement. He had always thought of himself as the family's protector. Had not his mother labeled him as such? Not truly prepared to accept Law's "big brother" announcement, Carter declared, "I will speak to Mrs. Warren in the morning." He certainly would not promise his brother anything upon which he could not later deliver.

When she had made her appearance on the landing, Carter's heart had stumbled to a halt. Arabella's gown fit Lucinda Warren perfectly, the material accenting each of her very lush curves. The gown of dark plum accentuated the honey umber of her eyes and the brilliant highlights of her hair. Her eyes danced with an inner fire, and Carter stared in mute fascination.

Noting his distraction, the lady made a face. "Do you not approve, Sir Carter?"

Awkwardness surrounded him, but he managed to say, "On the contrary, Mrs. Warren. I approve too much." He extended his hand in her direction. "I have waited for you so we might enter together. As you know none of Louisa's guests, I thought it best."

She placed her bare fingers in his gloved palm, which reminded Carter of the gift he had purchased for her. He brought the back of her hand to his lips. "You are nearly perfect," he said with a tease. When her eyebrow rose with curiosity, he added, "But I mean for others to see you as I do." He reached for the box he had left upon a side table. "These mere trifles will provide you the confidence to shine." He handed her the white gloves and the burgundy and gold ornate lace fan.

Mrs. Warren protested heatedly. "I cannot accept a gift of this caliber from a gentleman. It would be unseemly."

Carter sighed heavily. "We are not intimates, you and I. In fact, I would term us 'friends.' As your friend, I wish you an evening of perfect happiness, one in which you will not fear the judgment of others. Permit me to observe a smile upon your lips." He felt the strum of desire return, but Carter held no regret at presenting her the gloves and the fan. Nor when he thought on it, had he regretted kissing her at the inn. How could he? It was the first time he had felt alive in years.

"They are exquisite," she said wistfully, and Carter knew he had won.

"Only if they grace your hands," he whispered seductively.

His tone gave her pause, and she glanced up at him in disapproval, but even that gesture made Carter's heart stutter. "No more, Sir Carter," she said adamantly. "I shall accept these items as a symbol of our friendship, but I shall not have you think them more than that. Anything else, which has passed between us, must not happen again. Agreed?"

He smiled indulgently at her, but disappointment washed over him. "You are most astute, Mrs. Warren. I have acted as a cad, and I possess no excuse except your beauty. However, I promise on my honor as a gentleman not to treat you without respect ever again."

Louisa's dining hall was filled with the best of the neighborhood. "I understood Sir Carter owes his life to you, Mrs. Warren," Mr. Whisenant said from beside her. Louisa had placed Mr. Monroe on her right and Whisenant on her left. Both men had found Mrs. Warren's company delightful, much to Carter's chagrin.

The lady smiled with forbearance, and Carter thought it amusing he recognized the nuances of her gestures. "I assure you, Mr. Whisenant, your sources have erred."

"Oh, no, Mrs. Warren," Monroe added quickly. "I had it from Sir Carter himself. Did I not, Sir?"

Carter looked up as if surprised by the content of their discussion. How could he let it be known he had eavesdropped on their exchange? "Had what, Monroe?"

The young buck meant to impress the others at the table, and Carter fought the urge to remove him by his ear. "Heard how you shoved the ladies to the coach's floor when the attack occurred. How you returned for Lord Hellsman's servant. How Mrs. Warren jumped from a moving coach to come to your rescue."

Everyone at the table had gone silent. *Yes, it was time to box Monroe's ears.* The neighborhood meant to hear the tale from the participants. Mrs. Warren paled, and Carter wished to throttle Monroe for his insensitivity. With his flippant means to bring the glory to his own doorstep, Monroe had painted the lady in a negative light. "As we are both employed by the Home Office," he said pointedly, "it was my duty to investigate any attack on members of the aristocracy. As Lady Hellsman is my sister in marriage and Mrs. Warren is the daughter of a decorated military man who died in service to his country, I held a most honorable responsibility to act."

Carter sipped his wine to steady his resolve. He would turn the story to the lady's favor. "I discovered Hamby, but he was not seriously injured; however, it was necessary for me to examine the area for fear of further attacks. I was just returning to assist my brother's servant when another shot rang out. Before I knew what had happened, our attacker had placed me in a precarious situation." He noted Mrs. Warren's shiver of revulsion. Had the memory of his peril affected her?

"I expected to die, but Heaven had sent Mrs. Warren to rescue me. The lady possessed the good sense to seek me out after hearing our intruder's gunshot. Her appearance distracted the assailant long enough for the advantage to turn my way."

"Were you not frightened?" Mrs. Peoples, the vicar's wife, asked in awe.

Mrs. Warren discovered her voice. "Most decidedly so."

Carter added, "I am certain Mrs. Warren recognized Fear, as is reasonable in all humankind. Yet, the lady possesses a generous heart. As I fulfilled my responsibility as a servant of good King George, Mrs. Warren fulfilled her responsibilities as a servant of God."

"Here, here," several about the table said in admiration, and Carter turned his polite attention to his tablemate. Mr. Whisenant's sister, a pretty girl of some nineteen years, but his awareness remained with his traveling companion. Yet, to his chagrin, the topic had not run its course.

"What do we know of your attacker?" Mr. Peoples asked.

"Very little," McLauren shared. "We thought perhaps he was a wayward highwayman." Carter knew the earl had found an opening he meant to ply.

Mr. Linton, McLauren's closest neighbor, spoke with prejudice. "There are plenty upon the roads these days. So many from the war look for an easy means to line their pockets."

Mrs. Warren's gaze settled on the man. With disbelief, she said, "Do you suppose these men…these former soldiers…would not prefer to hold an honest occupation?"

The room's atmosphere shifted, and a cold stillness sent a shiver down Carter's spine. With a curl of his lip, Whisenant snarled his disapproval. "For all any of us know, your attacker could have been part of that Pentridge gang. Last I heard several of the leaders were still on the run."

McLauren had explained to Carter about the uprising, but now it was Whisenant and Linton who wove a tale of greed. Although Carter theoretically worked for Lord Sidmouth, the Realm was involved in more important seditious acts than those stirred up by a few disillusioned stockingers, ironworkers, and quarry men.

"These hooligans have made a nuisance of themselves from South Wingfield to Ripley to Codnor and to Langley Mill. There are rumors that one of the leaders, Jeremiah Brandreth, killed a servant just because the man's mistress refused to provide the rioters with weapons. Reportedly, the group even attempted to take control of the Butterley ironworks in Nottingham. Although they killed three senior managers and wrecked the place, the factory agent and a few constables sent them packing."

Mr. Whisenant appeared quite knowledgeable of the specifics of the march. So knowledgeable Carter wondered if the gentleman was an informant for Sidmouth. There were many internal rumors regarding the Home Secretary employing spies and paid informers to root out any acts of unrest.

Whisenant continued, "The 15th Regiment of Light Dragoons met the men at Giltbrook, where forty were captured. Unfortunately, the masterminds of the march escaped."

Miss Whisenant ventured, "My brother believes these groups only wish to create strife. They hold no true cause for their manipulations."

"No cause?" Mrs. Warren said in skepticism. "What of mass unemployment? Although the development of machinery has brought products to the marketplace in a more efficient time frame and even at a lower cost, we have lost the value of the worker. Men without occupations cannot afford even the most economically priced item." She paused but briefly, and Carter suspected she had thought long and hard on the issues facing England. "Permit me to use a very feminine example of what I speak. The lace on this gown, for instance, with its small imperfections is superior to one produced by the machines. Also, it provides girls, without a future otherwise, a skill upon which to define their existence."

She glanced to Carter as if seeking his permission to continue. When he nodded his encouragement, Mrs. Warren added, "The Corn Laws, which were meant to protect England from outside monopolies, have driven the price of bread beyond the reach of many working poor. The repeal of the Income Tax was another government idea, which held good intentions, but which has saddled the nation with rising prices for basic goods and services. And last year's unusual spring and summer have left the country short of supplies and farmers struggling to meet mortgages and rents."

Mr. Linton accused, "Then you would offer asylum to those who turn against the government? You speak treason, Mrs. Warren."

Carter meant to intercede, but the lady held her own; he was quite proud of her. The smile never left her lips, and Carter recognized how this spectacular woman had built a world around caring for others. "I love this country, Mr. Linton. My mother and I spent nearly two decades following the drum. I lost both my husband and my father in this last great war, and I will admit my experiences have colored my views.

"A war holds terrors one never shares with those who have not been involved. The men who stood up to tyranny deserve to return to an England that welcomes them with more than a hero's parade. They deserve to return to a meaningful occupation and a loving family. And if I possessed the means to improve their lots, I would do so gladly. I would wish our country's government would do likewise. If those are treasonous thoughts, I must ask your forgiveness for my father, the late Colonel Roderick Rightnour, taught me to value the sacrifices of England's most noble servants.

"Since my return to England as Captain Warren's widow, I have had an eye-opening schooling in the difficulties of the working poor. My limited income often forces me to choose between coal and cabbage. It is not a pleasant experience, Sir." She was nothing if not brutally honest.

Carter noticed how some at the table shifted uncomfortably with her disclosure, but he found her courage absolutely magnificent. She continued, "There are not many things I know with absolute certainty, Mr. Linton, but one idea rings true. The business of war makes a country strong economically. Jobs and reasonable wages await any man willing to put in a fair day's work. Yet, the reality of what happens when the war ends and the celebrations cease defines a country. In that matter, I pray England is as great as we Her citizens believe Her to be. "

Chapter Twelve

"May I request the honor of this dance, Mrs. Warren?" Carter had looked on as several in his sister's party had openly shunned the woman, and he meant to mark her with his approval. His brother, McLauren, and Mr. Monroe had all stood up with her, but the lady's earlier conquest of Mr. Whisenant had faded with her supper conversation. In his opinion, she had spoken quite eloquently, but he suspected Whisenant preferred his women to model his sister, Miss Whisenant, whose timid behavior had irritated Carter to no end. Yet, he was of sterner stuff. No weak-kneed sycophants for him. His mother had insisted each of his sisters should speak her mind, and the baroness's influence had defined his taste in women.

A strange expression crossed her countenance, and several seconds passed before she replied. "Are you certain, Sir Carter? My earlier speech did not leave your employer in a positive light or so Lord McLauren has informed me."

Carter glanced to his brother in marriage. He was not surprised by the group's reaction to her bold statements. "The earl does not speak for me. I suspect McLauren mimics Louisa's concern for her younger brother, but I assure you I admired your stance."

At his welcoming tone, the lady's shoulders relaxed. She smiled in response, and every muscle in Carter's body came to attention, especially the one that thought her irresistible. He forced himself to concentrate on his breathing. *Not so tense*, he chastised. "If you insist, Sir Carter." She placed her gloved fingers in his open palm.

As much as he wished to control his feelings, his breath hitched, and a smile crossed his lips. "Insistence is my specialty, Mrs. Warren." He led her to the makeshift dance floor. Louisa had cleared the music room of extra furniture and had hired the local music tutor to provide the entertainment. As the man ran his fingers across the pianoforte, Carter took her in his arms. "Do you waltz?"

Her expression was inscrutable. Shrugging a shoulder, she said, "I suppose we shall discover together. I know the steps, but Captain Warren was never much of a dancer."

Carter laughed lightly. "I retract my earlier statement: Dancing is my specialty."

"Vain, they name is Sir Carter Lowery," she teased.

He enjoyed her this way, a vibrant, sensual woman being playful. "Guard thy tongue, my Dear, or I may purposely present your poor toes with a heavy stomp."

"An excellent dancer never stomps, Sir Carter," Mrs. Warren countered. "In contrast, he makes a poor partner appear graceful."

"As you wish, my Dear." He turned her into a light embrace–his hand resting at her waist. Tentatively, she placed her gloved hand upon his shoulder. He would never confess to having slipped the music master a handful of coins to play a waltz, but the feel of her hand on the seam of his jacket announced the payment worth every penny. "I am a bit surprised you never possessed the opportunity to waltz. Even if Captain Warren preferred only to observe, I cannot imagine there being a lack of young officers who would not have gladly led you about the dance floor." The music began, and Carter guided her into the opening steps.

"Mr. Warren was quite adamant in his disapproval," she murmured.

A frown crossed her expression when she stumbled on the turn, and Carter caught her a bit tighter. "Count the steps in your head," he whispered close to her ear. "But do not concentrate so heavily. Instead, trust me. I will never fail you."

As if those were the words the lady required, Mrs. Warren gracefully followed his lead. For Carter, it was a moment like none he had ever experienced. His body coursed with awareness, as if this woman had etched her name on his soul. He would never deny the connection. Could not deny it. However, recognizing his desire for Lucinda Warren and acting upon it were two different things. Although he admired and even concurred with many of her opinions regarding a country's obligations to its poorest citizens, Carter was an agent of the Crown, and to tie himself intimately to someone who spoke of a different future than did the Home Office would be occupational suicide. *Of course,* he told his warring mind, *when you accepted a position to serve England, the Realm was not under the Home Secretary's oversight.*

Carter returned to his earlier question. "Was I too presumptuous when I asked of your lack of experience in the latest dances and styles. If I offend you in my curiosity, please tell me so at once."

She glanced up at him. He noted how she worried her bottom lip. Finally, she said so softly Carter had to listen with all his being to hear. "Captain Warren thought me a terrible flirt. My husband found my impetuous nature frustrating. The captain often criticized my easy tongue, and in order to know marital peace, I made an effort not to displease him. A rout would have been quite awkward as Mr. Warren served as one of my father's officers."

Carter's previous desire to know Matthew Warren long enough to beat the man senseless had returned. Her words had gone a long way in explaining the inconsistencies he had observed in Mrs. Warren's personality. One moment, the lady spoke freely to those about her, and the next, she held herself in private, as if she expected a sound chastisement. Carter said softly, "It was Captain Warren's loss to have held a beautiful light and not to have nourished it. Despite my consternation with the captain's actions, I am elated with the knowledge of being the first to lead you through a waltz."

She presented him a watery smile, but her eyes spoke of a bit of devilment. The combination was quite enticing. "No more than I, Sir Carter."

"Then permit me to demonstrate what my dance tutor playfully referred to as a 'double bubble.'"

Mrs. Warren feigned alarm, but her melodic giggle said she enjoyed his teasing. "A double bubble? Does your wordy description mean my toes will know pain?"

Carter leaned his head back to laugh heartily. "You will observe, my Dear, that what you termed as my vanity is truly my incomparable expertise," he declared as he spun her first one way and then executed a reverse, which brought them closer. Mrs. Warren's nervous snigger grew into a tinkling laugh— a laugh Carter found quite addictive.

Early Monday morning, three carriages set a course for Derbyshire. Carter had sent Mr. Monroe to Suffolk to pursue additional clues on the smuggling investigation. Much to Carter's perturbation, the man had offered Mrs. Warren a tender farewell.

"Are there children at Blake's Run?" Simon asked as the coach made its way north and west.

Carter looked on as the boy absent-mindedly rotated a wooden-and-string toy in his left hand. The child had not been happy to leave Maryborne's nursery: While in Lincolnshire, Simon had taken on the role of Lisette's defender against the older Ethan, a characteristic Carter had admired. It reminded Carter of his childhood, those times when he had defended his sisters against the neighborhood's worst ruffians.

"If you ask if Lord and Lady Hellsman have children awaiting their return, they do not. Their marriage is too new, but there are plenty of children about the estate."

Simon asked hesitantly, "Shall I be permitted to play with them?"

Carter thought about the request. "I see no reason you should not enjoy time with Cook's son or with some of the younger grooms. You will have freedom to roam the manicured park. We live in Derbyshire, near the Dark Peak. The land is wilder than what you have experienced in Kent. You must practice caution until you recognize the dangers, but do not fear God's hand in creating the land."

The boy glanced to where Mrs. Warren napped in the rocking coach. Carter had thought her delightfully alluring. The shadow of her long lashes resting upon her cheeks held him captive. Simon leaned forward to whisper, "Why does no one speak to me of God? Does everyone think me a heathen?"

Carter had never heard a child speak so maturely. He wondered where the boy had heard the word "heathen" and what a child could know of prejudice. It bothered him to think Simon might have experienced shame. "You wish to speak of God?" Again, the boy glanced tentatively at Mrs. Warren, but he nodded agreeably. "Very well." He paused to gather his thoughts. "When I was younger, my mother was one to say God was everywhere, and He meant something different to each man who walked the earth." He reached for the toy, an unusual contraption he had sent to Ethan when he was still in the East. The fact his nephew had readily parted with the gift both pleased, as well as disappointed Carter.

"Take this toy, for example. I found in an Indian marketplace and sent it to Lord McLauren upon Ethan's birth. Some in the East call it 'Gennai's

Wondrous Click-Clack.'" Simon giggled at the odd-sounding name. "Later, when I returned to England, an American diplomat proudly informed me the proper name for the toy was 'Jacob's Ladder.'"

The boy frowned dramatically. "Surely," Carter continued, "you know the story of the Biblical ladder to Heaven."

"Sulam Yaskov," the boy murmured.

Carter closed his eyes to recite, "Jacob left Beersheba and went toward Haran. He came to the place and stayed there that night because the sun had set. Taking one of the stones of the place, he put it under his head and lay down in that place to sleep. And he dreamed, and behold, there was a ladder set upon the earth, and the top of it reached to heaven; and behold, the angels of God were ascending and descending on it! And behold, the Lord stood above it and said, 'I am the Lord, the God of Abraham your father and the God of Isaac; the land on which you lie I will give to you and to your descendants; and your descendants shall be like the dust of the earth, and you shall spread abroad to the west and to the east and to the north and to the south; and by you and your descendants shall all the families of the earth bless themselves. Behold, I am with you and will keep you wherever you go; and will bring you back to this land; for I will not leave you until I have done that of which I have spoken to you.' Then Jacob awoke from his sleep and said, 'Surely the Lord is in this place; and I did not know it.' And he was afraid, and said, 'This is none other than the house of God, and this is the gate of Heaven.'" Carter released the toy to let it clack its way from one ribbon to the next. "After the American's explanation, I was pleased I had bought the Click Clack; I began to think on the toy as a symbol of my pledge to protect Ethan from all harm."

Simon's expression was one of regret. "I should not have accepted the gift."

Carter gathered the wooden squares in his large palm and handed them to the boy. "I suspect Ethan thought you required my protection more than he. Keep the toy and know I am near."

A single tear slid from the child's eye. "Will you protect Mrs. Warren also?"

Carter's eyes returned to the sleeping form. "Always," he said reverently.

Simon asked, "Have you ever known failure?"

The image of the youth he had left to the ravages of war sprung to Carter's head. "Once." He paused awkwardly. "We are all human and suffer from the weaknesses of the flesh." He swallowed the bile rushing to his throat. "In the war, I promised to return for an innocent, who should never have been placed in that position."

"What happened?" Simon whispered in awe.

Carter shrugged away the tension building between his shoulder blades. "I took an enemy bullet in the leg. The other soldiers carried my from the field before I could fulfill my promise."

"Did the person live?"

Carter said solemnly, "I pray daily he did, but I possess no knowledge one way or the other. I must trust God's goodness."

Simon's expression spoke of childlike confusion. Finally, he made his decision; the boy returned the toy to Carter's palm. "Tell me the story of God's ladder again. I wish to know more of the God of Abraham's greatness."

"It is beautiful, Sir Carter." Mrs. Warren sighed heavily. They had arrived in Derbyshire late the previous evening, and today he meant to show her and the boy a bit of his home. He had always loved the ruggedness of his ancestral estate. It had provided him and his sisters the possibility for great adventures, and as a youth, Carter had climbed every hill, scaled every rock face, and swam every stream. Each miraculous moment of his life was somehow linked to this place.

He smiled easily with her praise as Simon rushed circles around them. The boy scampered off, following one of Law's favorite hounds across the open field. "Quite different from Kent," he protested weakly.

"Yet, equally magnificent," Mrs. Warren countered.

He enjoyed the pressure of her hand as it rested upon his arm, and without realizing he did so, Carter cupped her hand with his free one. "I thought at week's end, we might travel toward Manchester and, perhaps, Liverpool. My sources say there are large Jewish enclaves in both cities. We will leave the boy under Bella's care."

"Do you think Simon's family could be found in the western shires?"

Carter shook his head in the negative. "Our purpose will be to ask questions. To learn more of how we might identify the boy's family. We must assume

Captain Warren met Simon's mother while serving in Spain and Portugal. We must determine where people emigrating from those areas settled in England."

She asked honestly, "How might I aid our search?"

"Do you hold letters from Captain Warren? Records of his service? I could send to London for the captain's files, but my interest could cause someone to take a closer look. I fear my position could signal others in the Home Office to wonder why Captain Warren would draw my notice."

Mrs. Warren nodded her understanding. "I received only two letters from Mr. Warren during those years. They were mailed to his parents and forwarded to me by Father Warren. At the time, I supposed Matthew considered it ill form to write to me directly before we were officially engaged. Afterwards, there was no reason to know of his regard. The captain's parents kept mine well informed of his success in the war. Those letters rest at the bottom of my trunk."

Carter frowned in frustration. "I had hoped Captain Warren had left a more thorough trail," he said dejectedly. He glanced toward the line of peaks. "I suppose it is equally foolish to hope for any irregularities in the captain's records."

"As my father was Mr. Warren's commanding officer, I would imagine the colonel permitted my husband great latitude." Her chin dipped, and Carter could no longer look upon her countenance, but the tightening of her fingers upon his arm told him the lady struggled with her emotions.

He leaned close to speak in private. "Tell me what bothers you. I remain your confidant."

She stumbled to a halt. When she released his arm to present him her back, Carter encircled her in his embrace. He spooned her body with his. A silent sob shook her shoulders, and so he nuzzled her ear. "I never meant to bring you grief." When her tears increased, he slipped his handkerchief into her hands before gently rocking her in his arms. She wrapped her arms about her waist and accepted his comfort. She fit him perfectly. The rounded curves of her body rubbed softly against the hard planes of his chest, while the heat flooded his groin. He tightened his grip and closed his eyes to the satisfaction of holding this particular woman to him.

The mention of those years of fruitlessly devoting herself to a man who had held her in contempt had swept away Lucinda's composure. After the years of deprivation, the baronet's touch was a salve to her badly bruised heart. Sir Carter Lowery was everything she had once thought Matthew Warren would be–strong and decisive, yet tender. The gentle sway of his body brought hers to life. Longing rushed through her veins, and although their actions spoke of inappropriateness, Lucinda wished to remain in the safety of his arms forever. She knew he was not immune to her, and for a woman who had never known a man's lust, Sir Carter's obvious desires were a giddy experience. His loins nestled in the crevice of her hips, and Lucinda wished she held some knowl-edge of how to entice the baronet to kiss her again and perhaps to…

She heard the sigh of regret and felt the gentle caress of his body go still. On a throaty rasp, he said, "If you have recovered, permit me to return you to the house."

In disappointment, Lucinda dashed the moisture from her cheeks. Stepping from his embrace, she said, "I apologize. My days with Captain Warren hold a myriad of emotions, but I promise to keep my personal thoughts under due control." She forced herself to speak to his sympathetic countenance. "I am not a watering pot. I shall not disappoint you."

I shall not disappoint you. He heard Mrs. Warren's voice echoing in his head as he dressed for bed. Carter suspected that particular phrase summed up the wom-an's life. Mrs. Warren had wanted so much to please her husband, and Captain Warren had abused the lady's trust. "I shall not disappoint you," he whispered. How many times had he said those same words? To his mother? His sisters? To Pennington? His fellow Realm members? His father?

The realization of their similar paths shook Carter to his core. Had Mrs. Warren considered herself a disappointment to her parents? Especially to her father? "Surely the colonel would have relished having a son to follow in his footsteps. Was that the reason Rightnour had turned a blind eye to his daughter's misery? Had thought Captain Warren a good replacement?" Carter did not think Mrs. Warren a good enough actress to hide her loneliness from those who wished to know the truth. "If nothing else, why did Rightnour not

offer his only child comfort once Warren passed? Had the colonel knowledge of the captain's duplicity? Did Rightnour attempt to hide Warren's other
life in order to protect his own reputation?" In frustration, Carter jammed
his fingers into his hair. "God, I hope not. Mrs. Warren will never survive
another betrayal."

"I have not requested a maid to accompany us," Carter whispered close to her
ear as he seated Mrs. Warren at the breakfast table. He had waited for her in
the main foyer. "By using the let coach, we will be less conspicuous than if we
used one of my father's equipages. I had thought a maid would draw attention
to our position, but if you would feel more comfortable with a chaperone, we
can certainly secure one."

A look of concern crossed her expression. "May I inquire to your plan?"
she said softly.

Carter straightened. In a voice meant for the waiting footman's benefit, he
asked, "May I prepare a plate for you, my Dear?"

"Just toast and perhaps an egg," she said sweetly.

Carter enjoyed the way in which she followed his lead. The lady was quite
intelligent. "Absolutely." He chose a plate before uncovering the various dishes.
Over his shoulder, he said, "Griffin, please pour Mrs. Warren her tea. The lady
is quite fond of tea." He winked at her.

She surprised him by countering, "What would you say if I chose chocolate
instead?" He heard the tease in her tone.

Carter's lips tugged upward. "I would say, Griffin, Mrs. Warren's wishes are
always to supersede my instructions."

He delivered her plate before filling one for himself. Returning to the
table, Carter excused the servants. "I possess experience in questioning
Jewish community leaders on prior occasions." He cleared his throat pointedly. "Unfortunately, some groups are not so welcoming, especially when confronted with members of the aristocracy." The lady nodded her understanding.
"I had thought we could travel as husband and wife or as brother and sister.
People of trade, without connections."

"Brother and sister," she announced after a brief pause.

Carter had preferred the idea of a pretend marriage; he had hoped to remain by Mrs. Warren's side without censure. "Brother and sister, it is. I assume you have packed items for overnight."

She granted him a slight nod of her head before asking, "Have you spoken to Lord Hellsman? Shall it be a nuisance to leave Simon behind?"

Carter good-naturedly patted the back of her hand. "The child will do well, even in our absence."

Within a half hour, they were on the road again. From his place upon the rear-facing seat, Carter watched her carefully. Last evening, as he spoke with Lawrence regarding his plans, he had marveled at what a wonderful sport Mrs. Warren had been. Throughout the chaos surrounding this journey, she had never complained. The lady had trusted him implicitly. From London to Kent to Suffolk to Lincolnshire to Derbyshire, and now to Manchester, and nary a word of grievance. No woman of the *ton* would have considered even being uprooted one time, but Mrs. Warren had readily done so six times in less than one month, and with each situation, the lady had blended in with those she encountered. It was quite remarkable.

"Why are you smiling?" she asked with a carefree tone.

Carter schooled his expression. "Just considering the pleasure of seeing Manchester with a beautiful woman on my arm."

"A beautiful *sister*," she corrected.

The corners of his lips turned upward. "Amazingly, a man may possess a bevy of beautiful sisters. Some of which he discovers in the oddest of places."

"Thank you for agreeing to speak with us," Carter said as Isaac Cohen slid into the place beside him. The man appeared oddly amused by being summoned to the private dining room of the Capalett Inn on the main road between Manchester and Staffordshire. When they had arrived in the Manchester area, Carter had called in at Chesterfield Manor. Charles Morton, Baron Ashton, had quickly located a leader of the local Sephardic community.

"The baron is an excellent patron of many of my compatriots, as well as an honorable man."

Carter's gaze spoke his earnestness, and the man presented him an almost imperceptible nod in response. "My sister and I have an unusual predicament, and we require both your assistance and your discretion."

Rigid with disapproval, Cohen's eyebrow rose in curiosity, but he said, "I would be pleased to be of service, Mr. Patrick." It was the name upon which Carter and Mrs. Warren had agreed.

Carter articulated the tale he had previously constructed. "I am a war veteran, Mr. Cohen, having served on several fronts, but before I entered the service, my sister and I followed our father from Portugal and Spain across the European continent." A knot of eager anticipation tightened in Carter's stomach as the stranger nodded his encouragement. "After one of the bloodier battles in 1812, my sister discovered a small babe, which was sheltered in a recessed area of one of the few remaining cottages of a burned out village. We used our limited resources to discover the child's family, but as the war raged onward, we could do nothing less than to take the child with us. Since the war's end, I have used my connections to the government to review every record of the aftermath of that particular campaign to locate the child's family." His mouth compressed in a frown. "The boy is five years of age, and we are willing to assume his care, but if he has family, then it would be best to place him with those with whom he serves a heritage. Even now, it will be difficult for the boy to call others family, but it would be unfair to wait until he is older."

Cohen asked with a mischievous grin. "I assume the child is Jewish."

Carter nodded, forcing a grateful smile. "Yes, I should have made the situation clearer. We were near a village outside of Salamanca at the time. Our enemy burned crops and everything in sight before the British-Portuguese forces under Graham drove them from the area. Most of the British troops gave pursuit, but my father's company was to push the straggling French sympathizers toward the prisoner ships."

"You were part of the force?"

"A lieutenant." Carter spoke in half-truths. In reality, he had finished up university in 1810 and had not entered his military service until 1813.

"And this was Spain?"

Was that suspicion Carter heard in the man's tone? Cohen sounded almost protective. "Yes," he said simply. "Realizing the child is Spanish is the basis of our seeking your advice. We must discover where members of your race from Algeciras might have settled in England."

If Cohen meant for Carter to question his decision to seek this man's assistance, he succeeded. "My people have worked hard to assimilate into English society, Mr. Patrick. Since the early 1700s, our schools have taught our children English, and many of our religious services are offered an English translation." Cohen paused before saying, "The Jewish world has known wars in central Europe, massacres in Poland, and expulsion from Bohemia, as well as daily persecutions elsewhere. We have come to England and have taken occupations no one else would do, just to demonstrate our usefulness."

Carter interrupted, "I assure you, Mr. Cohen, I mean no petty torment. If the boy remains as part of our family, he will be educated as a gentleman, but more importantly, the child will know the conversion of the Church of England. This will be our last effort to locate the boy's family. After this, he will permanently become a Patrick."

"But not have the look of a Patrick," Cohen said wryly.

Carter scowled, "No, but it is our God-spoken responsibility to see to the child's education."

Cohen studied their expressions, "And you feel likewise, Miss Patrick?"

Mrs. Warren shifted in her seat, but her voice was steady. "The boy has become a cherished member of our family, Mr. Cohen."

The man nodded curtly. "This will be no easy task, Mr. Patrick. Not counting those in London there are established Jewish communities in nearly every market town, seaport, and provincial center in England, as well as a sprinkling of families throughout most rural villages. Portsmouth and Plymouth are likely, but we could also be looking to Ipswich, Falmouth, Exeter, or a dozen other settlements. I will place inquires as to where those from Salamanca might have settled. How may I reach you?" He retrieved his hat from the empty chair.

Carter said casually, "I will leave my directions with Baron Ashton." He and Cohen stood together. Carter extended his hand in earnest gratitude. "We will appreciate whatever information you may secure."

With a brief bow, Cohen disappeared into the inn's interior. Carter watched him go before returning to his seat. "The conversation went better than I had expected."

"Do you think Mr. Cohen will prove valuable?" she asked in concern.

Carter said honestly, "Cohen may not trust us, but he will not wish to disappoint Ashton. I hold no doubt Cohen knows who to ask." He caught her hand in reassurance. "We will have an answer soon. Trust me."

"I do," she whispered.

Carter brought her knuckles to his lips. "Let us order our meal. I have secured rooms for this evening. We must wait until tomorrow to return to Derbyshire." His lips lingered upon her skin. He might have taken her into his arms if the door had not suddenly opened to reveal Mr. Bradleton, the innkeeper.

"Excuse me, Sir." The man bowed awkwardly as he approached Carter to speak to him privately. "I have the Earl of Charleton waiting for a room. Might I prevail upon you to share the private dining room with him?" Mr. Bradleton nervously shifted his weight from side to side.

Carter shot a quick glance to Mrs. Warren. She would not welcome what would happen in the next few minutes, but he would not permit Mr. Bradleton to know Charleton's wrath. Neither could he avoid Gerhard Rightnour, who held great sway among those in Sidmouth's administration. "Certainly, Mr. Bradleton." The innkeeper presented him a curt nod and rushed away to bid Charleton's entrance.

"What is amiss?" Mrs. Warren asked from where she sat.

Carter wished to observe her reaction to the earl and his to her. "Mr. Bradleton wishes us to share the room with a member of the aristocracy."

Mrs. Warren nodded and stood in obligation. Carter moved to brace her stance. He had touched her elbow just as Charleton strode into the room. The earl's easy smile faded quickly as he stumbled to a stop. "Sophia?" he said on a rasp.

"The Earl of Charleton," Carter whispered through tight lips, and he felt her recoil in alarm. He nudged Mrs. Warren into an awkward curtsy as he bowed. Then he waited for her response. In a sharp rebuke, she countered, "No, Uncle. I am Lucinda."

Charleton gave his head a good shake. "Of course…you are Lucinda… but you so resemble your dear mother…" he stammered. Another hard shake brought his shoulders back. "My God, Child! I held no idea you were in England. I have heard nothing of your whereabouts since Waterloo. I feared you had perished along with Roderick."

155

A brief flinch announced her discomposure, but she responded, "No, Uncle. I have been in London since my return from the Continent." Her voice spoke of calm, but Carter could feel the tension coursing through her muscles.

Charleton looked as if someone had struck him soundly. "Can I hope you were traveling to Lancashire to become reacquainted with your family?"

"I fear not, Sir," Mrs. Warren said defiantly.

Charleton's eyes finally rested on Carter, and recognition crossed his countenance. "I was told the room was occupied by Mr. Patrick and his sister. What play do you practice with my niece, Sir Carter?" The earl's gaze locked on Carter's hand on Mrs. Warren's arm.

Carter swallowed hard, but he said, "It is not what you think, Your Lordship."

Charleton scowled, "My niece is alone with a gentleman in an inn with nary a maid or chaperone in sight. It is exactly as I think, Sir."

"No, Uncle!" Mrs. Warren protested, but Carter interrupted.

Surprisingly, he expected panic, but somehow Charleton's poorly veiled suggestions did not go against Carter's own thoughts of late. He could do worse than Mrs. Warren as his wife. "Please join us, Your Lordship." Carter gestured to the table, but he purposely refused to release Mrs. Warren's elbow. "Permit us to make an explanation. Afterwards, if you still feel a need for my speaking my intentions, I will do so willingly."

"No!" Mrs. Warren turned pleadingly to him. "No! I shall not permit the earl to punish your kindness by forcing upon you a marriage proposal. Lord Charleton has no right to speak for me. I have had no contact with him for more than two decades! It is ridiculous! You deserve a wife not already steeped in scandal! Save your 'willing' proposal for a woman worthy of your regard. My answer is an unequivocal *No*."

Chapter Thirteen

He watched half in surprised and half in admiration as Mrs. Warren strode from the room. Their acquaintance was of a short duration, but Carter knew without a doubt she bit her lower lip to keep from crying. Her shoulders were stiffly straight, forbidding the emotions to show.

"Lucinda!" Her uncle called after her retreating form. "Child, I demand you return to this room immediately!" But the lady ignored the earl's command. "Bloody stubborn chit," he growled in disbelief.

"The lady is three and twenty, Your Lordship," Carter cautioned from behind him. "Mrs. Warren has lived on her own in London for some two years. She has been without a husband for four years and a father for two. She is a woman accustomed to seeing to her own decisions."

The earl's shoulders slumped in defeat. "I hired a man to travel to Brussels to locate her, but he could discover no information on my niece beyond the day before Waterloo. I was led to believe she had likely perished in the aftermath of the battle or perhaps Lucinda had known her own form of Bedlam after so many losses in a short span of time."

With sympathy, Carter replied, "Mrs. Warren has suffered greatly, but I can attest to the fact she is not lacking in her mind." *Nor in her body*, Carter thought, but he kept that particular fact from his argument. "She is one of the most intelligent women of my acquaintance."

The bite in Charleton's reply remained when he said, "I suspect you had better tell me what has occurred, which has brought my niece dangerously close to ruination. I expect to know it all, Sir Carter, or Mr. Pennington, as well as Baron Blakehell, will know my wrath. If Lucinda's actions mirror her mother's as closely as does her appearance, my niece will not reappear this evening. Her mother, Sophia, possessed the most annoyingly inflexible nature. She was a magnificent woman." A heavy sigh slipped from the earl's lips, and Carter wondered what Rightnour did not say of his sister in marriage. "Poor, Roderick. He never understood Sophia's need for independence and passion and adventure. My younger brother was our father reincarnated. I suspect a battle of wills often occurred in Roderick's household."

Carter again gestured toward the chairs. "I will ask Mr. Bradleton to send a tray to Mrs. Warren and to deliver our meal. We do have much of which to speak, Your Lordship. What I know of Mrs. Warren would agree with your earlier assumption, but I have also observed how someone in the lady's past has done his best to break her spirit."

Lucinda had rushed to the room Mr. Bradleton had indicated. Slamming and locking the door, she had thrown herself upon the bed to cry away another round of disappointments. Her dream had become her nightmare. Sir Carter had promised her uncle he would offer for her. The thought of calling the baronet "Husband" had led her prayers of late, along with a prayer for acceptance by the Earl of Charleton, in order to make her worthy of Sir Carter's regard; however, what had happened below had blurred her hopes into a murky bog. "Be wary for what you pray," she chastised on a hard sob. "God will laugh at a person's most decadent prayers and give them a twist of reality."

In truth, she held no laudable traits to make Sir Carter wish to know her beyond his duty to the Duke of Thornhill or beyond his lust. Lucinda knew he wanted her the way a man wants any willing female, but the baronet did not love her. No one had ever loved her in that singular manner. Never loved her enough to forgive her shortcomings. Never loved her the way Thornhill loved his beautifully impetuous duchess. The way Lord Worthing looked upon Lady Eleanor. The baronet felt compelled to "save" her, but Lucinda could not permit him to make the ultimate sacrifice.

"Carter," she whispered as she rolled to her back to catch up a pillow to hug. "I would love you unconditionally." Another round of tears burned Lucinda's eyes. It was a painful certainty: She would never know the splendor of real love.

Charleton leaned heavily into the chair. "My God!" he expelled in incredulity. "What have they done to my darling child? If I could find Roderick's grave, I would disinter my brother to beat him into the ground once more. He stood by and permitted Captain Warren to defame Sophia's daughter." Carter noted how the earl never spoke kindly of his younger brother; perhaps Mrs. Warren had the right of the feud, after all. Yet, however Charleton felt about Roderick Rightnour, the earl spoke fondly of the colonel's wife and child. Based on his interpretation, Carter thought hope existed for Charleton and Lucinda to forge a relationship.

"Much of what I have shared," Carter cautioned, "is based on speculation. Mrs. Warren has shared only bits of her life as the captain's wife, and the Duke of Thornhill has included his observations. Yet, none of what I suspect has been confirmed by the lady."

"I understand your hesitation, Sir Carter." The earl presented him a penetrating look. "At least, I understand your hesitation as to making assumptions of my niece's anguish. However, I pray you are not dithering with her emotions. Have you abandoned your thoughts of claiming Lucinda or was your earlier declaration only a ploy to stall my anger?"

Carter swallowed a scoff of dissatisfaction. "You heard the lady's response. I do not believe either you or I could press her into doing something not of her own invention." Carter's heart knew the vexation of Mrs. Warren's adamant denial. He had thought he might be compelled to kiss her into agreement; in fact, he had hoped for the pleasure of the lady's mouth. However, her protest had stung his pride. Carter knew he could not win Mrs. Warren's heart if he did not set her free to choose him.

Carter knew instinctively this evening could change his future. "If you wish me to claim your niece, then you must permit me to do so in my own manner. First, we must resolve the issue of the child and the reality of Mrs. Warren's marriage, and then I can pursue a relationship with your niece."

Charleton scowled in displeasure. "Do so if you truly wish it. I rescind my threat to make mischief with Mr. Pennington. I do not want Lucinda injured further because I am a stubborn old man."

Carter breathed easier. The earl would not force them into a stilted marriage. "I will assure you, my Lord, your niece has earned my fervent loyalty."

The earl made to rise. "It is best I do not call on Lucinda this evening. It would not do for the Earl of Charleton to be seen entering Miss Patrick's quarters, but her brother could see to the lady's comfort. Tell my niece I am most anxious to have her under my roof at Charles Place—to know the opportunity to prove it was never my idea to abandon her. If she wishes to bring the boy to Lancashire, I will welcome them both with open arms." Carter noted the tremble in the earl's words. Mrs. Warren's abject refusal to know her uncle brought the earl great pain. "You will send me regular updates of your successes and failures on my niece's behalf, Sir Carter. If you require additional resources, a nod in my direction will bring you a full company to command. I will move Heaven and Hell to right the wrongs done to Sophia's daughter."

"I am your family's servant, my Lord. I promise to protect Mrs. Warren's life and her heart."

"See you do, young man. Said company of men can be used to punish a wastrel as easily as it can be commanded to fight for the rights of my niece and the child."

It was late when Carter knocked upon her door, and although it was several minutes before she released the lock, he held no doubt she was awake. Her red, blotchy eyes told the tale, and so Carter simply stepped into the room and opened his arms. Immediately, she sought his comfort, and Carter found he had longed for her warmth along his body. He strongly suspected she was everything he required in his life. "I apologize," he whispered in her ear. "When Mr. Bradelton announced the earl's arrival, I could not refuse his joining us."

She nodded weakly as she stifled her sobs. "Of…of course." Her voice sounded hoarse as if she had not spoken for hours.

Carter's hands stroked her back as he murmured endearments. "I cannot stand by and watch you injured by the world. You must know I meant only to protect you."

Mrs. Warren stiffened in wary disbelief and pushed against his shoulder. Reluctantly, Carter released her. Turning her back on him, she asked, "Then the earl accepted…my refusal."

He could not tell from her tone whether the lady celebrated his announcement or regretted it. Either way, he scowled. "For now," he said noncommittally. "Charleton has no desire to bring more disdain to your door. The earl agreed we should continue the investigation, although Charleton insisted we practice propriety. As a widow, you would be given a pass by Society for some choices, but not for others."

Mrs. Warren kept her eyes downcast, but she managed a clear tone. With a stilted laugh, she said, "I am relieved, Sir Carter, you were able to reason with my uncle."

Carter caught her arm. "I have delayed Charleton's edict," he hissed, "but I would prefer your reaction was less triumphant. I am considered by many to be an eligible prospect."

When he had knocked upon her door, Lucinda had thought to bury her head further into the pillow. To smother her last breath and to make the humiliation and the pain disappear forever. *How many times*, she had wondered, was she to pretend the world had not ripped out her heart and stomped upon it soundly.

However, when the baronet had caught her in his embrace, Lucinda had succumbed to the security she always associated with the man, and for a moment, her dream flickered to life; but then he said, "You must know I meant only to protect you."

Protect! Her brain had screamed the word. Lucinda did not want his protection so she did the only thing she could: She had pronounced herself satisfied to be free of the baronet's obligation to her.

A beat passed as his eyes narrowed upon her lips, and Lucinda felt Carter Lowery's heat seeping into her bones. "Permit me to remind you, Sir Carter." Her lips were suddenly very dry, and she wet them with her tongue. The gesture enflamed the intensity of his stare, and Lucinda's mind stumbled to a halt.

"Remind me of what?" he said on a rasp.

Lucinda shuddered as she sucked in a deep, unsteady breath. "I would never celebrate any man offering for a woman he does not affect," she said brazenly. "It would not be conducive to a happy marriage."

The baronet scowled. "I thought you an intelligent woman, Mrs. Warren," he declared with a tightening of his grip. "Yet, you require multiple reminders of your own."

"Such as?" she challenged.

"This." His mouth came down hard upon hers. It was crazy, but he tasted delectable. A touch of wine and perhaps a bit of cinnamon. Warm and firm lips. A kiss that spoke of power and self-confidence. A kiss which spoke of all which lay between them. He leaned closer, the heat of his body and his manly scent implanted upon her, wrapping about her. With a groan of satisfaction, Lucinda leaned into him, her arms encircling his neck. Her mind screamed she should beware of permitting her heart to know this man, but her body fought for her complete acquiescence. His mouth claimed her as his. Carter Lowery would always be the man by which she measured every other male acquaintance.

Rallying her quickly fading defenses, she shoved against his shoulders to place distance between them. She could not entertain an affair with this man. Could not permit herself to weaken. "I have learned my lesson, Sir Carter," she said breathlessly. "You are a perfectly eligible catch, and I should be grateful you thought my reputation worthy of saving; but it is not necessary to seduce me to prove your argument."

Carter recoiled as if she had struck him. Why he tolerated this particular woman's shrewish tongue, he held no idea. Likely, because she tasted of heat and desire. All he wanted to do was to demonstrate a proper seduction—to pleasure her until she groaned his name in perfect delight.

He released her immediately. "I understand completely." He assumed a businesslike attitude. If the woman did not require his attentions, Carter would withdraw. He was not one to force his affections upon any woman. "Despite my moment of weakness," he admitted grudgingly, "I did not come to your room for a assignation. I meant only to verify you were not unduly distressed by what occurred earlier. I also meant to encourage you to renew your relationship with Charleton. The earl appears genuinely concerned for your well being."

"What of my father's objections?" she protested.

Carter's mouth turned down in a frown. "Rightnour has not forgiven the colonel for whatever tiff brought upon their differences," he confided. "Yet, the earl spoke fondly of you and your mother." Their gazes locked as he studied the depth of her resolve.

With a last bit of defiance, Mrs. Warren exclaimed, "How could the earl know anything of my life? He had no contact with my parents!"

"Charleton had no contact with the colonel," Carter countered, "but your mother wrote him regularly about your escapades. The earl recounted how you broke your arm when you climbed an apple tree at age five and how you never learned to play the pianoforte, but mastered the harp within a fortnight."

She swayed in place, but Carter resisted the urge to reach for her. "Why would my mother go against my father's wishes to contact his brother?"

"I have no informative response," Carter said honestly. "I suggest you speak to your uncle."

Mrs. Warren nodded slowly. "Has His Lordship retired for the evening?"

Carter took several steps toward the door. "Charleton has asked that we break our fast together." He knew she would not sleep until she had answers. "We will return to Blake's Run tomorrow, and then you may decide what you and Simon will do. Charleton has extended an offer to his niece and her ward. The earl is equally capable of orchestrating the investigation into Simon's parentage, as am I. He possesses unlimited resources and is willing to ply them upon your behalf. He reached for the latch. "It may be best if we part ways, Mrs. Warren."

It was satisfying to note how the dark circles under her eyes matched his. The lady had had no more sleep than he. Of course, her lack of nocturnal relief had come at her uncertainty of her future with the Earl of Charleton, while Carter's came with the shocking realization Mrs. Warren had not returned his interest. She was not immune to his persuasion, but Carter had reasoned her desires came from a woman accustomed to a man's touch. After all, she had been for several years without a husband in her bed.

But what if she possessed a lover? His mind tormented him. Such a scenario would go a long way in explaining her rejection of his advances, as well as giving credence to why she sought a man's protection. *What if the man was Thornhill?* The duke had written to Carter to explain a confrontation between the duchess and Mrs. Warren. Had the duke recognized Carter's interest in the woman? Although Thornhill had denied a romantic entanglement, had the letter been a warning for Carter to avoid the lady? An image of Brantley Fowler and Mrs. Warren engaged in a heated embrace danced freely before Carter's eyes. Instinctively, a scowl deepened the lines of his forehead.

"What pray tell have I done to bring about your displeasure, Sir Carter?" the lady asked with a heavy sigh of disapproval.

Carter's eyes fell upon the woman's countenance, which sported an opposing look of abjuration. He fought against the urge to turn her steps toward the stairs, to return her to her quarters, and to kiss her until she smiled upon him again. "I am concerned for how Mr. Monroe's investigation goes in Oxford."

"Then you mean to join your friend as soon as possible?" she asked in dispute.

Carter said adamantly, "I hold a position of importance in the British government. If you decide to join your family, then I must be away to oversee the operation I designed."

Before she could respond, the servant opened the door to the private dining room, and the earl rose to greet them. "Mr. Patrick. Miss Patrick. I am pleased you could join me."

Mrs. Warren curtsied, as Carter bowed. "Thank you for the invitation, Your Lordship."

Although his eyes remained on his niece, the earl gestured to the previously prepared table. "I took the liberty to order. Please forgive my presumption." Servants scrambled to set serving dishes upon a nearby table. "It does my heart well to see you have recovered, Miss Patrick," he said tentatively. The man wished to please his niece. The earl recognized an opportunity had arrived in the form of a chance meeting.

"The journey brought on fatigue," Mrs. Warren murmured, but she maintained eye contact with the earl, a fact of which Carter approved.

He nudged her forward to seat Mrs. Warren between them. "Permit me to prepare your plate," he whispered when she stiffened with the close quarters. The lady nodded weakly. "May I prepare something for you, Your Lordship?"

The earl shrugged off the offer. "I am content to enjoy my coffee and your sister's company," he said with a large smile.

Carter added coddled eggs, bacon, and toast to her plate. With his back turned to the pair, he heard Mrs. Warren softly say, "This is most generous of you, Your Lordship."

Carter returned to the table, as the earl ordered the servants from the room. When the last of Mr. Bradleton's help closed the door behind her, the earl said, "Sir Carter, your years in the diplomatic service have proved beneficial. You have provided an old man a moment he thought never to have. I am forever in your debt."

Mrs. Warren blushed thoroughly. "We should enjoy our meal, Your Lordship, and permit the company to develop naturally."

The earl said earnestly, "I am rarely a patient man, my Dear, but I have learned over time that the most precious gifts require nurturing."

Carter tapped Mrs. Warren's knee beneath the table, and she nodded her understanding. "I...I do not know...know how to begin, my Lord." She swallowed hard, and Carter felt instant sympathy. Her world would shift again, and there was no means for him to offer his safeguard. "Sir Carter has stated... stated that you...you have maintained a relationship with my mother, although the colonel always claimed...my father claimed you and he held a long standing disagreement." Carter recognized how she fought for control. "How is that possible, Sir?"

The earl sat forward and reached for her free hand. Carter was pleased to see her accept Charleton's gesture of affection. "Do you wish me to withdraw?" Carter asked, noting a pivotal moment in its conception.

Mrs. Warren shot him a pleading glance. "Please stay."

The earl, too, added his agreement. "It is time for my niece to know the reason for my break from her father." He examined the palm of Mrs. Warren's hand. "Even your fingers remind me of your mother's," Charleton said distractedly. He looked upon his niece's countenance for several elongated seconds before he began. "Roderick and I were always very much alike. Great friends, as well as brothers. That is until the evening of Aunt Caroline's fiftieth birthday celebration. That evening both Roderick and I took the acquaintance of Miss Sophia Carrington, the daughter of Viscount Ross. We were both quite struck by the lady's beauty and affability.

"Lady Sophia was the youngest daughter of a viscount and Roderick the second son of an earl. It was a perfect match, but that particular fact did not stifle my determination to make the lady mine. Roderick and I waged a mighty battle, each of us publicly courting your mother. Finally, before we came to fisticuffs, our father stepped into the fray. The old earl had his eye on Lady

Margaret Morissey, the eldest daughter of the Marquess of Rodfurth for me. The lady's dowry would solidify the earldom, and the former Charleton removed me from the play. A commission was purchased for Roderick, and my betrothal was announced. My brother married the woman I wished to name as my own."

Carter watched Lucinda Warren's expression change from mild curiosity to horror. "You are saying, Sir, my mother wished to marry you instead of my father?" her voice rose incredulously.

The earl held her hand when she attempted to pull away. "I am saying, Lucinda, I will never know who Sophia would have chosen had she the opportunity." He said the words slowly and with an air of authority, characteristic of men in his position. "I held a duty to the earldom, and so I married Margaret. Unfortunately, my wife passed in childbirth." Charleton's shoulders sagged. "Roderick and I parted with bitter words, never to speak again, but from Lady Sophia, I secured a promise to write to me of my brother's accomplishments, and also a promise to inform me if my brother required my assistance. Over the years, I lived vicariously through those letters."

"My father never asked for assistance," Mrs. Warren declared defiantly.

The earl patted the back of her hand. "Your loyalty speaks well of both your parents, and I do not mean for you to choose who to love best. I like to tell myself Sophia loved both Roderick and me. If your mother could open her heart to both Rightnour brothers, could you not do the same, my Dear?" He ran a finger along her cheek. "I have no other family, Lucinda, and neither have you. I would be honored to know the child my younger brother called 'daughter.' Please make the effort to reclaim your position in Society." He paused awkwardly. "Sir Carter has told me of your search for the family of your late husband's child. I am willing to assist you in your search. If we are unsuccessful, I will finance the boy's education and his eventual apprenticeship."

Tears misted her eyes. "It is all so much to comprehend, Your Lordship," she said softly.

Carter cleared his throat. "Obviously, Mrs. Warren must return to Blake's Run for the boy. Perhaps, Your Lordship might wish to join us there. The baron and baroness are on the Continent, but my brother and his wife are in attendance. I would think a week or so might be an excellent beginning. Time to reunite. To learn more of each other would do you both well in coming to a decision. I imagine there are many questions still to ask."

The earl appeared grateful for the offer, but Mrs. Warren frowned. "I would not wish to inconvenience Lord and Lady Hellsman."

"My brother and Lady Hellsman would be pleased to entertain the earl," Carter said confidently. "Hellsman means to expand his thoroughbred line, and Charleton is known for some of the best horses in England. I assure you, Mrs. Warren, Hellsman will sing your praises for the connection."

Mrs. Warren said weakly, "As customary, Sir Carter, you have solved yet another of my dilemmas."

Chapter Fourteen

"I apologize," Carter said compliantly. They had agreed the earl would tarry at the inn an hour or two before he followed them to Derbyshire. It would not do for "Miss Patrick" to be seen traveling with Charleton. After the stilted moments following Carter's suggestion of the earl's visit at Blake's Run, Carter had escorted Mrs. Warren to the let coach, and they had departed Manchester. Enduring her silence for some twenty minutes, he had finally sucked in his pride and offered yet another request for forgiveness. "I meant only to assist you."

She turned her head slowly to glare at him. Her eyes darkened with aggravation. Through tight lips, she said, "You say you mean to provide me choices, but then you snatch those options from my grasp before I have the opportunity to weigh them." Mrs. Warren returned her gaze to the passing terrain. "Despite what you think of me, Sir Carter, I am capable of executing a degree of caution."

Decidedly piqued, Carter chose his words carefully. "What would you have me do?"

A single tear slid over her cheekbone, and Carter clinched his fists rather than to reach for her. With a soft sob, she said, "Perhaps it is time you accepted your own advice: Return to your position in London and leave Simon and me to our chosen devices."

In many ways, Carter wanted nothing more than to walk away from her. Lucinda Warren was the most frustratingly desirable woman he had ever encountered. Yet, his heart wished to guard her from harm. "I cannot leave immediately. After all, it was I who extended the invitation to Charleton, and as the earl holds great influence with the Home Office, I cannot offer him an offense." He paused to examine her reaction, but Mrs. Warren refused to meet his gaze. "I will wait several days and then claim I have been summoned to London. Until then, I will limit our interactions to those with the company of others. I assume those terms will meet with your agreement."

"Do as you wish, Sir," she said bitterly. "You require not my permission to act in your best interests."

He gave a dramatic shudder. Nothing about the agreement to withdraw was in his best interest, but Carter kept his thoughts private. Rather than to argue further, he slid lower in his seat, crossed his arms over his chest, and closed his eyes. He did not appreciate the concept of being labeled a miserable failure. It was an odd sensation, but somehow he would find the strength to leave Lucinda Warren behind.

Lucinda waited until she heard his soft snore before turning her head to look upon his beloved countenance. In the late morning light filtering through the coach's window, she studied the lines of his face, attempting to memorize every small detail. His forbidding countenance reflected the strength of his character. In a few days, he would be gone, and she would likely never see him again. The realization tore at her heart, but she knew it was best. She held no doubt if she remained close to the baronet, Lucinda would succumb to her desire for him, and she would not compromise herself simply to know the pleasure of his embrace. Sir Carter's honor would demand he make her a second proposal when he discovered her not the experienced widow he thought her to be. No, Lucinda would not trap him into a loveless marriage. She had already weathered one disastrous joining; a second would destroy her. She set back into the well-worn squabs to study him closely. No other man would ever own her heart, but perhaps one day she might discover another, a man she could respect and with whom she could show affection.

"Welcome, Your Lordship." Lawrence Lowery led his wife, Carter, and Mrs. Warren in greeting their unplanned guest. When Carter had announced the impending arrival of the Earl of Charleton, Law had presented him with a look of scathing disapproval. "Arabella and I planned a speedy withdrawal to the dowager house," he had growled, but Lawrence knew duty better than anyone. He and Arabella had quickly organized the staff to accommodate the earl.

Charleton slowly disembarked. "You have a beautiful property, Hellsman. The Dark Peak creates a majestic backdrop." He shook Law's hand and air kissed the back of Arabella's knuckles. With an appreciative smile, Charleton said, "You have discovered a jewel, Hellsman. Wherever did you find the acquaintance of Lady Hellsman?"

Law gestured toward the house. Good-naturedly, he said, "It is a long story, Your Lordship. Perhaps over tea, you can persuade Lady Hellsman to share her version of our courtship. I am certain it varies from mine."

The earl chuckled. "It sounds delightful. My curiosity is piqued."

Law placed Mrs. Warren on his arm, while Charleton escorted Arabella inside. "Let us say the story begins with a rainstorm and a dark cave." Law laughed easily as Arabella blushed prettily. Mrs. Warren glanced over her shoulder to Carter, but he refused to acknowledge her questioning gaze. Despite Carter's best efforts not to know jealousy, his brother's marital happiness grated on Carter's well being. Rather than to follow immediately, he turned to give the earl's driver directions for the coach. He would eventually join them in the sitting room Arabella had designated for entertaining, but he would not readily rush into the revelry.

After an hour of polite conversation, Lord and Lady Hellsman and Sir Carter excused themselves, leaving Lucinda and the earl alone. As nervous as she had ever been, she asked, "May I send for the boy, Your Lordship?"

The earl appeared relaxed and content. "Might we wait a bit? I find myself full of questions and would wish to learn more of my niece."

Lucinda attempted to steady her breathing. "Certainly, Your Lordship. What do you care to know?"

"I suppose Sir Carter explained how I searched for you after Waterloo," he began.

She paused to collect her composure. She would not permit her uncle to observe her surprise. "I fear the baronet omitted that particular fact," Lucinda said with uncertainty.

Silence filled the space between them. Finally, the earl said earnestly, "In London, we had received reports of the chaos following Waterloo. A mass exodus of English citizens flooded our docks, but despite my relentless searches, you were not among them." Lucinda heard the crack of emotions in her uncle's voice, and she felt a twinge of guilt for causing him grief. "I sent several investigators to Brussels. They discovered neither you or your father had attended the Duchess of Richmond's ball."

"Before the battle, the colonel had been ill for a week or more," she confessed. "I could not leave him." Lucinda easily recalled how she had so wanted to attend the duchess's ball. To dance and to laugh and to be a girl again.

The earl nodded his understanding. "Was Roderick ill when he rode into battle?"

Tears clouded her eyes, and Lucinda worked hard to blink them away. "I begged Father not to go, but, of course, he would not abandon his men." She thought, *Yet, he abandoned you.*

Charleton's lips turned down. "Was Roderick unaware of the exodus of English citizens from Brussels? According to all accounts, Napoleon's speedy advance had surprised even Wellington. They say the duke rushed from the ball, leaving his hostess in a distraught state."

Lucinda lied, "I doubt Father was aware of the danger." She swallowed the urge to blush.

The earl did not appear convinced, but he said, "My men found no evidence you returned to the residence you shared with your father."

"No. I volunteered in the hospitals, tending the wounded. I have no idea how long I remained among the Belgium nuns who housed the most severely wounded, but one day, Sister Agatha announced the convent would close, and they were to remove to a southern province. By then, there was nothing remaining of my former shelter. The army had assigned it to another family. My few belongings were stored in the 'deceased' section of a military warehouse. I retrieved them before I convinced the paymaster to give me father's last pay; with the money, I booked passage home. Originally, I returned to Devon, but Father Warren refused to accept me in his home."

Her uncle's mild oath did Lucinda well. If she had been a man, she might have challenged Gideon Warren to a duel for his total disregard for her future. "Why did you not return to Merritt House?"

"Father had let the property when he returned to service, and I had always wanted to visit London. I purchased passage on a coach and made my way to the Capital. With my widow's pension and the small allowance from my mother's will, I did well until Simon appeared on my doorstep."

Charleton appeared quite vexed. "I should never have accepted the Belgium reports that you likely perished. Early on, I checked Captain Warren's files, but there was no news of your claiming his allowance."

"While he was still alive, Father would not hear of my accepting the allowance, but after Father Warren's rejection, I held no other alternative." Thankfully, her uncle did not comment on her refusal to seek his assistance.

"Did you not claim the rents to the Devon estate?"

Lucinda forced the lump in her throat away. "I had no rights to the property."

The earl's tone was kinder than she deserved. "I demanded the old earl bequeath the property to Roderick upon his marriage to your mother with the understanding it would be left to their child–their children. The house is yours if you wish it. At a minimum, the rents should be returned to you."

Moisture returned to Lucinda's eyes. She owned a piece of property. She felt her heart falter. Small, it was, but she was not destitute, after all. "The rents would do me well for now. I am not certain I would wish to live along side Coltman Hall and the Warrens."

Her uncle said by way of agreement, "I will send word to my man of business to learn what has become of the rents and to make arrangements for their immediate dispersement to you. That is if you hold no objections."

"That would be most kind, Your Lordship."

Contentment glittered in his nut-brown eyes. "This has been an superb beginning. Thank you, my Dear. I believe it is time I have the acquaintance of young Simon now."

Carter had not gone far. In fact, he had chosen an adjoining sitting room to read through the reports, which had arrived in his absence. Carefully, he had released the latch and set the door ajar so he might eavesdrop upon Mrs. Warren's conversation with the earl. He could not decipher the words, but he could hear the tone and knew satisfaction. No anger peppered their speech.

If the lady knew of his deviousness, Mrs. Warren would not appreciate his continued meddling, but Carter held little self-control when it came to the woman. He felt compelled to see her well. After all, bringing Charleton into her life had been at his urging.

Her soft sobs brought him closer to the door, and Carter debated upon whether to step into the room; but when she chose to respond to the earl's encouragements, Carter had resumed his pretense. It was odd to be so obsessed with anything beyond his work, and he was uncertain he liked the person he had become of late.

Finally, he heard the boy's uneven hop upon the steep stairs. The child looked up from where he held tightly to the balustrade. "You are home, at last," Simon said with an easy smile.

Carter smiled in return. "Mrs. Warren and I were absent but eight and forty hours."

"It felt longer," the child confessed. His expression changed to one of wonder. "Did you hear, Sir Carter? I am to greet an earl."

Carter lifted the boy from the stairs to set Simon before him and then knelt to straighten the child's jacket. "You have met an earl previously," he reminded the boy. "Lord McLauren is an earl also."

Simon's forehead scrunched up in disapproval. "This is different," he declared. "Lord McLauren is Ethan's family, and Lord Charleton is mine."

Carter loved the way the child reasoned. "Then it is important you not keep the earl waiting." He led the child to the sitting room door. "Should I announce you?" he asked conspiratorially.

The boy nodded enthusiastically. "Add a 'mister,' please."

Carter offered an abbreviated bow. "An excellent idea," he said as he tapped on the door. Swinging the door wide, he said with delight. "My Lord, permit me to present Mr. Simon Warren, recently of London, England." Carter rested his hand on the child's shoulder as a reminder for the boy to bow.

Charleton beamed with delight. "Come in, young man." He gestured Simon forward, and Mrs. Warren held out her hand for the child. Carter offered the room an exit bow, and with a wink of approval, he disappeared into Blake's Run passageways. Yet, he purposely left the door partially open; it was a habit he could not quite break. He should have been pleased: Mrs. Warren had discovered family; yet, Carter experienced a real sense of loss. Before the week was complete, the lady would have no need for his presence in her life.

"Come with me," Arabella caught Lucinda's hand. "I have a surprise for you."

Lucinda laughed easily. This amazing woman had opened her home and her heart to Lucinda. It was wonderful to have a true friend, something with whom she could share the trials and the triumphs of life. They entered one of the chambers located in the family wing. "And whose quarters are these?" Lucinda asked in comfortable companionship.

"This suite belongs to my husband's youngest sister, Delia. Is it not lovely?"

Lucinda turned a slow circle. "It is magnificent. I cannot imagine growing into womanhood in such a place. All I knew while following my father's military career were small cottages, officer rooms, and tents."

Arabella hiked her skirts to sit cross-legged on the bed. "Was it terribly dangerous? When I first heard you had followed your husband and then your father into battle, I was quite envious. Not many women have known such adventure."

Lucinda said ironically, "I am certain most ladies of the *ton* would think me a hoyden. In truth, much of the time was pure drudgery: constant mending of socks and uniforms. Preparing meals from meager commodities. Cleaning away mud and dirt. Yet, there were moments of valor among our men, and I bear witness to the best England has to offer." Instinctively, Lucinda thought of Carter Lowery. In her mind's eye, she easily imagined him on the battlefield, leading by example. Never accepting defeat.

"I can assure you, no one shall ever think me a lady of the *ton*," Arabella Lowery declared boldly. "I ride as if the Devil chased me. I speak when I should hold my tongue." She blushed before expelling an ironic laugh. "However, Lord Hellsman seems to prefer me without all the refined manners my cousin Annalee purports to possess." She whispered conspiratorially, "Baron Blakehell had shaped an alliance with Annalee's family; I was not the baron's choice for his son."

Oddly, from the moment of her acquaintance with the couple, Lucinda had thought the Hellsmans were a perfect match. "You are fortunate, Lady

Hellsman. Most men wish to change the women they affect," Lucinda declared. "If a woman possesses an original thought, she is seen as a bluestocking."

Arabella chuckled, "Most men would say it is we women who set our sights on reforming them."

Lucinda sat on the bed's corner. "Is the battle only to be lost?"

Lady Hellsman's eyebrow rose is curiosity. "You were a married lady, Mrs. Warren. You understand the need to compromise."

"*Compromise* is often another word for *obey*," Lucinda said bitterly.

Tentatively, Lady Hellsman leaned forward to capture Lucinda's hand. Arabella's touch was both comforting and intimidating. "I agree. Some men take their vows too seriously." She paused before asking, "Was Captain Warren one of those men?"

Lucinda looked away. The memory of her time with Matthew Warren always left her feeling wanting. "I cannot say Mr. Warren was particularly strict…" She bit her lower lip to ward away the wave of emotions rushing to her chest. "Actually…" Lucinda cleared her throat. "Actually, Captain Warren was often quite strict. We were betrothed from childhood, but I do not think my husband was pleased with the connection. I have thought long on it: Captain Warren could hardly break a promise to the daughter of his commanding officer. I foolishly held hopes that after the war—once we were on our own—we could have found a commonality. Unfortunately, Mr. Warren held the belief others only saw his achievements as being a result of his connection to the colonel."

Sympathy laced Lady Hellsman's voice. "Why is it we women find excuses for a man's poor behavior? Why do we place the blame upon our shoulders, as if we possessed the power physically to force them to act insensitively?"

Despite her low spirits, Lucinda smiled broadly. "Can you not see it?" she asked on a breathy inhale. "Matthew Warren, you must act the role of prat today!" She mocked as she shook a scolding finger at an imaginary figure.

Lady Hellsman joined in the silliness. Placing her fists on her hips she said shrewishly, "Lawrence Lowery, you are to confront your father regarding our relationship."

Lucinda burst into laughter. "I cannot imagine Lord Hellsman doing more than pulling you upon his lap."

Arabella blushed, but she nodded enthusiastically. "Likely swallow my sharp-tongued words with a kiss of dominance."

Lucinda had never had such a free conversation: She enjoyed the idea of speaking without censure; yet, she captured her laughter to ask, "Why have you brought me to this lovely room?"

Lady Hellsman swallowed her mirth to speak earnestly. "Because the former Delia Lowery is a most delicate woman," she declared as she scrambled from the bed. "When Lord Hellsman rescued my sister Abigail, my cousin Annalee, and me from Dark Peak, our bags remained at our inn; therefore, the baroness opened her daughters' wardrobes for our use. Delia is a tad shorter than I, more of your stature, and the dresses a bit too young, but I learned to love Delia's sense of style. I thought you might make use of several of those that remain. You cannot depart for the earl's estate with the looks of a poor relative."

Lucinda glanced at her well-worn day dress, and Arabella quickly apologized. "I meant no offense, Mrs. Warren. You are an incomparable woman, and few could claim your resilience."

Lucinda swallowed her pride. Arabella Lowery spoke honestly, and Lucinda had always claimed to respect frankness. "Perhaps you should show me the gowns and permit me to decide."

A smile exploded upon Lady Hellsman's lips. "Wait until you see Delia's riding habits. There is a blue one, which would do wonders in highlighting the golden tones of your skin." Arabella removed several gowns from the ones in the dressing room and laid them upon the bed.

In wonder, Lucinda fingered the fine cloth. Silks, satin, fine lawn, the best muslins. Regret rushed over her: She had lost so much by marrying Matthew Warren. "Oh, my," she sighed. "These are exquisite, but will not Lord Hellsman hold objections to your offering his sister's belongings to a stranger?"

Lady Hellsman waved a dismissive hand. "No man would notice if a woman of your beauty wore the same dress twice." She reached for the buttons on the back of Lucinda's gown. "Don a few, and then make your choices."

Lucinda wished to feel the soft cloth against her skin. She still held the memory of Sir Carter's eyes upon her entrance at the McLauren estate. She permitted Lady Hellsman to assist her to undress. Reaching for a delightful confection of the purest gold, Lucinda allowed the tawny yellow daydream to slide easily over her form.

"Your skin and hair makes it possible for you to wear nearly any shade, but I suspect the deeper hues are more to your liking."

Lucinda nodded mutely. In the mirror, her reflection told the story of a woman she had yet to meet. "The color...the color is perfect."

"That it is," Lady Hellsman said admiringly. "Carter will love it on you. Remove the extra row of lace, and you shall be a walking dream."

Lucinda's color deepened. "Do you really think...? I mean to say, it would please me to know the earl's acknowledgement."

Lady Hellsman frowned. "You wish only to please Charleton? What has become of my brother Carter?"

The flush upon her cheeks spread to Lucinda's neck and chest. "The baronet has stated his desire for us to part ways." Her voice sounded strangely unfamiliar. Was it the fear of never seeing Carter Lowery again speaking?

Arabella's lower lip formed a pout. "I held such dreams of Carter finding happiness."

Lucinda hid her expression by smoothing out the gown's wrinkles. "Sir Carter has chosen his mistress in the form of the Home Office."

Lady Hellsman also appeared embarrassed. "I suppose, but I had hoped to call you 'sister.'" She reached for the gown's laces and busied herself through the awkward moment.

Lucinda would have counted herself blessed to have Arabella Lowery as her sister. "We may remain friends," she assured. "When Simon and I depart for Lancashire, I would adore having a friend with whom to exchange letters and visits."

Arabella smiled comfortingly. "I would enjoy that also." She tightened the lower laces and straightened the seams across Lucinda's back. "Oh, look!" she exclaimed. "We must be sisters of the soul. I possess a similar scar upon my left shoulder. How did you come to yours?"

The vision of her boldness brought another rush of color to her cheeks. "It was in Belgium. I attempted to protect a wounded British soldier, and his enemy struck me for my brazen behavior."

Arabella gasped. "You were so close to the battle?"

Lucinda immediately realized her error, and her mind raced to cover her mistake. "I...I foolishly...foolishly sought my father's...my father's remains on the battlefield. I held hopes of giving him a proper burial, but I came upon a wounded soldier left for dead. Scavengers meant to strip him of his clothes and weapons. When I attempted to stop them, one of the men struck me with a whip."

"What happened next?" Lady Hellsman whispered into the room's silence.

Again, Lucinda lied. "The soldier died when they moved him too roughly. I failed him." She hated beginning her friendship with half-truths, but no one would understand how she regretted her decisions to prove herself worthy of being the colonel's daughter. With an ironic smile, she added, "War is not all glorious victories." Lucinda changed the subject. "And now you must tell me of your mishap." She turned to catch up Lady Hellsman's hands.

Arabella laughed self-consciously. "As I said earlier, I am a hellion by nature; my father taught me how to ride hard, and he permitted me my head. Upon my acquaintance with Lord Hellsman, my reputation for mischief proved true. Lord Hellsman had saved me from the rainstorm on Dark Peak, later from a fall into the estate's tarn, and then one of my suitors unseated him during the race to the hounds. Three soakings in less than a week brought on an ague and a high fever.

"While my Lord recuperated, the baron had placed a wager with Hellsman's university enemy for a horse race. If the Blake's Run stable lost, Lawrence would forfeit his favorite stallion, the one upon which my husband wishes to build his line. There was no one else to ride Triton so I convinced Sir Carter to dress me as a groom, and I would ride against Viscount Ransing. The viscount did not appreciate my aggressiveness on the horse. He meant to knock me from Triton's back."

"It is my turn to be stunned," Lucinda admitted.

Lady Hellsman grinned mischievously. "Lord Hellsman and Sir Carter arranged several 'accidents' to beset Viscount Ransing. The viscount is now married to my cousin Annalee and is theoretically 'family.' However, I do not suspect there shall be much interaction between the Lowerys and the viscount. Hard feelings remain between them."

Lucinda asked, "The same cousin who was intended for Lord Hellsman?"

Arabella laughed paradoxically. "Yes, we are all family now. Stranger things could occur, do you not think, Mrs. Warren?"

"And so you mean to leave in the morning?" Law said with disapproval.

Carter had joined his older brother in their father's study. He and Mrs. Warren had returned to Blake's Run three days prior, and he had effectively avoided her each of those excruciatingly long days. In fact, when he had received the missive from John Swenton, Carter had secretly celebrated having a legitimate excuse to depart. He required distance between him and the lady. "I am in the midst of several important investigations."

"And what of the attempts on Mrs. Warren's life?" Law protested.

"The earl can oversee the lady's safety."

Law paced the open area. "I do not like this change of events, Carter. It is uncharacteristic of you to retreat. In fact, I have never known you to walk away from a challenge. What has changed between you and the lady?"

Carter boldly asserted, "You misunderstood my relationship with Mrs. Warren. I have taken on her investigation as a favor to Thornhill."

His brother sat heavily. "Has the duke designs on the woman?"

Carter shook his head in denial. "Thornhill only affects his duchess." Even though Carter recognized the impossibility of Brantley Fowler holding an interest in Mrs. Warren, he had difficulty rebuking the idea.

Serious displeasure crossed Law's countenance. "I have observed the way you look upon the woman."

Carter fought not to squirm under his brother's steady gaze. "And how do you suppose I look upon Mrs. Warren?"

"As if you wish to swallow her whole."

Carter had not slept for four evenings, and his emotions had been wrung dry. His chest hitched as he sucked in a breath. He did not want to leave her. Even with their recent estrangement, he still enjoyed watching her move about a room—hearing the soft timbre of her voice as she spoke to those about her. He had thrived in her presence. When he had held Lucinda Warren in his arms, Carter had known hope. He wanted so much to know love—the same as his friends—but he feared he was not made to give his heart to anyone. "I admit I had thought to pursue a relationship." He knew he must give Law a justifiable explanation or his brother would not relent. "Yet, in Manchester, when the earl discovered the lady and I had traveled unchaperoned, I did what any gentleman would do. I offered to declare my intentions."

Law released a low whistle. "What did Mrs. Warren say?"

"No. No. No. The lady made it perfectly clear she held no interest in becoming the mistress of Huntingborne Abbey."

Law said cautiously, "It was not the most romantic of proposals. From what Arabella has shared, Mrs. Warren's first joining was a loveless one."

"I am not in love with the woman," Carter insisted.

His brother leaned into the chair's cushions. "Are you certain?"

Carter mustered enough resolve to meet his brother's searching expression. "Absolutely. I can never love another. Not in that manner. It would be too dangerous. Someone could use the person I affect to reach me." The women of his acquaintance concentrated their efforts on landing a titled husband. "It would be better if I must marry to seek a political connection, one such as those, which Louisa has suggested. Love would only complicate my desire to succeed Pennington," He said with little apology, but his mind went to the unmistakable physical reaction he always felt when Lucinda Warren was near.

"As you say, Carter. Perhaps your leaving is best for everyone."

Chapter Fifteen

Despite his protestations, he had hoped Mrs. Warren would see him off, but only Law and Arabella stood upon the manor's steps. The memory of her walking with him before Huntingborne's entrance clung to him with bittersweet longing. It seemed a century prior. Could it only have been a month? "I have asked Mr. Watkins to return the let coach to Kent," he explained, as his eyes swept each window praying to see her countenance one last time. It pained him to find each one empty. "I have spoken to Charleton, and the earl assures me he has earned Mrs. Warren's permission to act in her stead. The lady's uncle appears quite content at having his family restored to him." A twinge of guilt for failing her shot through Carter.

Law nodded his agreement. "Charleton has expressed similar sentiments to me. He plans to return to Lancashire on Monday."

Carter spared a swift glance toward the still opened doorway, but he knew she would not come. No other woman had ever affected him as had Lucinda Warren. The idea of how quickly he had come to depend on her scared the wits from Carter. Yet, at the same time, he recognized the perfection of his need for the lady. "Then it is time I am away," he said reluctantly.

Law extended his hand. "Be safe." It was what his brother had always said as Carter planned to depart. The familiarity brought another round of regrets.

Bella was more demonstrative in her farewells. "You must write often," she instructed as she wrapped her arms about his waist. "I am forever fearful. Do not remain away too long," she whispered. "Worrying is not good for a woman enciente."

Carter glanced to where Law looked on. His brother's smile told the truth of Bella's words. Carter laughed freely. "You must get thee to the dowager house," he declared dramatically. "With Louisa in lying in November, Maria in early January, and you in…"

"December," Lawrence supplied the missing information.

Carter exclaimed enthusiastically, "And you in December, I imagine the baroness has already set sail from Italy."

Law admitted, "We received a letter before we departed Scotland. Depending upon the weather, Blakehell and mother will return by mid July. I thought it best we return to Blake's Run and set up house elsewhere before the baron could take up his manipulations."

Carter nodded earnestly. "Excellent choice. Mother will be distracted with adding to the family, and the baron will be free to amuse himself. Do not permit our father to love you so much he destroys you."

Law flinched with Carter's pronouncement, but his brother said, "I have learned my lesson, and if I should slip into my old ways, Arabella has my permission to sharpen her shrewish tongue upon my back side."

Carter added with a bark of laughter, "I remain your witness, Bella."

His sister in marriage smiled easily. "I am pleased the Lowery men find me capable of taming the elder."

Carter looked up to find Mr. Watkins toting a large metal case. "Yes, Watkins."

"Mrs. Warren's case, Sir. It be locked in the space beneath the coach's bench. Thought it best to return it to the lady before I set out for Kent. That is unless ye wish me to send it on with the remainder of the lady's belongings."

Carter hesitated an instant. He could use the box, which he recognized as the one holding her father's papers, as an excuse to see Mrs. Warren again, but the wary expression on his brother's countenance told Carter not to venture into the fray again. "It appears foolish to ferry the box to Kent only to ship it north again. I am certain Lord Charleton will find room in his carriage for Mrs. Warren's belongings."

Law announced, "Mrs. Warren is in the blue drawing room. Ask Mr. Malcolm to show you the way, Watkins."

"Aye, Sir."

Carter watched his man disappear into the depths of Blake's Run. After another awkward pause, he mounted. "I mean to return to Suffolk to recapture the smugglers' trail, then I am to London."

"Shall you not call in at Kent?" Arabella asked in concern.

"There is nothing at Huntingborne for me now."

Lucinda had worked hard not to fidget under her uncle's steady gaze. Each breath caught in her throat. The familiar call of loneliness had returned. She had wanted nothing more than to beg the baronet to remain at Blake's Run—for another day—another week. Not to leave until it was necessary for them to part. She could see him in her mind's eye: the immobile lines of his back—straight and proud and ever so determined. Despite her despondency, one side of her mouth curled into a faint smile.

She forcibly swallowed a pang of regret. "When might we leave for Lancashire?"

"Tomorrow is the Sabbath. Monday will be soon enough," the earl said easily.

Fighting to quell her heart's thunder, Lucinda sighed heavily. Dutifully, she reminded herself to count her blessings, but even as she did so her eyes shot to the clock. Surely Sir Carter must have departed. A light tap on the door sent her heart reeling.

"Come," the earl ordered.

The door opened to reveal Mr. Watkins. "Pardon me, Your Lordship," he said with an awkward bow. "Mrs. Warren. But I be settin' out for Kent; yet, 'fore I do, I thought to bring ye yer box from the coach, Ma'am."

Never had she felt so alone: The box would be her last excuse to see Sir Carter again. Realizing the earl's eyes watched her every reaction, Lucinda smiled at the coachman. "Thank you for your kindness, Mr. Watkins. If you will leave the box on the table, I shall have it delivered to my quarters."

"Yes, Ma'am." The man bowed again. "Hopefully, we will see ye and Master Simon in Kent agin soon, Ma'am."

Despair slipped over her, and Lucinda tasted bitterness. "I think not, Mr. Watkins. Simon and I will be residing with His Lordship in Lancashire."

A final bow announced the coachman's exit. "Of course, Ma'am. Best wishes." And then he was gone. She regretted his departure for Mr. Watkins was a man who had placed himself between her and danger simply from loyalty to his master. Lucinda doubted ever to know such allegiance again.

"What is in the box, Lucinda?" the earl asked in curiosity.

She blushed thoroughly. "The colonel's papers. I managed to retrieve them before I departed Brussels."

Cautiously, he asked, "What do they contain?"

Her color deepened. "I am sad to say I do not know. I could never muster the courage to read them. My father's loss was too fresh, and then as time passed, I thought it disrespectful to his memory to read the colonel's most private thoughts."

Her uncle ventured, "Perhaps it is time. I cannot imagine Roderick keeping a journal. My brother was not a sentimental man. If Roderick retained only certain items, he deemed them important." Charleton paused awkwardly. "We could read them together. When the late earl made arrangements for Roderick's marriage and mine, I lost more than a woman I affected. I lost my brother, the other half of my childhood. If Roderick's papers, even dull letters of business, can fill in the gap between us, I would relish reading them. That is if you do not think my doing so is too reprehensible."

She felt the color drain from her face. Lucinda pretended to flick link from her gown. One part of her felt permitting Charleton access to the colonel's private correspondence was the ultimate betrayal, while another part told her not to offend the man willing to open his home to her and Simon. "If you would not term it as an affront, Sir, perhaps I might read them first before permitting your perusal. It is a duty I should perform on my own."

The earl swallowed hard, obviously in disappointment. "Of course, my Dear. Whatever you think best."

Monday, he thought as he swung his legs over the bed's edge. *Monday, the day Lucinda Warren was to travel north with her uncle.* Monday, the day that would end any hope to which Carter still clung. For six and fifty hours, his emotions had warred over the correct thing to do regarding the lady, and with each argument, he had come to the same conclusion: He should stay away from Mrs. Warren. The lady required time to settle to her new life—a life, which held no place for him. Yet, as often as Carter heard the words bouncing about in his head, just as often he recognized his heart would cease to beat if that scenario occurred.

A sharp rap announced John Swenton's arrival. The baron had been following Jamot's trail while Carter had been with Mrs. Warren. Pulling on his breeches, Carter made his way to the door. "It is about time," Swenton grumbled as he pushed past Carter.

"Good morning to you, Swenton." Carter resentfully closed the door behind his friend. He understood how much the baron wished to be at home on his Yorkshire estate. They were the last of their unit, the last to know the satisfaction of claiming family. Unlike Carter, Swenton had no siblings, and his parents had long since disappeared from the baron's life. In Pennington's eyes, Swenton had the least to risk, making the baron a valuable asset. What the Realm leader had overlooked was how Swenton's "aloneness" placed the barony in danger of slipping through John's hands.

If something happened to Carter, the Lowery name would survive. He was the spare. And if Arabella delivered forth a son, Carter was third in line. The Lowerys would continue on without him, but Swenton's estate would fall into the hands of a distant cousin, one who John Swenton loathed. Yet, Carter, too, had had enough of cheap inns, dirty clothes, and intrigue, and his sympathy had been worn thin.

"I require a meal and a bath and a real bed," Swenton grumbled. "After that, perhaps my good humor will return. You do realize it rained all night, do you not? I sat in a muddy puddle of rainwater and waited for that crazy Baloch to show, which he did not, by the way."

Carter shrugged away his friend's bad mood. "I will summon the innkeeper. Would you prefer to eat here or below stairs?"

"I have already given the man orders, and I refuse to climb those steps again," Swenton declared. "We will break our fast here. I also mean to claim your bed for a few hours. The inn keep swears he has no rooms available." Swenton scrubbed away his exhaustion with his dry hands.

"Then I suppose I should dress. Who is keeping watch? Monroe?"

Swenton scowled. "Yes, the all-too-willing-to-please Dylan Monroe has taken over for me. You know, Lowery, there is something odd about that man. Have you ever noticed how he seems to be wherever Jamot is sighted? Is it possible the Baloch has found an informant? Whenever a man is too anxious for a confrontation, my hackles take on an edge."

Carter's frown lines met. He said stiffly, "I had not thought of the possibility. Monroe came aboard after Pennington reconnected with Godown's aunt. He was recommended by Lord Sidmouth."

The baron's countenance held the expression of defeat. "Could Sidmouth have his spies in the other departments of the Home Office? Rumors say His Lordship employs provocateurs to search out sedition among the English citizenry."

"But why spy on British spies?" Carter argued, but he could easily imagine Sidmouth doing so.

Swenton rotated his shoulders to drive away exhaustion. "Who is to say? With Pennington's eventual withdrawal, perhaps Sidmouth has another candidate for the position. Mayhap Monroe is to identify your weaknesses. Or there is the possibility His Lordship means to combine the departments over which he has control. Disbanding the Realm could save a sizeable expense."

Carter held his breath. His jaw tightened. Had Swenton stumbled upon an idea Carter had long suppressed? What was the Realm's future? Could he continue its greatness? Would it crumble under his watch? "After you have bathed, we will discuss this further." Carter slid his arms into his shirt and let it drop over his head and shoulders. "Thank you, Swenton," he said thoughtfully. "Your keen sense of rightness has opened my eyes to a likelihood I have relentlessly denied."

While his friend slept, Carter reorganized his men in the area, having them concentrate their investigations on Jamot's associates rather than on the Baloch himself. He purposely did not speak to Monroe for he wished to observe his aide more closely. He drafted a letter to Pennington in which he used a secret code, of which only five men were aware. In it, he fabricated details of Jamot's sightings, as well as Carter's suspicions, regarding an unnamed aristocrat involved in the smuggling ring. He would ask Monroe personally to deliver the message to Pennington. Adding the innocuous words of "wherewithal" and "extraordinary" in relation to Dylan Monroe, without raising notice was a much harder task than Carter had anticipated. However, he supposed it was why Pennington had chosen the words, used within a certain order, to inform the reader something was amiss with the messenger.

In late afternoon, Carter looked up to see Swenton enter the private room. "You appear more congenial," he said blandly.

The baron slid into the opposing seat. "Appearances hold deception," he grumbled. He reached for the knife and hard cheese to cut away the crust. "What is my assignment this evening?"

"I expect you to find your own bed and know additional rest." Carter did not look up from his papers, but he heard Swenton's quick intake of air, indicating the baron's surprise. "Your eyes speak of distress, John. Is everything aright with your estate?"

The baron did not respond immediately. "Marwood Manor is prospering. Thankfully, I made shipping investments, which proved profitable and held us together during the last two harvests."

"Then what troubles you, Swenton?" Carter met his friend's gaze. "As always I am your servant and your confidant."

The baron shifted as if uncomfortable. "Someone for whom I care dearly has taken ill," he confessed.

"The lady in Vienna?" Carter asked cautiously.

Swenton shook his head in the negative. "No, not the one I visit regularly." Carter again wondered if the mysterious woman with the Austrian connection was the baron's mother. None within their unit knew the truth of Swenton's childhood. Rumors surrounded the former baroness's speedy exit from her marriage, but John Swenton had never spoken more than a few dozen words regarding the scandalous affair. "It is someone who does not welcome my protection."

Carter could sympathize with his friend's sentiments. "All we can do under such circumstances is to recruit another to act in our stead." *As you did with the Earl of Charleton*, he chastised. "Have you considered a family member who could lend the necessary assistance? Or a companion, as Berwick has done with his brother Trevor? The earl has promised Jeremy Ingram a settlement and a future position for Mr. Ingram's service to Trevor Wellston."

His friend stood to use the scene outside the window as a distraction. The clock accented the passing seconds. Finally, Swenton said softly, "It is a lady, who brings worry to my door, but Berwick's principle could prove useful. I could hire a genteel lady to serve my friend and later present the woman with a suitable dowry or a settlement after a few years' service. I will take the idea under consideration." The baron returned to the table. "Thank you, Lowery. At least, I have the beginnings of a plan." He poured a glass of wine. "And how goes your latest adventure with the lovely Mrs. Warren?"

It was Carter's turn to squirm. "I have taken my own advice: I have placed Mrs. Warren and Simon in the capable hands of her uncle, the Earl of Charleton."

"Amazing," Swenton said in awe. "I half expected you to make your addresses to the woman."

Carter schooled his expression. He spoke slowly, every word controlled. "The lady and I often disagreed. We would never suit," he announced hurriedly and returned to his papers. Carter had wrestled with his indecision for days, and although he was proud of his restraint in the situation, he could not say the words pleased him. Instead of being the shrew he had portrayed her to be, Lucinda Warren was everything he wanted in his life. The realization tightened his throat.

He glanced up to see Swenton grinning at him appreciatively. "Welcome to the world of lost causes," his friend said wryly. "However, if your stars change, do not hesitate to call upon me. I quite enjoyed playing cupid on Viscount Lexford's behalf."

Lucinda had packed her meager belongings before making an appearance in the morning room. Although her uncle had said they would depart early this morning, the earl's valet had indicated his master had taken to his bed earlier than anticipated the previous evening with a severe headache. "Lord Charleton has suffered from headaches his entire life." Mr. Priest whispered when she had answered the man's light knock upon her chamber door.

"I understand," she said sympathetically. "My father, the colonel, suffered likewise. Is there anything I might do to ease Uncle Gerhard's discomfort?"

"No, Ma'am. I am accustomed to seeing to His Lordship's needs."

Lucinda touched the man's hand in admiration. "The earl is fortunate to have such a man in his service. My father's batman was exceptional in resolving the colonel's suffering; however, my mother and I were quite adept at tending him. If it would not offend you, perhaps some day we could compare our knowledge of such remedies. I would enjoy hearing you speak of what brings Uncle Gerhard comfort. I know so little of the earl's life." She knew better than to tell Mr. Priest she likely held knowledge of medicine beyond the valet's experience.

"If the earl would not object, I would be pleased to speak on my service. For now, Ma'am, His Lordship wished for you to be aware of the possibility of a later start tomorrow or even a delay."

Not finding her uncle at the table, Lucinda had greeted Lord and Lady Hellsman before filling a plate. "His Lordship has not come down?" she asked.

"I have not seen the earl," Hellsman mumbled as he scanned his newspaper.

Lucinda sat where the footman indicated. "My uncle was ill last evening. We may be forced to beg for your extended hospitality." She prayed it would not come to that point, but Lucinda thought it only fair to warn the Lowerys of the prospect. "I apologize if our presence at Blake's Run has delayed your retreat to the dowager house." She shot a quick glance at Arabella Lowery.

Lord Hellsman took a long admiring look at his wife. "I assure you, Mrs. Warren, Lady Hellsman has organized our new home. Only a few personal items require transplanting. Whether we move into the manor later today or later this week will make little difference. If the earl requires another day or two to recover, we will be pleased for your company. My wife was despondent at having to lose her new friend so quickly," he said teasingly.

Yet, Lucinda was certain the couple had second thoughts when a familiar coach pulled into the circle before the manor house in late afternoon. "Father's coach," Lord Hellsman announced as he caught his wife's hand so they could greet his parents as a couple. Lucinda heard Arabella groan of displeasure, but Hellsman ignored his wife's qualms. "Come along," he said with encouragement. "We must portray a united front." A short, harsh laugh followed. "You, too, Mrs. Warren. You must assist Arabella in distracting the baroness, while I deal with the baron."

She frowned in confusion. "Me?"

"Of course, you," he stated as he tugged his wife toward the main entrance. Lucinda followed reluctantly. "I hold no doubt the baron called at McLauren's estate before proceeding on to Blake's Run. My mother will have heard of Carter's involvement in your life, and I would have the baroness's interest quickly appeased."

Lucinda's confusion turned to shock. Hellsman spoke of an apparent connection between her and the baronet. She glanced at her worn day dress, and her groan of discontentment joined Lady Hellsman's earlier one. The baroness would find her an unimpressive specimen of femininity.

The door swung wide, and the Blake's Run staff spilled out upon the main steps to greet their master and mistress. A footman scrambled to set down the steps, and an elderly man, whose looks spoke of a combination of Lord Hellsman and Sir Carter, stepped wearily from the coach. He was not as tall as either man, but he possessed the same full head of hair. Lord Hellsman's touch of gray at his temples would likely turn to the silver strands his father sported.

The baron turned to assist his wife to the ground. Lucinda came to the instant conclusion Lady McLauren was the image of the baroness as a young woman. It made Lucinda anxious to have Maria's and Delia's acquaintances to observe which parent held precedence in the younger Lowery girls' looks.

"Father!" Lawrence Lowery exclaimed. "I am pleased to have you safe at Blake's Run, Sir." He bowed before extending his hand to the baron. Lucinda immediately wondered what prevented their embrace. Surely, the Lowery men had resolved their earlier disagreement over Lord Hellsman's marriage.

She watched as her new friend, Arabella Lowery, dutifully stepped forward to greet her father in marriage. The baron presented Lady Hellsman a quick bow and a respectful kiss to her cheek. "Welcome home, Baron," Lady Hellsman said pleasantly, although Lucinda recognized the reserve in Arabella's tone.

"Thank you, Lady Hellsman. I have longed to look upon the Dark Peak again."

"The Alps were magnificent," the baroness interrupted. "I was sorry to curtail our adventure." She embraced her eldest son and caressed his cheek. "You look well," she said as she smoothed a line across his forehead.

"I am content, Mother. More so than words can express," Lord Hellsman declared as if to ward off his father's criticism.

The baroness patted his cheek. "I knew it would be so as soon as I laid eyes upon Miss Tilney." She reached for Arabella, who joined the baroness in a loving embrace. "I have returned to Derbyshire to be available to Louisa and Maria," she announced.

Lord Hellsman caught his mother's hand and brought it to his lips. "You will be required at Blake's Run also, Baroness."

Tears sprang to Lucinda's eyes as she looked upon Lady Blakehell's countenance. She would never know a mother's happiness at discovering herself a grandmother. "Oh, Bella," she gasped as she tightened her embrace on her son's wife. "When?"

"December," Arabella said softly.

"A Christmastide baby." The baroness's hand came to her mouth. "Did you hear, Niall? An heir for the title?"

Lucinda's eyes shot to the baron. His expression spoke of relief and pride. It was a telling moment. Baron Blakehell may not have approved of his son's marrying Arabella Tilney, but the man would celebrate the continuation of his family name. His gaze met Lucinda's. "I suggest we take our good wishes within."

With a touch of embarrassment, Lord Hellsman said, "Baron. Baroness, permit me to present our newest acquaintance, Mrs. Lucinda Warren, the Earl of Charleton's niece. His Lordship is quite ill and regrets being unable to welcome you home." Lucinda executed a proper curtsy. "Mrs. Warren, these are my parents the Baron and Baroness Blakehell."

She could tell from the baron's raised eyebrow Lady McLauren had filled her parents' heads with tales of Lucinda's involvement with Sir Carter. "I am pleased for the acquaintance," she said tentatively. "I hope Uncle Gerhard will be well enough to join us later."

Unease crossed Lady Blakehell's countenance, but she quickly recovered her feigned cordiality. The baroness asked what both she and her husband wished to know. "I understood Carter was in attendance at Blake's Run."

"My brother has returned to his position," Lord Hellsman announced. "Some two days prior."

Was that a look of reprieve, which crossed the baron's countenance? "I shall leave you to your happy homecoming," Lucinda said with as much poise as she could muster. "I should see to my uncle's recovery. Thank you for your graciousness toward His Lordship and me." She made a second curtsy before focusing her steps toward her uncle's chambers. Even if it offended Mr. Priest, she meant to see to the earl's speedy recovery. With a questioning look of disapproval, the baron had made it quite clear he thought her below his youngest son's notice. What hurt more than the baron's biased opinion was the truth behind Blakehell's unspoken objections: Sir Carter deserved someone infinitely more suitable than she.

Chapter Sixteen

When she reached her uncle's chambers, Lucinda found the earl asleep. Mr. Priest greeted her kindly. "I thought I might relieve you for a few minutes," she whispered. "I am certain you have additional duties, especially as the baron and baroness have returned unexpectedly from the Continent."

"Thank you, Ma'am. You are correct; His Lordship will wish to greet his host and hostess properly dressed."

She peeked at the resting form on the bed. "Permit me to retrieve a book to keep me company, and I shall return to sit with Uncle Gerhard."

"Of course, Ma'am. The earl will be most appreciative."

Lucinda nodded before scurrying away. Her uncle's illness would serve her well in avoiding the Lowerys, at least until she and Charleton could make their exits. Entering her now familiar quarters, she realized she had returned her book to the library in anticipation of their leaving. With a frown, she glanced about the room. "There is nothing to be done," she chastised herself, "but to hope the Lowerys have not gathered in the manor's library."

As if in answer, her eyes fell upon the locked box containing her father's private papers. "Better than encountering the baron and baroness again so soon," she declared aloud. "And I did promise the earl I would read Papa's papers before I shared them with him." Resigned, Lucinda removed the key from a string about her neck and unlocked the metal clasp.

She thumbed through the papers, many of which she barely recalled seeing previously. After the devastation she had witnessed and the pain of losing her father, she had been so distraught when she had refused to return to the quarters she had shared with her father. A group of Belgium nuns had taken her in. She recalled crawling into the bed they had provided her and had cried for what must have been days. Finally, a member of her father's staff had called upon her to inform her the army had assigned the small set of rooms, she had once shared with the colonel, to another family. "Where am I to go?" she had asked in bewilderment.

The strict military protocol had defined the obvious: "You should return to England, Ma'am. Surely you possess family who are anxious for your return." What the man had not understood was her complete desolation had arrived.

"How long?" she had whispered.

"Four and twenty hours," the officers had said in clipped tones.

And so she had packed her personal belongings and those few remaining items she wished to retain of her father's. Having witnessed the scavengers on the battlefield who stripped the bodies of their clothing, jewelry, and medals, Lucinda had sold many of her father's uniforms and personal effects for enough money to book passage to England. Without time to decipher properly what papers held the most importance, she had emptied a metal box her mother had used to store clean bandages and medicinals and placed all the colonel's correspondence within, and there they had remained until this day.

Her eyes scanned the stack of letters and business papers, finally resting on a thin leather covered journal. "Best to start with something innocuous," she declared as her eyes filled with tears. "Papa likely spoke of burnt meals and plans for battles," she assured her aching heart. "I do not think I could bear to read the letters he kept from Mama and me. At least, not immediately." She swallowed the bile clogging her throat. "Once he is feeling more himself, perhaps Uncle can make sense of the papers from Papa's man of business."

Thus decided, Lucinda returned to the earl's room, the journal tucked neatly at her side. Mr. Priest placed a chair beside the window so she could have advantage of the light. The rest of the room remained in darkness. She recalled how her father preferred total darkness when he suffered likewise. Within seconds, she was alone with a man she barely knew.

Over the past week, Lucinda had searched her uncle's countenance for the similarities between the earl and her father. The earl was several inches shorter than the colonel's military stature, and he was more effeminate in his features. His hair was lighter and his lips thinner. Roderick Rightnour's weather-beaten countenance would have looked odd upon the earl's shoulders, and Lucinda certainly could not imagine hardened soldiers snapping to attention when Gerhard Rightnour issued an order. The earl had the soft-spoken authority of the aristocracy, while Roderick Rightnour could quell the most dangerous enemy with his raging intensity. It was as if Nature had known their roles prior to their births and had presented each with the perfect countenance and frame. She had come to the conclusion over the past several days her mother had been fortunate to spark the interest of two such diverse men.

When the earl had first pronounced his affection for Sophia Rightnour, Lucinda had been both incensed at her uncle's forwardness and curious on how things had come to pass. She had to admit it had been freeing finally to have an explanation of what appeared to be a foolish feud between brothers, a feud more than two decades old, and although she remained fiercely loyal to the colonel, she had appreciated Gerhard Rightnour's honesty. He could have presented her a lie and waited for her to discover the truth. Instead, the earl had spoken from his heart and had ultimately endeared himself to her.

She sighed heavily when she opened the journal to the first page. Her father's familiar script brought fond memories rushing forward to catch her heart in a tight grasp. Unshed tears tightened her throat, and Lucinda blinked several times before her eyes could focus on the words. She read quickly through the early entries, which described her father's joy at having claimed Sophia Carrington as his wife. The colonel spoke of their days together as the happiest he had ever known.

7 August 1794 ~ The day has dawned at last. My darling Sophia has delivered forth the most beautiful child God has ever touched. Lucinda Isabella Rightnour came into this world at two of the clock on the new day. Sophia thought I might be disappointed not to claim a son, but everyone knows a wee lass can claim a man's heart with her first breath. My daughter's hair is a golden fluff, and her eyes are blue, but Sophia assures me both will change with time. Thank you, God, for your benevolence.

Lucinda smiled easily. She recalled the feeling of love when she curled up in her Papa's lap in the evenings. The smell of cigars clung to his jacket, and she would bury her nose into the cloth. Those early years were idyllic. They lived in Devon and enjoyed the life of a genteel family. Papa never claimed his aristocratic roots. He was Captain Rightnour then, and the neighborhood envied the goings on at Merritt House.

Over the next hour, Lucinda read the dated entries. Her Papa did not write in the journal daily, only when he had something of note he wished to mark. Lucinda relived her first birthday, the time she fell into the small tarn behind the house and her Papa diving in to save her, the swimming lessons, which followed that incident, her governess's praise at the quickness of Lucinda's mind, and the moment the dream began to crumble.

7 August 1804 ~ My darling girl has turned ten, and the day began in glorious anticipation on both our parts. I have bought Lucinda a pony, and I mean to teach her to ride.

Lucinda remembered the day well. Her father's gaze had held his happiness when he lifted her to the specially made saddle. Yet, her mother had not been pleased at the colonel's daring. "What if she falls and breaks her neck?" Sophia Rightnour had pleaded.

Lucinda's father had scoffed at his wife fussiness. "I will walk beside her every step. You must know I would never permit anything to happen to my Lindy Girl."

Later that evening there had been a terrible rout. Lucinda had always thought the fright had stemmed from her mother's continued objections. That is, until she read her father's words.

Sophia and I have been living a lie. I have discovered her betrayal: My wife has maintained a correspondence with my older brother Gerhard. As I have celebrated each of Lucinda's accomplishments, Sophia has shared those same events with the man whom she once preferred over me. I had thought we had carved out a satisfying life together, but I have been a fool.

Why? Lucinda wondered. *Why had her mother risked her marriage by secretly writing to a man to which the colonel had purposely parted ways? It made no sense.* Even if Sophia Rightnour continued to love Gerhard, what would have driven her to bring pain to a man who adored her?

A stirring from where the earl rested upon the bed brought Lucinda scrambling to her feet. She tucked the journal behind a cushion. "You are awake, at last," she said as she rushed forward to assist him to a seated position. She fluffed the pillows behind his back.

"Where is Mr. Priest?" he asked cautiously.

"The Baron and Baroness Blakehell have returned from their journey. I permitted Mr. Priest time to prepare your clothes. I assumed you would make an appearance at supper." She busied herself with pouring her uncle a glass of water.

"That is most kind of you," he said unsurely. "You are correct; I must place myself forward to greet my hosts." He sipped the water she had given him. Returning the glass, the earl caught her wrist. "Something has occurred to upset you. Please tell me what is amiss. It disturbs me to see you so often in distress; I would ease your pain if you would permit it."

Lucinda's eyes fell on the long slender fingers holding her hand in place. *What could she say? Should she ask him how he had managed to steal her mother's heart from her father?* Somehow, the words would not come. She would finish the journal to discover more of her parents' pasts before she confronted the earl. Earlier, Lucinda had remarked on her uncle's earnestness. She did not doubt his previous tales, but perhaps the earl had omitted some important fact. *As did your mother and father,* she silently cautioned.

The earl waited patiently for a response; therefore, with a small shrugging motion, she told him a half-truth. "The baron did not approve of Lord Hellsman's joining with the former Arabella Tilney. He held plans for the eldest son to wed Bella's cousin Miss Dryburgh, who holds connections to Lord Graham."

Her uncle reasoned, "But I heard Lord Hellsman say his wife was the Earl of Vaughn's granddaughter. The Vaughn title can be traced to the early Anglo Saxons. Graham's only goes back three or four generations. Miss Tilney holds the more considerable lineage."

"True," Lucinda granted. "And if Miss Tilney's family was not acceptable company, what of mine?" The earl frowned. "I did not mean it as such," she said quickly. "Our connection is an exceptional one. However, the Blakehells have spent several days with their oldest daughter before returning to Blake's Run. I am certain Lady McLauren has filled her parents' heads with tales of my situation with Simon and of Sir Carter's involvement. They must think Arabella infinitely more appropriate than I."

"If what you say proves true, we will depart immediately. I would not have you subjected to more censure. You are my precious girl."

Her uncle's endearment was so reminiscent of her father's sentiments Lucinda could not hold back the tears forming in her eyes' corners. "You should know I have begun to read Papa's journal." She confessed. She saw anticipation flare in the earl's gaze, and she swallowed her boiling lack of confidence. "I still wish time alone with Papa's personal thoughts," she cautioned, "but the box has many letters from Papa's man of business. I thought they could shed light on the condition of the Devon estate. If your offer remains, would you assist me in deciphering them? Previously, I had thought to ask the Duke of Thornhill's or Sir Carter's man of business for assistance." Lucinda paused awkwardly. "Now I possess other options. More important options." She smiled to relieve the tension between them. "I prefer your expertise."

The earl released her wrist. "And I prefer you, my Dear, to all others," he said with an answering smile.

She bent to kiss his forehead. "Thank you for understanding. We shall deal well together, you and I."

Although obviously still suffering from his headache, the earl made an appearance at the Lowerys' supper table. Lucinda was quite pleased with how well Charleton handled the awkward situation. The earl was the flawless aristocrat, speaking pleasantly, but firmly.

"We were agreeably surprised by your presence at Blake's Run," the baron ventured.

Charleton held his soupspoon in ready. "I am certain, Blakehell, you have been apprised of the reason for my following my niece to your door. There is no need to pretend ignorance of Sir Carter's orchestrating Lucinda's and my reunion. If you have specific questions, I would be honest in my response, but I should warn you, I will not tolerate any reproach of my niece. Lucinda possesses the most noble heart; she has not always known peace, but my precious girl is a better person for rising above her difficulties."

The last line was directed to Lucinda, who sat opposite her uncle. His words caused her to wish for things never possible. No one had ever spoken so eloquently of her. She mouthed a silent "Thank you."

The baron blustered, "If either you or your niece, Charleton, thought we meant to rebuke Mrs. Warren, you have erred. However, you must admit it appears odd to have met a niece in a Manchester inn."

The earl nodded his agreement and sipped his wine. "I sent for Lucinda after Waterloo, but those I hired convinced me my niece had perished in the battle's aftermath. I was not aware she was alive and in England until I entered the private dining room occupied by your youngest son and my niece."

Lucinda expected the baron to speak to the inappropriateness of her and the baronet sharing such intimacies. Instead, Blakehell asked, "And why did you not seek out your uncle, Mrs. Warren?"

Before she could respond, Charleton answered for her. Normally, his suppressing her freedom would have riled Lucinda, but today she welcomed the earl's interference. "I am ashamed to say my brother and I stubbornly permitted an old feud to fester, and over the years, Lucinda was rarely in my company. If you ask her, my niece will tell you, she thought I would not welcome an impoverished relative. I fear Lucinda's beliefs speak poorly of my character, not hers. My previous implacable nature is a trait I mean to change." Her uncle had shouldered the blame for her immaturity. He was kind and generous, and Lucinda felt the regret of ever holding unchristian thoughts regarding the man. It was wonderful to have someone willing to protect her.

The baroness gave her husband a warning glare. "None of this is our concern. I, for one, have always trusted Carter to make astute judgments. If my youngest son thought Mrs. Warren's cause one he would champion, then I am persuaded it is the right thing to do. No family history has a perfectly smooth course. It is how family members ride out the storm, which leads to merit. I shall hear no more talk of distress. Instead, I wish to celebrate the acknowledgement of Lawrence and Arabella's coming together and bringing forth an heir to the title."

"Here, here," Lord Hellsman declared from beside Lucinda.

"Oh, Arabella, I am so pleased," Lucinda said in earnest. "You deserve such happiness." However, Lucinda knew a bit of envy. She kept what she hoped was a welcoming countenance, but she had the vague fear the world knew her not worthy of an honest man's love.

Bella beamed with contentment. "Papa is beside himself with anticipation. It shall be his first grandchild. He speaks of how Mama must be smiling down from Heaven."

"Bella and I mean to call upon the Earl of Vaughn next week," Lord Hellsman filled in the awkward silence. "I will not have Bella making such a long journey in bad weather or in the latter part of her lying in."

The baroness overrode any response her husband intended to make. She evidently meant to keep "hostile" words from the conversation, and Lucinda admired the woman for her deft handling of what could have been an awkward moment. She was still not certain whether Lady Blakehell approved of her or not, but Lucinda appreciated how the woman took command of the evening. She prayed some day to possess as much aplomb within her own household.

After supper, the earl spoke of the need to return to his bed, and Lucinda begged to be excused to tend him. His step was a bit unsteady on the stairs, but his wit was in tact. "An interesting evening," he said tongue in cheek.

"Not one I would care to repeat," she confessed. "But you were truly brilliant, Sir."

He patted her hand upon his arm. "It is time I serve as your guardian. It is a role I have long waited to assume." They reached his chambers. "What say you retrieve Roderick's papers, and you and I will begin our perusal?"

"I thought you ill."

Always the perfect gentleman, her uncle smiled upon her. "I would be a fool to squander one moment with you. Give Mr. Priest time to assist me into something more comfortable, and then return with the box."

Lucinda had changed into a simple gown without her stays and hurried to her uncle's room. The earl lounged in a lush robe and sipped his cognac. "Welcome, my Dear," he called from the table, cleared for their purpose. "Mr. Priest means to attend to my wardrobe while we work. I hope you hold no objections."

Lucinda smiled easily. "Of course, not. Mr. Priest has proved himself most worthy. I appreciate his tender care upon your behalf." She crossed to sit opposite her uncle. "When had you thought to depart for Lancashire?" she asked casually.

"It would be unseemly to leave on the morrow. Very poor manners indeed, but I hold no doubt the following day would serve us well."

"I am anxious to see Charles Place for the first time," she said as she unlocked the box and set several bundled stacks upon the smooth surface.

"Actually, you were born in the east wing of the old section of the house," the earl said unceremoniously. He untied the ribbon on the bundle she placed before him.

Lucinda sounded unconvinced. "Truly? I thought Mama and Papa were in Devon." She thought of her father's entry regarding her birth. The colonel had not spoken of his location; she had just assumed they had been at Merritt Hall.

"You may take note of your baptism in the local church records," her uncle said as he read through the first document. "This is the deed to the Devon property. The land is paid free and clear. I should have my man of business peruse it; I have previously posted a letter to Mr. Shadwick regarding the rental arrangement."

As the earl read the next document, Lucinda quickly scanned the deed. She thought it important to be knowledgeable of her father's estate. While Charleton studied the multi-paged document, Lucinda released the ribbon on a smaller stack. She lifted the first one to examine it more closely. It was exactly like the many service reports she had seen among her father's correspondence over the years. It was a summary of the colonel's annual service and a pay accounting. This one was dated January 1804, some seven months before her birth. Her eyes skimmed the details a second time, and then the truth of the page struck her: Her father had spent the last six months of 1803 following Lord Arthur Wellesley at Assaye.

In September 1803, Scindia forces had lost to Lord Gerard Lake at Delhi and to Wellesley at Assaye. The colonel, a captain then, had departed for England before Lake defeated the Scindian force at Laswari, followed by Wellesley's 29 November success over Bhonsie forces at Aragon. "If Papa departed northern India in early September, he could not have been in England for my conception," she murmured awestruck. The earl had suddenly gone still, and Lucinda's chest squeezed tighter. In a panic, she sprang to the chair she had occupied earlier to retrieve the journal from where she had left it.

Flipping through the pages she had skipped previously, she intently read the entry her father had written of being summoned home by his father to speak his vows to his betrothed Sophia Carrington. Instead of the lengthy journey around the Cape, Roderick Rightnour had set out on a three-month land and sea journey, traveling every day for long tedious hours to do his father's bidding. "I am elated to claim Lady Sophia as my wife. I am the most fortunate of men," he had written. The colonel and her mother had spoken their vows on 30 December 1803.

"Uncle Gerhard," she said stiffly. "Was I an early baby?"

The earl blinked in surprise. He rose slowly to stand dejectedly. His voice was taut. "I should say you were," he spoke on a tearful rasp, "but…" He paused to excuse Mr. Priest from the room. With the valet's exit, the earl straightened his shoulders. "My father thwarted my plans to travel north with Sophia to Scotland." His stance was stiff, but his lips trembled. "The old earl had noted my growing interest in Viscount Ross's fourth daughter and had sent for Roderick's return. Charleton and Ross had previously come to an agreement for Roderick and Sophia's joining, but young hearts are not always obedient. When I learned of my father's plans, I risked everything to claim Sophia as my own."

Lucinda's heart stumbled to a halt. Her eyes sought his, while a vague hollowness filled her chest. "Roderick Rightnour is not my father." Her knees buckled, and she sank into the chair.

As if by magic, the earl knelt before her. A sad, painful vestige of a smile graced his lips. "It was never my wish not to claim you. In fact, Sophia and I thought we could change our parents' objections; however, my father held other plans. He demanded what he termed a 'temporary separation' and sent me to the West Indies to survey our properties there. It was my punishment for betraying Charleton's wishes. When I returned some ten months later, Sophia had accepted Roderick, and you had made your appearance. Roderick did not know, at least, not initially; you were always so petite, it was easy for others to believe your birth an early one. Then one day, Roderick caught Sophia crying while I embraced her. We fought, our blows destroying Mama's favorite antiques. The old earl said it was best if Roderick remove his family to Devon. With my encouragement, Father made arrangements for my brother to claim Merritt Hall. Roderick never returned to Charles Place."

"Papa kept the secret," she whispered. She swallowed hard the pang of reality, which clutched at her heart.

"Yes, and Roderick loved you unconditionally. I admire how my brother separated his hatred for me from his love for my daughter. In many ways, he was a much better man than I. He made the best of a terrible situation, and from what I know of their marriage, your mother and Roderick were fiercely devoted to each other and to you. Sophia came to love her husband as much as he loved her. She told me so in one of her letters."

Lucinda wrung her hands. "Mama wrote of my accomplishments..." Realization flooded her senses. She looked upon the earl's countenance–so much like her own. Why had she not seen the similarity previously?

"Sophia thought I possessed a right to know of your life. Even over Roderick's objections..."

Lucinda could make little sense of anything she had discovered. "I do not wish to be your daughter," she said bitterly. "I cannot betray Papa's memory."

The earl reached for her hand, and she attempted not to flinch at his touch. "I would never rob Roderick of his legacy." Lucinda brushed away the tears streaming down her cheeks. "You can never be my daughter without my destroying every fiber of your reputation. Forever, you are Roderick's child and my niece." He swallowed hard. "Please say you can tolerate Gerhard Rightnour as your uncle. I do not believe I have the strength to release you again. This past week has been the greatest days of my existence."

Lucinda panicked. "I...I do not know. It is all so...so much more...than I can say." She glanced around the room, blindly searching for an exit. "I must go." She stood quickly. "I require time to think on what is best." She stumbled toward the door, never looking back. "Please...please pardon me."

Chapter Seventeen

The nightmare had returned, and Carter woke in a cold sweat. Even after his body jerked him from his sleep, terror still held him in its grip, and Carter worked hard to steady his breathing. He gulped for air and swallowed the bile burning his throat. He did not turn his head or flick a muscle; He had learned over time if he did not move too quickly, the details of the dream would reveal themselves.

He stared hard at the dark drape of the inn's four-poster, and the images danced before his eyes. He rode the twisting trail between the two military outposts, Wellington's orders securely tucked away in his jacket, only to stumble upon a scene of brutality. The English battalion had encountered an under-sized French regiment. "What the...?" he growled as he looked down upon the scene. His countrymen, greatly outnumbered, were trapped with the hill upon which he sat at their backs. They would all know Death if he did not act.

Without considering the consequences, Carter had kicked his horse's flanks to join the skirmish. He had departed Wellington's army some fifteen months prior, but he was still fiercely loyal to the man. Shouting orders, he rode between the lines of Englishmen who had turned tail to run. He did not think he would make a difference, but somehow Darek Merriweather had heard Carter's frantic pleas, and the man who now served as Carter's valet, caught one man after another and turned each around to fight again. Within minutes, the retreat had turned to an assault. Merriweather rushed forward and back, rallying his fellow soldiers to fight on.

Meanwhile, Carter had discovered Colonel Rightnour's bloody body. Of course, at the time, he had not known it was Rightnour. In fact, he had never heard of the long-time military man before that eventful day. All he had known was the English battalion's commander had made an elementary error, leaving his men too exposed. The colonel had lost his leg, and a gaping hole spoke of the man's brutal death.

The boy covered the colonel with his own body. The officer's horse rested along side its master. The animal, too, had met a horrid death. "Come with me," Carter had ordered while the boy had clasped tightly to the man's body.

"My father?" the youth had questioned.

Carter had looked upon the destruction. Bodies polluted the ground with seeping blood and guts. The French advanced, and there was no time for grief. "Would expect you to live," he had said defiantly.

He had caught the lad by the arm and had dragged him to safer ground. "I will come for you when this is over," he had assured before returning to shore up the English lines in anticipation of the next French assault. Yet, the devastation found in the boy's eyes had never left him. At any given moment, Carter could summon the image as if the lad stood before him.

The acrid smell of blood and gunpowder and the deafening sound of exploding ammunition flooded his senses, while a shiver of fear racked his spine. He had never felt so inept, but he had fought beside Merriweather and the other outstanding soldiers on that Belgium battlefield.

He had witnessed charge after charge by the French, but his fellow Englishmen had fought honorably. As the French withdrew, Carter had permitted himself the liberty to look to the place where he had deposited the boy. A bit of the lad's shirt had shone from behind the tree. Earlier, he had thought neither of them would survive the day, but hope had flared, and he had made his way along the line to retrieve the lad.

With his eyes closed to recover the dream, Carter could visualize his approach. Crouched over. Touching a soldier's shoulder. Redirecting the man's line of fire. Instructing Merriweather, whose name he had not yet learned, to send men to block the French stragglers from escaping. Every detail rang clear. The smells. The sounds. The air thick with smoke and humidity and Death. The cries of men meeting their Maker. The mud. The soldiers in lines. Bayonets at a ready. The squares formed tight to withstand the French assault. None of it escaped him.

He could plainly see the look of surprise upon his countenance when he caught sight of the lone French cavalryman barreling down upon the boy. Could see his panicked response as he raced to the spot where the lad clung to the tree, never once suspecting he was in danger. Could hear the snap of the Frenchman's whip as it came down heavily on the youth's back. Could hear the lad's scream, fiercely shrill. Could read the curse upon his own lips as he charged up the slope to reach the boy's side. Could feel the desperate need to protect the innocent youth, who had witnessed the worst of society's manipulations.

His body jerked hard as the bullet struck his thigh, effectively cutting him down–keeping him from reaching the lad. The gaping hole in his leg. As he lay wreathing upon his side, Merriweather had appeared over him, a rifle aimed at the advancing Frenchman. Without notice, Carter's newfound comrade fired, striking the Frenchie in the throat.

Carter had never remembered the details so clearly. Even now, he could feel the burning pain, and the sensation of blood oozing from the wound was so real, he unconsciously reached for the deep scar, which marred his skin, only to find his leg dry. "Bloody hell!" he hissed into the room's silence. His pulse raced as he made himself turn upon his side. With a heavy sigh, he squeezed his eyes closed, this time to drive the images away. His body exhausted from the experience.

As he inhaled and exhaled measured breaths, he heard Merriweather's distant voice ordering men to make a litter for him. Heard his future valet offering words of encouragement as he pressed an already bloody handkerchief to Carter's wound. "You were a God send," Merriweather's voice trembled with the effort to staunch the blood flow. "I would follow you to the end's of the earth. I mean to see you well, Sir. Tell me your name."

Carter, who had thought he would die of his wound, wanted his mother to know how he met his end. It would have killed her for him to disappear without her knowing of his being with Wellington. He caught Merriweather's arm before saying clearly. "Lowery. Carter Lowery. My parents are the Baron and Baroness Blakehell in Derbyshire." The effort had cost him dearly, but he added, "Promise me you will tell my mother she was in my final prayers."

"I mean to see you well, Sir," Merriweather had insisted.

Yet, Carter had persisted, "Promise me."

Merriweather had met his desperate gaze. "I will stay with you to Brussels. If the worst proves true, the baroness will know of your heroism."

And Merriweather had kept his promise, had stayed by Carter's side, often abusing officers who did not respond quickly enough to Carter's need for care. Kerrington later reported having arrived at the hospital to claim Carter's wounded body to find Merriweather standing guard over him. "I had to pull several strings," Kerrington had shared later, "to keep Merriweather from knowing a court martial for his insolence." The man who had saved Carter's life that chaotic day had sung Carter's praises to Wellington himself, and Carter had been declared a hero by King George, but Carter knew it was Merriweather's determination, which had saved his fellow soldiers, as well as Carter's life.

Fully awake, he reluctantly rolled from the bed and stood slowly. He rotated his shoulders to release the tension. The dream clung to the back of his mind, but he made his way to the tray, which held a decanter of brandy. Pouring himself several fingers of the liquid, he tossed it back before sitting heavily in a nearby chair. Burying his head in his hands, Carter allowed the last remnants of the dream to drift away into the room's darkness.

"At least, I no longer need fear the dream's end," he said aloud. With a deep sigh, he looked about the room he had occupied for the last week. Dawn's fingers peeked through the closed drapes. "Time to start another day."

Again, he stood: This time to open the drapes to welcome the light. He hoped to hear from Pennington soon. Carter had sent the Realm's leader the secret message, two days prior, regarding Carter's suspicions of Dylan Monroe. "It will be difficult to put Monroe off for much longer without raising suspicion," he acknowledged. When Monroe returned from London, Carter meant to send his assistant to The Rising Son Inn to question Blackston and several locals. Carter did not expect to learn anything new on the smuggling ring, but the ruse would keep Monroe from under foot while the Realm discovered a means to deal best with his likely betrayal.

Turning back to the room, he poured water into a basin so he might wash away the sleep from his eyes. He would like to have Merriweather with him now: He could use the former infantryman's good advice. "I should send to London for Merriweather to join me," he remarked as he lathered the soap ball against a cloth. But the thought of London brought forth the memory of meeting Mrs. Warren there. He desperately missed the woman—missed the spark in her eyes and even the disapproving scowl, which often graced her lips when she spoke to him.

Carter despised being so susceptible to her. "Nothing to be done but to live with the lady's admonishments," he acknowledged with regret. He finished his wash and used a small towel to dry his chest and arms and legs, taking time to examine the scar; yet, the motion brought forth a final memory: It was the boy's countenance, tears streaming down the youth's cheek. Eyes filled with anguish and remorse: The eyes that had haunted him for more than three years. "My father?" he heard the now familiar timbre as clear as if the lad whispered in Carter's ear.

His heart stuttered with the realization. "I did not know the officer was Colonel Rightnour," he confessed as his hands began to shake. "Not until at the hospital when Merriweather spoke of his former commander." Carter's breath hitched. "The boy said, 'My father.'" He exhaled sharply. "But Rightnour had no son, only a daughter." He shuddered with the realization. "No wonder the lady's eyes have haunted me from our first acquaintance." His head and emotions awhirl, Carter dropped the towel across the back of a chair. *Had Lucinda Warren recognized him as the man from the battlefield? If so, why had the woman not acknowledged their former connection? Had Mrs. Warren purposely hidden her role in her father's demise? And what did all her secrets have to do with the recent attempts on his life? Or even those on her life?*

"Your Lordship!" Arabella Lowery looked up in surprise when she observed the Earl of Charleton's pale features. She rushed to his side. "Please, my Lord. Permit me to see you to a chair. Should I send for the apothecary? You appear quite distraught."

He sat heavily. "You must assist me, Lady Hellsman," he said passionately. "I cannot make my niece see reason."

Arabella poured the earl a glass of wine. "Drink this," she encouraged. "And then explain how I might serve you."

The earl's hand trembled, but he quickly composed his expression. "It is with a heavy heart I must involve you in my family's shame, but I cannot permit my youthful foolishness to ruin Lucinda's life." He paused to sip from the wine. "My precious girl deserves better than she has received from me," he said with deep remorse.

Bella suspected Lucinda's secrets were ones not easily dispatched. She caught the earl's large hand in her two smaller ones. "I would be Mrs. Warren's friend."

Charleton nodded shakily "I have observed you with Lucinda. My girl respects you and will listen to your advice. I must ask you to speak in my behalf."

Arabella recognized the desperation in the earl's voice, and she steeled her spine for what he meant to tell her. "It would be best, Sir, if you simply spoke your fear."

Defeat crossed the man's countenance, but Charleton accepted what he must do. "Last evening, after we retired, Lucinda and I explored her father's private papers. While I searched the records of the Devon estate, Lucinda chose to read through Roderick's military records. I will spare you all the sorted details, but Lucinda has discovered the true reason for my and Roderick's feud. She left my quarters in quite a fever." He wiped his forehead with his hand-kerchief. "I should have insisted Lucinda remain with me, but I could not look upon her pain without doubting my strength. Again, I took the coward's trail, but this morning, Lucinda will not accept my apology. She refuses to unlock her door—to permit me admittance. How may I explain away her fears, if Lucinda will not speak to me?"

Arabella remained uncertain as to whether she should interfere in a per-sonal matter, but she knew she must offer her friend a shoulder upon which to cry. "You wish me to convince Mrs. Warren to accept your apology?"

The earl shook his head in denial. "I would not ask you to choose sides in the conflict, but if you could persuade Lucinda to permit me the opportunity to speak to her in private, I would be forever in your debt."

Bella breathed more easily. She would not deny the earl his request, but nei-ther could she, with a clear conscience, place Mrs. Warren in an uncomfortable situation. "If you are well enough for my leaving, I would seek Mrs. Warren's approval."

Charleton caught her hand, bringing the back of it to his lips. "You are an angel. I can never express my full gratitude."

Bella tapped lightly on Lucinda's chamber door. She had no idea what she would say to her friend. "Lucinda," she said reassuringly. "It is I, Arabella. Please permit me to speak to you." Bella pressed her ear to the door to listen for Lucinda's approach, but she could detect no movement within. "Lucinda?" she said louder and rapped more forcibly. "Lucinda? Mrs. Warren? I insist you open the door at once!"

Arabella did not like the urgency she heard in her voice. Again, she listened closely, but heard no response. She caught a passing maid. "Madge, please ask Lord Hellsman to join me here and tell Mrs. Grayson to bring her keys. Mrs. Warren may be ill."

"Yes, Ma'am." The girl rushed off to do Bella's biding.

"Mrs. Warren?" Bella jiggled the door's handle. "Lucinda!" she called as her fists tapped out a heavy tattoo against the wood paneling.

Law finally appeared beside her. "What is amiss, Bella?" He caught her up in a loose embrace.

Tears streamed down her cheeks. "Mrs. Warren and the earl…" she wailed. "Something terrible happened between them. The earl believes Mrs. Warren is distraught, and he asked me to speak in his behalf." She looked frantically to the still closed door. "I have pleaded for admittance, but Lucinda does not respond. Oh, Law!" she gasped. "I hear no one moving about within. Could Mrs. Warren have done something foolish?"

Her husband's countenance darkened. "I will not have you upset. I will handle whatever crisis has arisen. I insist you to go below," he said gently.

"I cannot," she pleaded. "Please do not ask it of me."

Law cupped her cheek with his large palm. "Bella…" he whispered. "You must consider the child. I know you mean well, but whatever has occurred here… I must argue that you not risk your health in your rush to serve your new friend."

Reluctantly, Bella nodded her agreement. In the few short months of their acquaintance, Lawrence Lowery had brought her such great happiness. "May I wait in the hall?"

He smiled that special smile, the one he only used when he looked upon her. "You know I can deny you nothing."

Mrs. Grayson interrupted their tender moment, and reality jarred Bella to her senses. "You sent for me, Lady Hellsman?" As if she had run up the narrow servant stairs, the woman clutched her side.

Her husband set Bella from him. "Please open Mrs. Warren's door," Law demanded. "The lady does not respond."

"Yes, Sir." The housekeeper removed a ribboned ring attached about her waist. Upon it were several dozen keys to the various locked pantries and doors for which the lady held responsibility. She searched the ring for the correct key, finally settling on a well-worn one. "Do you wish me to enter first, Sir?" Bella thought it amusing Lawrence had not considered the fact Mrs. Warren could be unclothed.

Bella knew the second her husband came to the same conclusion. "If you would, Mrs. Grayson." He stepped between Bella and the unopened door to block Bella's view, and despite it being unnecessary, she appreciated his over-protective nature.

Although she could see nothing but her husband's broad shoulders, Bella could hear the door open, could hear the housekeeper's tentative steps, and then the confused silence. Law gently shoved her further from the opening. "Promise me, Bella, you will not move until I know it is safe for you to enter Mrs. Warren's quarters."

Yet, before Bella could utter her promise, Mrs. Grayson announced, "Mrs. Warren is not within, Lord Hellsman."

Bella darted around Law's stance to come to a stumbling halt. What Mrs. Grayson said was true: The room was deadly quiet in its emptiness. "Where could Lucinda have gone?" she asked in disbelief.

Law presented a reproving glare, but he spoke the obvious. "The balcony door is open."

Bella flinched. "You think Mrs. Warren…?"

Her husband pointed a finger of obedience at Bella, very much as he often did with his hounds, and she would have laughed at his attempt at mastery if the situation were no so dire. "I will look, and you will wait here," he said slowly and distinctly.

"You have my word, Lawrence," Bella said placatingly. "But be quick about it." She shooed him toward the open door.

With anticipation, Bella watched Law bend over the balustrade to examine the ground below. Her husband stretched lower, reaching for something apparently from sight, and Bella knew images of her friend's broken body. When Lawrence turned around, he held up a thick ball of bleached material.

"Our Mrs. Warren has used the bedding to make a rope," he proclaimed as he stepped into the room. Bella's vivid imagination brought forward an image of a hangman's noose. "The lady has used the baroness's favorite linens to design an escape."

Bella shook her head in denial. "Escape from what? If Mrs. Warren wished to leave, she is of age. Even Lord Charleton could not prevent her withdrawal. None of this makes sense.

Law handed the rags to Mrs. Grayson. "Where is the earl?"

Bella explained, "Lord Charleton awaits below. He asked I convince Mrs. Warren to permit him an explanation. They have experienced some sort of rout."

Law caught Bella's arm. "You and I will speak to His Lordship. Mrs. Grayson, I want you to first examine this chamber and to report anything unusual you discover. Afterwards, I want a thorough search of the manor and the immediate grounds. I will send Griffin to assist you, and please keep this in secret."

"Of course, Lord Hellsman."

With that, he escorted Bella from the room. Upon the stairs, he brought her to a halt. "Whatever is amiss, you must permit the earl to see to his niece's safety," he insisted.

Bella said defiantly, "Carter would expect us to serve the lady."

Her husband scowled, "My one and only concern remains your health. I will do all possible to assist Charleton, but I will not permit you to place yourself in the way of danger."

Bella did not agree, but she permitted her husband his masculinity. They found Lord Charleton pacing the open area between the chairs and the window seat. He turned in anticipation, but his countenance fell when his niece did not appear. "Lucinda remains angry with me," he said dejectedly. "I prayed for her forgiveness."

Law seated Bella before responding, "Mrs. Warren's room was empty; it appears she has climbed down a makeshift rope, although why your niece would go to such lengths makes little sense."

The earl swayed in place. "What of the boy?" he asked in concern. "Lucinda would not leave Simon behind. She has claimed no affection for the child, but my niece would never abandon the boy. It is not in her providence to deny her responsibilities."

Bella nodded her agreement. "I shall visit the nursery, but surely if Simon were not above stairs, the maid in charge of the boy would inform us."

Law suggested, "Do not permit Simon to know of Mrs. Warren's absence. While you are above, see if Mrs. Grayson has learned anything of import."

The rough jostling shook her awake, but Lucinda still possessed no idea of her whereabouts. She attempted to move—to stretch her legs and arms—but the closed quarters in which she found herself would not permit her any freedom of movement. Another jolt sent her stomach rolling, and Lucinda pressed her mouth against her shoulder to stay the bile rising to her throat.

She attempted to make sense of where she was and how she had come to be in the enclosure. Concentrating on the last evening's events, her crazy world came crashing in. The earl had disclosed the truth behind her birth, and Lucinda had felt the betrayal foisted upon her by her mother, the colonel, and the earl. She had blindly made her way to her chambers, but much of what occurred after she entered the room eluded her.

A noise had alerted her she was not alone, and Lucinda had turned to sound an alarm, but an arm had caught her about the neck, while a large, meaty hand had covered her mouth. With the assumption her assailant meant to kill her, she had fought her attacker. Had she not received a note announcing her the target of a madman's plan? Yet, despite her best efforts, she was no match for the man who easily outmaneuvered her. He tightened his grip about her neck, and although she had clawed at the exposed skin of his arm, her strength quickly faded. Lucinda's ability to breathe had reached the point of terror when she collapsed against the man who would declare today her last on this earth.

Even now, the skin upon her neck burned from the intensity of her struggle. She wondered if anyone at Blake's Run was aware of her absence. Was anyone searching for her? The earl? Lady Hellsman? Sir Carter? Would any of them give a care if she disappeared from their lives? Lucinda held no doubt of her own insignificance, but the illusive dream of normalcy had seemed so real she had begun to believe Captain Warren had erred in his estimation of her. She had lived the past decade as the backdrop for the games her husband had executed. All about her, those who claimed to cherish her had robbed her of a purpose. She had drifted through life, accepting what came as being her only option.

The space in which she rested suddenly stopped its rocking motion. When a slit of light invaded the space, Lucinda shielded her eyes by turning her head to the left. "Awake are we?" an unfamiliar voice boomed into the tight space. Alert to what would follow, Lucinda kept her face hidden and waited to meet the stranger's next assault. "Remain quiet," he hissed. "We will be on our way again soon."

Lucinda searched for a memory that might match the man's identity, but nothing about his speech or voice held familiarity. Stretching her eyes wider, willing them to look upon her abductor's countenance framed by the light, she asked, "Do I know you?"

The man leaned closer. She was in some sort of locked box, and her assailant had used a latch, which permitted a hinged opening. "No, Mrs. Warren; you know me not. Yet, I know of you. I knew your late husband, and I know your lover."

"I have no lover," she protested. However, her captor dismissed her objections by slamming the latch closed. Within seconds, Lucinda felt the box shift, as if she was in a hack, and the rocking motion resumed. "What lover?" she screamed, but no response was forthcoming. *So her husband's ghost had followed her to Derbyshire.* A quavering ache filled Lucinda's chest. The thought of how alone she was tore at her heart; as usual, she would be expected to face her perils without the assistance of others.

Chapter Eighteen

Lawrence Lowery closed the drawing room's door behind his wife. "Now, Your Lordship, I think it time you explain what has caused this upheaval in my father's household." He directed the older man's steps to the grouping of chairs.

The earl sat heavily. "I cannot express my regret, Lord Hellsman."

Law's irritation rose quickly. "I want no more words of remorse, Lord Charleton. I am willing to place my resources at your service as long as your family's crisis does not create difficulties for Lady Hellsman. My wife and our future family are my priority." He schooled his expression. "Please speak of what has happened to send your niece out into the night."

Charleton nodded curtly. "Very well, Hellsman. As I explained to your lady, Lucinda and I examined Roderick's personal papers last evening. Everything appeared to be going well; my niece has shown more trust of late, and I held great hopes we would soon close the chasm we inherited. Unfortunately, Lucinda read something in her father's military records, which upset her. I made my attempts at an explanation, but being unaware of how my brother Roderick and I came to feud so violently shocked her so much, Lucinda stormed away in tears."

Lawrence listened carefully to what His Lordship did not say. "And you think this alarming news drove Mrs. Warren from her chambers?"

The earl scowled in disapproval. "I would not think it of Lucinda; I suspected to face a barrage of contemptuous remarks today, all well deserved I might add, but I am more than surprised my niece has chosen retreat. Roderick would never have approved, and my niece has always struggled to please him."

"I thought you unaware of Mrs. Warren's upbringing," Law said suspiciously.

Profound sadness crossed the earl's countenance. "Lucinda's mother kept me informed of my niece in lengthy, newsy letters. It is true I do not know her well, but what I do know of Lucinda does not speak of cowardice."

Law added, "If not for Mrs. Warren's quick thinking my brother would have a met a dreadful end. In reality, I can easily imagine the lady rushing into the struggle, not the reverse."

The earl nodded eagerly. "I fear Lucinda's disappearance only complicates the situation."

"True," Law reasoned. "But surely she is somewhere about the estate. I would think Mrs. Warren has taken refuge in one of the follies rather than to risk being alone in the dark." He doubted a brisk walk in the night's middle was the lady's true destination, but if Mrs. Warren had departed on foot, they would quickly locate her. *Unless, she sought out the solitude of Dark Peak or the bottom of one of the estate's tarns*, he thought. Carter would be livid if Law had permitted the woman to know danger.

Anxiousness returned to Charleton's countenance. "What is being done to locate my niece?"

"I have asked two of my most trusted servants to search all the rooms. First, we must ascertain whether Mrs. Warren is on the immediate grounds. If that search proves fruitless, I will call forth the hounds."

Bella reentered on a rush. "I have discovered a note," she said out of breath. She thrust the paper in Law's direction, but he was more concerned with the paleness of Bella's lips, all color drained from her cheeks. He caught her about the waist and set her firmly in a nearby chair before accepting the note she held firmly in her grasp.

The earl rose slowly, almost as if he expected the worst. "What does the message say, Lord Hellsman?"

Law unfolded the single sheet to read aloud: "Tell the baronet if he wishes the lady's return, he will learn to look elsewhere. If he comes closer, the lady will die."

Charleton's pallor spoke volumes. "In what type…of investigation…has Sir Carter involved my niece? I thought their only connection was the location of Simon's family," he accused.

Law said defensively, "It was Mrs. Warren who received the threat when they were in Suffolk. My brother nearly died saving your niece!"

220

Bella snapped, "It does not matter who is to blame. You must send for Carter right this minute. There is no time to lose! Only the baronet can resolve this chaos."

Lawrence reached for the bell pull. "You write the message, Bella, and I will make arrangements for a rider."

"Two riders," Bella insisted. "Lord Worthing is in Derby. He can be at Blake's Run within hours."

Law nodded his agreement. "Perhaps we should send for Viscount Lexford and the Marquis of Godown also. The last I knew, Carter was in Suffolk, but that was a week prior. We require someone with knowledge of Carter's investigations."

"Meanwhile," Charleton asserted, "If you hold no objections, I would ask several of your men to organize a search."

Law cautioned, "Do not in your frenzy to locate your niece run the risk of ruining her reputation."

"Tell Mr. Sack Mrs. Warren has gone for a walk and you fear she has lost her way in unfamiliar country," Bella reasoned. Law smiled at her: His wife was a woman made for crisis. "Now, hurry," she encouraged.

Aristotle Pennington's appearance at the Suffolk inn did not surprise Carter so much as it amused him. "I thought it best if we speak in person," the Realm leader assured. "I could not assume the chance we had more than one possible spy working within our ranks."

Carter poured them both a drink. "It was Swenton who questioned Monroe's motives," he confessed. "I fear I did not recognize what the baron easily observed." Uncomfortably, he added, "I have failed you again." He shivered with trepidation.

The Realm's leader's eyes flashed in annoyance. "Dear God, Lowery!" Pennington said with a huff. "You will never be perfect. The best any of us can do is surround ourselves with the best people we know. You have done that with Swenton."

Carter corrected, "You chose the baron long before I was part of the Realm."

Pennington shook his head in disapproval. He regarded Carter narrowly. "But it was your leadership which presented John Swenton with new possibilities. Until you joined the unit, I often wondered if the baron would sabotage our best-laid plans simply because he had previously known nothing but misery. Swenton has never had a family or someone he admires. The baron sees that in you; you have provided a sail for his sinking ship." He slugged down the drink. "Enough of your questioning your ability to lead this organization. Concentrate on what you do best, and all else will fall where it may. You cannot control every situation. Unfortunately, upon occasion, innocent people suffer. It is a fact against which you must wage the battle, but it is also a fact you must accept when even your best efforts are not enough. Now, retrieve the letter Mrs. Warren received and permit me to compare the handwriting to that of Monroe's reports."

Carter did as he was told and within a few minutes they poured over the samples Pennington had brought with him. It was in such moments Carter cherished his relationship with Aristotle Pennington. If he were younger, he might have wished his own father had been cut from the same cloth as the Realm's stoic leader, but Carter had not had Pennington's acquaintance until the man quite literally snatched Carter from the battlefield.

"What is your business with a lieutenant in King George's army?" Carter had defiantly thrust off the hold James Kerrington had had upon his arms.

"Easy, Boy," Kerrington had hissed. "No one means you harm."

Carter jerked the line of his coat straight. "I am no one's *boy*!"

Pennington had immediately diffused the situation by walking away. "Perhaps you are correct," he had patiently remarked. "You are not a *boy*, but you have yet learned the ways of a man. *Boys* solve disharmony with violence; *men* with reasoning."

At the time, Carter had possessed no choice but to follow the man. Kerrington and Marcus Wellston had kidnapped him from where Carter had overseen the watch and had transported him to a deserted area behind enemy lines. If he did not quickly ascertain what the crazy Englishman meant, he might lose his life, and so he had trailed after the man the others had called "Shepherd."

"What if I wish to be a *man*?" Carter had challenged.

Pennington had paused to wait for Carter's approach. "Then you will dine with us this evening and decide if you wish to be an integral part of something larger than Wellington's army." Carter had known confusion, but something in Pennington's countenance had spoken of confidence–had made Carter abandon his doubts–had created a desire to know Aristotle Pennington's approval.

"Note how the author of Mrs. Warren's letter has attempted to forge your script, but there are characteristics of his hand which betray his efforts." Carter examined the points to which Pennington pointed. "Your tutor, Mr. Brady, taught you well regarding the necessity of a neat hand." It no longer surprised Carter to hear the Realm's leader speak casually of personal facts regarding his agents. He had learned since joining Pennington at the Home Office the man had kept meticulous files on those he had chosen as Realm members. "You never leave a smear from too much ink on the pen or a dull point."

Carter finally recognized what Pennington did. "It is as if our unknown author paused to construct his thoughts." There were thicker letters where the ink pooled. "I never allow my *a*'s to lie so flat along the line," he remarked.

"Nor your *c*'s and *d*'s." Pennington unfolded one of Monroe's most recent reports. "You can easily note your assistant's lazy script."

Carter felt ill; he hated to believe they had erred in choosing Dylan Monroe. He could not say he held a true affinity for the man, especially after Monroe's attentions to Mrs. Warren, but Carter understood the expense of their specialized training. "Why?" he asked. "Why send Mrs. Warren on a dangerous mission?"

Pennington sat the papers aside. "We must approach this situation carefully. If we play our cards too quickly, we might not discover the depth of Monroe's betrayal. Does the man work alone? Does he have connections to foreign agents operating in England?"

Carter asked immediately, "Such as Jamot?"

Pennington's grave dissatisfaction crossed his countenance. "My guess is any connection on Jamot's part is purely coincidental. Yet, my suspicions say the Baloch plays a role in this madness."

Carter scrubbed his face with his dry hands. "Where do we begin?"

"Send for Swenton. I want the baron involved. As you have previously noted, John Swenton possesses the knack for quickly analyzing the fine nuances which define an indignity."

When Carter returned forty minutes later, Pennington had retreated to his room. "I thought it best if others did not know of my presence in Suffolk," he admitted as he drew chairs about a small table. "Before coming here, I instructed Monroe to return to his duties."

Swenton grumbled, "I am grateful for the reprise. Staring upon an empty farmhouse for hours takes its toll on my patience."

Carter and Pennington exchanged a knowing glance. It had been over a year since the baron had last seen Lady Yardley's twin sister, Satiné, and Swenton grew more withdrawn each day. Only Carter and Pennington recognized the baron's unease. The others knew Swenton held a "lost love," but none suspected the baron had developed an affection for the scandal-ridden Satiné Aldridge. Their acquaintance had been of short duration, but Pennington had made Carter aware of Swenton's frequent secret correspondence with the woman. It was the reason Carter had earlier suggested a companion for Swenton's "ill friend."

"I thought it might do me well to make a list of what we know and what we have yet to discover," Pennington suggested. "Would you mind serving as scribe, John?"

Swenton shrugged from his jacket and rolled up his sleeves. "Feed me, and give me drink, and I will obediently be your clerk." His friend's shoulders relaxed with the familiarity of the routine. He reached for the paper Pennington had placed upon the table. "I see you began without us," he said with a taunt.

"Writing assists me in organizing my thoughts." Pennington poured them each a drink. "I will not apologize for knowing my strengths and weaknesses."

Carter read over Swenton's shoulder. In addition to the questions Pennington had previously voiced, the Realm's leader had added: Has Monroe forged other documents or letters in SC's name? Is DM involved in the smuggling ring? Who are DM's contacts in the Realm? In the Home Office? Are the attacks on Mrs. Warren related to those on SC? Does Simon Warren's sudden appearance play into the attacks?

Swenton released a slow whistle. "Appears we have a multitude of questions to answer."

Pennington moved his chair closer. "No time as productive as the present. I wish to know every detail, no matter how insignificant."

Some five hours later, no conclusions had been reached, and Carter had, in truth, lost interest in the multiple conversations. Having taken a short respite to dine, they lounged lazily afterwards. Swenton had propped his feet upon Carter's abandoned chair, while Pennington had partaken of an imported cheroot. Unable to tolerate the idea of how many facts he had ignored, Carter had lain across Pennington's bed. His legs dangled over the edge, and he covered his eyes with his forearm. All the talk of Lucinda Warren had brought images he had spent a week suppressing, and Carter wanted nothing more than to sleep long enough to finish his dream of making love to the woman. Pennington had not asked of the lady's connection to the events at Waterloo, and Carter had made a private promise not to implicate her further.

As he accepted his obsession with the woman, an exquisite image of Lucinda in passion filled his mind, and Carter felt the responsive tug in his groin. He wondered if Swenton entertained such moments in response to a memory of Miss Aldridge. It was certainly not a topic men readily discussed. The bizarre thought brought a smile of amusement to his lips. The world assumed men held all the answers when, in reality, there was no manual on how to attach a woman's affections. The female population was a fickled sect. "Fickled enough to accept Dylan Monroe's attentions over yours," he grumbled silently. Recognition of the man's influence over the woman Carter desired brought a curse to his lips. "Monroe!"

Pennington turned from the window. "What of Monroe?"

Carter pushed to a seated position to stall for he had not meant to bring his jealousy to the conversation. "I was…I was wondering how Monroe came to be so…so highly placed. It is not like you, Sir, to permit a man with ulterior motives so close to our operations." Immediately, Carter wondered if he had said too much.

Although Pennington scowled, he did not appear offended. "Occasionally those who practice nefarious purposes manage to invade our inner structure. However, Monroe came to us via a recommendation from the Duke of Portland, and I had Monroe thoroughly investigated, and there were no questionable connections."

Swenton asked, "Who is his family?"

Pennington ticked off the names of several minor aristocrats. "The Goodwins, the Woodvines, and the Dymonds."

Swenton observed, "Those families only go back two or three generations."

Pennington's frown liens deepened. "Although we prefer those with strong ties to England's history, deep ancestral lines are not a prerequisite for service."

Carter asked, "Which Dymonds? Those in Staffordshire or Cornwall?"

Pennington responded, "Those in Cornwall, but I would suppose the Staffordshire branch on the same family tree."

It was Carter's turn to frown. "Cornwall is close to Devon, from where both the Warrens and Roderick Rightnour hail," he said slowly as if tasting the words. "And the current head of the Dymond family in Staffordshire is Franklyn Dymond, the Earl of Whitrow, Hugh Dymond's father."

An icy eyebrow rose, and Swenton asked, "Hugh Dymond, as in Viscount Ransing?"

Carter watched as Pennington made the connection. "It cannot be. I specifically turned away Ransing's overtures to join us."

"When did Hugh Dymond seek admittance to the Home Office?" A cold shiver ran down Carter's spine. He prayed he had not underestimated Law's former enemy. If so, Carter's family was in danger.

"Then we are agreed?" Pennington asked. They had spent several frantic hours planning what action to take. "I will ask Monroe to escort me to London. Once there, I will observe him more closely and set about finding our answers regarding the depth of the man's deception. Swenton will travel to Oxford and make contact with Ward Dartmour. They will oversee the investigation into Cyrus Woodstone's most recent dealings, and you will explore Viscount Ransing's involvement in this twisted web."

It had taken all of Carter's well-honed patience to sit through the procedural meeting. His emotions screamed for his immediate withdrawal to Derbyshire to ensure his family's safety. "Agreed," he said through tight lips.

A light tap on the door interrupted Carter's dark thoughts. Swenton opened the door to a sour-faced Symington Henderson. "I beg your pardon, Sirs," he said in obvious nervousness. "I bring poor tidings. Mr. Monroe is no where to be found."

Before Pennington could respond, Carter had taken up his jacket and his hat. "You three may make the best of this madness; I am to Blake's Run." He took several tentative steps, uncertain how his actions would translate on paper. Would the Selection Committee think his choice the sign of a weak leader?

From beside him, Swenton whispered, "Your duty is to home first."

With a curt nod, Carter raced from the inn to the stables; within minutes he pressed Prime to a gallop.

Despite the danger on the road, he had ridden throughout the night, attempting to stretch Prime's stamina to its limit, but with dawn's appearance, Carter had quickly come to the conclusion he could not knowingly cripple his favorite stallion; so he had reluctantly turned Prime toward a place, which would welcome him, at any hour: the circle before Linton Park. Carter slid to the ground as Lord Worthing's grooms rushed forward. "Thank you, Prime," he whispered as he stroked the lather from the animal's neck.

"Sir Carter." The head groomsman acknowledged.

"I apologize for the interruption of your duties," he said as he walked briskly toward the main entrance. The man trailed behind him. "I will require a fresh horse immediately. Once Prime recovers, someone must take the animal to Blake's Run." He pressed a coin into the man's hand. "I will speak to Lord Worthing briefly and then be on my way."

The groom shook his head in the negative. "Lord Worthing departed late yesterday, Sir."

Carter frowned. He had not time for a social call, but he could not simply order the Earl of Linworth's staff about without some sort of explanation. Fortunately, the main door swung wide, and Eleanor Kerrington, Lady Worthing, motioned him into the house. "Other than the servants, few are awake at this hour." As if she had been expecting him, she slid her arm through his. "Come join me in the morning room."

He had no time for a leisurely breakfast. "You must forgive me, Lady Worthing, but time cannot be spared. I would not have called at Linton Park if I had not required a fresh horse."

The viscountess ignored his protest, and so Carter had walked with her to where breakfast awaited. It was difficult for a gentleman to refuse a lady, even when his mind screamed for his abrupt withdrawal. "Ah, I am an indulgent mother, Sir Carter. My darling Amelia is producing her first teeth, and so I mean to introduce her to something more substantial than gruel." She gestured to where Worthing's daughter rested in a small cradle.

Despite the adorable countenance of Amelia Kerrington staring up at him, Carter's frustration rose quickly. "Please, Lady Worthing…" he pleaded.

Once they entered the room, Kerrington's lady excused her servants and closed the door. "Tell me how goes the investigation?" Her eyes spoke of her own anxiousness, and Carter knew instant regret of not recognizing the lady's ploy.

"Which investigation?" he asked. He could not imagine Kerrington sharing Realm business with his wife, but the viscountess had been present at more than one Realm rescue, including her own. She would hold some knowledge of her husband's role in the organization.

Her countenance scrunched up in dissatisfaction. "Your brother sent word to Linton Park yesterday afternoon. He sought James's assistance with a disappearance."

Carter's heart slammed hard against his chest. "What sort of disappearance? A kidnapping?" Could Ransing have executed another form of revenge? Since he had made the connection between Dylan Monroe and the Dymond family, Carter had expected the worst. "What has occurred? Is it Lady Hellsman?" Law would be devastated.

"No. It was my brother's former friend, Mrs. Warren." A punch in his gut would have been kinder. "I thought you brought a message from my husband."

Carter forced himself to concentrate on her words. "Kerrington is with Law?"

"Of course. James left immediately upon receiving the message."

Instinctively, he presented her a bow of respect. "I must depart," he said distractedly. "Please forgive my lack of manners, Lady Worthing." With that, Carter was striding toward where the groom held a waiting horse. He had promised Simon he would protect Lucinda Warren with his life, and once again, he had been found wanting.

Chapter Nineteen

H e had pushed Lord Worthing's horse to its limits and had been rewarded by reaching Blake's Run in record time. Tossing the horse's reins to one of the younger grooms, Carter was on the ground and running, mounting the main steps two at a time. Mr. Malcolm barely had released the door's latch before Carter burst into the interior. "Law! Arabella! Anyone here?"

Carter looked up to find his mother descending the main staircase. The scene was so commonplace that for a few seconds he had forgotten his parents had recently been on the Continent. "Mother, thank God!" He raced to meet her. "Tell me Lord Worthing and Law have located Mrs. Warren."

His mother extended her hands to him, and Carter instinctively entwined their fingers. "I am pleased you have arrived. This situation is most unusual."

"Forgive my manners, Baroness, but where is Law?" he demanded.

"Your brother, Lord Worthing, the earl, and several others have set out to locate Mrs. Warren."

Carter scrubbed the road dirt from his cheeks with his handkerchief. "Do you know when they departed? Where they meant to search?" Exhaustion tugged at his senses, but Carter's work was not complete.

"Bella could tell you more than I," his mother admitted. "She is in her sitting room. Lawrence has ordered his wife to bed. He fears for his health."

Carter kissed his mother's cheek. "Thank you for not chastising me for bringing danger to your doorstep," he whispered. The Baroness Blakehell was always his foundation. If he could find a woman of the same nature as Fernalia Lowery, Carter would consider himself a fortunate man. His mother was a dangerous lioness when the world "attacked" her family, but she was a loving, gracious, supportive female in other times.

"Nonsense," she said affectionately. "Now, go speak to Arabella. Lady Hellsman will be thankful you have arrived; our Bella has prayed for your safe return." She continued down the stairs. "I assume you will require a fresh horse," his mother said with a knowing smirk.

"Yes, please." Her businesslike manner eased some of the tension knotting Carter's shoulders. "And ask Cook for some bread and cheese. I am starving." He did not wait for his mother's acknowledgement: The baroness was a doting mother. She would see to everything necessary. Within seconds, Carter was tapping on Bella's exterior door.

"Come." Carter slipped into the room. His brother's wife looked up in anticipation. "Thank Goodness, you have come. The messenger found you in good time."

"What messenger?" Carter crossed to sit beside her.

"Law sent a rider to Suffolk to locate you," she explained. "If you hold no knowledge of a Blake's Run messenger, how did you know to come?"

Carter shook off the question. "I have no time for a long retelling. Simply know I have discovered Mr. Monroe holds connections to Viscount Ransing. I rode to Derbyshire because I feared for Law's safety, only to discover from Lady Worthing that a monumental occurrence had driven Lady Eleanor's husband to my ancestral home." He caught Bella's hand. "When we finish, I wish you to approach the baron and baroness regarding shoring up Blake's Run's defenses until this madness is complete. I suspect Ransing has planned something devious."

"Whatever you say, it will be done."

Carter nodded curtly. "Now apprise me of what has occurred."

For the next several minutes, Bella explained how the earl's illness had delayed Charleton's departure, how Charleton had sought Bella's assistance after he and Mrs. Warren had argued, how Bella had discovered Mrs. Warren's absence, and how they had sent for his associates, including Worthing, Godown, and Lexford, to assist with the investigation. "Lord Worthing says there is no possibility Mrs. Warren climbed down the makeshift rope. The knots remained securely tied, but not pulled taut from the lady's weight. The viscount assured your brother someone draped the rope off the balcony as a ruse."

Carter's mind was six steps ahead of Bella's explanation. "Then why leave a note?"

"Lord Godown says the intruder is offering you a challenge you cannot refuse."

Carter agreed with the marquis's estimation. "I had best trail the others," he said as he stood.

Bella followed him to her feet. "Bring Mrs. Warren back to us. My friend must be terribly frightened."

Carter swallowed his own fears. He thought of how he had left the lady behind in Belgium–how he could have insisted on Merriweather's retrieving "the boy"–how he had been so consumed with his own survival he had forgotten his promise to the youth until after Merriweather had escorted Carter from the field. He made no promises this time. "Please pray my best will be good enough."

Bella trailed behind him. "Simon and I will do just that."

He brushed his lips across his cheek. "Take care of yourself and the child. I will bring Law home safely."

Tears of anxiousness flooded her eyes, but his sister in marriage's voice remained steady. Arabella Lowery remained incomparably strong in the midst of chaos. "I want both Lowery brothers together under Blake's Run's roof."

Within another quarter hour, Carter was following the trail left behind by seven horses. He was uncertain as to the identity of the other two riders, but he assumed one was the family steward. Mr. Beauchamp was an excellent hunter, and the man knew the land better than anyone in the neighborhood. It was odd. In the half hour he had spent at Blake's Run, his father had not sought him out, if for no other reason than to charge Carter with Law's care or to accuse Carter of delivering scandal to the baron's door. The knowledge of Blakehell's lack of interest in the turmoil only proved how removed from Carter's life his father remained.

Lucinda had concentrated her efforts on deciphering where her abductor had taken her. She knew when they had departed the untended country roads and had moved along one of the turnpikes. No longer violently jostled about in the small box, she had accessed what she could do to escape.

She began with inspecting the latched opening only to find it secure. Next, she pushed against each of the boards above her head and the ones on her left. None gave even an inch. Unable to turn to address those on her right, Lucinda reluctantly accepted the fact she could not manage an escape while still in the box. Therefore, she must keep her wits about her when she reached the planned destination.

Her abductor had said he had held Mr. Warren's acquaintance; yet, Matthew had passed some four years prior. If a connection existed between her late husband and her captor, it was one of long duration. The man had also claimed knowledge of Sir Carter, but not necessarily the baronet's acquaintance. Lucinda held no doubt the "lover" to whom the man referred was Sir Carter. To the best of her knowledge, Mr. Warren and the baronet had had no prior connection. Sir Carter was some four years junior to her husband, and so an acquaintance similar to the one Matthew Warren held with Brantley Fowler was an unlikely possibility.

Then what connection did they possess? Even she had not known Sir Carter until that fateful day in Belgium. Therefore, a connection between the two could not have existed. She was the only link between Sir Carter and Mr. Warren, which meant her abductor thought Lucinda held information regarding Matthew Warren's actions—actions that would have piqued Sir Carter's interests. Now, all she had to do was to determine what deception Captain Warren had practiced right under her nose.

For a brief second, Lucinda had experienced the shame of her foolish naiveté, but she quickly placed her blame on hold. She would have plenty of time to berate her actions, or lack thereof. Instead, she replayed every interaction she had had with Sir Carter. She would focus upon what the baronet had said of his investigations. Somewhere in Sir Carter's most casual speeches were hidden clues to this madness.

He had ridden hard and had overtaken his brother's search party, which had rested their horses while studying a map of the land. He slowed his horse to a walk so as not to surprise them. Kerrington had heard Carter's approach before the others and had looked up. "Reinforcements," he had said to Godown and Kimbolt, and the other Realm members came forward to greet him.

Carter dismounted swiftly, and although his body ached from the pounding it had taken in the saddle, it was encouraging to know these three men had interrupted their lives to support him. He extended his hand to Kerrington. "I am pleased to discover you here."

Kerrington clapped him on the back as he accepted Carter's gesture. "We prayed you would receive word to join us. We are in a quandary as to what has occurred. Apparently, someone has taken Mrs. Warren from your father's estate, but we do not understand the 'why' or the 'wherefore.' Hopefully, you can share some details, which will explain what we face."

Carter frowned, "I am not certain I am as knowledgeable as you assume. Let us refresh the facts and see what develops." He stepped past Kerrington to greet his brother, Charleton, and Mr. Beauchamp. Finally, his eyes fell on the last rider, his father. Carter schooled his expression. "Thank you, Sir," he said simply.

As if his actions should have been self explanatory, the baron declared, "I could not permit harm to come to Lawrence."

Carter swallowed the bitterness rushing to his throat. "Whatever your motives, Sir, I am proud to ride at your side." With that, Carter returned to where Kerrington gathered the others about a small opening. They sat upon fallen tree trunks, large rocks, and the ground. The familiarity of working with his Realm brothers assisted Carter's concentration. "Perhaps you might quickly tell me what you have discerned, Worthing. I am aware of how Lady Hellsman came to discover Mrs. Warren's disappearance."

Kerrington quickly summarized what Carter had previously discerned from Lady Hellsman before adding, "There were signs of a struggle: water from the basin on the carpet and fresh marks on the door face."

"Anything else of note?"

Law explained, "The message left behind speaks of your ignoring what must be a current investigation."

"Other than the search for Simon's family, Mrs. Warren and I hold no connections." He held each man's steady gaze to permit him the truth of his words.

Lexford asked, "Is it not a fact the attempts on Mrs. Warren's life began after she assumed guardianship of the boy?"

"Your question holds merit, but I am still unconvinced the child is the key to solving this madness," Carter responded. "We must be overlooking an important clue."

Kerrington asked, "I understand protocol, but could you not share a bit upon what cases you have been pursuing?"

Carter knew Lord Worthing would not ask unless he was certain a connection existed, but Carter did not relish breaking confidences. He hesitated, choosing his words carefully. He held no qualms on discussing the matter with his Realm brothers, but Carter had always carefully hidden the dangers of his position from his family, who looked upon him as nothing more than a glorified clerk. He would not have them worry unnecessarily. "In Suffolk, we have been searching for Murhad Jamot among a local smuggling ring. Dylan Monroe and I cornered Jamot and his contact in a Lincolnshire inn, but Monroe was wounded, and Jamot escaped."

The marquis's countenance darkened. "That does not sound of you, Lowery. How did the Baloch manage to slip your grasp?"

Carter paused again. "Jamot held Mrs. Warren prisoner?"

It was the earl's turn to frown. "What pray tell was my niece doing at a disreputable inn, and why would you place Lucinda in danger?"

Carter fought the urge to squirm. He would prefer the others would not know how much his heart had ached to see her again and how frightened he was when he encountered Jamot holding Mrs. Warren as his prisoner. "While I was in London, Mrs. Warren received a letter from someone who forged my hand. It asked her to meet me at The Rising Son Inn, stating I had discovered Simon's family. As the lady had no knowledge of my script, and as I had been actively searching for the boy's family, Mrs. Warren had no reason not to believe the message."

The marquis summarized, "Someone knew of your assisting the lady and used that information to usurp your efforts. The move was not coincidental. Have you discovered the identity of the forger?"

Again, Carter would prefer not to disclose all the facts until he knew the truth. Reluctantly though, he said, "Swenton brought something suspicious to my attention: Mr. Monroe is in close proximity whenever there is a sighting of Murhad Jamot. The baron's observation has led Pennington to take Monroe into custody. We believe Monroe is the letter's author."

Kerrington's scowl lines deepened. "Why would Monroe involve Mrs. Warren if he is in Jamot's pocket?"

Carter swallowed his pride. "Perhaps Monroe thought if Mrs. Warren and Simon were present, I would forsake my investigation in order to protect the lady."

Law asked, "Was it not in Suffolk that Mrs. Warren received her death threat?"

Charleton demanded incredulously, "What threat of death?"

"The note of which my brother speaks was a barely literate attempt at intimidation," Carter explained.

Lexford stretched his legs and poked a stick at a clump of grass, but Carter recognized the viscount's disguise of nonchalance. Aidan Kimbolt had latched onto the incongruity in Carter's story. "Was it Jamot who shot Monroe?"

"No. An elderly gentleman. Well dressed, but likely not of the aristocracy." He spoke to Kerrington in hopes his former captain would realize the predicament in which Carter found himself. His position with the Realm required he keep his silence on certain matters. "The man who followed Mrs. Warren in London described his employer in a similar manner. I have attempted to disregard the possibility Mrs. Warren has become involved in some grand scheme, but..."

Kerrington finished Carter's thought, "But we could be walking into some sort of trap."

The earl sputtered, "You think my niece practices treason!"

"The lady spoke quite eloquently on the oppression of the Corn Laws and the government's suppression of the poor," Law stated defensively.

It did Carter well to have his older brother defend him; he had always admired Lawrence Lowery's strength of conviction, but Carter could not permit any of the group to malign Lucinda Warren. The woman had quite thoroughly engaged his heart. "Mrs. Warren said no more than what half the country says daily. However, I do believe Mrs. Warren possesses information, which has placed her in danger." His decision made, Carter added, "I know of no connection between Mr. Monroe and Mrs. Warren other than my former assistant taking note of my genuine concern for her and the boy."

The marquis's countenance held puzzlement. "What are you not telling us regarding the lady and Monroe?"

Carter glanced to his brother. What he would share would affect Law and Arabella, and it grieved him to remind his brother of a long, unspoken feud. "In truth, I hold no knowledge of import regarding Mrs. Warren beyond what I have previously shared. I have, however, discovered a troubling fact regarding Mr. Monroe. This particular point was what drove me to Derbyshire. I knew nothing of Mrs. Warren's disappearance until I rode into Linton Park at dawn."

"Just tell us," Lexford said irritably. "We are losing precious time, as well as daylight."

Carter nodded curtly. "Pennington disclosed Mr. Monroe's family included the Dymonds in Cornwall and likely those in Staffordshire." A shocked silence followed.

Law asked in disbelief, "As in Hugh Dymond?" His brother made an expressive shudder.

Carter spoke honestly to his brother. "It has come to my attention Pennington rejected Viscount Ransing's bid to join our ranks, but when Pennington's attention to the duchess drew him away from London, Lord Sidmouth and the Duke of Portland installed Monroe as my assistant."

The implications were plain, and no one spoke the assumptions. However, Blakehell appeared unconvinced: His eyebrows sailed upward toward the baron's receding hairline. "You are saying your brother's university feud with Hugh Dymond has translated into some sort of traitorous plot? This is too bizarre, Carter. You have erred."

An awkward silence ensued until Charleton cleared his throat. "Mayhap not so bizarre, Blakehell."

"Would you kindly explain, Your Lordship?" Kerrington asked suspiciously.

Charleton glanced nervously about the group. "Last evening, Lucinda and I shared her father's private papers. In those, my niece read something in her father's military records, which brought on extreme sentimentality on Lucinda's part." Carter thought the earl's description of Mrs. Warren in error, but he held his tongue. "After my dearest girl returned to her quarters, I broke my promise to her: I finished reading Roderick's papers. I would not have Lucinda injured again unnecessarily. I mean to keep her from harm."

The marquis suggested encouragingly, "And something in Colonel Rightnour's papers refers to Hugh Dymond?"

"In fact, they do. " Again, the earl paused before explaining, "It is of great importance my niece's reputation is maintained. I would not wish what I share to become common knowledge."

Kerrington assured, "We want only to save the lady and return Mrs. Warren to your care."

The earl nodded curtly. Charleton's clear, straight gaze met the others, daring each man to dispute his words. "In Roderick's papers there are references to my brother discovering a deep secret regarding Captain Warren. Roderick wrote of Warren being part of a group bringing European artwork and pottery from the plundered war cities to England. Many of the pieces were quite rare. Roderick concealed his discovery to protect Lucinda's reputation."

Carter's attention piqued with the mention of stolen European artwork. The thought of solving more than one investigation thrilled him. "And Hugh Dymond held connections to Captain Warren?"

"The viscount's name is mentioned among several others. The only one on the list of which I had a previous acquaintance was Cyrus Woodstone, whose father is a well known Member of Parliament for Dorset."

Kerrington looked at Carter sharply, and Carter suspected Lord Worthing knew more of Carter's investigation than the viscount pretended. He said, "Now that we have a glimmer into what we are stumbling, I suggest we remount. Lexford is correct: We have lost our momentum."

Without another word, seven men retrieved their horses. Mounting, they waited for Carter's orders. Although he was the youngest, they had placed their combined faiths in his ability to lead. "Mr. Beauchamp, if you would take up the trail, we will follow; but as we become closer, I will assume the role. Whoever has Mrs. Warren has named me as his enemy, and I do not mean to disappoint the lady's assailant."

Kerrington guided his mount to come abreast of Carter's horse. "Is there anything else you wish to share?" Their pace had slowed as they reached the first plateau. Their group followed the wagon's trail, which meant whoever had taken Mrs. Warren would soon make a decision: A wagon could not traverse the passes of Dark Peak. Mrs. Warren's abductor would choose either to abandon the lady or to abandon his chosen transportation.

"I hold my own conclusions, but you know the gist of what has happened." He glanced behind him to where the others studied the landscape for possible clues. "Have you a theory?"

Kerrington adjusted his seat as his horse began to climb once more. "I was just considering how easy this trail is to follow. I am not one who prefers 'easy.'"

Carter bit back his reply: He did not enjoy the feeling of having no control over the lady's rescue. "I am certain the marquis and Lexford have taken notice, but not the others." He glanced to where Mr. Beauchamp leaned low upon his horse to search the ground. "So, we are likely riding into some sort of trap."

"Yes," Kerrington commiserated. "Yet, at the moment, we hold little choice. Mrs. Warren's life is in danger."

Carter's self-chastisement and indignation had arrived. "The lady knows peril because I thought myself superior to Viscount Ransing, and I practiced petty foolishness upon the man," he hissed.

Kerrington scowled, "This situation has roots deep in the past. If what the earl shared proves true, Ransing has been involved in nefarious dealings for many years; his using the feud between him and your brother is purely a ruse— an excuse to even the balance when the viscount has clearly lost his reason."

Carter lowered his head. It appalled him to think his actions had cost Mrs. Warren her freedom. "I should not have taunted Ransing with my superiority. It was a shallow endeavor. I used my power with the Realm to make Ransing pay for his arrogance." He sucked in a sharp breath of self-anger.

Kerrington shook off Carter's self-censure. "You cannot permit the negative thoughts to ride with you, or you will know failure." It bothered Carter that Kerrington paused for emphasis. Carter did not require more responsibility heaped upon his shoulders; he felt weighed down by his duties. "Do you recall day when Wellston and I pulled you from the battlefield watch to join the Realm?"

It struck him as supremely ironic Kerrington chose to remind him of his young, impetuous self. "How could I not?" Carter replied dejectedly. "I have not had a day's peace since."

Kerrington mustered a wan smile. "I cursed Pennington that day as much as you," the viscount admitted. "I had argued vehemently we did not require a seventh man, and even if we did, Kimbolt had brought us Lucifer Hill. Wellston argued you were too young–you had barely reached your majority, and you were so green."

Carter gritted his teeth. He had been a damn fine junior officer; he had proved that particular fact at Waterloo. He hoped if he made some clever remark, perhaps Kerrington would abandon this line of conversation. "It is pleasant to discover in hindsight I was not a welcomed addition to such an elite group." It was irreverent to encounter the truth now that they rode together into what was likely an ambush.

"Nonsense," Lord Worthing declared. "It had nothing to do with you personally; it was just the tediousness of having to open our operations to yet another stranger; and at the time, your record had shown you a passionate soldier, but not a particularly adept military strategist." Carter grudgingly recognized his sometimes angry, self-destructive self in Kerrington's description. "I had already spent a lifetime tempering Fowler's hastiness, and I could not imagine beginning anew with you."

A frown of alarm and regret creased Carter's brow. "Then why did you change your mind? You were never one blindly to follow nonsensical orders."

Kerrington urged his horse forward. "It was Pennington. Our own 'Shepherd of lost souls' who convinced me you were the Realm's future. He said you possessed the innate insight to lead England against those who could corrupt it to its core. In truth, I thought Pennington had lost his reason, but now I thoroughly agree. Without men of your caliber, Lowery, this country is doomed."

Chapter Twenty

Their progress had slowed to a crawl, and Lucinda wondered where her abductor meant to take her. Although it remained stiflingly hot, the temperature inside the box had cooled somewhat. She was miserably cramped and miserably stuffy and miserably regretful. Everything in her life had been turned upon its ear, and now that she knew for certain she loved Carter Lowery she would likely die.

The horses whined from the strain of pulling the wagon, and Lucinda braced herself against the obvious incline, which would follow. Her journey had been one of straining to stay in place against gravity's pull upon her position, and Lucinda held no doubt they approached the Dark Peaks behind Blake's Run. During her confinement, she had examined everything she knew of the baronet and of her late husband, but not one connection showed itself. It was extremely frustrating for if she could discover the "tie," Lucinda might be able to use it to bargain for her release.

Suddenly, the wagon's forward movement halted, and Lucinda's heartbeat increased in anticipation. She waited, part in panic and part in relief, for her release from her wooden cell, but no sound came from the outside world. She strained to hear her abductor's approach; yet, only silence reigned. Within seconds, realization arrived: She was alone and locked in a box with no means of escape.

Although Carter had warned her to take precautions, she had admittedly not thought it possible for danger to strike a second time in so few hours, and so Arabella had made her way around the orangery toward the dowager house, where she meant to unpack more of the trunks she had sent over previously as a means to distract her heart from the disarray of her friend's abduction. She had convinced herself if she went about her normal duties, everything would return to how it should be. Her thoughts remained deeply seated upon the situation between Carter and Mrs. Warren, and she prayed for the search party's success. The couple, obviously, affected each other, but Bella easily recognized the gulf between them. "Very much as it was between Lawrence and me."

Lucinda Warren had been systematically abused by her late husband, the woman's self-confidence chipped away by a man who thought only of his own comforts. Lawrence had explained what Law had termed to be Carter's growing interest in the woman and how truly unsuited they were for each other. "I fear my brother's heart will know disappointment," Law had declared as he sat Bella upon his lap. "He is young; yet, I have held the hope of Carter finally knowing love. He has always harbored the idea the baron does not recognize his worth. It would do Carter well to know the love of a woman fiercely loyal to him, and him alone."

"In the same manner, I am with you?" Bella had teased as she pulled her body closer to his.

Law's hands had skimmed her hips, lifting her center to his erection. "Exactly," he had rasped. "Such a woman can change a man's stars."

Remembrance of what had followed brought a flush to Bella's cheeks. She paused to stare blindly at the back lawns and to imagine her husband striding toward her. He was always so confident—so assured of his role in his family and in Society. Bella held no doubt he could have claimed any woman he wished. The fact Lawrence Lowery had chosen her never ceased to amaze Bella, and she thanked God daily for bringing them together. "Come home safely," she said on a sigh.

It was the last thing she recalled before the terracotta squares leading to the orangery had come up to meet her fall. She had slammed hard against the tiles, and even the cool surface of the bricks had offered no comfort. A groan. A hand across her mouth. A cloth about her eyes. It had all happened so quickly, Bella had had little time to react. Someone swept her from the floor and had thrown her roughly over his shoulder.

Unable to see her attacker, Bella had fought for escape, but whoever had grabbed her had had an accomplice, who had quickly bound her hands and legs, turning her into a living sack. She resented how the second man had fondled her ankles as he tied them together; however, she ignored the intrusion and listened to the whispered exchange between the men.

"Hurry, before someone comes looking for her."

"She is a wild one, more passionate than her cousin."

Which cousin? Bella wondered. She had cousins in England's southwest shires, those generations residing within the Earl of Vaughn's reach, as well as those in Staffordshire, an extension of Lord Graham's family. All were less impetuous than she.

The men were running. She assumed they raced from the gardens, away from any hope of her rescue. With a gag in her mouth, she could not scream for assistance, and as Bella bounced hard against her abductor's shoulder, she knew instant fear. She prayed the man's rough handling would not harm the child she carried. Above all else, she must protect Lawrence's issue. Thus resolve, Bella ceased her struggle. Instead, she went limp in the man's grasp, easing the harsh blows to her body from his jostling her roughly. Later, she would concentrate on escaping. For now, the child's welfare took prominence.

"Sir Carter!" Mr. Beauchamp beckoned Carter forward. Carter, along with Kerrington at his side, joined the family steward. When he and Worthing reined in their horses, the man said, "We are entering some sort of enclave, Sir, and it appears the wagon we seek has taken a turn into this horseshoe enclosure. I do not like it, Sir."

"Neither do I," Carter declared. "Whomever we pursue has made no effort to conceal his trail."

"What do you wish us to do, Lowery?" Kerrington asked.

His "captain's" words still clung to Carter's shoulders: It was time he proved himself worthy of Pennington's respect. "I would wish to be of Thornhill's nature and storm into the battle," he said with a knowing nod to Kerrington. "Yet, a bit of caution is necessary. Lord Worthing, if you, Godown, and Lexford would lead the others in a circular approach, I will follow the trail to its end."

Kerrington did not question Carter's decision. "As you wish. Give us a quarter hour to take up protective positions before you set out again." Kerrington motioned Beauchamp to follow him, and within a minute, the other riders had dispersed.

Carter would have preferred to dismount and to rest his horse, but he thought better of it. He held no idea whether he faced one culprit or several. Whether the person he followed was the infantryman, who had attacked him previously. Whether Mrs. Warren's abductor held him in his sights. Carter would not know until he rode into the shelter's narrow opening. Until he exposed himself to the lady's attacker.

Instinctively, Carter checked the pocket watch he carried in his pocket. It was the one his father had presented him on Carter's eighteenth birthday. A very ornate timepiece, the baron had explained had once belonged to Nigel Lowery, Carter's irascible grandfather. According to the baron, Carter's appearance had been a profound relief to Niall Lowery, who had bemoaned the need for a spare after three successive female births. Carter had carried it every day since; in his reasoning, it was a symbol of his connection to the Lowery family, perhaps even a symbol of Niall Lowery's love for his second son. "Ten more minutes," he said to remind himself of the task at hand.

"Dear God," he said reverently aloud, "in your eternal goodness, protect those who ride with me and share your benevolence with Mrs. Warren. I failed her in Belgium, but with your permission, on this day, I mean to fulfill that long ago promise to the lady." Returning the watch to an inside pocket, Carter's eyes scanned the open trail. The idea he could be riding to his death did not frighten him. This was the life he had chosen, and Carter held no regrets. His legacy would be one of life–the lives he had saved and the lives he had changed. "It is enough," he declared. "Even if Pennington's prediction never proves true, I will continue on. I will do what is right for each English citizen: I will do my duty."

He caught the horse's reins more firmly in his grasp and used his knees to nudge the animal forward. Retrieving his gun from the holster strapped to his chest, Carter set the trigger for a quicker response. He felt very exposed, and he sat lower in the saddle to make himself a smaller target. With each tap of the horse's hoofs against the smooth pebbles and twigs, Carter's heart pounded out a fearful staccato. He licked his dry lips and set the horse's pace to a gallop. "Time to free Mrs. Warren," he said as he rode hard into the opening.

After hearing nothing for what felt like hours, when the shot rang out, Lucinda had jumped—her body responding to the sound of the recoil. She had heard enough rifles to recognize the sound. Instinctively, she jerked her knees upward, only to have them bang against the side of the box and sending a radiating pain shooting through her already numb limbs.

Suddenly, the box in which she rested shifted, and she fought to stay in place as the wagon beneath her tilted, pitching the box downward to slam into what she assumed was the hinged back drop. The sound of wood ripping told her the back would not hold her weight mixed with that of her enclosure. The question was what would happen if the wagon shifted again?

A second shot brought another reaction and another tilt of the box followed by a scream and her bracing her hands against the sides of her enclosure. The box was angled some five and forty degrees, and Lucinda stiffly pushed against the box's rear to hold herself in place.

When a third round of gunfire ensued, Lucinda breathed through the desire to recoil. Instead, she concentrated on conjuring up an image of Carter Lowery's beloved countenance. "Do not forget me," she whispered as she closed her eyes to hold his image before her.

Carter bolted from the horse and dove for protection as the dirt sprayed upward about the stallion's legs. The animal bucked and then rose up on two legs. It pawed the air, and Carter rolled away before the stallion could strike him.

Within seconds came answering fire, and Carter knew one of his friends had taken up the fight. Scrambling to his feet, Carter ran toward where he had seen the flash of light—where his enemy lay in wait. It had never been his way to rush heedlessly into the skirmish, but this time was different: Lucinda Warren had suffered because of him, and Carter meant to set her world aright. He owed her as much. "Never again," he growled as he ducked behind a stand of trees. A third round of gunfire told him the others had engaged the resistance, but Carter ignored the melee. He possessed no doubt his family and friends would prevail in the altercation. He remained focused on only one task: the saving of Lucinda Warren.

He cautiously approached a small "survivor's hut," as those from the area called the structures. The shelters were nothing more than four walls and a dry roof. Occasionally, one might find such a hut with a wooden floor, but most had been designed purely to provide shelter from the elements.

The dust-encrusted windows blocked his view, and so Carter possessed no other option than to enter the unknown. With a sigh of resignation, he kicked the door, but it did not give. Expecting to encounter an armed opponent, Carter jumped to the side to avoid a counter attack, but silence prevailed. Again, he kicked the door; this time, the splinter of wood rewarded his efforts. With his shoulder to the panels, he shoved with all his might, and the door gave a little, but it remained frustratingly impenetrable.

As he stepped away to kick it a third time, Law appeared by his side. "On three," Law declared, and Carter nodded. Even in this madness, it was comforting to be standing shoulder to shoulder with his brother. "One. Two. Three," he pronounced. This time the door sprung wide, slamming into the wall, and Carter led the way into the darkness.

Gun at-the-ready, the empty room brought instant disappointment. "Where is she?" he growled as he turned in a gallingly silent circle.

"I have no idea," Law responded in bewilderment.

"Lowery!" He heard the desperate call of James Kerrington.

Following the sound, Carter rushed from the hut, in search of his friend. A second shout drew him further into the enclave. Bursting through an untamed stand of bilberry bumblebee and bog asphodel, he came to a stumbling halt beside his father. Perched on the edge of a steep drop off sat a wagon, its rear draped over the cliffside, precariously teetering forth and back.

"Stay alert," he cautioned as he slowly approached the wagon. He wished to rush to the cliff's edge and make certain Lucinda's was not lying crushed on the rocks below, but Carter had learned his lessons well. His eyes scanned the ground searching for traps, and he was rewarded when he discovered a perfectly concealed fuse line, running beneath one of the wagon's wheels in the direction of several large boulders. "Lexford!" he pointed toward the ground and to the rocks, and viscount moved guardedly along a circular route to examine the situation.

"Give me a moment," Lexford instructed as he bent to the task.

Carter motioned the others to hold their positions while Lexford defused whatever awaited them. The viscount had always held the steadiest hand when it came to gunpowder combinations.

"It is clear," Lexford announced as he stood. "An elementary attempt." The viscount's cocky smile told Carter the fuse line had been no more than a convincing decoy.

"Hold your positions," Carter warned. He did not need to look to know Kerrington, Lexford, and Godown had their backs to him. His friends surveyed the area: Their party was in an exposed position. Although he had not asked, Carter realized Mr. Beauchamp stood guard over whomever his friends had captured earlier.

He sidestepped, keeping the hill to his back. As he drew nearer the wagon, Carter's breathing eased. There was nothing from the ordinary about the abandoned wheeled vehicle. The tongue faced the back of the hut, and there was a storage box for farm tools upon the bed. One wheel hung off the cliff's edge, but nothing else appeared suspicious. Perhaps, the culprits had made an effort to hide the wagon, and he and the others had interrupted their plan. It appeared those they pursued had meant to send the wagon over the cliff. Or perhaps this was a weird coincidence—an abandoned wagon was not solid evidence. "Mayhap we followed the wrong trail," he called. "There is nothing here."

The sweat beaded between Lucinda's breasts, but she held herself stiffly in place. She supposed it was possible if the box slid from the wagon it would simply land roughly upon the ground, splitting open and freeing her from her "prison." Yet, something in her gut told her an escape would not come that easily. Not only had the box shifted, but also had the wagon upon which it rested. She did not know what awaited her, but Lucinda was determined to delay the inevitable for as long as she could.

She schooled her mind to conjure up the image of Sir Carter again. She had longed him. It was an intense, irrefutable need she could not eliminate. The baronet's loving countenance had a calming effect on her heart. If Lucinda admitted her obsession, *calm* was not the term she might have used; but despite how thoughts of the man always made her emotions stutter–the tension tight between them, such a flood of delight filled her when in Sir Carter's presence she found comfort in her desire for him. She easily could recall his scent–strong and masculine, clean soap and sandalwood. His voice–quiet, but firm–a tone, which would quell the most dangerous of men and seduce the most unwilling female.

"Mayhap we followed the wrong trail. There is nothing here."

Lucinda's eyes sprung wide. Had she imagined he had come for her? Surely if it were her imagination she would dream of Sir Carter professing his love. She listened with her whole being. Muffled voices–too far away for her to delineate what they discussed. Lucinda held her position. *What if the stranger–her abductor–had returned?*

"Then we should question those you have captured."

Sir Carter's voice. Lucinda was certain of it, and he was close. She opened her mouth to cry for his assistance, but nothing came out.

"What of Lucinda?" Charleton asked as he looked about dejectedly, and Carter knew a similar sinking feeling: He had failed her again.

"Beauchamp has two men tied up on the other side of the clearing," Godown explained.

"Then we should question those you have captured." Reluctantly, he turned his back on the cliffside. Carter's mind raced to catch up with the reality of their futile chase. Had his enemies meant to play a game? "I thought…" he began. As he took the first step to walk away, the obvious arrived. "Wait!" he ordered. Carter knew all eyes had fallen on him.

Tentatively, he edged closer to where the wagon teetered upon the ledge. Placing a steadying hand on the wooden side, his free hand reached for the box. "Lucinda?" he said on a rasp of disbelief. "Lucinda, are you within?" His fingers clutched at the joint holding the box together.

A sob answered his question. "Carter?"

"I am here," he said anxiously. "Do not move. I mean to have you out soon." He turned to the others. A strange reticence invaded his heart. Despite her perilous position, Carter had found her. A moment of profound silliness brought a smile to his lips. "She is within the box. We must secure the wagon before it tumbles to the rocks below."

Immediately, Kerrington and Godown caught the wagon tongue to brace it. The wagon sat on a slight descent, leading to the cliff's edge. Lexford instructed, "We require rocks behind the wheels."

Carter, Law, the earl, and Blakehell retrieved several of the larger rocks, which peppered the hillside. "Hurry!" the earl pleaded as he huffed and puffed under the weight of a large stone. Carter admired the man's dedication to his niece. Not many men would turn their worlds inside out to welcome a poor relative. Carter dropped another stone at Lexford's feet. The viscount had crawled under the wagon to stack the stones so as to block the wheels backward movement. "That should be enough," Lexford declared as he scurried from beneath the wagon. "Captain, you and Godown must make certain the wagon tongue does not tilt upward."

"We have it," Kerrington assured. "Just roll the damn thing our direction!"

"Everyone, use your shoulders!" Carter instructed. He purposely placed himself where he might observe her enclosure. He was not certain what he would do if the box suddenly pitched to the side, but he meant to be in a position to save Lucinda Warren if Fate presented them another debacle."

"Lucinda!" Charleton called in desperation as he grunted against the effort of moving the wagon.

"I am here, Uncle," she responded in a hopeful voice.

"Hold my darling girl!"

"Again!" Carter shouted as the wagon rolled forward a few inches and then rolled back into place. It would be so much easier if all four wheels were on solid ground.

Godown asked, "Should I retrieve a horse?"

Carter pressed his weight against the side of the wagon. "There is not time." He held onto the side of the wagon so tightly his knuckles cramped from the strain.

Kerrington ordered, "Everyone, on two. One! Two!" Carter could feel the desperation coursing through his veins. He could lose her forever. His muscles twitched with the exertion as his heels dug into the rocky surface.

"Carter!" Her voice plaintively called, and he doubled his efforts. Even with the desperation of her tone, he relished the sound of his name upon her lips. Slowly, the wagon inched forward.

When the wheel touched the solid ground, he encouraged. "Almost there!"

Again, his friends and family responded, and Carter realized how blessed he was to know such devotion. His gloved hands caught the wheel and directed it along the ground until it rested upon the rock surface. He straightened to mark how far from the cliff edge the wagon sat. "Enough!" he called as he scrambled into the back of the wagon. Kneeling beside the box, Carter took a careful examination of the situation. "Lexford, assist me in lifting this damn thing from the wagon. The rest of you be prepared to keep the wagon from rolling backward again."

"Permit me to wedge these logs between the spokes." Godown lifted a broken tree limb to slide it between the openings in the wheels.

When the marquis had finished, Lexford tentatively climbed upon the seat. The wagon inclined, and Carter felt the wooden seat shift beneath his feet. "Do not move, Mrs. Warren," he warned. He spoke to the side of the box. "Lord Lexford and I mean to hand you down, and then we will release you."

"I am frightened," she wailed.

He felt his heart falter. "As are we all," he said ironically, "but this is no worse than we experienced at Waterloo. We prevailed then, and we will prevail now."

She remained silent for several elongated seconds. Carter hoped she understood his implications: He knew her secrets. Instead of responding to his declaration of their connection, she said, "Tell my uncle I wish to go to Lancashire."

"I am here, my girl," Charleton said in relief. "I mean to have you safe at Charles Place soon."

Carter wedged his fingers beneath the foot of the box, while Lexford took the head. With a nod of agreement, they used their knees to lift upward. The movement caused the wagon to shift, and they paused until the movement ceased. "Easy," he whispered roughly.

Carefully, they edged toward the right side of the wagon. It was more stable than the left because the wheels were buried in the grass tuffs between the rocks. Godown and Law scrambled to position themselves to accept the box. "Lower it slowly," Carter cautioned. It amazed him how light the weight. Lucinda Warren could not be more than nine stone. Bending as one, Carter and Lexford lengthened their reach to sit the rough box into the marquis's and Law's outstretched arms.

"We have it," Godown announced as he adjusted his grip. Carter and Lexford jumped down to assist the pair in setting the box firmly on the ground.

"Thank God!" Charleton expelled on an exhalation, and Carter understood. All the strength had seeped from his limbs. He rotated his shoulders to relax his muscles before he crawled toward the still closed box.

Kerrington ordered, "We must find a means to open this latch. Mrs. Warren must be smothering within."

"Are there tools in the hut?" Godown asked.

The baron volunteered. "I will have a look."

Carter knew his father did not approve of the situation, which was steeped in scandal, but Carter did not care. All he wanted was to release Lucinda Warren from her wooden cell and to hold the woman in his embrace once more. It felt a lifetime had passed since they had last come together.

"There is a small opening between the slats," Lucinda instructed, and Carter noticed how her voice spoke of her resolve to survive.

Lexford announced, "I have a hand shovel attached to my saddle." The viscount shrugged. "An old habit. From when we were in Persia. Should I retrieve it?"

Carter nodded his agreement. He was on his knees beside the box, looking for the opening Mrs. Warren had indicated. We must wedge something into this space." He gestured wildly. "Everyone should look for a sturdy log or a sharp rock." As the others stepped away, Carter crawled closer to the opening. He required a moment to speak privately to Mrs. Warren. "Lucinda?" he said on a rasp. "Did they hurt you?" He prayed her captor had not violated her.

"Lots of bruises and aching muscles," she confessed. "And my hair is in terrible disarray."

Carter smiled easily. Only a woman would worry upon her hair. "To me, you are always beautiful."

"You are a delightful flatterer, Sir Carter," she said primly.

Each of her rebukes was like coming home. Carter had missed her more than he had thought possible. When he heard her desperation, there was such a feeling of bewilderment and guilt and disbelief that he had to respond. With Lucinda Warren, he experienced a fierce need for possession. Even with the box separating them, Lucinda was dangerously arousing. "I should assist the others. I want you free." His voice was raw with desire, and Carter swallowed hard.

Lexford returned, carrying the metal shovel, no more than twelve inches in length. They each had carried one when they had been in the field. It was similar to the ones soldiers used to bury their dead. "We can wedge the tip behind the slats and use a rock as a hammer." Lexford was on his knees beside Carter. "Mrs. Warren, cover your eyes."

"I cannot move my arms," she admitted. "The space is too confining."

Lexford mumbled a curse. "Then turn your head as far to the left as possible. Squeeze your eyes shut and clamp your lips tightly closed."

"I understand."

Carter assisted Lexford in inserting the shovel's tip between the slats and holding it in place. Lexford retrieved a flat rock from those beneath the wagon. "Hold it steady," he said as he used the rock to pound the metal into the opening.

Carter felt the vibration through his whole body, but the sound of the wood ripping away made the pain worthwhile. "Again," he encouraged.

Kerrington reappeared. "Use this one. It has less slate in it and will not crumble so quickly."

Lexford changed out the rocks. He lifted the new one with both hands and let it strike the handle's tip. The opening increased.

Kerrington instructed. "Move the tool's tip closer to the joint. We must free the nails."

Carter yanked the shovel from the opening and wedged it again in the small space between the two slats forming the right corner. "Do you have it, Lexford?"

"I am prepared." This time, the viscount struck the metal a powerful blow. When the nail pulled away from the wood, Carter and Kerrington caught the freed slat and tugged it from the box's side.

"The next one," Carter instructed as he placed the metal wedge behind the second slatted joint.

With two more strikes of the rock, the second slat came free. Charleton and Godown had returned, and they joined in the battle to liberate Mrs. Warren.

"Stay safe, my girl," the earl said through joyful tears.

Unable to wait for the third slat to be removed, Carter and the earl caught the wood and tugged. They were united—the two men who loved Lucinda Warren. When the board gave way, sending him and Charleton tumbling onto their backsides, Carter laughed in relief, while the tears pooled in his eyes. He had not failed her.

He righted his position to sit beside the box to see Kerrington and Godown assisting Mrs. Warren from her enclosure. They, literally, had their hands beneath her head and feet and sliding her sideways toward them, and then she was free. A beautiful woman lying upon the grass. Carter wished to cover her with his body and kiss her senseless, but with others looking on he held for a few awkward seconds. And in that time, her uncle moved to cradle her in his protecting arms. Mrs. Warren's body rocked with sobs of relief, and Carter's fingers instinctively reached for her.

"Where is father?" Law asked. The others looked on awkwardly.

Carter pulled his gaze from the domestic scene. "The baron sought tools to free the lady. He meant to search the hut."

"I will find him," Law announced.

Carter stood and knocked the dust from his breeches. His body craved a hot soaking bath—preferably one he could share with Lucinda Warren. "No, I will do it. It will provide the baron the opportunity to address my irresponsibility." He glanced to where Charleton assisted Lucinda to her feet. Mrs. Warren clung to the earl's lapels. "Gather everyone. We should return the lady to Blake's Run as soon as possible." Reluctantly, Carter turned his steps from the woman he desired.

He strode purposely toward the structure, but his mind remained on the cliff's edge and a war widow. Therefore, when he entered the still open door, Carter did not expect the scene upon which he stumbled: The baron stood against the wall, his hands raised to his shoulders, and Cyrus Woodstone pointed a gun at the baron's heart.

"We have been waiting for you," Woodstone said coldly.

In that instant, Carter was grateful he had not permitted Law to seek out their father. Carter's training could prove the difference. "You provided us many challenges," he said evenly as he sidestepped slowly toward his father.

"You are a worthy opponent," Woodstone announced. "It has taken a decade for anyone to take note of our operations."

Carter asked, "How will you stop the others from killing you?" He would not antagonize Woodstone with a personal taunt—not when the man still held a gun on Carter's father.

Woodstone's confidence rose quickly. "I need only to make an example of you." The man turned the gun on Carter, and despite the danger, Carter breathed easier. His father would be spared. "And I am not afeared of your friends' revenge."

Carter ceased his sideways movement. It was essential to protect the baron at all costs. "You think yourself invincible?" he asked with feigned nonchalance.

Woodstone shook his head in denial. "I require no shield of invincibility. You have underestimated me, Sir Carter. After all the elaborate plans you have witnessed this day, did you think I would approach six men without some form of assurance?"

Carter's heartbeat hitched faster. If Woodstone spoke of six men, he had likely incapacitated Beauchamp. "As I know you are dying to tell me, please explain your proposal."

"Very well." Woodstone gestured with the gun. "Our removal of Mrs. Warren from Blake's Run has served its purpose. While you rescued the lady, my associates have removed Lady Hellsman from the manor." Carter had anticipated something similar, but he had rushed away before putting security in place. "If I do not join my friends by midnight, Lady Hellsman will pay the price. So, I am certain you can convince your companions to permit me my freedom."

Carter could hear his father's anxious breathing. "You cannot injure Lady Hellsman," the baron asserted. "She is the title's future."

Woodstone declared, "Then you best hope I arrive in time."

Carter's mind raced in search of answers. "Ransing means to have his retribution?" He hoped his bold assertion would rattle Woodstone's composure as much as the man had rattled his.

A flicker of doubt crossed Woodstone's expression. "You have discovered the viscount's involvement?"

"Of course," Carter declared. "But I do not understand a man who makes an innocent woman his target." He regarded his enemy with a hint of suspicion.

Woodstone's jaw line tightened, and Carter took note of the man's inherent disapproval. "Ransing means for your brother to know grief for his many manipulations. Hurting Lady Hellsman will destroy the future baron."

"Arabella…" the baron began.

"Is a strong woman." Carter hoped to keep the news of Bella's upcoming lying in a secret from these men.

Woodstone gestured with a nod of his head. "Blakehell, you must carry my terms to the others."

Carter glanced to his father. "Do as he asks, Sir." He hoped to remove the baron from danger; only then could Carter act.

"I will not leave you, Carter," Blakehell declared.

Carter attempted to reason with his father. "Sir, Lawrence will require your guidance. Law is your heir."

"And you are my youngest son," the baron insisted as he stepped menacingly toward Woodstone.

"No!" Carter shouted, but it was too late. Woodstone reacted to the baron's charge; he turned the gun and fired.

Chapter Twenty-One

From his eye's corner, Carter saw his father stumble backward, clutching at his chest, but Carter had no time to tend the baron's wound. He lunged for Woodstone, taking the man to the ground. His opponent struggled valiantly; yet, Carter's training prevailed. A few well-placed blows to Woodstone's kidneys sent the man reeling with pain. When his father's assailant used a hand to protect his side, Carter delivered a solid punch to the point of Woodstone's chin, and the man spun to the ground with a heavy thud.

Chest heaving, Carter stood over Woodstone waiting for his attacker's next move. Behind him, he heard his father groan, but Carter purposely did not turn his head. He was the only defense between Cyrus Woodstone and Niall Lowery.

"What the…" Kerrington's voice boomed over the silence. His friends had arrived, and Carter's shoulders relaxed.

"A bit of trouble," he said through tight lips.

"Father!" The desperation in Law's voice drew Carter's eyes from the culprit who had shot the baron. He turned to see his brother pressing a handkerchief to their father's shoulder.

Quickly, he joined Law on his knees beside his father's body. "What happened?" Law demanded.

Carter had no right to feel offense as his brother's tone: It was his fault his father had known danger. His enemies had made those Carter affected their targets. "Woodstone meant to prevent my involvement in an investigation of a grand scale. I attempted to remove the baron, but father placed himself between me and Woodstone." Carter still could not believe he had failed to protect his family. What good were his skills if those he loved still could know harm?

"I have Woodstone secured," Kerrington announced.

Carter felt the divide between Carter Lowery, governmental agent, and Carter Lowery, dutiful son, widen. "Send someone to where Beauchamp held the others. I suspect Woodstone has seen to his accomplices' release."

Godown nodded his understanding. "Lexford and I will see to the others and return Mr. Beauchamp and his captives to Blake's Run."

Mrs. Warren, supported by Charleton, appeared in the open door. "What is amiss?"

"Father has been shot," Law shared. "But I cannot tell the extent of the injury."

She straightened her shoulders with renewed resolve, and Carter recognized the determined Lucinda Warren had returned. "Carry the baron outside where the light is better. I shall examine him there."

Charleton argued, "Lucinda, I must insist we remove…"

She laid a comforting hand on the earl's arm, and Carter instinctively wished she would look kindly upon him. "Uncle, I appreciate your wish to protect me, but I have nursed men with wounds previously. I am not of such a frail nature as to have my sensibility offended."

Charleton reluctantly nodded his agreement.

Kerrington suggested, "Let us use the broken door as a litter."

Carter and Law carefully lifted their father to the wooden panel. With Kerrington's assistance, they carried the baron into the light.

"Set him down under the tree," Mrs. Warren instructed. She released her hair and quickly rewrapped it into a tight knot at the back of her neck, but the few seconds it had hung loose about her shoulders added to Carter's fantasies of her. "I shall require you knife, Sir Carter." She extended her palm in his direction.

"What makes you believe I carry a knife?" he said just to watch the gamut of emotions crossing her countenance. The lady did not disappoint: first disenchantment and then irritation.

She extended her hand further. "Your knife, Sir, and then I will require clean water or brandy for the wound."

"I have a flask and a roll of bandages in my saddle's bag," Kerrington acknowledged. "I will bring the horses about."

Carter instructed, "Ask the marquis and Lexford to locate the wagon's horses. We will require them to transport my father home."

As Kerrington moved off, Mrs. Warren said, "I shall require your assistance, Gentlemen. I do not wish to move the baron any more than necessary. One of you must cut away his jacket and shirt."

Carter recovered his knife from her hand. "I will see to the baron." He knelt where he could reach the wound. Blakehell's countenance held his pain, and Carter wondered how long the lines had covered Niall Lowery's forehead and eyes. In Carter's mind, the man he called "Father" had never aged, but, obviously, Carter had erred. The gentleman lying upon the wooden litter was firmly in the latter part of his life. The thought grieved Carter: they had wasted so much time with contention.

Kerrington returned with the necessary supplies. Mrs. Warren replaced Carter at Blakehell's side. He shuddered with pain, and Lucinda brushed his hair from his damp forehead. "Baron, I must examine your wound," she said softly as her fingers probed the opening.

The baron swatted her hand away. "You may do your worst, Mrs. Warren," Blakehell said through tight lips. "But first I must speak to my sons."

She glanced over her shoulder to Carter, and he nodded his agreement. He knew without a doubt what the baron meant to say. Therefore, Carter permitted Law the preference of the contact.

"You must permit Mrs. Warren to tend you, Sir," Law encouraged. He caught the baron's hand in his, and despite his best efforts, Carter knew the twinge of jealousy. When Niall Lowery passed, Lawrence would hold the memories the baron's other children had been denied.

"I am not avoiding Mrs. Warren's care," Blakehell assured. "But neither you nor Carter can spare the time to oversee the lady's efforts." The baron swallowed hard, his Adam's apple visible.

"Carter and I mean to see you well, Sir," Law reasoned.

Realizing his father's intent to tell it all, Carter interrupted, "The baron is correct, Law. You and I must escort Woodstone south. We have an encounter with Viscount Ransing to keep."

Puzzlement crossed Law's countenance. "I do not understand. What care I for Lord Ransing?"

Carter scowled. He was not certain he believed Woodstone; he could not imagine Ransing could "walk" into Blake's Run and simply steal Arabella away. Such a move would be unprecedented. "In his ploy for freedom, Woodstone claimed if he did not meet with Ransing by midnight of this day, the viscount would kill Lady Hellsman."

"Bella?" Law said in disbelief. "How in bloody hell…did Ransing achieve… access to Arabella?"

Carter admitted, "I remain unconvinced Ransing has Bella; I think Woodstone means to play me."

Law managed to untangle his tongue. "Yet, we cannot simply ignore the possibility."

Carter argued, "Ransing would not dare…"

"To violate or to kill my wife!" Law exclaimed incredulously. "The man planned to ruin my future by stealing Triton from my stables. He married Miss Dryburgh because the viscount thought I would claim the woman. And do not forget Bella had a hand in turning Ransing's manipulations to folly. Personally, I find the viscount quite capable of the ultimate revenge, especially if Charleton's earlier disclosure proves true. Ransing would have little reason not to complete another crime."

Blakehell grunted, "You must hurry. Lady Hellsman carries the title's future."

Kerrington encouraged, "Charleton, Mrs. Warren, and I will see to the baron. You must finish this, Lowery. Close out the investigation, which could assure you of your future with the Home Office, and settle this feud forever."

Mrs. Warren laid her hand gently upon Carter's arm, and the customarily unsettling tension sparked between them. "Much of what I have overheard makes little sense," she began. "But Lord Worthing is correct: You are the answer to all this chaos. I promise my best care for Baron Blakehell, and I charge you to offer the same for Lady Arabella."

He would dance through fire for this woman. "Of course, we all have our duties," he said regrettably. All Carter wanted was a few minutes alone with Lucinda Warren before she slipped from his life forever. Reluctantly, he instructed his brother, "Assist me with hoisting Woodstone onto a horse, Law. I suppose Ransing has retreated to his property in Dove Dale."

Godown appeared with the wagon's horses. "Beauchamp, likely has a broken leg, but your steward managed to follow his escaped prisoners. He and Lexford have everything in hand."

"Then we have use of your special skills," Carter said knowingly. "We have another lady to rescue. I will explain as we ride."

Godown smirked, "I am beginning to think you see me as being cut from the same cloth as Thornhill."

Lucinda handed Carter the reins for the horse upon which they had tied Woodstone. "You are to return safely to your father, Sir," she said softly.

Carter leaned down to speak to her ears only. "Promise me you will remain at Blake's Run until we can speak privately."

"I am at the earl's disposal," she protested. "I can offer no such promises." The lady looked to where Charleton fed Blakehell small sips of brandy. "Lord Charleton means for me to know a home. It has been six years since I have experienced such devotion."

Carter knew her correct: When thrust into the worst of circumstances, Lucinda Warren had responded with courage and resolve. She deserved time to be pampered by a doting uncle. He nodded curtly to release her. "My father is not much of a drinker: The baron abstains beyond what is served with his meals," he cautioned. He would act the role of gentleman. Carter would withdraw; he would accept the impossible: He would move on with his life.

"Then I should return to the baron's side," she said dutifully. "Know care, Sir Carter."

"And you, as well, Mrs. Warren." With that, he kicked his horse's flanks. He did look back to see her hand rise in a final farewell. Deep in the pit of Carter's stomach was the sinking feeling of dread: He had just ridden away again from the woman he loved. Surprisingly, the realization he loved Lucinda Warren did not scare him half as much as what he thought it might. In reality, the idea felt "right"–more right than anything else he had ever known. However, his future was named: He would continue to concentrate on his goals within the Home Office and forget his aspirations of calling Lucinda Warren "wife."

Lucinda reluctantly returned to Baron Blakehell's side. Raw and unadulterated grief filled her heart: There had been no time for her to express her gratitude to Sir Carter for risking everything to save her. She still held no idea of how Sir

Carter had come to ride with Lord Hellsman and the earl. It seemed whenever she knew trouble, the baronet appeared in her life.

"I am quite capable when it comes to gunshot wounds," Lord Worthing announced. He returned her gaze. "It comes from many years in service to England while on foreign shores."

Lucinda assured, "I am glad for the assistance." She rinsed her hands in a bit of the brandy before using her fingertips to probe the opening more thoroughly. "It appears the volley has passed through the baron's shoulder and out his upper arm." She touched a particularly sensitive spot, and Blakehell grimaced. "A sliver of shrapnel is lodged against the collar bone. Where is the closest village where we might find a surgeon?"

Kerrington shook off her unspoken suggestion. "The closest surgeon, to my knowledge, is in Hayfield."

"I fear for infection if the metal is not removed efficiently," Lucinda whispered.

Lord Worthing asked in concern, "Do we have the means to remove it?"

Lucinda glanced about them. "The conditions are not ideal. If we had a fire where we might heat water…"

Worthing assured, "Sir Carter would not have left his father in your care if he did not believe in your ability to persevere."

"There was the need to rescue Lady Arabella."

"Sir Carter holds the reputation for thwarting the baron's plans," Worthing confided. Lucinda wondered why she had not previously recognized the source of the pain so often found in Sir Carter's voice. In his eyes, there was always the mask to disguise the agony of guilt–that is unless he looked upon her. They held a great passion in those few stolen moments, and such a thought brought a flood of exquisite yearning to Lucinda's heart.

She accepted Viscount Worthing's explanation without comment. "Then we should not disappoint the baronet."

Within minutes, she cut the skin of the baron's shoulder, opening the wound further and permitting it to bleed again. The blood would assist in cleansing the injury. It was not exceptionally deep, and, thankfully, Mr. Woodstone had not been an accurate shot, but Lucinda recognized the seriousness of the situation. She had witnessed many men die from lesser wounds, and the conditions were far from ideal. In addition, Baron Blakehell had passed the prime of his life. "I can see the tip," she announced. "I will require your assistance, Lord Worthing."

The viscount adjusted his position, keeping Blakehell's upper arm braced under his leg. "Tell me what you require."

"Dip your knife in the brandy and then use it to flay open the skin while I cut around the metal to loosen it." She glanced to the pain contracting the baron's countenance. "We must work quickly."

"I am at your disposal, Ma'am." Lord Worthing followed her instructions perfectly, and Lucinda wondered if he should not have been the one cutting into Blakehell's flesh.

Slowly and meticulously, she cut the exposed tissue to free the piece of metal. Finally, she caught the tip between her index finger and thumb. Gently lifting upward, Lucinda released the shrapnel from the skin. Holding it tightly in her grasp, she slipped it into a pocket in her day dress. "Hand me the bandages," she instructed. Her uncle passed the rolled strips of muslin to her. Lucinda cut a section from the end of one roll and folded it several times to pack the opening and to staunch the blood flow. Next, she drizzled more of the brandy over the wound. "Permit me to wrap the baron's shoulder so he cannot move it, and then we should set a course for Blake's Run."

"I will see to the horses and the wagon," Kerrington announced as he stood. Lucinda thought it miraculous Sir Carter's associates—all men of the aristocracy—possessed skills of the common man. She had seen more than one aristocratic military officer without even the ability to mount his steed unless his batman gave him a boost.

"Thank you, Ma'am," the baron said through dry lips.

Lucinda nodded her acceptance. "Rest now, Baron. We shall return you to the baroness's care as quickly as possible." Lucinda stood and rotated her shoulders. Every muscle in her body ached. "I mean to find a private setting," she whispered to the earl.

"Not too far, my Dear," he warned.

Lucinda smiled easily at the man—her natural father. He was truly a good man. She had lost everyone for whom she cared, and it was wonderful to discover Lord Charleton would risk everything for her. "Just a moment to compose my emotions," she said lamely. She squeezed the earl's hand and wandered off into the wood line. Dutifully, Lucinda tended to her personal needs and straightened her clothing. It had been nearly four and twenty hours since she had agreed to share the colonel's papers with her uncle. In that short time, her life had taken another drastic turn.

She reluctantly admitted in hindsight, Matthew Warren's selfish nature had thickened into a carapace, no longer easily disguised. Her late husband had taken what he wanted with no consideration for others. Captain Warren was not half the man Sir Carter Lowery was. "Even when he was nothing more than a young Lieutenant Lowery, the baronet walked with confidence. He is a natural leader. Even his older, titled associates bow to the baronet's wishes." And despite her best efforts, Lucinda had come to adore the man's customarily mocking smile.

"The baronet is a dangerous man," she whispered a chastisement. "Dangerous to any woman's heart." She was too aware of him, and Lucinda feared one day she would succumb to his charms. "And then where shall I be? Sir Carter can never choose me. Even with Lord Charleton's approval, I am steeped in scandal. It is best for me to accept my 'uncle's' kindness and carve out a life of caring for the earl and possibly for Simon. It shall be enough—more than for which I could have hoped when I departed Brussels." Yet, her acknowledgement of the truth did little to allay her despair. What Lucinda feared most was how her heart would burst from no longer knowing the baronet.

From the Peaks to Dove Dale was another long, exhausting ride, and Carter could no longer feel his legs. Numbness had invaded every pore of his being. It had been a very silent journey. Law's desire to secure his wife's safety had driven Carter's brother to distraction.

"It is the way of men," the marquis had said sagely. "I would have ridden from one shore to another if in doing so it would have returned Grace to me. A man's physical comforts are nothing without a woman to share them." In January, the marquis had foolishly driven his wife from his home in a jealous rage, and Lord Godown had spent nearly three months searching for the former Grace Nelson. It had been quite the humiliation. The infamous Marquis of Godown had married the destitute sister of Baron Nelson, a man on the brink of bankruptcy.

"What if a woman's reputation is so riddled with scandal she becomes an encumbrance?" Carter had asked tentatively.

The marquis scowled—a rueful grimace. "You must recall how I tormented myself and all those within earshot over what I righteously believed to be Lady Godown's betrayal. Yet, even as I openly listed Grace's supposed faults, I knew I would never know happiness without her. A bit of outrage will die away with time, but there will never be another Grace. She is my other half."

Carter paused, marshalling his thoughts of Lucinda Warren into articulate images. "Then you hold no regrets?"

Godown shook his head in amusement. "Do you know with a simple smile, my wife can drive away my most foul mood? That Lady Godown can turn that simple smile into a seductive proposal? I have no means of knowing how she has the ability to dispel gloom and fill my house with cheer, but she does. My only regret is Grace will sleep alone in our bed this night and my son will not know his father's nightly kiss for the first time in his short life. Everything I require in life can be found at Gossling Hill."

Law joined them as they dismounted. "What should we do with Woodstone?"

"Tie him to a tree, and keep the gag on him. We do not want him sounding an alarm."

Godown said, "I will see to our prisoner. It will give you time to develop a plan, Lowery."

Carter nodded his appreciation. He and Law watched the manor for movement. "Assuming Woodstone has not led us on a fool's task, we must discover where Ransing holds Arabella," he whispered.

Law confessed coldly, "I hope Woodstone speaks with two tongues for if not, I mean to kill Viscount Ransing this evening."

Carter had never heard his brother speak with such icy tones. They studied the drive. It wound its way through the woodland. "We must devise a plan to tease Ransing and his men from the house," he thought aloud. "A rider-less horse, perhaps. Or a fire in the stable."

"How would a rider-less horse draw the viscount from the manor?" Law asked with a touch of impatience.

"If we remove the saddle, it will appear the horse has lost its way and simply seeks a stall and hay. As a horseman, I think Ransing will respond. In addition, the ploy will provide us with a better idea of how many men we face."

"What of Lord Godown?" Law remarked sourly.

A determined smile found a home on Carter's lips. "His Lordship possesses unique skills. Lord Godown can access the manor and search it for Lady Hellsman."

Law took a deep breath and raised his gaze to meet Carter's. "There is so much of your life and that of your associates of which I was never privy. I am quite discomposed by the reality."

"Pennington brought together a group of men whose talents complemented those of the others. It was Pennington's genius, not mine."

"And what is your particular skill, Carter?"

Carter frowned, "I am not convinced I possess any—certainly none as developed as Godown's stealth or Berwick's ability to scale all sorts of heights."

An unspoken understanding passed between them. "Design the plan to recover my wife. I await your suggestions."

"It is agreed?" Carter asked.

"Permit me a quarter hour to enter the house," the marquis instructed. "If I discover the lady, I will deliver the signal."

"What signal?" Law demanded.

"Lowery knows the signal," Godown said with a smirk before strolling away toward the back of the manor.

The marquis's nonchalance stole Law's words from his lips. If the situation had not been so dire, Carter would have laughed. Instead, his gaze followed his friend's shoulder line. "Godown really is quite remarkable at intrigue," he said to reassure his brother. "We often called him the 'Ghost.' The marquis will not fail us." Law nodded curtly. "It is time I prepare the fire and the horse." They had decided to set fire to the dried hay in the barn to attract the servants from the manor. If that did not produce Ransing, then they would send in the unsaddled horse.

"Ransing will think the two events in such close proximity cannot be coincidental," Law argued.

Carter agreed, "And the viscount will panic. He will expect a full assault, and to protect himself, he will retrieve his bargaining tool in the form of Lady Arabella."

"You will place Bella in more danger!"

"If she is within, your wife is already in peril. We cannot save Bella if we cannot find her. We will force Ransing to deliver her to us."

Chapter Twenty-Two

Carter watched the manor for either the marquis's signal or his reappearance. When neither came, he worked his way toward the barn and exercise ring. By his estimate, it was eleven of the clock, but even so, several of Lord Ransing's men remained awake. Three played cards about a makeshift table inside the barn's open door, while a fourth sat upon a low bench watching the curve of the drive. *Perhaps Woodstone had not spoken an untruth. Mayhap the servant expected the aristocrat's return.*

On silent feet, Carter made his way along the back of the structure. Slipping into a side door, he held for several elongated seconds before moving forward. His eyes quickly adjusted to the filtered darkness, and he climbed the lone ladder to the loft. It was odd: as a child, Carter had always loved playing in the Blake's Run loft. It had made him feel invincible to look out upon his father's land. To stand above those performing their duties below. To fulfill his mother's promise of his overseeing all their lives. The memory was a good one, one he would like to share with his own children some day.

Of course, the thought of children brought the image of Lucinda Warren's sweet countenance. He wondered upon the look of their children: He was tall compared to many Englishmen, while the lady was quite petite. Carter chuckled with the prospect of short sons and Amazon daughters. It would be justice for a man of his stature to have daughters similar to his middle sister, Maria, who was tall and statuesque. As long as they were healthy, he would know satisfaction.

The noise of someone moving about below reminded Carter of his mission. He waited for the sound to recede before he edged slowly forward. His nerves vibrated, as taut as plucked strings. Careful not to be heard by the card players, Carter knelt to gather the dry straw into a mound. Removing the flint and striking block from an inside pocket, he rubbed the two hard against each other seeking a spark. With a flash of light, the fire flared, and Carter quickly used several sticks of straw to capture the flame. Shoving the sticks into the gathered straw, he sat upon his heels to watch the flames catch first one straw strand and then another. Satisfied the fire would easily spread upon its own, he gathered the striking block and returned it to his pocket.

Standing slowly, Carter examined his work once more. It would not take long before the loft would be engulfed in smoke and fire. Turning his back on his work, Carter edged toward the opening, which held the ladder. He would be descending into the darkness. He set his gun's trigger and lowered his weight upon the ladder's upper rung.

Step by step, he moved cautiously into the darkness. Above him, Carter could smell the smoke filling the loft and see the pale glow of the fire consuming more of the barn's contents. He had reached the last rung before a sound off to his left froze him in place. A sinister growl warned Carter one of the estate's dogs had discovered his intrusion. Normally, Carter would have cautiously knelt to extend his hand to the animal so the dog could smell it and find him non-confrontational. But this was not a "normal" situation. He could not call the animal over and make friends. Although he could not see it clearly in the poorly lit barn, Carter could estimate the size of the dog as being perhaps four stone.

Slowly, he placed the toe of one boot on the packed earth before set-ting his weight flat upon the ball of his foot. His movement brought another warning growl from the dog, along with a barring of the animal's teeth. Carter bit back the urge to say, "Easy, Boy." He must remain quiet or risk drawing attention. Keeping the animal in sight, he stepped from the rung to stand alert. As casually as his frayed nerves permitted, he edged toward the still open side door. Although he pretended to ignore the dog's warnings, Carter kept his gun pointed at the animal. It would pain him to kill the dog, which only acted from instinct; but Carter would choose Bella's life over the animal's.

At a safe distance, the dog trailed behind him, but Carter reached the side door and slipped into the night. Purposely, he closed and locked the door to keep the animal within. He heard it whine and scratch at the door, but Carter had made his escape. Crouching low, he ran bent over toward the cover of the tree line. Reaching the privacy of a stand of oaks, he permitted himself a moment to take stock of his work. He could recognize the glow from the fire had grown more noticeable, and even from the distance, the odor of burning wood and hay could be detected. It would not be long before those inside would sound an alarm, and Carter's plan would either know fruition or failure.

As he made his way through the woods to rejoin his brother, Carter wondered upon how things had progressed at Blake's Run. He had no doubt between James Kerrington and Mrs. Warren's efforts, Blakehell had survived. He wished he could have been there to comfort his mother when the baroness discovered the peril her husband had encountered. And Carter wished personally to know if Mrs. Warren had suffered beyond the obvious. There had been no time to speak to the woman in confidence. In addition, he required time to examine his father's actions. The baron had reacted in a manner, which Carter had not anticipated. It frustrated him to know somehow he had misinterpreted his father's motives. It was not like him. Carter was known for his analytical skills, and he had misjudged one of the most influential people in his life. When this madness knew an end, he and the baron would be long overdue for a father-son encounter. Carter dreaded the likely confrontation. He had always kept his own counsel when it came to the baron, but, obviously, he had erred in his estimation of Niall Lowery.

"How much longer?" Law asked anxiously.

Carter knelt beside his brother. "Tolerance is not easy, but I must plead your patience. I am certain the marquis has placed himself in a position to rescue Arabella when the fire draws the estate into action."

Law did not turn his head. His eyes remained on the manor's dark windows. "It should be I who saves Bella."

Carter placed a comforting hand on Law's shoulder. "I know not your despair, but I do know your intelligence. You want what is best for your wife, and in this matter, Lord Godown is the best choice. He has received specialized training in extracting others from difficult situations. Lady Arabella's chances of escape have greatly increased simply from the marquis's involvement."

Law's scowl deepened. "For the immediate future, I bow to your advice," he said grudgingly.

"Fire!" The alarm sounded. "Fire!" They watched as one of the card players rushed to take up a metal bell to warn the others.

"It is nearly time," Lord Ransing said on a taunt.

Despite her desire not to permit the viscount his satisfaction, Bella could not stifle the words quickly enough. "Time for what?"

"For you to die," Ransing announced with a smirk. "It will be a shame for you to suffer because of Hellsman's folly, but such is the way of men. Women are indispensable."

Bella bit back the panic rushing to her throat. "Is that how you view my cousin, Lord Ransing? As indispensable?"

Ransing stretched out his legs and sipped his claret. "Lady Ransing is the lesser choice," he declared. "It is another manipulation I can place at your husband's feet. He and the baronet led me to believe Hellsman meant to make Dryburgh's daughter his own."

Bella knew it was not wise to rile Lord Ransing, but she would not tolerate the viscount's disparaging either Annalee or Lawrence. "If I recall, you practiced your own exploitations, my Lord."

"If I had known of Hellsman's interest in your assets," he said as he seductively surveyed Bella's curves, "I would have called upon you instead."

She hid the shiver of disgust racing down her spine. Bella said defiantly, "I would never have accepted your attentions. After all, I had knowledge of the depth of your vengeance."

Ransing made no effort to apologize for his behavior. "It pleases me to know I left my mark on your back. I imagine taming a woman with your spirit would be most satisfying." His eyes raked her figure again. "Perhaps I will have my way with you before I kill you. Anything would be better than begetting your cousin with an heir. I have never known a woman so stiffly unresponsive."

Bella could easily imagine the degradation her cousin suffered at the viscount's hands. She had been fortunate to escape such a fate. "Perhaps Annalee requires a bit of tenderness," she protested.

"Mayhap I should consider using my whip upon Lady Ransing," he baldly countered.

Before Bella could respond, a persistent tapping at the door interrupted her thoughts. "Come," Ransing called lazily.

The door swung wide to reveal the same servant who had assisted the viscount with her abduction. "Pardon, my Lord," he said anxiously, but word has come from the stables. The barn is on fire."

Ransing shoved to his feet. "I am surrounded by idiots! If I have told Stoy once I had told him a hundred times, I will not tolerate his men smoking where we store the hay and the wool." He jerked his waistcoat into place. "Do we have enough men to fight the fire?"

"You should decide for yourself, my Lord," the servant said judiciously.

"If I hired a deaf mute, would he be more responsive to my needs? I cannot imagine him to be less so than you, Styl."

The servant bowed again. "As you say, my Lord." Bella admired the man for diffusing Lord Ransing's temper. She imagined the viscount's man had had a multitude of experience in doing so.

"Stay with the lady," Ransing ordered as he strode from the room. With the viscount's exit, Bella breathed easier. She thought possibly, the fire indicated her husband or Sir Carter had arrived.

"Would it be acceptable if I had a small glass of the viscount's claret?"

His eyes sparkling with mischief, the man known as Styl exclaimed, "I hold no objections, Ma'am! In fact, I mean to join you." He poured the wine into a short glass and took a swig and then topped it off. He poured a second glass and handed it to Bella.

She took a sip as Mr. Styl slugged down the liquid. "Is the manor in danger from the fire?" Bella asked innocently.

"Not likely," Styl assured. He strolled casually toward the open door. "The barn is set well behind the house," he said cockily. "In fact, there is no one near. No one to disturb us."

Bella's breath hitched in fear. "Lord Ransing would frown upon your assuming liberties," she dared.

"I will tell the viscount you thought to escape," he said with confidence. "Moreover, I know too many of Lord Ransing's secrets for His Lordship to stay angry with me." He reached for the door to close it.

Bella watched him carefully in anticipation of the man's next move. She chastised herself for having felt safer with Lord Ransing's servant. He had appeared quite innocent upon his entrance, but she now realized her error. "You must know, Sir, I shall fight you with every ounce of strength I possess."

"Your efforts will not be necessary, Lady Hellsman." A baritone voice in the shadows materialized in the form of the Marquis of Godown. Bella's knees buckled in relief as Lord Godown jammed a gun to the back of Mr. Styl's head. "Please give me a reason to pull this trigger," the marquis said sinisterly.

Styl raised his hands slowly. "I am your servant, Sir."

Lord Godown warned, "I have no need of a Janus in my service." He prodded the man forward. "Lady Arabella, if you would assist me."

"Certainly, my Lord. What do you require?"

"Bring me the tasseled ties about the drapes and be quick about it," he ordered.

Bella raced to do his biding. When she returned to his side, Lord Godown handed her the gun. "Do not hesitate to use it," he said softly, and Bella nodded her agreement. The marquis quickly used the ties to hobble Styl's legs and to wrench the servant's arms behind his back.

"Lord Ransing will hunt you down," Style boldly declared, his speech peppered with colorful language.

"Tell your master I look forward to the acquaintance." With that pronouncement, Lord Godown retrieved his gun from Bella's grasp and used it to strike Styl across the back of his head. Ransing's servant collapsed face first upon the Persian carpet. "Come along, Lady Hellsman," he said as he captured her hand. "Your husband awaits you in the woods."

It had taken their small party several hours to reach Blake's Run. Lucinda had ridden in the back of the wagon, tending to Baron Blakehell and Mr. Beauchamp. Her uncle and Lord Lexford had ridden ahead, leading the two prisoners, who were tied to their saddles; therefore, when Lord Worthing turned the wagon into the entrance circle, the baron's household awaited their master's return. The baroness stood wringing her hands while groomsmen and footmen ran along side the wagon. Lord Worthing brought the wagon to a halt and jumped down to assist Lucinda from the back.

"Oh, my Dear," Lady Blakehell exclaimed as she caught Lucinda up in a tight embrace. "How may I ever thank you? Lord Charleton has shared how brave you were."

In a daze, Lucinda asked, "Has someone sought a surgeon? The baron shall require more than I could provide him."

Her uncle appeared at her side. "A groom has gone for the magistrate and the surgeon. You must come with me; Lady Blakehell will see to the baron." He slipped his arm about her waist, and Lucinda gave herself up to the comfort of his concern. "You require tender care, and I mean to see to your recovery."

"You, too, Sir. You should find your bed and a much needed rest," she murmured.

"After you are safe within," Charleton encouraged her forward.

Lucinda glanced over her shoulder to where Lady Blakehell hovered over her husband. "Is there any word from Sir Carter?"

Charleton followed her gaze. He whispered close to her ear. "It is a good sign that Hellsman, Godown, and Sir Carter believed Woodstone. Lady Hellsman disappeared earlier today. Lord Lexford and I arrived to find a household in complete chaos. The baron's return will focus the Blakehell staff and the baroness on the immediate future. It will provide the gentlemen with time to perform their duties."

With an expression of impatience, Lucinda said, "Sir Carter's investigation has brought tragedy to his family. The baronet will not rest until he rights this wrong."

The earl's hand stilled their progress on the entrance steps. He directed her from the activity. "Although I have no desire to bring you more pain, there is something of import of which you should be aware."

Lucinda's heart beat agonizingly fast. "I am not certain I am strong enough for more intrigue."

The earl caressed her cheek, and Lucinda leaned into his loving touch. It was quite surreal to look into Gerhard Rightnour's eyes. She saw her father's countenance, and the lines blurred. She was determined to think of the man as her uncle—not to betray Roderick Rightnour's devotion—but as she looked upon the earl, the word "father" filled her mind. "I would postpone saddling you with more responsibility if it were possible. As your dearest family, I would gladly shoulder all your troubles; yet, information regarding Captain Warren has surfaced."

Lucinda clung to his thick fingers, so like those of the colonel's. She shut her eyes and drew in a deep breath. "Tell me quick."

She did not miss how Charleton's lips tightened in self-chastisement. "In my foolish need to protect you, I have presented you a disservice, one for which I must beg your forgiveness." The earl swallowed hard and shifted his shoulders in that characteristic slant, which spoke of his resolve. Lucinda found it odd she had come to know Charleton so quickly. "When you stormed from my rooms, I broke my promise to you. I continued to read Roderick's papers. Please believe me, I meant only to shelter you. I feared my brother's papers held other secrets, which would bring you more anguish. I could not bear the pain upon your lovely countenance."

Lucinda paused, shepherding her thoughts. "I am not angry, Sir. It is strange to have someone who wishes only my benefit, but I am pleased by your concerns. However, I plead for you to share what you have discovered of Captain Warren."

The earl nodded curtly. She admired how he never denied his responsibilities. "Roderick speaks of discovering how Mr. Warren had come to be involved with a group of unscrupulous men. The baronet's investigation has revealed Cyrus Woodstone served as a purveyor of European artwork to English collectors. My brother's papers show Captain Warren supplied Woodstone with many pieces."

"I knew your late husband, and I know your lover," her abductor had taunted. Lucinda shivered with dread. "Did Matthew's parents know?" Questions raced through her mind. "Why did the colonel not put a halt to Captain Warren's manipulations?"

"Because, like me, Roderick loved you. He hid the captain's perfidy to preserve your reputation."

Lucinda considered Charleton's assertion. "I thought Papa displeased with me," she confessed. "I could never understand why the colonel had turned so cold; I thought him grieving for Mama. He was oddly unrepentant of his poor opinion of Mr. Warren as an officer after my husband's untimely death. It all appears so reasonable in hindsight. Keeping Mr. Warren's secret must have eaten at Papa's soul. He was always so honorable."

The earl directed her steps to the still open door. Blakehell's men had carried the baron to his quarters, and Viscounts Lexford and Worthing waited. "We will speak more of this when we are alone," her uncle whispered.

"Lady Blakehell has asked her cook to set out a light meal," Lord Worthing indicated. "Lexford and I mean to wait for the magistrate. If Hellsman and Sir

Carter have not returned by the time we finish with the local authorities, we will follow them to Dove Dale."

God bless the servants. Lucinda glanced about the main hall. Lady Blakehell trailed her husband to his quarters, and the servants appeared quite preoccupied with their duties. "I am famished. I have not eaten since last evening. If you will excuse me, I shall make myself more presentable. Shall I ask Mr. Malcolm for rooms for you and Lord Lexford to refresh your things?"

"I have previously addressed our needs," Lord Worthing assured. "It is quite common for Derby neighbors to call on one another."

Lucinda nodded her understanding: She held no status in Blakehell's home. It was a sobering reality. She often thought her connection to Sir Carter placed her in an elevated position among the baron's household, but she was nothing more than an inconvenient guest. "Then I shall see to my ablutions."

Lord Worthing caught her arm. "May we speak privately?"

She turned to see her uncle and Lord Lexford entering the morning room. "Is something amiss, Lord Worthing?"

The viscount led her from the way of servants crisscrossing the entrance hall. He spoke softly. "I have…on our journey…I have been considering how efficiently you treated Baron Blakehell's wound. How adept you were in the crisis."

Despite wondering how to respond, Lucinda held Worthing's gaze steadily. "My mother and I often assisted the camp surgeon."

Lord Worthing's countenance was ashen, his eyes narrowed. "I do not speak of generalities, Mrs. Warren. I speak of a particular wound. Of a particular man. Of the aftermath of Waterloo."

Lucinda's cheeks reddened, but she managed to say, "I fear I do not understand, my Lord."

The viscount's shoulders stiffened, and he spoke earnestly. "Do not think you will dissuade me with mild protestations, Mrs. Warren. You were in the hospital where the military brought Lowery after the baronet replaced your father upon the battlefield. Darek Merriweather spoke of the boy who had followed Sir Carter's litter to Brussels." Lucinda's knees buckled, and Worthing caught her arm. "Sir Carter's man described how the boy had contributed to the removal of the bullet from Lowery's leg."

She thought to deny the viscount's assertions, but the words would not come. "Lieutenant Lowery had been cut down because he meant to save me from a French cavalryman. My father had perished when he protected me during the initial charge. I could not permit Lieutenant Lowery to die also. Please, you must not speak of this to the baronet."

"Lowery is unaware of your involvement?" Worthing said in incredulity. "Do you not understand the baronet has suffered for years with thoughts of having failed the boy from the battlefield? The baronet believes the boy—you—died at Waterloo."

Lucinda schooled her expression to dispassion. "If Mr. Merriweather knew of the boy at the hospital, why did Sir Carter's man not share that particular fact with his master?" she accused.

"To my knowledge, no one beyond the Realm knows of Sir Carter's personal hell."

"Not even his family?" A deep, sickening dread spread through Lucinda's veins.

Lord Worthing shook his head in denial. "No one other than those with whom he served." The implications of the viscount's assertion played heavily against her chest. "You must tell Sir Carter the truth—to release the baronet from his nightmare."

"I cannot," she protested. "It would destroy everything. Do not ask me never to know Sir Carter's benevolence again." Before she could say more, the sound of running feet upon the stairs drew her attention from the viscount.

"Ma'am! Oh, Ma'am!"

She instinctively opened her arms to Simon. The child rushed into her embrace, and Lucinda closed her eyes to the pleasure of holding the boy. "I am well," she whispered as she rocked him. She had never permitted herself to care for the boy, but somehow Simon had snuck beneath her defenses.

"I thought," he said on a watery sob. "I had lost you, too."

"I apologize, Mrs. Warren." The maid came to a stumbling halt before her. "One of the grooms told Master Simon what occurred. He has been distraught with fear."

Lucinda wiped Simon's cheeks free of the tears with the sleeve of her dress. "It is well, Sarah. I shall return Simon to the nursery after he joins the earl and me in the morning room for a late night meal."

Simon whispered loudly, "Could I not stay with you?"

Lucinda brushed the child's hair from his forehead. "Would you like that?"

"I will protect you," Simon declared.

"I could ask for no better knight," she said sweetly. "Come. You will join the earl while I freshen my things. Then we shall have a treat together."

Lord Worthing extended his hand to the boy. "I recall when my son Daniel was your age. He could eat at any hour. Let us permit the lady her privacy. I am certain Sarah will be happy to assist Mrs. Warren."

"Would you, Sarah?" Simon asked hopefully.

"It would be my honor."

Simon tugged on Lord Worthing's hand. "Come. I wish to express my gratitude to Lord Charleton. He brought Ma'am home safely."

Lord Godown led the way through the empty passageways, and Bella scurried to keep up with his long strides. "As the household has rushed to extinguish the fire Sir Carter has set, we will exit through the study. Stay close," he whispered. "Once we are outside, stay before me until we reach the woodland." He tightened his grip upon her hand. Not waiting for a response, the marquis entered the dark study and adeptly led her about the scattered furniture, and Bella marveled at his ability to see in the pitch-black room.

A brief pause announced his release of the lock, and Arabella looked behind her to what should have been a deserted hall. Instead, a dark figure filled the doorframe. In spite of her best efforts, Bella sucked in a sharp breath. She could feel the muscles of Lord Godown's back tighten. Instinctively, the marquis shoved her behind him.

"Leaving without a farewell?" Viscount Ransing sneered.

The marquis slipped his gun into Arabella's hand before he responded. "You appeared busy with more pressing matters," Godown spoke with an air of superiority.

The viscount stepped into the shadows. "I knew immediately the fire was a ruse. Of course, I thought Lord Hellsman would come for his wife in person. I should have known the future baron to be a coward. Lawrence Lowery has always permitted others to face the dangers." Only the marquis's fingers digging into her skin kept Bella silent.

"What plan have you for us?" Lord Godown demanded. While he spoke, Bella set the trigger.

The thin wall sconces kept Lord Ransing in silhouette, and Bella could not discern his facial expression or his gestures; yet, she recognized the danger. "Am I to assume you set the fire also?" A bit of doubt played in the viscount's tone.

"I possess many talents," the marquis boasted. Bella noted how Lord Godown slipped his hand into a side pocket.

Ransing chuckled. "Furtiveness is not one of them."

"Are you certain?" Lord Godown taunted. "Perhaps I have laid a trap among the furniture." He shifted his weight and for a moment Bella felt quite exposed. Then she realized he meant to draw Lord Ransing's attention from her.

Ransing stepped boldly into the room. "I will assume my chances." His arm rose to chest high, and even in the dim light, Bella could see the gun pointed at the marquis. Lord Godown had given her his weapon and left himself without a defense. The viscount cocked the gun.

Without a second thought, Bella squeezed the trigger of Lord Godown's gun. The explosion rang in her ears, while the room filled with gray smoke.

"Run!" Lord Godown ordered and shoved her through the partially opened patio door. Bella lifted her skirt and ran toward the tree line. Somewhere in the woods was her husband, and she meant to find Law. Behind her, she heard Lord Godown involved in a melee; the sound of broken glass and items being thrown about easily recognizable.

A single shot whizzed by her head, and Bella doubled her efforts. She glanced up to see Carter and Law rushing to her side. Sir Carter reached her first and caught her about the waist. He was alert to a possible assault, but no one had followed her from the house. "Stay with Law," he ordered as he shoved her into her husband's arms. "Where is Godown?"

"In the study," she called to Carter's retreating form. "The patio doors!" Then she collapsed against the man she loved.

Carter raced toward the unknown. It was a common scenario, and that familiarity gave him confidence. Two rough-looking farmers rushed him, but Carter barely noticed. He struck the first one a clasped hand blow to the man's throat, sending his assailant to his knees. The second received the heel of Carter's hand to the man's nose and then an upper cut to his chin. Both had lost their momentum, and Carter vaulted over their broken bodies to charge the incline to the balcony.

From within, he could hear the fracas. In the darkness, several men struggled. Pausing only long enough to identify Godown's recognizable form, Carter grabbed the nearest assailant about the neck and gave the man's head an opposing jerk. A loud crack announced the man's demise.

"Here!" Godown shoved another of Ransing's men in Carter's direction. Intuitively, he caught the man by the back of his hair and slammed the culprit into the wall. A loud grunt of pain said Carter had incapacitated another of Ransing's henchmen.

Turning to rejoin the fight, only Godown remained standing. "Ransing ran out when his men rushed in. He was limping from Lady Hellsman's gunfire," Godown announced. "I will settle things here. You should find Lord Ransing before he reaches the lady."

"Bella," Law pleaded, "are you injured?" His wife sobbed uncontrollably. Law's jaw tensed: He would kill Ransing for the viscount's insult to his family.

"I shot him!" she forced out on an exhalation.

Law tightened his arms about her to quell her fear. "Who? Who did you shoot?"

Bella whispered harshly, "The viscount."

"But you did not kill me, Lady Hellsman," a voice declared from the darkness.

Law strained to remain alert. He could hear the desperation in Ransing's tone and could smell the fear on Bella's skin. "It is I you seek, Ransing. Leave my wife untouched."

The viscount stepped further into the ring of moonlight, and Law noted how his enemy favored his left leg. Although he had not fully comprehended her earlier assertion, Bella had made contact. "Lady Hellsman knows of my involvement with Woodstone. I cannot leave witnesses."

Despair wrapped itself about Law's heart, each beat nearly tearing it apart. "I cannot permit you to harm my wife."

Ransing gave a hard laugh. "Then one of us will die."

Law placed Bella behind him. He had never shot anything other than a fox or a deer, and Lawrence was uncertain he could look a man in the eye and pull the trigger, but he was all that remained between Ransing and Bella's safety. Neither Carter nor Lord Godown had emerged from the house. A violent pendulum of emotions coursed through his veins. He concentrated on Lord Ransing's stature, attempting to anticipate the viscount's attack. Behind him, Arabella's soft sobs spoke of her despondency.

Law swallowed his fear. His senses sharpened as never before. Pure murder spread across Lord Ransing's countenance. Slowly, Law raised his gun. His gaze narrowed and honed. Ransing was breathing heavily, and Law noted the flicker of hatred in the viscount's eyes, which signaled his finger twitched upon the trigger. In the space of a single breath, a flare of light split the blackness, and Ransing toppled forward to kiss the dirt.

Law looked to the gun he still held tightly in his grip to find it unused and then to his right where a puff of white smoke hung upon the night's air. As the graying mist thinned, Law's eyes rested upon his younger brother. Glowing white hot, Carter's gun reflected the moonlight.

Chapter Twenty-Three

Carter had insisted that Lawrence remove Arabella to the nearest inn. He was not certain who had experienced the most shock–Arabella or Law? When he had stumbled upon the scene, Carter knew he must kill Lord Ransing. Despite his older brother's protestations, Carter had known Ransing's death would change Law. Carter had experienced more deaths than he cared to acknowledge, and in his line of work, it was a foregone conclusion; yet, each time he was forced to use extreme violence, he had to justify the loss of life. If Law had been the agent of death, Carter's older brother would have always second-guessed his actions. So, when Law paused as Ransing prepared to shoot, Carter had taken the choice from his brother: He had shot Lord Ransing in the head.

"We must send for Pennington," Godown reminded Carter of the investigation.

Carter looked upon those they had captured. "I asked Law to send for Sir Phillip Spurlock. He is the magistrate Viscount Stafford befriended near Pemberley. Sir Phillip is man I trust. He was at Blake's Run when Ransing attempted to steal Triton from Law. Sir Phillip is an honest magistrate."

Godown scowled. "You know my opinion of Viscount Stafford, but I will follow your lead in regard to Sir Phillip." The marquis's eyes narrowed. "How long do you expect it will be before we finish this investigation? I should send word to Lady Godown of my delay."

Carter shrugged noncommittally. "We are in the middle of nowhere, and it is not as if we can send one of Ransing's men with a message."

Godown's countenance was not peaceful in response. "I am warning you, Lowery, I will not have Lady Godown in a state of worry so I advise you to discover a reliable messenger, or I will be on the road to Staffordshire myself."

Carter arched an eyebrow. "If you assist me in moving the prisoners to the root cellar, then you may ride into the village and secure a messenger for Lady Godown. I require an update on Hellsman and Arabella, and if we are to remain behind until Pennington responds, we will require food while we wait."

Some three-quarters hour later, Godown had departed, leaving Carter alone with his thoughts. Before the marquis's exit, Carter had quickly scribbled a note to his parents to explain he must remain in Dove Dale until the authorities could take possession of the prisoners. He had wanted to return to Lucinda Warren's side immediately, but duty insisted he remain behind. He assumed Law would escort Bella to Blake's Run later in the day, but he wanted the baroness to know she was in his thoughts.

He wondered how long Mrs. Warren would remain in Derbyshire. He had asked her to wait for his return, but Carter knew she could not go against the earl's wishes. Reluctantly, he grudgingly admitted, "Fate has offered me another test: A personal taunt. The lady is my private temptation, and I remain uncertain as to whether I will succeed in either winning her heart or banishing Lucinda Warren from my life forever."

The viscounts had spoken to the local magistrates, making arrangements for Woodstone's men to be gaoled until governmental agents could assume custody. When Lord Worthing had tapped on her door at eight of the clock, Lucinda had had but three hours sleep; however, she welcomed the viscount's willingness to treat her as a capable woman.

"Lord Lexford and I will set a course for Dove Dale, but I wished you to know the local magistrate will call upon you this afternoon to hear your statement. I have led Mr. Ramsey to believe your abduction was a ruse to draw Blakehell's household from the manor."

Lucinda nodded her understanding. "You have spoken the truth: Lady Hellsman was always the object."

Worthing shook off her statement. "I suspect Sir Carter's enemies recognized the baronet's allegiance to you."

In spite of the worry gnawing at her composure, Lucinda said, "You shall assure Sir Carter first of my deepest gratitude for his quick thinking in saving my life and, secondly, for his devotion to my and Simon's plight."

Lord Worthing frowned deeply. "I would gladly deliver a more private message to the baronet if you wish to write one."

She wrestled with the hope, which flared in her veins. Would Sir Carter welcome an overture from her? Or would he see her as an obligation? Lucinda could not bear to claim him in duty only. The anxiety in her chest tightened. "It is best I speak only of my gratitude," she said blandly.

"As you wish, Ma'am." The viscount bowed to exit. Lucinda wished to call him back, but she loved Carter Lowery too well to saddle him with the widow of an art thief—one who had brought shame to his country and his uniform. She had made her choice. She and Simon would leave for Lancashire soon. She glanced over her shoulder to where the child slept heavily. Curled into a tight ball, he hugged a carved horse. When she had asked him of the gift, the boy had admitted Captain Warren had sent it for Simon's third birthday. Although she despised the captain's betrayal, Lucinda merited her late husband's gesture of love.

Lucinda joined Lady Blakehell in the morning room for a late mid-day meal. "Good afternoon," she said as she entered the room. "I hope your presence at table indicates Baron Blakehell is recovering nicely."

The baroness smiled that secret smile of women secure in their worlds. "The baron is snapping at everyone," she said with a satisfied smirk. "Poor Mr. Selwyn received an earful when he announced Niall must remain in bed for a week. By the by, the surgeon sang your praises. He has instructed Mr. Everett, the baron's man, on how to change the wound regularly. Now, if Mr. Selwyn would simply provide Niall a large dose of laudanum, the household could rest easier."

Lucinda sat to the lady's left. "It is my experience men are poor patients. How they respond is a matter of pride."

"So, true," the baroness said sagely. "Heaven forbid it were the male domain to deliver forth children."

Lucinda blushed with the intimate conversation. "I would imagine you correct, Baroness."

"Oh, I apologize. I had forgotten you have no experience with child bearing. As a married woman I assumed you knew of such things."

Lucinda's cheeks reddened. "I have witnessed childbirth," she confessed. To lighten the situation, she said, "I would think the world less populated if men were responsible for procreation."

The baroness spread jam on her toast. "We women are the more powerful sex. We simply allow our men the illusion of dominance."

Lucinda chuckled, "Obviously, we cannot permit males the secret of our manipulations." Although she knew nothing of the ways of strong-willed women, Lucinda enjoyed the camaraderie.

Mr. Malcolm entered to extend a silver salver. "The recent post, Ma'am."

The baroness accepted the three missives. "Thank you, Mr. Malcolm." She thumbed through the message. "Thank Heavens! This one is from Lawrence." She used her knife to break the wax. Lucinda looked on with impatience as the baroness retrieved a pair of spectacles in order to read Lawrence Lowery's message. "They have found her!" she said on a rush of air. "Lawrence says Arabella is not injured, but he means to stay another day in Dove Dale. Lady Hellsman is exhausted and is shocked by the turn of events."

Lucinda could not hide her real interest. "And what of Sir Carter?"

The baroness scanned the two-page letter. "Lawrence writes both the marquis and Carter are unharmed, with nothing more than bruised knuckles and sore jaws. Carter will remain in Dove Dale until Mr. Pennington arrives to settle the investigation." She frowned deeply. "Carter killed Lord Ransing to prevent the viscount from harming Law and Arabella." The baroness pressed the letter to her heart. "I certainly never wanted such a life for any of my children, but especially for Carter. We Lowerys sometimes forget how seriously Carter takes his role in this family. I would pray for my youngest finally to know peace. To laugh as he once did. To permit others into his life." Lady Blakehell sighed heavily. "A mother never stops worrying for her children." She refolded the letter. "I should share Lawrence's news with the baron. He was quite distraught he could not protect Arabella and Lawrence."

The baroness's unrepentant response surprised Lucinda. She did not wish to offend, but she had witnessed Sir Carter's struggle with his father, and she meant to caution the baroness. "Did not Baron Blakehell have a care for Sir Carter's fate?"

The baroness's eyebrow rose sharply. "You speak eloquently on my youngest son's behalf."

Lucinda knew she should eat her words, but she could not permit the moment to pass. If the baroness truly "dominated" her husband, it would be Baroness Blakehell who would change Sir Carter's perceptions. "I mean no offense, Ma'am," she began softly. "But Sir Carter silently suffers the mark of not knowing his father's love. As such, I do not believe Sir Carter will ever achieve the happiness you desire in his name. Anyone with an idea for detail can easily observe how your youngest son strives for the baron's attention."

Lady Blakehell appeared irate. "You have no right to criticize my husband. You have no knowledge of how the baron feels about his children."

Appreciative of the baroness's declarations, Lucinda said, "I have no desire to place my opinions against your own. I can only speak to what I have observed. Please accept my apology." The baroness's eyes filled with tears. It was hard for Lucinda to maintain her indignation in the face of such agony. "Please think on what I have shared. I only want what is best for the baronet."

Lady Blakehell dashed the lone tear from her cheek. "I should ferry Law's message to the baron. Enjoy your meal, Mrs. Warren." With that, the baroness disappeared.

Pain cut Lucinda deeply; she prayed she had not widened the wedge between her and Sir Carter's parents. "It is not as if you will ever be a part of his family," she chastised under her breath. Feeling awkward and sad, Lucinda stood to return to her quarters. She would avoid the Lowerys until it was time for her departure. Sir Carter's family might tolerate her in their lives, but they would never accept her as the baronet's future mate.

As she stepped away from the table, her eyes fell upon the two remaining posts. One was addressed to "Mr. Patrick." Her heart slammed against her chest wall. Although the letter held Sir Carter's assumed name, Lucinda knew the contents concerned her family. Surreptitiously, she slipped the letter into her pocket. Lucinda would share the letter with Lord Charleton. The earl was her family now. Her uncle would settle Simon's future. She was no longer Sir Carter Lowery's problem.

Carter looked up in relief when Worthing and Lexford rode into the entrance of Ransing's small manor, which was not much larger than a hunting lodge. Having thoroughly inspected the place, Carter suspected the late viscount had used it for trysts and gaming nights. He and Godown met the viscounts before the main steps. "How is my father?" Carter ignored the customary greetings.

"Mr. Selwyn has treated the baron's wound and expects a full recovery," Worthing explained as he dismounted. "Mrs. Warren's attention to detail saved the day; Mr. Selwyn verified the dangers of returning the baron to Blake's Run with the bullet fragment still in his shoulder. The lady demonstrated remarkable aplomb."

Carter held no doubt Mrs. Warren would excel at all she attempted. "And the lady? And Mr. Beauchamp?"

"I spoke to Mrs. Warren before we departed. The lady appeared pale, but strong of limb. She sends her gratitude for your involvement in her rescue." Carter could not hide the frown crossing his brow. He did not want the lady's gratitude; he desired her love. Worthing's mouth announced his disapproval, but his former leader spoke no more of Mrs. Warren. "The steward's leg will know several months to heal."

Carter nodded his understanding. "When did you leave Blake's Run?" Despite his disappointment at not receiving a personal message from Mrs. Warren, Carter asked, "When will Charleton set a course for Lancashire?"

Lexford said as he tied off his horse's reins. "We departed at eight. No one else was awake. It was a long night. The magistrate has taken Woodstone's accomplices into custody. As to Lord Charleton, the earl said he would not depart until his niece was capable of traveling." Carter's expression sobered. Worthing had just professed Mrs. Warren's stable health. She would likely leave Blake's Run before he could return. The thought brought another round of frustration.

Schooling his expression, Carter assumed a businesslike slant to his shoulders. "We have captured several of Lord Ransing's men. I suspect many did not know of their master's tendency for larceny."

"And the viscount?" Worthing asked cautiously.

"Dead," Godown responded. "Lady Hellsman wounded him in the leg before Lowery thwarted the viscount's attempt to end Hellsman's and Lady Arabella's lives. I was a witness. Sir Carter possessed no other option."

Carter knew the marquis had just perjured himself. Godown was in the house with the other prisoners when Carter confronted Ransing, but his friend meant to protect Carter from censure. He had killed a peer of the aristocracy, a feat, which could be punishable by law. That particular fact had played into Carter's decision to keep Law from delivering the fatal blow to the viscount. Carter prayed his governmental position would protect him. Otherwise, he would be living on the Continent in the near future. "There are several paintings in the attic, which I suspect are part of those removed from Spain."

Worthing said, "We should decide what we mean to share with Pennington and how we might spin this tale upon its head to protect your reputation and that of your family, as well as Lord Charleton's niece."

Carter led the way into the house. It was comforting to know these powerful men meant to keep him safe. He was blessed to have their allegiance. Not many men could claim such devotion.

Lucinda tapped upon her uncle's door and was pleased he was awake and enjoying a tray in his room. "Come in, my Dear," he called when Mr. Priest opened the door to her. "I was just going to come looking for you. How is the boy?"

"Simon slept soundly. I woke him earlier and returned him to the nursery. I did not want Simon to sleep the day away and then be awake all night."

"Having one's days and nights confused is difficult to correct." He motioned her to a nearby chair. "Is there any word on Blakehell?"

"The baroness reports her husband will recover quickly, assuming they can stave off infection."

"Excellent," the earl declared. "I am very proud of you, my Dear."

Lucinda shared, "The baroness received word from Lord Hellsman. He, the baronet, and the marquis rescued Lady Arabella, but Sir Carter killed Lord Ransing in the chaos."

The earl's expression darkened. "I hate to know the baronet has stumbled into a scandal. It will be difficult to avoid the gossip."

Lucinda's eyes filled with wariness. "The scandal will taint your door also, Sir. If you wish to withdraw your protection, I shall understand."

The earl peered at her with irritation. "I will not hear such protestations. You are my dearest girl. Roderick would never have abandoned you, and neither will I."

Lucinda looked away before her tears could betray her. She had become quite the watering pot of late. With a great effort, she presented her uncle a tremulous smile. "I must plead for your assistance, Uncle." Lucinda reached for the letter. "This came for Sir Carter. It bears the directions the baronet gave when we sought news of Simon's family. Would you do me the favor of reading it?"

"Would you not wish to read it first?' He accepted the letter, but made no move to open it.

Lucinda shook off his suggestion. "I have been anxious to be free of Simon for nearly seven months, but now that the possibility exists of his leaving, I find I would miss him sorely."

Charleton nodded curtly. "Then permit me to be your emissary." He chipped the sealing wax from the closure and unfolded the single page. Lucinda bit her bottom lip in anxious anticipation. "This is from a Mr. Cohen."

"That is the man Sir Carter and I met in Manchester," she explained. "He is a respected member of the Jewish community. The baronet told Cohen we found a babe in one of the Spanish villages, and we had assumed responsibility for the boy."

Her uncle nodded absent-mindedly as he read the message. "Sir Carter honestly shared his interaction with Mr. Cohen when I questioned him in Manchester."

"Has Cohen found Simon's mother?" she asked in exasperation. The not knowing was worst than the knowing.

Her uncle held the letter while he paraphrased. "Mr. Cohen believes he has located Simon's grandparents. He is concerned because the Cottos' story does not coincide with the one the baronet has shared; yet, Cohen expresses confidence in his find. He asks Mr. and Miss Patrick to meet him on Monday at the same inn as previously. He will bring the boy's grandparents with him."

"This is Friday," Lucinda reasoned. "Should we travel tomorrow or Monday?"

The earl motioned Mr. Priest to fetch paper and ink. "I will write to Cohen immediately and arrange a late afternoon meeting. I prefer not to travel on the Sabbath."

Lucinda could not hide the disappointment. "Then we will remain at Blake's Run for two more days."

The earl's eyebrow rose in question. "I thought you would wish to wait for Sir Carter's return—to assure yourself of the baronet's health."

"I would," she admitted reluctantly. "I am just anxious to begin my new life as your niece."

"You are already my family," he said lovingly. "There is no waiting necessary."

"We are agreed." Worthing controlled the conversation, but it had been Carter's ideas upon which they had settled. "We cannot keep Mrs. Warren's name from the investigation, but we will tell everyone the earl discovered Colonel Rightnour's suspicions regarding his daughter's husband. When Charleton shared the colonel's private papers with his niece, Mrs. Warren turned over the information to Lowery."

"It is good to bury a lie deeply within the truth," Godown observed. "But we should send word to Charleton to secure any papers which could prove otherwise."

Carter nodded his agreement. "I will see to it. As Law will not return to Blake's Run until tomorrow, I will ask him to ferry the message to Charleton."

Lexford played with the stem of his glass. "We must locate more of the paintings. Even if we are correct about the two in the attic, we must prove there are more pieces in question. It is necessary to portray Ransing as the vile creature he was."

"It goes to say we must search the viscount's residence in Staffordshire, as well as his father's manor in Cheshire," Godown reasoned. "I could oversee the Staffordshire search and Lexford the one in Cheshire."

Carter rationalized, "We must also search Woodstone's property in Oxford and Monroe's in Cornwall. It would be best if we organized the searches, coordinating them to occur on the same day and time. Doing so would prevent word spreading and providing a warning to the others."

Lexford added, "We should look also into the minor estates. If I had stolen artwork, I would hide it in a less obvious place."

Godown reasoned, "I am certain Pennington will be aware of all the appropriate properties."

Worthing pursued the topic further. "What of Captain Warren? He must have had an accomplice in England. Someone beyond Cyrus Woodstone."

Worthing's words circled in a loop in Carter's mind. *Where would Warren hide artwork? Who would he trust not to betray him?* "I know," he said excitedly. "His parents' home in Devon. When Mrs. Warren returned to England, her husband's family turned her away, claiming their grief too severe. They would not admit her into their home."

"Sounds as if the Warrens had something to hide," Lexford observed.

Kerrington agreed. "Did you not say Monroe held connections to those in Devon? Perhaps there are several sites in close proximity."

A renewed wave of protectiveness caught Carter off guard. "I wish to lead the investigation into the Warrens," he declared. "It would do me well to right the wrong they presented to Mrs. Warren."

On Saturday, Lord and Lady Hellsman returned to Blake's Run, but Sir Carter did not, and Lucinda knew instant disappointment. She had celebrated Arabella Lowery's arrival for Lady Hellsman remained Lucinda's dearest friend. "It was terrible," Bella confessed as Lucinda assisted her friend into a clean dress. "I was certain Lord Ransing would kill Hellsman, but Carter completed the deed before Lawrence could react.

Lucinda tied Bella's laces. "How did Lord Hellsman respond to his brother's sacrifice?" Lucinda asked tentatively.

In the mirror's reflection, Bella could observe Arabella's pronounced frown. "Lawrence knew shock. I believe my husband felt robbed of his manhood; Hellsman meant to save me, but Lord Godown freed me, and Carter ended Lord Ransing's threats."

Lucinda ventured, "I would imagine Sir Carter meant to spare his brother the pain of knowing death first hand."

Bella nodded knowingly. "I have said the same to Hellsman. My husband's brother is a man built to protect those he affects. I am certain there will be less controversy with Carter's position than if Lawrence delivered the deadly blow. My husband and the viscount held a long history of animosity."

"Lord Hellsman's reputation could suffer," Lucinda reasoned. She despised how her late husband's perfidy had tainted the lives of the Lowerys. The thought added to her resolve to place Sir Carter from her life. *But never from your heart*, she silently chastised.

Bella straightened the seams of her dress. "We shall weather whatever comes our way." She turned to face Lucinda. "Am I presentable enough to call upon the baron?"

Lucinda smiled weakly. "You are exquisite, but I am certain Baron Blakehell would easily have accepted the smudges on your other gown. The baron has worried for your return."

"I carry the title's heir," Arabella said petulantly, "but my father in marriage's concern is a welcomed step in bringing the family together." She squeezed Lucinda's hand. "I shall see you at supper. I am most anxious to learn more of your rescue and your bravery."

On Monday, Lucinda and Lord Charleton made their farewells as the baroness and the Hellsmans looked on. A message had come from Sir Carter, but Lucinda was not privy to its contents. It was meant for the baroness only. She knew it was improper for him to write to her, especially when she kept company with his family, but a part of her had wished for a small gesture upon which to hang her hopes. Despite recognizing how well they would not suit, Lucinda could not forget Carter Lowery.

"We should be in Manchester within the hour," Lord Charleton announced.

Lucinda placed her wayward thoughts away on a mental shelf. "It shall be wonderful to have this matter settled." She stroked Simon's hair. The boy had tired of asking questions of her and the earl and had settled upon the bench seat beside her for a nap.

"The boy could remain with us," Charleton suggested.

Lucinda's hand stilled. "I appreciate your willingness to assume Simon's care, but I cannot help but to think the boy should be with his family."

"Family is important," Charleton agreed. "And I understand the pain of losing those important in one's life."

"As do I," she said softly. "I imagine Simon's grandparents most anxious to be reunited with their daughter's child."

Chapter Twenty-Four

Sir Phillip had arrived on Friday and Pennington on Saturday. The magistrate agreed they could not contact Ransing's family until Pennington could organize the governmental counter raids. Carter had been pleased the magistrate had acted so sensibly. Because of the smell of decay, which had already set it, they had wrapped Ransing's body, as well as the two other men who had lost their lives that evening, in several sheets and placed them in the barn.

With the pressing need for secrecy, they also agreed to keep Ransing's associates imprisoned at the viscount's estate. The fewer people who knew of their plans the better. "At eight of the clock on Wednesday," Pennington confirmed. The Realm's leader had thought the coordinated raids an excellent idea and had praised Carter's ingenuity.

"We should depart," Godown reasoned. "If we tarry too long, I suspect the locals will begin to question our presence in the area."

Pennington agreed, "Henderson and Van Dyke will escort the prisoners to London. I will send one of our men to take possession of Woodstone's associates later in the week. From what Lexford and Worthing have shared, I suspect the two who assisted with Mrs. Warren's abduction were nothing more than a pair of unemployed lackeys."

The mention of Mrs. Warren had Carter clenching his teeth against the desire and the guilt. Although he would never admit it, he had been distracted and short tempered since he had left her behind to return to his duties. With each day that passed, Carter remained unsettled and unsatisfied. He knew his expression was often intense, but he hoped it also unreadable. "What of the dead?"

"We cannot move them until this matter is settled," Pennington said with a bit of regret. He asked Lexford, "Do you suppose we could impose on Lucifer Hill to stand guard over this place until we can execute our searches?"

Lexford laughed softly. "The man has been married for some seven weeks—long enough for Hill to be itching for something other than farm work. He is less than fifty miles removed."

Carter retrieved his hat and gloves. "As I have the longest ride, I will leave first; if you wish I can send a message to Hill from one of the neighboring villages. Less suspicious than sending one from Dove Dale."

Godown grumbled, "Lexford and I should return to our homes and make arrangements for Wednesday's assaults."

Lexford said what they were all thinking, "The marquis and I have ready wives at home."

"And you think neither Worthing or I do?" Pennington protested good-naturedly. "Did you hear them, Worthing? I am too old to appreciate Mrs. Pennington's charms, and you, too, with Lady Eleanor."

Worthing laughed comfortably. "I am the most insulted. I claim only four years upon Godown and five on Lexford."

"Be off with you," Pennington gestured. "Lord Worthing and I can maintain the ruse of country gentlemen enjoying the hunting and cards."

Godown grabbed his hat. He obviously required no further prodding. "Give Aunt Bel my best," he said as he caught up his gloves and crop. "I will oversee everything in Staffordshire. And for the record, Pennington, I hope the sun does not scar the image of your enjoying my aunt's charms into my memory." Without looking back, he was gone.

Lexford smiled knowingly. "It does me well to observe Godown's devotion to my wife's sister."

Worthing said sagely, "When a man of the marquis's temperament falls in love, it is with complete abandon."

Pennington observed, "I believe your statement, Worthing, could apply to each of the Realm. We who serve without notice and often without honor must find pleasure in life's basics: a man and a woman living with devotion."

Carter heard the self-satisfaction in each man's voice. It was all he could do not to saddle his horse and race hell bent after Lucinda Warren. Yet, there were matters still to settle—matters through which Carter meant to protect her. Somehow, he had to convince his irrational desire that time would not destroy his chance to possess what his comrades knew. "I should take my leave. As I am no one's senior and have yet to claim a bride, I have business in Devon, which will bring me no notice and less honor, but business of import nonetheless. Gentlemen, until we meet again in London, ride safe."

"Are you certain you wish to have the acquaintances of the Cottos?" Lord Charleton asked. "You may leave this matter in my hands. I will act honorably on the boy's behalf."

Lucinda squeezed the back of the earl's hand. They had decided to leave Charleton's driver, Mr. Higgins, with Simon until after their meeting. Worrying for Simon's state of mind, Lucinda had argued, "What if the Cottos are frauds: I would not have Simon's hopes dashed."

"I hold no doubts you would serve Simon well," she said kindly. "However, my curiosity must know satisfaction."

Her uncle smiled easily. "Your mother often spoke fondly of your insatiable inquisitiveness." He motioned a waiting servant forward. "Please send in Mr. Cohen and his guests."

"Yes, Your Lordship."

Within minutes, Mr. Cohen escorted a man and woman of some fifty years into the room. "Lord Charleton." He led the couple into a proper bow. Lucinda noted his surreptitious glance in her direction. Obviously, Cohen possessed no idea of her real identity.

Her uncle rose casually to gesture to the other three chairs about the table. "I assume you are Mr. Cohen," he said with his customary patrician air.

"I am, Your Lordship." A second glance in Lucinda's direction spoke of Cohen's interest.

Charleton said, "I believe you hold a prior acquaintance with my niece."

Cohen's eyebrow rose in surprise. "Ours was but a brief acquaintance, my Lord, not of long enough duration to hold knowledge of the lady's name," he said judiciously.

"Mrs. Warren," she murmured.

A look of complete understanding crossed Cohen's countenance, and Lucinda was pleased not to answer additional questions.

"And your guests?" the earl prompted.

Cohen responded politely, "Your Lordship. Mrs. Warren. May I present Mr. and Mrs. Cotto? Solomon and Reina. The Cottos believe they hold information of the boy you brought to my attention."

A second time, Charleton indicated the chairs where Cohen and the Cottos should sit. "Please. We have business of import." When they were seated, her uncle continued, "First, Mr. Cohen, would you explain how Mr. and Mrs. Cotto came to your attention?"

Cohen nodded his head in compliance. "Although Mr. Patrick provided only basic information, our sect has in place a means to communicate with others of our race. Whereas, you have more than a million possibilities, our presence in England is not so prominent—a mere eight thousand." He smiled with what appeared to be satisfaction. "With the assistance of our rabbis, we possess a means to contact any of our race."

He continued, "Those of our like in the organized provincial centers affiliate themselves at the outset with one of the London conventiclers, generally the Great Synagogue, where the bulk of our race attend upon the solemn occasions. The Cottos have most recently come to worship in Portsmouth, and although many from Portsmouth affiliate themselves to London's Hambro Synagogue, the spiritual head of the Great Synagogue is the High Priest throughout England."

As Lucinda looked on, Charleton turned to those who would place a claim on Simon. "May I ask of your reason for choosing Portsmouth, Mr. Cotto?"

The man, who reminded Lucinda of the "Rag" men, she had once observed at Rosemary Lane, near the Tower of London, sat perfectly straight. "First, Your Lordship, please excuse my English," he said with a thick accent. He spoke slowly, enunciating each word carefully. "I read your tongue with more efficiency than I speak it." Charleton nodded his head aristocratically, and Cotto continued. "I do not possess the learning of Mr. Cohen and many of my countrymen. I am a simple man from a small Spanish village in the Soria Province. My wife and I traveled to England some ten months prior, but as it was in my homeland, work has been difficult to find. We have journeyed across England, but I have known no success."

"And what is your occupation?" Lucinda asked when no one else spoke. She did not wish to place Simon with a family who could not support the boy. Simon had thrived over the last month with no more bare meals.

"In Spain, I trained the horses for Vizcendo de Ariba, a man of high rank who met his end at Salamanca. De Ariba prided himself on owning the finest line in the province."

Lucinda knew little of thoroughbreds–had only even considered their value to the aristocracy after having the acquaintance of the Hellsmans. Lady Arabella had explained how men saw their horses as an extension of their personalities. An aristocrat setting astride his thoroughbred declared to the world his lineage equaled that of the animal. She could understand how a man accustomed to training such animals could find work scarce as the animals themselves, especially if the man was a Jew. Unfortunately, Cotto's explanation did not ease Lucinda's qualms.

"Would you please explain how you believe you hold a connection to the boy my niece has made her ward?" Charleton's expression showed none of the emotions Lucinda's did.

"Many years prior, during the war that raked our homeland raw, our daughter," Cotto gestured to his wife, "met an English lieutenant. When she brought the man home for our approval, neither her mother or I could accept Sadia's choice."

"Because the gentleman was an English military officer?" Lucinda asked indignantly. Why she felt any allegiance to Matthew Warren, she could not explain. Perhaps it was the fact Lucinda had never considered the possibility others would object to an English gentleman.

"No, Ma'am," Cotto explained. "The man…" Cotto paused awkwardly. "I mean no offense, Ma'am. From your introduction, I recognize you possessed a connection to my daughter's husband, and you hold an allegiance to the man." He glanced at her significantly. "Our objections are difficult of which to speak. The man Sadia chose was of Judaeo German extraction. Matthew Warren held Ashkenazim origins."

Lucinda's lips trembled. She struggled to hide how much pain coursed through her chest. She had come to accept Captain Warren's betrayal as being the man's great love for another woman, but this was another layer of deceit. She had the acquaintance of Matthew Warren her entire life, but she had never really known the man to which she had been betrothed.

Her uncle captured her hand, and Lucinda concentrated on his features. They were nothing like her father's. The colonel would have been fuming by now, but the earl had schooled his expression to one of sensibility. "You mean to tell us the Warrens are of Jewish descent? How is that possible? I know from both my brother's words and those of his wife the Warrens regularly attended services at the Church of England. My, God man! My niece and Matthew Warren spoke their vows before the clergy of the church."

"Long after he, obviously, spoke his vows to our daughter before a rabbi," Cotto declared.

Lucinda found her voice. "If you objected to your daughter's marriage, how did it come to pass?"

Cotto's eyes narrowed and his mouth thinned to a tight line. "Lieutenant Warren held no honor. He claimed my daughter before vows were spoken." The man's words ripped at Lucinda's composure. Once again, she despised her husband for denying her the intimacies of the marriage bed. If it were not so unladylike, Lucinda would spit upon Matthew's name. "When a woman antici-pates her marriage no good can come of her joining," Cotto declared into the silence. "I said as much to Sadia, but my warning knew deaf ears. My beautiful daughter lost the child she carried only weeks after speaking her commitment."

The man's words made little sense. "Simon is but…"

"Six years of age," Cotto finished Lucinda's protestation. "The first child was a daughter."

Lucinda had trusted Matthew Warren unconditionally. She had bought into the fairy tale, and now all her walls had crumbled to dust.

Charleton empathized, "It is difficult to permit a child her mistakes and not wish to rush in."

Cotto closed his eyes, and Lucinda noted the pain and disillusionment, which crossed his countenance. She had observed like emotions in her mir-ror's reflection. "Mr. Warren took our Sadia away on the day of their joining, and Mrs. Cotto has known no peace since that eventful day. We received but a half dozen letters from Sadia in those intervening years. One explaining the untimely death of her daughter. Another holding news of her second child. A third announcing Simon's arrival. Another speaking of Captain Warren's demise. A fifth pleading for our assistance when our Sadia took ill. A final one from a physician explaining Sadia's passing. We knew nothing of the lieutenant's abandonment or of the Englishman's dual life. It makes me sad to think our daughter accepted Lieutenant Warren's unfaithfulness."

Although she thought it impossible, Lucinda felt pity for Sadia Warren. The woman's parents had turned their backs on their only child. She could hear the bitterness in the earl's tone when he asked, "You did not rush to your daughter's side when you discovered Captain Warren's desertion?" She knew Charleton had searched for her after the colonel's death, and he had welcomed her despite Lucinda's many faults. It was a sobering reality.

Mrs. Cotto shot a furtive glance at her husband. "Sadia's choice was not in keeping with our faith," she said softly. "But we did send for the child after learning of Sadia's passing."

Apprehension riddled Lucinda's question. "You have never set eyes on the boy?"

"No, Ma'am." Mrs. Cotto wiped her eyes with a small handkerchief.

Another long, uncomfortable pause followed. "Yet, you had sought the boy?" Lucinda searched for a flicker of hope in the Cottos' tale.

"We were too late," Cotto admitted without emotion. "Sadia had sent the child away, leaving no record of where he might be. However, our daughter did leave an account of her husband's activities. Neither Sadia or Mr. Warren acted honorably, as such, we feared retribution and fled our home." Lucinda noted Mr. Cotto's expression of anticipation. The man thought his tale would spark the earl's interest. Little did Cotto realize the earl would never pay to hush information, which would soon become public record.

The Cottos had protected their reputations, but did nothing to shield their daughter or Simon. Lucinda's heart felt caught in Sadia Warren's fierce bleakness. Evidently, Matthew had spoken kindly of Lucinda to his legal wife, and Sadia Warren had chosen a complete stranger rather than permit her parents access to Simon.

She shot her uncle a brief, anguished glance, and Lord Charleton responded in love. "My niece and Simon are saddled with Captain Warren's perfidy." The earl spoke to Mr. Cohen rather than to the Cottos. "As an earl, I can protect Lucinda from the shame she inherited from her late husband. I would be willing to extend the earldom's influence to Simon."

Cohen's eyes sharpened with interest. "Yet, the Cottos possess family connections." His protest sounded less than honest, and Lucinda recognized

Cohen's dislike for the Cottos. Evidently, the Jewish leader disapproved as violently as she of the Cottos' actions.

Charleton ignored Cohen's dispute: Both the earl and the Jewish leader negotiated for the same outcome. It was freeing to recognize how well her uncle knew her heart. "True," the earl said simply. "Yet, I doubt an English court would hand a boy over to impoverished grandparents, who have never set eyes upon the child, when an English earl wished to adopt the child."

Cohen did not even flinch from her uncle's pronouncement. Instead, he turned to the Cottos. "I agree with Lord Charleton. As sorry as I am to say this, no English court will recognize your plea."

Cotto's cheeks reddened with indignation. "You would take the boy from his family?"

Charleton's expression displayed his profound distaste for Cotto's false familial concerns. "The boy affects my niece, and she cares for him tenderly. He thrives under Lucinda's care, and she has faced the censure of Society to protect the child. Yet, I am not insensitive to your claims. You have a legitimate connection to Simon and should be reimbursed for relinquishing your rights to the boy."

Before Cotto could object, Cohen asked, "What do you propose, my Lord?"

The earl sat forward to press his point. Lucinda marveled at his confidence. "As Charleton, I hold connections beyond my estate, especially in the world of thoroughbred horses."

Cohen explained for Cotto's benefit. "Lord Charleton has an exceptional line, one renown throughout England." The news brought greed to Cotto's eyes, and Lucinda knew her uncle had won. Her eyelashes swept downward to conceal her relief.

The earl nodded his head with refined assurance in acknowledgement of Cohen's praise. "I am willing to assist you in securing a position with a well-respected breeder and present you with a settlement for your renouncing your claim to the boy."

Cotto asked suspiciously, "How large a settlement?"

"A thousand pounds."

It impressed Lucinda how the earl could speak so calmly on such an important matter. The sum was a phenomenal offer, and she recognized how her uncle meant to control the negotiation.

"A thousand pounds and a lucrative position," Cohen reiterated.

"And your promise never to contact Simon. Once I accept him into my household, the child will be reared with my values."

A myriad of emotions crossed Mrs. Cotto's countenance, but the lady held her tongue. Lucinda wondered why the woman had permitted her husband his stubbornness.

Cotto hesitated, obviously debating whether he should refuse the earl's offer, while knowing he had few options. Finally, he said, "How should we proceed, my Lord."

Disappointment and elation fought for control of Lucinda's heart. Disappointment that the Cottos would not fight for their grandchild and elation at having the boy as part of her family.

"I assume you trust Mr. Cohen to arrange the legal details on your behalf," Charleton said with more amiability than Lucinda thought necessary. "I will have my man of business contact Mr. Cohen. The gentleman will know what is best for the child and for your family."

Cohen evidently understood his role for he stood immediately. Lucinda held no doubt the earl would reward the Jewish community handsomely for Cohen's service. "Thank you, my Lord. Mr. and Mrs. Cotto and I await word of the negotiations." The Cottos followed Cohen to their feet. Each offered a bow of respect before Cohen ushered the couple from the room.

Long after their departure, Lucinda stared at the still open door. Every protective instinct she held flared to life. Protective of Simon, who had not known they had just bargained for his future. And protective of her uncle, who had risked a fortune to assure her happiness. "Your generosity never ceases to amaze me," she whispered.

"Even if your heart was not part of the agreement, I would never have permitted Simon to live in a household filled with prejudice," the earl declared.

"We cannot protect Simon from the world's censure," Lucinda responded.

Her uncle recaptured her hand. "Yet, we can provide the boy a safe haven, one where he will know respect and worth." He kissed her temple. "Let us send for the child. I am certain he is quite famished; boys are always hungry."

Lucinda chuckled, "Lord Worthing said something similar on the evening of our return to Blake's Run."

Charleton stretched his arms over his head. "I will write to Mr. Shadwick this evening. Tomorrow, we will set a course for Charles Place. I am most anxious to welcome you to your new home."

The Wednesday raids had proved quite successful, and Carter had received fabulous praise for his uncovering of the theft ring. Although he had pleaded with the others to accept their portion of the honor, each of his friends had refused the accolades.

"My name has known enough renown," Godown grumbled. "I am happy to be nothing more than the Marquis of Godown, a member of the House of Lords, and father to Renard Crowden."

Carter had not asked how his friends had recovered so many treasures. He suspected they had been relentless in their searches for they recognized the consequences of failure. In Staffordshire, Godown had uncovered a dozen pieces of suspect; Lexford another five from the Earl of Holderman's manor. Worthing found several pieces of pottery and more than a score of figurines in Oxford, while Carter had discovered eight paintings and another half dozen statues under Gideon Warren's roof.

"What is it you wish at such an ungodly hour?" The man had still worn his dressing robe when Carter had demanded admittance at Coltman Hall.

Carter had taken great pleasure in the anxiety upon Warren's countenance when Carter announced his position and his purpose. He wished Mrs. Warren had been present to witness the exchange. Throughout his search, he had thought of Lucinda Warren and how her late husband's family had treated her so poorly. His final revenge, taking Captain Warren's parents into custody, proved exceptionally satisfying. His only regret had been the knowledge Gideon Warren had not been the man with Murhad Jamot at Suffolk's Rising Son Inn. Carter had assumed the Warren's had marked Lucinda for death in order to protect their participation in the art thefts.

"You have a message, Sir, from the Earl of Charleton." Carter looked up to see Symington Henderson, his new assistant. They had experienced a set back during the coordinated searches with the complete disappearance of Dylan Monroe, but Carter held no doubt they would eventually prevail. The Realm held extensive resources, and there were few places in the world Monroe could hide for long.

"Thank you, Henderson." Carter accepted the letter. He would have preferred the message had come from *her*, but, at least, the connection remained in tact. It was too soon for word of their discovery to have reached all the shires; therefore, Carter supposed Lord Charleton simply responded to the news Carter would portray Mrs. Warren in the most positive of lights. "Remind me an hour before I am to meet Prinny at Carlton House. Prince George does not like to be kept waiting."

"Likely, it will be you who waits," Henderson said jovially.

Already breaking the seal on the letter, Carter nodded his agreement. "Not likely," Carter corrected. "It is an assurance." The Prince had already sent emissaries to several foreign governments, inquiring of their claims of missing artwork. Prinny saw their recoveries as excellent diplomacy.

Henderson discreetly slipped from the room, and Carter leaned heavily into the chair, prepared to have even second-hand knowledge of Lucinda Warren.

Following the customary greetings, the earl wrote, "I thank you for your allegiance to my niece. Lucinda would think herself undeserving of such kindness, but I am pleased you see beyond my niece's façade to her real vulnerability."

Carter realized how difficult it was for Lucinda Warren to permit anyone to observe her fears. Obviously, he and Charleton knew the woman well.

"Please send word when you have settled the business with Captain Warren's parents. I wish to prepare Lucinda for the news." Carter had previously posted a letter to the earl within hours of confirming his suspicions regarding the Warrens.

"I have much news of which you will take an interest," Charleton continued. "First, Lucinda and I met with Mr. Cohen for the man had located young Simon's grandparents." Carter's heart raced. He knew it would be difficult for Lucinda to part with the child, and with Simon bearing Captain Warren's name, the boy would know great censure unless the child's grandparents took care.

"I will explain in more detail in another letter, but please know neither Lucinda or I would see Simon placed with Mr. and Mrs. Solomon Cotto. The first Mrs. Warren's parents spoke with vile prejudice, and they sought the boy from duty, rather than love.

"I have, therefore, paid the Cottos to abandon Simon to my care. I have purchased passage to the Americas for the Cottos who boarded ship on Friday. Simon will remain with me. I have promised the boy a gentleman's education and a future, more than he would know with the Cottos.

"One point of concern from the conversation with Mr. Cotto may prove of importance to your investigation. Cotto freely shared the news of his objection to his daughter Sadia's marriage to then Lieutenant Warren. The man's narrow mindedness came not from Sadia Cotto's joining with a foreigner—an Englishman, but rather from the feud among Jewish tribes. The Warrens have passed themselves off as good Englishmen, when, in reality, they are Ashkenazim German Jews. Cotto's family is Sephardic."

"Damn!" Carter muttered. "I had never considered the possibility. No wonder the Warrens forced their son to marry Lucinda Rightnour. Lieutenant Warren could not return from the war with a Jewish wife, especially one of Spanish descent. Their son's actions would have brought notice to the family's differences; Matthew Warren would have ruined all for which the parents had suffered."

"On a more personal note, I plan to bring Lucinda into Society soon, as my niece, she has a prominent place to claim. My heir is a distant cousin, who is my senior. As said cousin is a bachelor of some repute, Lucinda's issue could one day inherit the title. Her return to Charles Place has renewed my resolve to outlive Cousin Edmund. Despite the scandal of the moment, I imagine when word of her importance to the title is known, Lucinda's worth to the *ton* will increase. I also plan a sizeable dowry to sweeten the interest of eligible gentlemen. However, I will not give my blessing unless Lucinda's heart is engaged. My dearest girl has known enough sorrow."

Notwithstanding his emotional upheaval, Carter read the closing, but his mind remained on the woman who had captured his heart. She would enter Society as Rightnour's niece—the only family of the Earl of Charleton, a wealthy and powerful aristocrat. In many ways, Carter celebrated Mrs. Warren's entrance into Society. She was truly one of a kind, and the lady deserved proper recognition of her worth; yet, Carter felt the sword of Damocles hanging above his head. "Dozens of would-be suitors will fill the lady's dance cards and sit in her parlor. Gentlemen with more powerful titles." His baronetcy was of short duration, and Carter was simply the second son of a baron. It twisted his gut to think upon her sharing her affections with another or to consider the possibility he would one day greet her as an indifferent acquaintance. It would be unlikely Mrs. Warren would choose to be Lady Lowery when she could expect to be a baroness or a viscountess or a even a countess. Carter possessed a small country estate with a manor house in need of repair and a governmental position, which demanded much of his time. He had little to offer the wealthy niece of the Earl of Charleton.

Chapter Twenty-Five

Lucinda morosely looked out over the manicured lawns of Charles Place. She had been in Lancashire for a little more than a month, and he had not come, nor had he sent his greetings. Once the news had arrived of Sir Carter's successful operation, Lucinda had expected the baronet's appearance in her uncle's sitting room, but his absence had spoken volumes. Initially, she had made the obligatory excuses for his withdrawal: There was still much to do with the investigation; his father's recovery should take precedence; and the baronet's responsibilities to his estate during the growing season were more pressing than dancing attendance upon a lady.

Unfortunately for Lucinda's foolish heart, there had been the occasional snippet in the London papers delivered regularly to Charleton's morning table. Sir Carter Lowery had been seen enjoying the opera in the Duke of Thornhill's box and in the company of Lady Cecilia Pickford's family, and Sir Carter Lowery had been among the guests at the Nichols-David musicale where he spent the evening with Lady Marguerite Nichols-David. "The baronet remains the dutiful son," Lucinda had told her crushed ego. "Sir Carter will choose among those who shall add impetus to his career." Had not Lucinda heard his companions' names mentioned repeatedly by Lady McLauren? Louisa Hutton had smartly warned Lucinda not to permit her heart to know Sir Carter, but Lucinda had foolishly ignored the countess.

"Ma'am?" Simon called from the open doorway. As she had suspected, the boy had thrived at Charles Place. "May I go to the stables to visit with Mr. Higgins?"

Charleton's coachman had taken a liking to Simon, showing the boy all he knew of horses. Simon's inclinations appeared natural, based on what she knew of Mr. Cotto, and the earl had fostered the boy's interest by offering to purchase a pony for Simon from one of the neighboring farms.

"Have you completed your lessons?" She asked in that maternal tone, which had appeared one day when Lucinda had tended a bloody scrape on the boy's knee.

"Yes, Ma'am."

Although they had agreed to keep some facts confidential until Simon was older, she and the earl had had an honest talk with the boy upon their arrival in Lancashire. "We were not successful in discovering those of your mother's family," she had explained. "But Lord Charleton has expressed an interest in your residing with him. The earl will hire a tutor and see you have a university education."

The boy's forehead had scrunched up in disappointment and then in elation. "I will stay with you and His Lordship?" Simon had asked in disbelief.

"Of course," Charleton had said in that characteristically authoritative manner, which Lucinda counted among his most endearing qualities. "This house has spent too many years without a boisterous boy roaming the halls." And with that, Simon had accepted his new life. It amazed her how resilient the boy was—in reality, much more resilient than she.

"No more than an hour," she said in admonishment. Lucinda had quickly learned if she did not place a limit on Simon's time in the stables, the boy would sleep among her uncle's cattle.

"Yes, Ma'am," he said with the crooked grin, which would one day break a woman's heart. Simon scrambled from the room, darting between two of the housemaids who polished the silver knobs decorating the earl's main staircase. Only yesterday evening, Simon had fallen asleep on the earl's lap, as Charleton had shared his line of horses with the boy. When one of the footmen had carried Simon to the nursery, the boy had repeated the animal's facts in his sleep. It was all quite comical, and Lucinda had taken comfort in the knowledge her Uncle Gerhard would no longer be alone.

"I have word from Mr. Shadwick," her uncle announced as he entered the room. "There are several new horses being placed for sale at Tattersalls at month's end. I thought we might travel to London for the sale. Might even take in part of the short Season before returning to Lancashire for Christmastide."

Lucinda stiffened in open rejection. She held no desire to travel any-where near London and Sir Carter Lowery. Moreover, she did not want to face the recent scandal surrounding her late husband's activities. Despite Sir Carter's masterful manipulation of the facts, many of the *ton* would snub her. She closed her eyes, willing away her anxiousness. "Should I not remain with Simon? Surely you will not tarry long in London," she said lamely.

"Simon's tutor and his nurse will see to the boy's needs," her uncle asserted. "Your future is calling. You have spent the last decade nursing an ailing mother, serving attendance upon an ungrateful husband, waiting upon your father's every whim, and caring for another woman's child. It is time for you to assume your place in Society, Lucinda."

"But all of Town knows of Captain Warren's deceit," she pleaded. "How shall I ever face so many critical strangers?"

"Straightforward. You will address them while on my arm," Charleton declared without censure. "Greet them as my niece. As a woman who placed her love of King and Country over her marriage vows. Yes, the *ton* will find you a novelty at first, but they will quickly see you as an intriguing, as well as a most handsome, woman. The longer you delay, the more the tales will grow with absurdities. Trust me. I have already heard from Prince George, who repeated the story Sir Carter provided him. The Regent wishes your acquaintance, and as Prinny goes so does the *beau monde*."

Lucinda had always considered herself an outsider, but her uncle meant to chip away at her veneer; and despite her fear of the unknown, she prayed the earl successful. She had tired of the forced fragile woman façade, which she had assumed with her late husband. "Are you certain, Uncle? I would not wish to dishonor you by bringing disdain to your door."

Charleton caught her hand in his two large ones. "If I had faced scandal years past, you would not be in this position," he declared boldly. "It is time I discover upon whom I can count as friends. I suspect I will have less respected associates when this is over, but I will be richer with you in my life."

Lucinda caressed his cheek. "You deserve a better niece—a better daughter," she said softly.

He brought the back of her hand to his lips. "No man could have a better daughter. You are perfection." He kissed her knuckles a second time. "I failed you once, but never again. I know your heart, Lucinda. I know the goodness of the woman you have become."

Tears misted her eyes. "I wish I had trusted my mother's well-honed intuition and had come to you straight away after leaving Brussels. We lost two years together."

"Yet, we have today," the earl countered. "And this is a beautiful day for a ride across the estate."

She frowned in confusion. "A ride across the estate?" As a child, Roderick Rightnour had been her rock, even during the turmoil after her marriage to Matthew Warren, but now it was Gerhard Rightnour to whom she clung.

A swift smile flashed across his mouth. "When I purchased the pony for Simon, I came across a mare of golden blonde, very much the color of your hair." He stroked a stray strand of fluff from her cheek. "I thought the animal an excellent match for my dearest girl."

"You purchased a horse for me?" She released the breath she held in a sigh of disbelief.

"I mean to spoil you," he whispered as he gathered Lucinda into his embrace. "So much so you will find a riding habit awaiting you in your quarters."

Lucinda laughed through her tears. "When?"

The earl's laughter reminder her of the colonel's—rich and dark. "When Mrs. Benton came to take your measurements for the new gowns, I took the liberty of asking the woman for a proper riding habit. I gave Mrs. Benton permission to choose the color and style. I hope it is acceptable."

Lucinda went on tiptoes to kiss his cheek. "It is the first riding habit I have ever owned; therefore, I shall be pleased no matter the color."

Charleton's eyes closed slowly, and his breath came in a soundless sigh. "And that is my first kiss from my beautiful daughter," he whispered. He laughed softly. "The gesture makes me wish I had ordered a hundred habits just to know the pleasure of your smile. To see you filled with innocent delight."

"Save your money," she whispered as she kissed his cheek a second time. "My love is free of encumbrances."

Carter stared at the blank page. He had returned to London late yesterday evening, having accompanied Pennington on a duty call to Thorn Hall. The Duke and Duchess of Thornhill had welcomed a son into their household, and although Carter had celebrated his friend's good fortune, he experienced the deep loneliness, which had clung to him since leaving Lucinda Warren behind.

"He is a handsome boy," Pennington had declared as he cradled the sleeping child in the crook of his arm. "You are a fortunate man, Thornhill."

The duke appeared bleary eyed, whether from lack of sleep or from emotions Carter could not say; yet, a look of complete abandon covered Fowler's countenance, and Carter felt envy creeping through his veins. He wished to discover a similar expression in his mirror's reflection. "My wife is phenomenal," Fowler gushed.

"Then it was an uneventful delivery?" Pennington asked.

Fowler collapsed heavily into a chair. "I would not say the duchess did not have the whole household on sixes and sevens," the duke confessed. "I am happy to have a son with the first child; I envision the duchess will not look upon another lying in with such idealistic aspirations."

Carter was delighted to have been in London when Velvet Fowler had delivered the child. He could easily imagine the duchess's excessive cries for attention–her unreasonable demands–and the duke's futile attempts to please her. If he had been in residence in Kent, he was certain Thornhill would have looked to Carter to solve the situation, and Carter could never claim competence in such an intimate matter.

"A message from His Royal Highness, Prince George, Sir," Henderson announced as he entered Carter's office. "The third one in a fortnight," his assistant said with a bit of awe.

Carter motioned the man forward. On some days, he felt much older than his four and twenty years *Five and twenty*, he corrected in another sennight. He wondered if he had ever been as "green" as some of the Realm's newer recruits. "Prince George wishes to use the recovered art as the basis for future treaties," he had said in explanation. Only he and Pennington knew the depth of Prinny's demands. "That shall be all for now, Henderson. Perhaps you might check with the Home Office for an updated list of the pieces we have identified from the Woodstone-Ransing affair." Several aristocrats had turned over the artwork they had legitimately purchased from Lord Ransing, without knowledge of the viscount's sources. Even the Earl of Holderman had convinced many within the Home Office of his innocence in the matter, claiming he was unaware of his son's nefarious activities.

With Henderson's exit, Carter opened the message: An invitation to one of Prinny's famous fêtes, one where Carter, his comrades, several key players in the investigation, including his brother and parents, and Lord Charleton, as well as Mrs. Warren, were to be Prince George's guests.

A light tap on the door brought Pennington's entrance. "I see you received a separate invitation," the Realm's leader said as he dropped into an empty chair. "I do not like it when Prinny exposes agents to public notice."

Carter agreed. "How might we temper the prince's enthusiasm?"

Pennington assured, "I will remind him England has numerous enemies. It will be a difficult conversation; the Regent is a stubborn man, but not an unreasonable one."

"One of the prince's parties in which we all just happen to attend would be acceptable," Carter suggested. "I am quite fond of Prinny's parties," he said with more levity than he felt. "If not for our prince's idiosyncrasies, I would not own Huntingborne Abbey."

Pennington flipped the invitation over and over, feeding it through his fingers. "I thought the changes you have made in the guest chambers at Huntingborne inviting, yet quite sensible."

Carter schooled his expression. "In my absence, Mrs. Warren assisted Mrs. Shelton in the design."

Pennington's eyebrow rose in curiosity. "I was unaware you had asked the lady for her opinion."

"I questioned Mrs. Shelton regarding the changes, and my housekeeper assures me Mrs. Warren *wrote* to me, seeking my permission for her intervention."

Pennington nodded his understanding. "Likely another of Monroe's ploys."

"When I heard the tale, I assumed Monroe had used the opportunity to establish his attempts at forgery. I now comprehend why Mrs. Warren so readily accepted Monroe's sending her to the Rising Son Inn in my name. "

"And you hold no objections to the lady's efforts?"

Carter thought of Lucinda Warren's lovely countenance. "I find few faults in Mrs. Warren's opinions," he said honestly.

"Yet, you have not called upon Charleton's household?" Pennington said archly. "You were aware the earl and Mrs. Warren had come to London?"

Carter spoke through tight lips. "I was aware. Lord Charleton and his niece were listed among those attending Portuous' musicale on Tuesday last." Although he acknowledged the attraction privately, Carter still could not explain his obdurate captivation with the woman. Each night, he made love to Mrs. Warren in his dreams. He felt the urge to stake his claim on her, which was the reason Carter had avoided calling upon the lady. He doubted, upon renewing his acquaintance, he could refrain from declaring his proposal.

"I see." Pennington leaned across the desk. "Then it is as I suspected, Mrs. Warren is the one."

Carter ignored Pennington's assumption. The idea he would speak his wishes to the woman did not alarm him as much as he thought it might. His only qualm came with the realization Mrs. Warren might refuse. "May I ask a question?"

Pennington offered no argument.

Carter chose his word carefully. "If the former duchess had come to you when you were five and twenty and had agreed to become your wife, which would you have chosen: Rosabel Crowden or your position with the Realm? Knowing what you know now, would you have risked your opportunities?"

"In a heartbeat," Pennington answered without forethought. "I am attempting to recapture a lifetime of lost memories. Just think, I could have returned home each evening to the welcoming arms of my wife and children. I could have known the comfort of Bel's body lining my chest every night. Now, all I pray is Lord Damon will permit to play the role of grandfather to his children. Yet, as wonderful as that would be, it will never be perfect because Adrian Murdoch's children will hold not one drop of my blood in their veins. They will always belong to Lawrence Murdoch; I will forever be the outsider. Do not mimic my mistakes, Lowery. I should have fought harder for Bel."

However, despite Pennington's emotional advice, Carter had not called on Mrs. Warren. Stubbornness filled his body with unyielding tension. He made excuse after excuse until the time had slipped by, and then he knew he was too late the moment he had entered the hall at Carlton House and had seen her holding court, surrounded by a bevy of English gentlemen.

Lucinda knew Sir Carter had come before the prince's herald had announced his name and station. His family surrounded him, and she could not completely conceal the look of longing crossing her countenance. She wished to rush to Lady Hellsman's side—to hear Bella's friendly chatter—to discover the reason Sir Carter had turned from her, but Lucinda's pride would not permit her to do so. Instead, she focused on Viscount Lerhman's story of his hunting dogs, plastering a welcoming smile upon her lips. She expected tears at the knowledge she had lost the baronet forever, but none threatened. Perhaps she had shed her last regret. She stood amiably with the viscount and the Barons Clarkson and Lavelle. All three men were sons of Lord Charleton's closest acquaintances, and her uncle had carefully orchestrated the men's attentions to display her in a flattering light.

Since her first appearance at a *ton* event, the gentlemen had called upon her regularly, along with a half dozen others who were equally devoted to her dowry. Her uncle had let it be known he intended to present her husband with a substantial settlement, and as Charleton had predicted, many of the *ton* had turned their heads from the scandal and sought her acquaintance. In fact, Lucinda's drawing room held many hopefuls, but not one man who set her blood afire. Sir Carter Lowery held that position in his solitary grasp.

She looked up from Lord Lerhman's smiling countenance just as Arabella and Lawrence Lowery offered her a bow of respect. "Lady Hellsman," she said politely. "I am so pleased to find you in health." She noted how Arabella Lowery had chosen a bell-shaped gown, one that concealed her blossoming figure. Women of the *ton* were generally sequestered away from prying eyes once their pregnancies became evident. Obviously, only an invitation from a prince would have induced Lady Hellsman to make an appearance in public.

"As happy as ever," Bella bubbled with excitement, and Lucinda knew a moment of envy. "You will join us for supper?"

Lucinda shook off the suggestion. "I am to remain as part of my uncle's party." Immediately, she regretted the lie. While at Blake's Run, Lucinda had wanted Bella as her dearest friend. Now she pushed Lady Hellsman away because Lucinda's foolish heart had fallen in love with the lady's brother in marriage.

Lord Hellsman caught his wife's arm; he stiffly said, "We should leave you with your company, Ma'am." Arabella nodded her agreement, but Lucinda noted the flash of disenchantment in her friend's eyes. The Hellsmans presented Lucinda a brief bow before withdrawing. Rather than returning immediately to her suitors, she watched them as they conversed with other couples in the crowd. She realized belatedly she had not even thought to ask of Baron Blakehell's health or of the baroness's plans for the lying in of her daughters. Essentially, Lucinda had become one of the women she had always despised: self-centered and without empathy, and it was all Sir Carter's fault.

His mother nattered on about finally having the acquaintance of the Prince Regent, but Carter had studied the interplay between Lucinda Warren, Law, and Lady Arabella. He forced the disapproval from his countenance. The encounter had not gone well. Carter recognized the irritation held tightly in the slant of his brother's shoulders. At that particular moment, he had despised how his relationship with Mrs. Warren had affected the lady's response to Arabella's overtures of friendship. Could Lucinda Warren not see how much it grieved him to withdraw from her? Could she not separate *their* relationship from the one Arabella offered? He was miserable, and now Arabella suffered also, and it was all Lucinda Warren's fault.

"Why do you not speak to the lady?" Kerrington asked. As was their way, Carter, his associates, and their ladies had sought one another's company during the supper hour. Even Pennington and Crowden's Aunt Bel had joined them. Mrs. Warren, her uncle, several of the lady's suitors, and Crowden's other aunt, Rosalía, Viscountess Gibbons, who according to Mrs. Pennington had a long-standing acquaintance with the earl, had chosen a table across the crowded room, and despite his best efforts, Carter's eyes drifted to where she sat.

"There is nothing to say," he repeated stubbornly. Both Swenton and Kimbolt had asked variations of the same question previously, and each time, Carter had given the same response.

Lady Worthing's brow knitted in disapproval. "You could ask of the lady's health or that of the boy," she suggested.

"Or of the horse she rode in the park this morning. Aidan says it was a fine mare," Mercy Kimbolt added.

"Or you could speak of your obvious infatuation," Grace Crowden declared.

His good humor evaporating, Carter's façade of indifference transformed to one of controlled ire. "I hold no fascination for the lady," he insisted through tight lips. "I am only concerned for the scandal dogging Mrs. Warren's steps. The lady has experienced enough drama for one lifetime."

Unfortunately, the women ignored his protestations. "Nonsense," Crowden's bride said dismissively. "I would venture to say Mrs. Warren is stronger because of her trials."

"And as I am fond of saying," Crowden said as he kissed the back of his wife's hand, "it takes a woman with sense, as well as sensibility, to find contentment with men of our ilk."

Kimbolt agreed, "When a woman comes meekly into the marriage, there is no basis upon which to build a relationship. Challenges faced together are the foundation for future bliss. A woman must exercise her choices."

Carter groaned. "I suppose it is foolish to declare my disinterest."

Swenton lifted his wine glass in a salute. "Although I know nothing of the contentment the others describe, I would be blind not to recognize you are besotted with the woman."

"Enough!" Carter said sharply. He prayed his response betrayed little but his insistence. "It is my life and my mistake to make. I appreciate your concern, but I must follow my original inclinations."

Lucinda worked hard to keep her countenance absent of the emotions coursing through her. The evening was more than half over, and Sir Carter had yet to join her even for the briefest of moments. In fact, he had not crossed an invisible line, which separated the room. Earlier, she had assumed he might seek a dance, or, at least, address his well wishes to her uncle. His parents had spent several minutes with the earl, but the baronet had ignored their previous connection.

"I understand you hold an acquaintance with my nephew," Lady Gibbons said quietly. Uncle Gerhard had claimed the woman's attentions throughout the evening. The viscountess's late husband had been the earl's long-time friend, and her uncle and the viscountess shared many acquaintances. The impish spark in Lady Gibbons' pale eyes spoke of the woman's quick mind. She was as petite as Lucinda and the perfect complement to Lord Charleton's boxed frame, and Lucinda had noted her uncle's tender care of the woman.

Lucinda leaned closer to keep their conversation private. "I am, Viscountess. Lord Godown assisted Uncle Gerhard in my rescue from Cyrus Woodstone."

"And his wife?" Lady Gibbons thankfully ignored the opportunity to speak of the scandal.

Lucinda glanced to the table where Sir Carter kept company with his associates. She had once dreamed of being accepted by the other men's wives. "I fear not, Lady Gibbons, but I have had the acquaintance of both Lady Worthing and the Duchess of Thornhill. I attended their joint Come Out ball as the guest of His Grace."

The viscountess's eyebrow rose in amusement. "I cannot imagine the current duchess looked upon Thornhill's bestowing his attentions elsewhere very kindly."

Lucinda thought of the duchess's venomous attack at Huntingborne Abbey. "I would agree," she said simply.

Lady Gibbons' snort of contempt surprised Lucinda. "The girl is all that is insecure. She used my nephew to turn His Grace toward jealousy—although I am certain Godown participated in the ruse of his own free will. In some ways, I suppose we, the marquis's family, are fortunate: The woman would have bored Godown within a week. Likely, my nephew meant to taunt young Fowler. He and the duke have had an ongoing 'competition' since their days at university. Now that I think on it, Thornhill and the duchess are a perfect match. The lady requires constant reassurance of her beauty and her worth, and the duke holds a compulsion to prove himself as a daunting knight, who rights the wrongs of ladies in distress. Perhaps when they both mature, they will find they have little in common."

Lucinda held few good thoughts of the duchess, but the duke was a different story. "His Grace has served me well over the years, even when I knew him upon the Peninsular front."

Lady Gibbons's lips pursed in dissatisfaction. "Do not misread my opinion of His Grace, my Dear. Thornhill has saved my nephew's life on multiple occasions, as has Gabriel done for each of the others in his group. The men share a pronounced allegiance to one another. Yet, except for the duke, those of Godown's governmental unit have abandoned their idealistic youthful dreams and have taken gigantic steps toward manhood. Sometimes, in my very biased opinion," she said pointedly, "I think Thornhill has had an easier return to his life than have had the others. Lord Worthing lost his wife and now faces the imminent death of his father. The Earl of Berwick lost his father, his older brother Myles, and his twin sister Margaret, while Viscount Lexford returned home to find his father incapacitated, his brother dead from a scandalous duel, and the woman he intended to marry pregnant with his brother's child.

"And Godown never thought to return to England after a devious woman accused him of the most vile of interactions. In his absence, my brother Renard passed, and the title rested in limbo without a clear successor. In comparison, Thornhill was always the heir to the dukedom. He protested he would not accept it because of his father's infamous reputation, but with a bit of prompting on his sister's part, Fowler reclaimed his position without resistance. The duke never grieved for his father, a man he despised. If any in the Fowler family suffered, it was Lady Worthing.

"The current Viscountess Worthing ran the dukedom in her brother's absence and faced Society's censure of their father. The Countess of Berwick knew only punishment from her uncle, a religious zealot, and our dear Grace and her sister, Lady Lexford, escaped from a brother who meant to 'sell' them to pay his gaming debts. Neither Thornhill nor his duchess has known the devastation the others have encountered. Lord Yardley, Viscount Lexford, and Sir Carter are minor sons, who never expected to inherit. I am a strong advocate for the concept that strength and merit are earned through adversity."

Lucinda listened closely to the viscountess's tale. Although it was shocking to have another speak earnestly on privileged matters, it was comforting to hear someone give voice to Lucinda's private thoughts. "I appreciate your honesty, Lady Gibbons. I, too, believe life's never ending twists and turns mold a person's mettle. "

"Mrs. Warren." Lucinda looked up to see Baron Lavelle bowing to her and the viscountess. "The Prince means to lead his revered guests in the next set." She could hear the musicians tuning their instruments in the distant ballroom. "Would you do me the honor of the dance?'

Lucinda would prefer to wait for the possibility of Sir Carter's appearance. Despite how he had ignored her all evening, her heart still hoped for a miracle. Yet, when her uncle nodded his approval, Lucinda dutifully placed her gloved fingers in the baron's outstretched palm.

"Please excuse me, Lady Gibbons," she whispered before standing to follow the milling crowd into the ballroom. It was a glorious room. The sheer magnificence spoke of a world of which she had never thought to know. She gazed upon her spectacular environs, every nerve aflame with joylessness. It was only a room if she did not share it with Sir Carter. He brought life to her days.

The Regent and Lady Shanleigh assumed their position at the head of the centerline of dancers, while Lavelle directed Lucinda's steps to a newly formed line at the ballroom's side. Instinctively, her eyes searched for Sir Carter, but the baronet was nowhere to be found. Just as she thought he might not participate in the dance, he bowed before a woman Uncle Gerhard had earlier identified as Lady Marguerite Nichols-David. A knife to her heart would have caused Lucinda less pain.

She turned her head to see the earl escorting Lady Gibbons toward a bank of chairs. The viscountess walked with a cane, and Uncle Gerhard took great care with the viscountess's steps. It appeared Lord Charleton had discovered a touch of love. *Everyone but me*, Lucinda thought morosely.

As she returned her gaze to her dance partner, Lucinda caught a brief glimpse of the baronet and the dark-haired woman on his arm. He and Lady Marguerite and the Kimbolts formed a foursome for the set. Quickly, Lucinda pulled her eyes from the scene. She wished the night would end soon so she might return to the Rightnour townhouse, where she might spend her night crying into her pillow.

"When do you return to Lancashire?" Baron Lavelle asked dutifully.

Lucinda bit her bottom lip to drive away the pain. "I am at my uncle's disposal," she said through a weak smile.

"Until that time, I pray you will permit me to call upon you at Nour Hall."

Lucinda attempted to place the wave of emotions from her expression. She was sorry she had accepted the baron's request for the dance–better to hide in the women's retiring room than to face the sight of the baronet enjoying himself with another. To disguise her anguish, she murmured her assent before looking away. Whether she preferred it or not, she was aware of every nuance of Sir Carter's interactions. She recognized every tic of his muscular stance. Lucinda searched for something–someone–upon which she could concentrate. To discover something which would distract her from the terrible tableau forming before her eyes. Then a familiar countenance came into focus. It was only for a few brief seconds before the man turned away, but she had seen him nonetheless.

Fear and anxiousness swarmed her chest. "Excuse me," she murmured as she walked speedily from the floor, leaving the baron looking on in disbelief.

"What is amiss?" her uncle asked as he caught her by the arm. His expression troubled. "Are you ill?"

Alarm exploded, as her mind raced to find a solution. "No." She shook off his hand. "But I must warn Sir Carter," Lucinda whispered uneasily. "Mr. Monroe is in the room, and he is dressed as one of the prince's footmen."

Charleton caught her again and shoved Lucinda gently in the direction of Lady Gibbons. "Join the viscountess," he ordered. "I will warn the baronet and the others. I want you safe." He strode away without looking back.

Lucinda paused to search the crowd again for Mr. Monroe's familiar countenance. Finally, she spotted him, slipping through one of the open laced draped doors leading to a raised terrace. With a staying hand to the viscountess, who struggled to her feet, Lucinda rushed to where she had last seen the man, who had once treated her as if she were a desirable woman, but whom she now knew as Sir Carter's embittered enemy.

Chapter Twenty-Six

Carter watched Lucinda as she walked arm-in-arm with Baron Lavelle toward the dance floor. "Lady Marguerite has no partner," Law had whispered. "You should not offend the prince by not partaking of his hospitality."

Carter knew his brother correct, but he had no desire to dance with anyone but Mrs. Warren; yet, with resignation, he nodded his agreement, before making his way to the woman's side. "Lady Marguerite," he said with a bow, "if you are not previously engaged, may I claim the next set."

The lady dipped into a proper curtsy. "You may, Sir," she said with her usual sweetness. No spark. No challenge. No shrewish barbs. Nothing like Lucinda Warren. Instinctively, he extended his hand to the woman. When she placed her fingers in his, Carter prayed for the slightest trace of tension between them, but only blandness existed. He shoved the sigh of disappointment from his lips; instead, he directed the lady's steps toward the dance floor. "You have been from London, Sir?"

After news of Mrs. Warren's arrival in the City had come, Carter had spent all his evenings alone, preparing his response to her. "Some," he said noncommittally. "I was recently in Kent on estate business." Not a total fabrication. He and Pennington had called on Thornhill, while staying at Huntingborne.

The lady smiled. "I would be pleased to one day see Huntingborne Abbey."

It was not necessary for Lady Marguerite to announce she would welcome his plight; Carter was well aware of his family's and her family's expectations. "A bachelor household is no place for a lady," he said with more irritation than he intended. *Yet, you willingly escorted Lucinda Warren to your home, and you would do so again in a heartbeat*, his foolish yearning announced. Placing Lady Marguerite beside Mercy Kimbolt, Carter took his place in the line of gentlemen; yet, in doing so, his eyes fell upon Lucinda. She stood directly across from him, and the thread, which was missing from his connection to Lady Marguerite, reached across the distance to where she partnered Baron Lavelle. Selfishly, he willed her to meet his eyes, but when she turned her head in obvious pain, Carter regretted the gesture. He shook his head sadly.

Ignoring his desire to race to her side and catch Lucinda up in his embrace, Carter turned his attention on Lady Lexford. He could not betray Lucinda in his heart by turning so quickly to Lady Marguerite. "Will you remain in London until the end of the Short Season?" he asked politely.

"I think not," she said with a nod to her husband. They had been married but six months, and Carter envied the bliss on Lexford's countenance. "The viscount and I plan an elaborate Christmastide celebration," she announced. The way Lexford's lady looked upon her husband, Carter wondered if she, took, knew the happiness of an expected heir.

He smiled easily. Carter was truly happy for Aidan Kimbolt, who had experienced more than one trial in his journey to happiness. "I will anticipate my invitation," he said with a taunt. However, his mind remained on the woman who had turned her back on him.

The last of the musicians' preparations filled the air. Carter set his mind to spending the next half hour with Lady Marguerite, but a flash of color—a blonde head turning to rush to her uncle's side caught his interest: with difficulty, he forced his feet to remain still.

A gasp from Lady Lexford diverted his attention for mere seconds, and when Carter looked again Lucinda Warren had disappeared. *Where is she?* Carter's heart lurched into high gear. He turned in place to search the entire room before he spotted her exiting through one of the lace-draped portals. *Did Mrs. Warren plan some sort of tryst?* The idea of her seeking the attentions of another man rebelled against everything holy within him.

From beside him, Lord Lexford questioned his wife, and Carter drew his eyes from the spot where he had last seen her. "What is amiss?" Lexford demanded.

"That man!" Lady Lexford whispered harshly, nodding toward the front of the room.

Carter and Lexford looked to where she indicated. "Which one?" the viscount asked anxiously.

Mercy Kimbolt caught her husband's arm. "The one standing behind His Highness," she hissed from her mouth's corner. "He is the one from the card game with Lord Stafford in Oxford."

"The one who approached you?" Lexford asked with distaste. The viscount's hands fisted and unfisted at his side.

"Yes," she whispered. Carter and the Lexfords completely ignored Lady Marguerite, who looked on in confusion. "His name is Mr. Monroe. He was the one from whom Viscount Stafford offered his protection."

Unconsciously, Carter repeated her words. "Monroe. Oxford." He could hear the urgency springing to his words. In a panic, he glanced to where the man now flanked Prinny. Closely. Too closely. Dressed in the garb of one of the prince's "invisible" servants was the man who had shot Dylan Monroe at the Rising Son Inn. A muscle twitched in Carter's jaw. Had the injury been a ruse for the older man to make his escape? During the incident, Jamot's capture preoccupied Carter's interest. "Escort the women to safety," he whispered his orders to Lexford. "It could not be a coincidence; the stranger must be Dylan Monroe's accomplice."

"Bloody hell!" Lexford muttered as he caught his wife and Lady Marguerite by their arms to rush them away.

"What is amiss?" Pennington stepped before Carter.

Carter ran his tongue along the sudden dryness of his lips. "I believe the rumors of an assassin are coming to fruition this evening. The man behind the prince is known to Lady Lexford and Viscount Stafford as 'Monroe.' Likely, Dylan Monroe's father," he said urgently. "Send someone to follow Mrs. Warren. She stepped onto the terrace. Where the father is, so must be the son." Fresh despair filled Carter's chest.

Pennington nodded and rushed away. Steadying his breath, Carter caught a glass of champagne from a passing footman before staggering in the direction of their country's royal prince, the heir to the English throne. He bumped into first one couple and then a second, presenting the ruse of his having imbibed too much. He hoped Lexford rushing the women from harm would add to the image of his inappropriate behavior. He also hoped his pretense would signal the others to take action. "Ex...cuse me! Pardon!" he said too loudly for polite Society.

With a final lurching step, he came abreast of Prince George. The fact the prince stood stiffly erect did not bode well. "Your Royal Highness," Carter slurred the words and swayed in place. Those around him retreated in disapproval, all except the man from the Suffolk inn. Carter cursed himself for not having taken note of the obvious: Dylan Monroe's wound was too clean–as if it had been perfectly placed. He executed a sloppy bow, and in doing so, he caught a glimpse of metal pressed against the prince's back. "Thisss is a wonferdul party!" he declared with a too familiar draping of his arm about Prince George's shoulder. Other than a collective gasp, the crowd had gone silent.

The prince said dismissively, "You have drunk too freely of my champagne, Sir Carter," but Carter recognized the Regent's silent plea for assistance.

"Yet, it's excellent cham...champagne." He raised the glass as if to examine the crystal; instead, Carter used the glass's shine as a mirror to examine the room for other accomplices. He permitted his weight to nudge the prince to the right, not an easy task considering Prinny's girth, but the assailant shifted also.

Fortunately, Prinny honorably excused Lady Shanleigh. "If you will pardon me, my Dear. I must speak to the baronet privately."

"Of course, Your Highness." With a deep curtsy to display her full breasts, the woman walked away.

Prinny caught Carter's arm in desperation, but the prince played his role. "We must find your family, Sir Carter."

Carter shot a quick glance about the room. He noted his father's approach, but Law stayed the baron with a whispered warning and a shake of his head. The entire party looked on. He and Prinny played a deadly game of dare, held together in an odd embrace and the assassin pressed closely behind them. "Monroe," or whatever the man called himself, had said nothing, but Carter could smell the fear on the man's rapid exhalation.

"It 'pears, Your Highness," he said with another hopeful lurch, "my family 'as deserted me." He noted Pennington had returned to the front of the gathering crowd. With a nod, he said he had followed Carter's orders. He hated the fact he could not rush to Lucinda's side, and he prayed she was not in danger–just a moment for a breath of fresh air–as opposed to Prince George's life. "What should I do?" he said morosely as if he was a "pity" drunk.

"Remain with me, my Boy," Prinny said through tight lips and a fake smile.

Through the champagne glass's shine, Carter noted how James Kerrington had crossed the musicians' raised dais to stand some ten feet behind the prince's attacker, and John Swenton approached slowly from the man's right.

The prince's assailant hissed, "Walk away, Sir Carter. I recognize your ruse."

Carter, too, spoke in hushed tones. "You will not live another day."

"Yet, I will die a happy man."

Carter heard Prinny's breath hitch. Unfortunately, Carter was not in a position to reach the gun before "Monroe" pulled the trigger; therefore, he did the only thing he could.

Lucinda paused for a few brief seconds to permit her eyes to adjust to the night's darkness. She scanned the area. There were no steps to the lower gardens, nor was there a connecting passageway. "Where has he gone?" she thought aloud. Carefully, she sidestepped to the balustrade to search the ground below. Nothing but rose bushes–lovely, but not conducive to Mr. Monroe's escape. Using the shadows to hide her presence, she traced the half circle of the raised terrace, constantly scanning the grounds, as well as the open door to the ballroom. No music filled the night air, which meant something was amiss–something involving Dylan Monroe. A flicker of light on her left caught Lucinda's attention. A low-cased window remained open, likely for cross ventilation, but a shadowy figure announced the opening was being used for something more than a cooling breeze.

Silently, she approached the window. It was designed so a person could step through; therefore, she lifted her skirts to enter the space. Inside, it was barely wide enough to stand without bumping the walls. She had never seen anything like it, but she had read of such architectural features–a space between the outside façade and the inside walls–used as an escape in case of fire on the upper levels. A person could pass through the narrow passage quickly if a fire prevented a more conventional escape.

The flicker of light, which had caught her attention previously, showed above her, and Lucinda dropped into the shadows. Her heart pounding a tattoo, she clung to the wall's sandy mortar. A dark staircase led to an unknown end, and Lucinda debated whether to follow the moving light. Surely her uncle had warned Sir Carter and his friends. They would search for Mr. Monroe, but what if they had not seen what she had? She must discover the reason for Dylan Monroe's presence under the prince's roof and report back. If no one else knew where in Carlton House the man hid, it fell to her to expose him.

With a deep breath to steady her frayed nerves, Lucinda began a slow and careful climb. Using one hand to steady her step, as well as to announce a turn in direction, she searched the blackness for the light and for where Sir Carter's enemy had disappeared. "Please God," she whispered. "Protect those who Mr. Monroe hunts."

Finally, she came to a dead end. For a few panicky seconds, Lucinda thought she had unknowingly sealed off her escape, but then reason arrived. If she were on a staircase, there must be a connecting passageway and a door. Cautiously, she ran her hands over the wall before her–only permitting her fingers to skim the surface–searching for a latch. When she grazed the thin piece of metal, she released the breath she held. Grasping it firmly, Lucinda turned the bar to the right. A soft click set her heart pounding double time, and she paused to listen for any indication of what awaited her upon the door's other side; yet, no sounds penetrated the space. With another steadying breath, she turned the handle far enough to release the latch.

Again, Lucinda paused; yet, only silence filled the air. With effort, she pushed against the door. It moved easily, but she did not. Fear incapacitated her. A narrow strip of light no more than an inch filled the staircase, and Lucinda took a moment for her eyes to adjust. She peeked through the opening. The passage glowed as if dawn had broken. Multiple lighted candles reflected off highly polished crystal and gold. She was above the ballroom.

Curious, Lucinda edged the door further, as more light invaded the stairway. With cautious steps, she slipped through the opening.

She was on a balcony, overlooking the prince's ballroom. It was narrow, likely no more than five or six feet wide. In addition to providing a decorative element to the room's design, the balcony would be used for servants to clean the painted ceiling of pesky spider webs and dust. A similar balcony ran along all four sides of the long room.

Clinging to the wall, Lucinda searched for Dylan Monroe. The glare from the magnificent chandeliers half blinded her, but she found him, squatted by a support, where those below could not observe him. In his hand, the man she had once thought all that was amiable held a long gun.

A familiar voice said too loudly, "It 'pears, Your Highness, my family 'as deserted me." *Sir Carter!* Yet, he sounded inebriated, something Lucinda thought impossible. "What should I do?"

As she looked on, Monroe edged closer to the decorative balustrade. He cocked the gun's trigger.

"Remain with me, my Boy!" A voice sounding very much of the prince's breathy squeak sent a feeling of dread down Lucinda's spine. *Dear God!* she thought. *Monroe means to kill the prince or Sir Carter, and I am the only one who can prevent the interloper's success.*

Carefully, she inched closer, assuming cover behind a draped support pole. Lucinda tucked her dark cinnamon gown about her legs to prevent it being seen by Monroe, while she peeked through the draperies' folds to determine the man's next move. She held no weapon—nothing but her mind and her determination. If necessary, she would throw herself upon the man. Lucinda could not permit Dylan Monroe to harm England's future king or Sir Carter Lowery.

When Monroe stood to take a shot, she prepared to propel herself into his back, hopefully knocking Monroe onto the floor below and not following him over the edge. Squeezing her eyes shut to the reality of the situation, she dropped her skirt tail and stepped into the open, but before Lucinda could react a gloved hand covered her mouth, stifling her warning scream. She had failed.

Carter's hold on the prince's shoulder tightened. Above all other actions, it was his duty to protect England's future sovereign.

"You will not live another day," Carter hissed as the man prodded the prince with both a taunt and a threat.

"Yet, I will die a happy man," the stranger declared baldly.

"You cannot kill us both," Carter argued. He searched the area for assistance. All of his men remained too far removed to prevent the interloper from firing.

"Not true," the prince's attacker said with confidence. "Look to the heavens, Sir Carter."

Carter's heart lurched as his eyes rolled skyward. Above him stood Dylan Monroe, a long rifle held confidently in his former assistant's grasp. The elder "Monroe" would place a bullet in Prinny's back, and the Realm-trained marksman would shoot Carter where he stood. Pennington must have followed Carter's gaze for the Realm's leader motioned Kimbolt to take the shot to kill Monroe, but Carter knew Kimbolt's efforts would come too late. Both assailants had known the risks of such a grand plan; they were prepared to die to achieve their goals.

Lucinda thought to struggle, but she opened her eyes to Lord Godown's beautiful countenance. He motioned her to silence, and Lucinda nodded her agreement. From where he had come, she did not know. She had certainly not heard his approach. He placed her behind him before silently withdrawing a polished knife from a case beneath his jacket. Motioning her to step away, Lord Godown caught the knife by its tip.

"Monroe!" he said with a deep threat. The next few second held pure chaos; yet, she witnessed it all as if in slow motion.

At the sound of his name, Sir Carter's former assistant spun toward them. He fired, but the bullet lodged in the ceiling with plaster raining down upon them. Amazingly, Lord Godown did not even flinch. He stood before her, a conquering Adonis. A flick of his wrist was all that moved—the knife turning end over end to lodge in the soft part of Dylan Monroe's throat. Blood sprayed upon the man's white shirt and footman's garb. A second shot followed, and a hole opened in Monroe's forehead; he tumbled over backward, arms spread like a vulture's wings.

The sound of a collective scream, a third gunshot, and a solid thud announced the crisis was not over. She and Lord Godown rushed to the balustrade to peer over the side. Both the prince and Sir Carter laid sprawled upon the polished floor, which held a trail of blood. Directly below them, Monroe's contorted body lay sprawled upon the floor. Lord Godown caught her to him, and Lucinda buried her face into his chest. She could not look upon the broken body of either Mr. Monroe or Sir Carter Lowery.

One second Dylan Monroe had held a gun upon Carter, and the next the man turned away. Carter did not wait to learn the reason. It was his opening. He caught the back of the prince's finely tailored coat and yanked hard as he shoved Prince George to the side. The double ring of exploding gunfire from above announced a change in the situation, but Carter had no time to consider his actions. As he tumbled after England's future monarch, a third shot caught his right shoulder, but Carter held on tightly to the prince, instinctively, covering the future George IV's body with his own.

Screams filled the room, both before and after a loud thud, which vibrated the wood around him. With a sharp inhalation to ward off the pain shooting through his shoulder, Carter's head popped up to survey the scene. The sound of retreating footsteps and additional screams had him turning to see the elder "Monroe" racing toward a side entrance.

"I have the prince," Kerrington ordered from beside him, as Carter worked to free himself from Prince George's amazingly strong grasp. "Catch the attacker."

Carter broke the prince's hold and rolled away from the rotund Regent, sprawled upon his back. "Swenton!" Carter called as he scrambled to his feet to give chase. "The other entrance!" He pointed to the servants' passage. Carter held no doubt his friend would respond.

Blood dripped from his shoulder, but he ignored the wound. He chased the prince's attacker through passages he did not know existed. He could not understand how with the prince's many servants, no one appeared to slow the man's progress.

Although years older than Carter, the elder "Monroe" had had a significant start upon him, and Carter's wound prevented him from using both of his arms to balance his run. The man overturned expensive statues and vases, leaving Carter to vault the debris. The water from the flowers turned the marble into slippery footing, but he refused to abandon the gambit.

The man turned to his right, and Carter followed only to see the elder "Monroe" bursting through a patio door leading to the garden. As he ran, Carter fished his gun from its holster, but he thought only to use it if he knew a clear shot. The prince's attacker followed the groomed path, while Carter forced his way through potted palm, rose briars, and clinging vines. A small wall announced the Carlton House stables on the other side, and his assailant deftly climbed the bricks at its lowest point.

Carter could hear the man drop to the other side several moments before he vaulted the wall with more energy than he possessed.

Jumping down from the barrier, Carter raced toward the stables, making the ready assumption the culprit had had a horse waiting for his escape. It might have been better for his attacker if the man had turned toward St. James's Park, which fronted the prince's home—more room to hide, but Carter was thankful for the confined space of the stables for their confrontation. With gun in hand, he raced into the prince's stables to search the stalls. Moving cautiously along the closed gates, he quickly surveyed each enclosure, some with animals and some without.

Heart pounding from his run, as well as from fear, Carter slowed his steps: The man he chased had nothing to lose—the elder "Monroe" would fight fiercely. Reaching the last of the stalls, he caught the gate's latch, but a sound behind him told Carter he had missed the obvious. His attacker broke from one of the first gates, running along side the saddled horse to prevent Carter a clear shot.

"Damn!" he growled as he gave chase. Exiting the stables, Carter scanned the area. In the distance, the elder "Monroe" pulled himself into the saddle. Carter's heart knew instant regret; the man would escape. However, before he could return to the stable to claim a mount, a shot rang out, and the man who had created havoc within the prince's palace slumped over the saddle's horn. With the man's lose hold on the reins, the animal bucked, throwing the prince's attacker to the ground with a bone-crushing slam to the hard dirt.

"Mrs. Warren…" Lord Godown urged. "Look!"

Lucinda turned to see Sir Carter fighting his way to his feet, and her heart soared. Lords Worthing and Hellsman, Viscount Lexford, and a man she did not recognize had surrounded the prince, guns evident in their grasps. Although pandemonium reigned, her heart celebrated the fact Sir Carter lived. However that moment of elation quickly faded when she noted the blood upon Sir Carter's shirt and dress coat. "He in injured!" she gasped and turned to race to the baronet's side.

Lord Godown caught his arm. "Where do you think you are going?"

From her eye's corner, Lucinda saw Carter race from the room. "Wherever the baronet goes," she said defiantly.

The marquis warned. "It is too dangerous. I will go."

Lucinda held his gaze. "Did you not see the blood?" she demanded. "Sir Carter requires my assistance."

"Lowery is trained for such conflict," he argued.

Never before had she felt such urgency. Any delay could cost the baronet his life. Tears filled her eyes, but Lucinda held them at bay. She whispered hoarsely, "Do you not understand? Sir Carter could die without my telling him…" Her voice broke, and despite her best efforts, a single teardrop slid down her cheek.

He stared at her for several elongated seconds before understanding dawned. The marquis examined her countenance closely, and Lucinda permitted him to see the depth of her unspoken affections for the baronet.

"We will go together," Lord Godown insisted. However, he did not immediately release her. Instead, the marquis turned to the disorder below them. Leaning over the balustrade, he called, "Grace!"

The woman Lucinda had learned to be the Marquise of Godown looked up. She certainly was not the most beautiful woman in the room, but even to Lucinda's untrained eye, she took note of the lady's natural elegance, a trait that would easily attract a man such as Lord Godown. "Yes, my Lord?"

"You hold my deepest regard," he said intimately as the room looked on.

"As you do mine, my Lord," Lady Godown said boldly.

The marquis nodded his acceptance. "Assist Lady Worthing, Lord Lexford, and your sister," he told her. "I will return soon."

Lady Godown's chin rose in command. "Be safe, my Lord. Renard and I await your presence."

He bowed to his wife before turning Lucinda's steps toward the narrow stairway. She had never experienced anything so beautifully tender between a

man and a woman. Across a crowded ballroom and in the midst of commo-
tion, the Marquis and Marquise of Godown had openly declared their love.
No artifice. No censure. No care for the opinion of others. Just pure emotion.
Lucinda prayed Carter Lowery felt even half what the Godowns shared. If so,
their future would be secure.

She tripped along behind him, the marquis never releasing her hand.
Reaching the still open window, they stepped through to stand upon the still
deserted terrace. From within the ballroom, they could hear various servants
and what sounded of Lords Worthing and Lexford barking orders to the
prince's guests. "Please follow Lady Lexford into the circular dining room."
"This way, please." "The prince will recover. There is no reason for alarm."

The marquis meant to lead her through the throng, but Lucinda pulled
him toward the terrace's balustrade. "Look there!" She pointed to where the
moonlight broke through the tree limbs to form a circle. Within it, a solitary
figure crossed without stopping. Within seconds, another figure appeared, this
one holding his right arm with his left.

"Carter..." she whispered.

The marquis tugged her to the far side of the raised terrace. "We do not
have time to chase after the baronet through Carlton House's many passageways. We will take a shorter route."

"We cannot," Lucinda protested.

"You wished to speak honestly to Lowery. That action requires we overtake
him." Without Lucinda's permission, the marquis lifted her to cradle Lucinda
in his arms before draping her over the terrace's edge. "Avoid the rose bushes,"
he warned before he dropped her to the ground clutter below. Lucinda had not
had enough time to be frightened or even outraged. She landed like a cat on
all fours. It was an exhilarating sensation. Since having the baronet's acquaintance, she had faced multiple situations only a lady author of a Gothic novel
could devise. She found she liked the challenges, which proved she was much
more of a competent woman than Matthew Warren could ever have imagined. Colonel Roderick Rightnour would have been extremely proud of her. "I
am coming down," the marquis cautioned, and Lucinda scrambled to her feet.
Within seconds, he stood beside her.

"Some day I wish to know how you move so quietly," Lucinda said with a
smile.

He presented her a cocky grin. "Only Lady Godown is privy to my most intimate secrets."

Lucinda answered his taunt. "Then I mean to make Lady Godown my dearest friend."

He smiled his most beguiling smile. "You will do very well for Sir Carter. Lowery should have a bit of mayhem in his well-ordered life. The baronet spends too much time making plans for all contingencies. Let us find the man and tell him his bachelor days are numbered. Somehow, I suspect, he will not mind." He led Lucinda in the direction the two figures had gone.

She double stepped to keep abreast of the marquis's long strides, but even then, Lucinda struggled not to fall flat upon her face. Within a minute, he boosted her over a low wall. Her hand came away from the bricks smeared with blood, likely Sir Carter's, and the realization caused her knees to buckle. "Which way?" she asked numbly. Carlton House stables followed one path and St. James's Park the other.

"The stables," he declared with confidence and strode away. She followed until they drew near the building. "Wait here," he ordered. "And remain from sight."

Lucinda wished to find Sir Carter, but she did as the marquis said. Obviously, Lord Godown was not a man accustomed to having his instructions denied. She squatted behind a row of hedges, ones where she could view His Lordship's cautious search. Yet, before he could examine the building, a rider less horse emerged through the open door.

From her vantage point, Lucinda could see a man running beside the animal; however, before she could warn the marquis, the baronet burst through the door to give pursuit. He staggered–his gait indicating his exhaustion and loss of blood. Immediately, she was running toward him–the danger the least of her worries.

The baronet swayed in place, and she meant to steady his stance; but the sound of a gunshot froze the marquis, Sir Carter, and her in place. To her horror, the man the baronet sought tumbled from his horse to strike the ground hard. Lucinda stifled her scream with a fist to her lips. Instantly, she looked to Lord Godown, but he held his gun loosely at his side: He had not had time to take aim. Then her eyes rested on the man she loved; yet, Sir Carter could not have delivered the fatal shot. He was too weak.

Godown pushed past Carter to investigate the shooting, and for once, the baronet did not follow. Instead, he sank to his knees. Lucinda rushed to his side. "Carter." She braced him to the ground.

"Lucinda?" he asked as he lay back.

"I am here," she said unbuttoning his dress coat. "God," she prayed aloud. "Assist me to stop this blood flow." Her fingers tore open his waistcoat, sending the buttons flying. She tugged his shirt from his breeches. "Your knife," she demanded.

"A pocket in my boot," he murmured weakly, not protesting her forwardness, which told her he was severely injured.

Lucinda caressed his cheek, her fingers leaving streaks of blood upon his skin. "No leaving me, Carter Lowery," she said adamantly. "I shall not tolerate it." She clasped his face in both her hands. "Your games end here."

He gave an exhaustive sigh, but Lucinda thought she recognized a hint of a smile upon his lips. Frantically, she wrestled the knife from his boot and cut strips of cloth from the tail of his shirt. Without asking, she worked his dress coat from his shoulder and down his arm, cutting parts of it away. Although they cleaved at her heart, Lucinda ignored his groans of pain and his guttural protests.

Using the knife, she slit the shirt's sleeve to his shoulder. "Oh, Carter," she moaned. "You are the most stubbornly infuriating man of my acquaintance." As she spoke, Lucinda folded the cloth strips across the seeping wound and used her weight to press it hard enough to staunch the blood flow. "Do you realize how many times I have tended your wounds?" she asked, but he did not respond. Anger coursed through her. She could have lost him on this night–lost him before they had truly known each other.

Frustrated, she placed the palm of one hand over the back of the other to hold the bandage in place. "Assistance will arrive soon," she encouraged, but he lay lifeless upon the ground.

"I swear, Carter, if you die on me, I mean to revive you and kill you all over again. How could you be so foolish?" Despite her words, Lucinda bent forward to kiss his lips softly.

"Harp…harp…harp," he said through a weak smile.

His expression eased her worried heart. "You must admit you have missed my harping." Her words came upon a cracked whisper.

"Absolutely."

"Please do not force me to spend my life worried for your safety," she pleaded through her tears.

Without warning, with his free hand, he pulled her down where she might rest her head upon his chest. She could hear the small shudder in his breathing: It matched hers. Silently, he stroked her head, and Lucinda felt her world complete. The steady beat of his heart filled her. "Lucinda," he whispered, and she raised her head to look upon his pale countenance. "I can only promise to love you with each breath I take." Despite his wound and the situation, he regarded her with an implacable finality, which somehow gave her comfort.

"And I love you, Carter Lowery." She leaned over him to brush her lips across his a second time. His eyes closed again, but this time in contentment, the tension draining from his expression. He had given himself up to her care.

Lucinda swallowed hard and returned to tending the wound. As she dressed it, she told him of how she wished to proceed. She hoped her assurances penetrated his unconscious state. "My uncle has been so good to me," she said through tight sobs, "I would prefer to postpone our joining so I might spend, at least, one Christmastide with him and Simon at Charles Place."

Chapter Twenty-Seven

It was late the following afternoon when Carter opened his eyes. He was in his room at the family townhouse, and his mother and Arabella tended him. For a moment, Carter wondered if he had dreamed of Lucinda's declarations of love. He recalled closing his eyes to listen to her melodic voice speaking of her hopes for their future and to wait for his rescue, but he could recall little beyond that gesture.

When Bella realized he was awake, she leaned closer. "Thank Goodness," she said with a smile. "We thought you might sleep through the night again."

"Lucinda?" he whispered. He caught Bella's hand to keep her from moving from focus.

"We sent Mrs. Warren home with the earl," she said as she straightened the blanket across his chest. "I fear you must marry the woman, Brother Dear." The hint of a joyful taunt laced her words. "The lady quite shamelessly refused to leave your side until Lord Charleton threatened to have his footmen carry her to his coach. The earl was quite distraught for his niece's health. The whole scene was reminiscent of my hoydenish ways with your brother."

"How long?" he asked through dry lips. He forced his eyes open to concentrate on what Bella shared.

"Some twenty hours."

"Do not tire him," his mother warned, but all Carter could consider was Lucinda had sat with him for a full day. She did love him: His ramblings had not been a dream.

"Send her word…I am awake…and I look forward to seeing her…tomorrow," he said with difficulty.

"I will do so immediately," Lucinda declared. "Permit the baroness to show her youngest her concern. I shall inform Lawrence and the baron of your recovery. They have waited most impatiently. I shall also send word to Mr. Pennington. You are quite the hero, Carter. The prince sings your praises."

He nodded his understanding. When Bella withdrew, his mother pulled a chair closer to the bed. She intuitively smoothed his hair into some semblance of style before she sat to wrap his hand into her two smaller ones. "I was so frightened, Carter," she whispered on a rasp. "I believe I liked it better when I did not know the dangers you encounter in your position with the Home Office."

He did not look at her. "I am sorry…to give you pain," he confessed. "I meant only…to bring honor to the family name."

She brushed the hair from his forehead. "Oh, my, darling boy. Please do not think I criticize. You were magnificently clever and astoundingly brave: Without you, Prince George would be lying in state. However, no mother wishes to think of her child in peril."

Carter laced his fingers with hers. "Without the government's specialized training…I would likely have died…on one of Wellington's…many fields of battle. Rather than to think…on how I might know Death…think of how my abilities…keep me safe. A man without…my training…would have met his end…last evening."

"I shall do my best to accept it. My only consolation is when you replace Mr. Pennington, you will spend your time in the office rather than on active investigations."

"You mean *if*…I replace Pennington," he corrected.

His mother laughed easily. "Trust me. Prince George means to have you close if trouble reoccurs."

A light tap announced his brother's arrival. "Are you awake enough for another visitor?" Carter nodded his welcome. "Perhaps, Baroness, you might ask Cook for some broth to bolster our patient's strength."

Their mother stood to make her exit. "I know when my boys wish to spend time without a parent." As she passed Lawrence, she added, "Do not tire him too much. Carter requires his rest."

"Yes, Mother," they said together, and the baroness smiled knowingly.

Law watched her go before asking, "May I retrieve something for you?"

Carter turned his gaze to the side table. "Some water."

The task appeared to set Law more at ease. He gently lifted Carter's head and uninjured shoulder, bracing Carter against his chest, before holding the glass where Carter might drink his fill. When finished, Lawrence reversed the process. "I told Merriweather I would assist him with your ablutions tomorrow if you are feeling well enough. Your man was most obliging while the surgeon tended to your wound."

"Darek is...a loyal member of my staff."

Law finally assumed the seat vacated earlier by their mother. "I am better when I speak earnestly; polite babble bores me," Law confessed.

Although Carter's mind kept an image of Lucinda's countenance close, he attempted to anticipate his brother's concerns. "I am a captive audience, Law." His energy waned and waxed.

"It is the lady, Carter. Although the family appreciates Mrs. Warren's efforts to save you, neither father nor I will have you marry if it is not your desire. Bella speaks of the lady's forwardness as if it is an accepted absurdity of your proposal, but Mrs. Warren's reputation is the earl's concern, not yours."

This was not a conversation Carter wished to have when his heart finally knew happiness. "Why is it...I recognized your desire...for Lady Hellsman, but you know nothing...of mine for Lucinda Warren?"

Law's expression spoke of surprise. "Then Bella has the right of it. You have always denied your connection to the woman."

"The right of it. The wrong of it. The everything of it. At least, Arabella understands love." Carter squeezed his eyes shut in frustration. "Tell the baron...I mean to have the woman...and he should set his mind to it." He turned his head away. "I believe...I will forego the broth...for more sleep. Please send Merriweather in...to sit with me."

Law stood slowly, but Carter chose not to look upon his brother. Against all Carter's hopes, Lawrence had slipped into his old ways, acting as the baron's agent. "I meant only to protect you, Carter," Law said lamely in apology.

He did not open his eyes. "Last evening should have proved...I am quite capable of persevering...even during the most difficult situations. I do not require...either Blakehell's or your protection."

When next he woke, it was daylight, and Merriweather was carrying in a tray holding hot coffee, toast, and eggs.

"Good morning, Sir." His valet placed the tray on a side table before bracing Carter to a seated position. "It is good to see a bit of color returning to your cheeks, Sir."

Carter ran his free hand over the two-day stubble bristling his jaw line. "Some food and then a shave," he said in response. "Do you know what time Mrs. Warren means to call?"

"I believe I overheard Lady Hellsman tell your brother the lady is expected at one, Sir." Carter glanced to the clock on the mantel. Only half past eight. Plenty of time to speak to Pennington and to have the inevitable "talk" with his father. As if he understood Carter's thoughts, Merriweather added, "Your family is still abed, Sir."

Carter nodded his gratitude. "I am famished."

"I chose items which did not require a second hand for cutting," Merriweather explained as he set the lap tray across Carter's legs. "I did not think you would appreciate my having to feed you."

Carter tossed a grin in Merriweather's direction. "I am long beyond the gruel years."

Merriweather's mouth compressed into a thin line. "As I suspected, Sir."

He had been truly famished, but the food, along with his ablutions, had proved the trick. By the time Pennington ushered Kerrington, Swenton, Crowden, and Kimbolt into the room, Carter had improved enough to maintain the conversation.

"Did we discover who shot the prince's assailant?" he asked one of his more nagging questions.

Swenton handed Crowden a five pound note. "I told you the baronet would cut straight to the unknown," the marquis said with a smirk. Crowden slipped the note into his pocket while amusement filtered through his tone.

Carter raised his eyebrows. "You placed a bet upon my response?"

Swenton chuckled. "It was only between Crowden and me. At least, we did not add your typical fare to the books at White's. By the way, I bet you would first ask of the prince."

Pennington sat heavily in a nearby chair. "Bets aside, Crowden had a most unusual encounter when he left you at the stables."

Although curiosity gnawed at his composure, Carter kept his expression perfectly neutral. He knew the marquis would answer in good time. "I chased after a sound rather than a shadowy figure as you had. A distant footstep. A crunch of gravel."

"Which led to…" Carter encouraged.

"Leave him be," Kimbolt warned, his smile roguish. "You know how Crowden loves to embellish a story with his many accomplishments."

It was comforting to be in a room with men secure enough in their company to leave titles behind. It was almost as it was when they were in the field together–before duty and responsibility had called each man home. "You were saying something of a superior sense of hearing." Carter's lips twitched with amusement.

Crowden gave a mock wince. "And my superior sense of investigation."

"Of course, I could never deny your ability for detailed inquiry."

It had taken several more minutes and more teasing before Crowden disclosed, "It was Jamot. He took his revenge on the man who meant to blame the Baloch for the attack on the prince. His story made little sense until I examined the pockets of the man you chased. The prince's assailant carried several documents, which appeared to be written by Murhad Jamot, but as we all know the Baloch has learned to speak our tongue, but has not mastered our script, I knew the items to be forgeries."

"Jamot?" Carter did not know why the tribesman's presence in this matter surprised him. Since the Baloch's appearance on English shores, many of his investigations led to Jamot. Likely, the man from the Suffolk inn had befriended the Baloch with the purpose of diverting the Realm's investigation into the assassination of the English prince. From what Carter knew of Mir's man, the Baloch would have been singular in his retribution. "Jamot has taken a liking to you, Crowden," Carter taunted.

"Not so much," his friend assured. "I place the changes in the fact the Baloch has lived in England for more than two years. With each of his interactions, Jamot appears to see Englishmen without the taint of Shaheed Mir's prejudice. In reality, the Baloch appreciates an honorable opponent."

"Did Jamot escape?"

Crowden flinched self-consciously. "The Baloch is a wily man."

Pennington scowled. "I prefer not to think on the possibility." He gave Crowden a deathly glare of disapproval. "In reality, we solved two different investigations: Ransing and Woodstone's art thefts and the Monroes' threat to the prince," he said all businesslike. "It was a fluke as to how the investigations overlapped through distant cousins."

"Then the man who shot me was related to Dylan Monroe?"

"His father," Pennington explained.

"What have we uncovered regarding the Monroes?" Swenton grinned widely. "Admit it: That was your next question, Lowery."

Carter threw a pillow at the baron. "I require a new circle of friends," he taunted. "Ones who do not presume to know me so well."

Like an indulgent father with several boisterous sons, Pennington ignored the banter. "The Monroe family are French émigrés who lost everything with the Glorious Revolution. The Monrets, as they were known upon the Continent, fled France with nothing. Apparently, the Earl of Holderman provided minimal assistance, but, generally, distanced himself from both father and son. Somehow, the Monrets came to the convoluted conclusion their strife came at King George's hand. That George III could restore them to their lost fortunes if the King wished to use his power for good. Killing Prinny was to be their revenge."

"The Monrets' complaint is one we have heard previously, but the family have taken it to the extreme. It appears there is more than a bit of Bedlam in Holderman's family tree," Kerrington observed. "I expect the man to withdraw from Society for an extended period."

After the debriefing, the conversation turned more cordial. Each of his friends meant to return to their country estates. "Too much notoriety," Crowden grumbled. "Grace hosted a drawing room full of nattering gossips this morning. I am unaccustomed to such notice."

"I imagine Lady Godown can handle 'nattering gossips.'" Kerrington assured. "Your wife is more than capable."

"Lady Godown is magnificent." Crowden's countenance bore his recent besotted state. Carter had to remind himself the Crowdens had been wed but nine months. The Kerringtons some eighteen. The Fowlers twelve. The Wellstons eleven and the Kimbolts six. The connections often appeared those of longer standing.

Kerrington asked, "Have you spoken your proposal to Mrs. Warren."

"Not officially." Carter laughed nervously. "I mean to do so today."

"Linton Chapel is at your disposal when you are prepared to speak your vows. It has brought each of us phenomenal fortune."

Carter nodded his gratitude. "I will speak to my lady."

Soon afterwards, his friends departed, and his father appeared in the opened door. "Are you well enough for company?"

Carter motioned the baron forward. "The bullet went through the flesh. If the surgeon would permit it, I would be up today and at my desk."

"Your mother will be pleased to have you speak so. Fernalia has been beside herself with worry." His father accepted the seat Carter indicated. "I suppose you know the reason I wish to speak to you. Lady Hellsman says Mrs. Warren and the earl mean to call at one."

"So I have been told." Carter would insist his father broach the subject first.

With a sigh of resignation, the baron began, "Mrs. Warren has my eternal gratitude—first, for saving my life and then yours, but…"

"The lady has saved my life three times," he interrupted. Carter had decided his father should be made privy to all the scandal surrounding Lucinda Warren. The baron was one to ferret out each damning detail and use it again and again to prove his point. Carter meant to diffuse his father's attack. "Once in Suffolk and again two evenings prior."

"You said three times." Blakehell studied Carter suspiciously.

"On the battlefield. Mrs. Warren is the boy I left behind."

The baron shifted uncomfortably. "I thought you said Mrs. Warren saved you? What in blazes was a female doing on a battlefield?"

Carter knew his father held very antiquated ideas about women and their roles. How he meant to shock the baron brought a smile to his lips. "Colonel Rightnour had been ill before the battle, and Mrs. Warren would not permit his following Wellington without her assistance. It was a foolish decision upon both the lady's and the colonel's parts. The colonel fell in battle, and I stumbled upon his regiment. I attempted to protect the boy I found grieving over the colonel's body. When I was shot, the boy followed my litter to Brussels and assisted in my care."

"And she sought you out after all these years?" Accusation filled his father's words.

"Mrs. Warren does not know I am aware of her identity," Carter confessed. "I will not speak of it, and neither will you," he added. "When Lucinda is prepared to trust me, she will reveal the truth."

The baron shook his head in disbelief. "You would begin a marriage knowing your wife practices a deception?"

"It is not a deception," Carter added adamantly. "Lucinda has not forgiven herself for her part in the colonel's demise, and until she does, she will not speak of her role in the colonel's inability to lead his men."

"The woman should be thankful you saved her father's reputation," Blakehell asserted.

Carter turned his father's comment. "And I mean to save Lucinda's reputation by keeping all her secrets."

Blakehell snorted his disapproval. "There are other secrets? I should have known."

"Oh, Mrs. Warren's secrets are aplenty." Carter laughed ironically. "To begin, Lucinda is not Mrs. Warren. Oh, it is true she married Matthew Warren, but the good captain omitted one vital fact. He had married Simon's mother some two years prior to his pronouncing his vows with Lucinda Rightnour—a fact of which Mrs. Warren was unaware until Simon appeared upon her doorstep. Yet, despite the complete betrayal of Captain Warren, Lucinda has opened her heart to the boy, who is the child of a Sephardic Jew and an Ashkenazic one."

"You mean to say the Warrens hid their race to insinuate their way into English society?"

"The Warrens are not the first to do so," Carter warned. "It is time, Father. England is changing: Its shores are teaming with many nationalities."

"And you plan to keep the confidences of a woman who has seen too much of the world to be an asset to your career? And worse, you mean to make her Lady Lowery!"

"I do," Carter said simply. "As I keep your secrets—keep our family secrets, I will do the same for Lucinda."

The baron blustered, "What secrets do you think we Blakehells have?"

"Secrets of your father…" Carter taunted. In reality, he did not know the reasons for his father's obsession with titles and land, but he was certain with a bit of investigation he could discover the truth. He would begin with the papers the baron left for Lawrence when his parents sailed for the Continent. He meant to "persuade" Blakehell to accept the futility of his objections to Mrs. Warren. Carter would use all the resources he had at his disposal to change the baron's opinion.

"What of my father?" Blakehell asked suspiciously.

He countered, "No one has an exemplary family tree."

"Yet, this woman brings nothing to the marriage but scandal. Surely, you can see the foolhardiness of your choice," the baron protested.

Carter bit back the caustic remark on the tip of his tongue. "True. Mrs. Warren has rumors of scandal surrounding her, which will make Lucinda more interesting to the *ton*. Many of the *beau monde* will clamber for the connection. Yet, she has more 'persuasive' qualities which you should consider."

"Such as?" His father said skeptically.

"Lucinda is the niece of the Earl of Charleton, a powerful associate of Lord Sidmouth. In addition, she has a sizeable dowry, which would more than turn Huntingborne Abbey into a showcase, and as Charleton's only relative, Lucinda's issue—our issue—will inherit the earldom."

"Impossible," Blakehell declared.

"I have the information from Charleton. The earl's current heir is a distant cousin, who happens to be older than Gerhard Rightnour. Even if the cousin would outlive Charleton, there are no other males available. Lucinda's son would be the heir apparent. Just think, Father, your grandchildren will not only control the barony, which you have nourished, but they will inherit two viscountcies and two earldoms." Carter knew he had struck a familiar chord because his father twitched with anticipation.

"If the cousin dies before Charleton, you could act as the boy's regent until your son reaches his majority." Carter wanted nothing from the earldom. He meant to teach his son of the baronetcy first, but he liked the idea of his oldest accepting the earldom and the possibility of the younger son receiving his title. Perhaps he had a bit of his father's conniving in his blood, after all.

"We will face that particular possibility if it becomes a reality," Carter declared. "For now, I wish to claim Mrs. Warren and rid her of that hateful moniker. I beg you to accept my decision with magnanimity. I know it was not your wish, but I do care deeply for the woman. She will serve me well as Lady Lowery."

The baron rose stiffly. "You are of age," he said judiciously, "and I have never been able to reason you from a decision." He extended his hand to Carter, and Carter gladly accepted it. "As always, the baroness and I will extend our support."

With his father's exit, Carter managed a short nap prior to Mrs. Warren's arrival. Bella escorted Lucinda into his room with the announcement of how she meant to chaperone their time together.

Carter lifted a shoulder in a noncommittal shrug. "I hold no objection to your playing chaperone," he said easily, "but you will permit Mrs. Warren and me a few moments of privacy prior to assuming your post."

Bella's hands fisted at her waist. "You must realize, Carter, I cannot go against the baroness's wishes."

"Arabella," he said calmly, "a man requires a quiet moment when he speaks his devotion to a woman, and I mean to claim mine even if I must tell my mother how Lord Stafford and I came upon Law's unconscious body."

Bella's eyes sharpened into a deadly glare. "I have never liked you, Carter Lowery," she declared petulantly.

"And yet, I hold you in deepest regard," he said with a smile.

Bella rolled her eyes in disbelief. "I shall be outside the door," she said grudgingly. "No more than a quarter hour."

When Bella disappeared, Carter motioned Lucinda to sit beside him on the bed's edge. He caught her hand in his. "I pray you suffered no injuries," he said when she settled her weight next to his. The customary heat returned, and Carter tugged her closer.

"A few scratches and bruises," Lucinda said with a blush. "Lord Godown dropped me over the side of the terrace into the garden." The marquis had explained how he had pursued her to the balcony, how he had delivered a knife to Dylan Monroe's neck before Lord Lexford had shot the man, and how he and Lucinda had followed Carter and the elder Monroe.

"The marquis spoke highly of your bravery," Carter shared.

Again, she flushed with color. "I thought to call upon Lady Godown if you think she would accept my attentions. I wish to extend my gratitude to His Lordship for his assistance."

"If you mean to call upon Grace Crowden, you should do so by week's end. The Crowdens return to Staffordshire. The marquis is not one for notoriety."

Lucinda laughed lightly, and Carter found it a delightful sound. He meant to hear it often in their lives. "I would not imagine the possibility for Lord Godown made a very public declaration of his affection for his wife. The *ton* must be atwitter with the news."

Cater looked confused. "When was this?" No one mentioned the incident when his friends called earlier.

"It came after the marquis and I argued over whether to give chase. I said you must know my opinions…" She stammered to a halt. "Then…then His Lordship turned to the crowded ballroom to speak his deep regard for Lady Godown. Much in the way of Romeo and Juliet, but in reverse. The marquis was on the balcony and his lady in the middle of the dance floor." She sighed a romantic sigh, another sound Carter wished directed at him. "In truth, if what I observed of the marquis's handling of a knife speaks of Lord Godown's ability with a sword, few would dare to tease him."

Carter chuckled. "Your assumption is most astute, my Dear. Godown and Kerrington are both unequaled with a blade." He reached for Lucinda, capturing the nape of her neck with his free hand. "And now to the crux of our time together." He nudged her closer for he meant to kiss her once he proposed. "I recall professing my love," he said softly, "but you deserve a proper proposal: Lucinda Rightnour, would you do me the great honor of accepting my hand in marriage."

Surprisingly, her forehead scrunched up in confusion. "Why did you use *Rightnour?*"

Carter frowned also. He had expected her positive response. "Because we both know you were never a *Warren* and because I mean to drive the captain from your memory."

Lucinda worried her bottom lip. "You know the majority of my secrets, but before I extend my agreement to your proposal, I must share one last truth. My telling may cause you to have second thoughts. If so, I wish you to know you may withdraw without censure."

"Speak on," Carter said evenly. He expected her confession regarding her presence at Waterloo, but he had not thought to know Captain Warren's true deceit.

"My husband," she began, and Carter shifted nervously. "Matthew…he kept his marriage vows to Sadia Cotto."

The lines above Carter's brows deepened. "I do not understand what you wish me to know."

"Do you recall…recall our first kiss?" she asked awkwardly.

He confessed, "Quite vividly. I clung to the memory for many weeks."

She smiled weakly at him. "It was…it was my first kiss."

Carter thought of the kiss. She had not been exceptionally experienced, but, in truth, he had celebrated the opportunity to teach her what pleased him. He certainly could not claim the reputation for womanizing that had hounded Gabriel Crowden, Brantley Fowler, or to a lesser extent James Kerrington, but he knew a woman enjoyed the foreplay of kissing. Suddenly, what she shared slapped him across the cheeks like an icy rain. "Your first kiss?" he asked suspiciously.

"Yes." Her eyes remained downcast.

"No kiss from Captain Warren? Ever?"

"No."

"It is not unusual for a man not to kiss his wife other than during conjugal relations. Not even then?"

Her color deepened, and she looked away. "Not even then."

Carter pulled her to lie upon his chest. She sobbed silently. In comfort, he stroked her back. "No kisses and no conjugal visits," he said in disbelief. "Even after two years of marriage, you are an innocent."

She rasped, "Are you disappointed?"

Carter bit back his retort, one directed at the late captain, rather than her. "*Disappointment* is not a word to describe my thoughts. I assure you there is not a man alive who would not wish to be the first to claim you as his wife. In truth, it has taken several long self-chastisements to accept the fact you had previously known another, and I am delighted to discover I have no reason for disdain. What troubles me is how selfish Captain Warren was. He robbed you of a proper marriage, as well as having neglected his obligations to Simon's mother. What could he have thought would happen when the war ended? Did he expect to live with both you and Miss Cotto? If I could bring Captain Warren to life again, I would see him drawn and quartered for his many offenses."

Lucinda said quietly, "You shall not be dissatisfied if I do not know how to proceed."

"You need only to do what feels natural," Carter assured. "In the marriage bed, we will feel no shame in what we share."

Lucinda raised her head to look upon him. She was quite beautiful, with long, thick lashes, silky-soft skin and full lips. "Such as?"

Carter smiled easily. Her purely innocent question brought images of them naked together. "First, you must accept my proposal; then I will provide you a taste of bliss."

"Oh, yes, Carter. I can think of nothing I wish more than to become your wife."

Carter claimed her mouth. He had wanted her for what felt forever, and now she belonged to him. Fierce need had him deepening the kiss; his hand sliding up her waist so his fingers might graze the underside of her breasts. The image of her mesmerizing eyes had remained with him for the past two years, and with their joining, Carter could lose himself in their depths without censure. Her vulnerability tugged at Carter's natural need to protect.

Desire flooded his mind. He was lying in bed with the woman he loved—her mouth pressed to his and her hands stroking his chest and arms. It was like nothing Carter had ever thought possible. True, her delectable body fired his blood, but Lucinda was more than simply a desirable woman: She was intelligent, resourceful, and compassionate. More importantly, she made him forget about his responsibilities to anything but her. Claiming Lucinda Warren would be the pinnacle of his life.

A light tap on the door warned him Bella meant to return, and Carter reluctantly released her mouth and nudged Lucinda to a seated position. Having but one mobile arm hampered his efforts, and Bella entered while they still clung to each other.

"I assume Mrs. Warren accepted your proposal," Bella said cautiously.

"And I assume you wish my lady as your new sister?" Carter countered.

Bella smiled largely. "Decidedly so. Now straighten your appearances before Lord Charleton and the baron join us. I believe the gentlemen are negotiating in your names."

Chapter Twenty-Eight

It had been the four longest months of his life. From his mid-September proposal to her mid-October departure for Lancashire, Carter had floated through the days. He had escorted his betrothed on picnics, riding through the park, outings to museums, exhibitions, and lectures, as well as the "required" appearances at the theatre, balls, and musicales. With each, Carter had stolen kisses, claiming he required a supply of memories to bolster his spirits in Lucinda's absence.

He had purposely taken additional liberties to acquaint Lucinda with the feel of his body near hers—to build her trust in him, but never once had Carter placed her in a situation where Lucinda might question his motives. He had come to realize how Captain Warren had ripped away every layer of self-confidence Lucinda possessed as an appealing woman. It was Carter's mission to undo the damage.

After her departure, they had written frequently, several times per week. Carter had become accustomed to ending his days with thoughts of her while sitting at the small desk in his suite at the family townhouse.

Ernest Hutton had traveled to London prior to Louisa's lying in, bringing word of Carter's oldest sister's disapproval of his choice of brides, although both Delia and Maria had applauded his actions.

"Ignore Lady McLauren," Arabella had declared when she learned of Louisa's vituperation. "Louisa thinks only of titles and connections. I suspect she is more like the baron than any of your siblings." His sister in marriage wrote her own letter to Lucinda, sharing the townhouse's study with Carter while Lawrence tended to business. Her pregnancy was quite evident, and as was customary, she had withdrawn from social engagements. His brother meant to return to Blake's Run at week's end. "Thankfully, Hutton adores Louisa, and she is quite attached to Lord McLauren. However, sometimes I wonder if another man of equal or higher rank had proposed first if Louisa might not have accepted the title before the man."

Carter chuckled lightly. Bella had always n her mind, and she remained a most excellent foil for Louisa's manipulations. "My oldest sister prefers to laud over us how she is a countess and even outranks Lawrence."

Arabella sniffed in disbelief. "Even Delia and Maria as viscountesses out-rank Lawrence, but my husband remains the head of the family. Delia and Maria understand the social structure, while Louisa attempts to bend it to her own devices. Lady McLauren is shortsighted: A woman carries her husband's title, not the reverse, as Louisa would like the world to believe."

Carter wondered what Louisa would do when she discovered his son would outrank hers. Charleton's title could be traced back some five hundred years, where McLauren's was only a hundred and fifty years in existence. The future Earl of Charleton would take precedence over Ethan Hutton. In many ways, he viewed the possibility as a satisfying reality. It would also mean Lucinda, as the child's mother, would hold more sway in Society, even as the wife of a baronet, than would Louisa.

With Bella and Law's withdrawal and the approaching winter months, Carter settled into a routine. He had made several journeys to Kent to order additional repairs for his estate, in preparation for bringing his wife to Huntingborne in late January. They had chosen 14 January as the date of their joining. At first, Charleton had resisted Carter's suggestion of Linton Park as the location, but a personal note from Worthing's father, the Earl of Linworth, had explained the significance of the chapel to Carter and the others, and Charleton had relented.

Finally, the day had arrived, and he waited anxiously for the Charleton coach to appear upon the Linton circle. "You will wear a hole in Lady Linworth's Persian rug," Lexford teased. Only the viscount and the marquis had accepted Carter's invitation to attend his nuptials. The Wellstons were expecting their first child in March, and the Earl of Berwick would not permit his wife to travel, especially across snowy Northumberland roads. Lady Worthing suspected twins could be more the truth, as both Wellston and his lady were twins, but no one knew for certain. Since their marriage, the couple had effectively withdrawn to their estate. Carter had not seen either since Marcus Wellston had recruited his wife's uncle, Charles Morton, Baron Ashton, to head the

Manchester investigation of the opium rings. That had been some ten months prior. Although Fowler's son was some five months of age, the Duchess of Thornhill had claimed "weakness" from her delivery, and Brantley Fowler had not attended the nuptials.

"Velvet does not suffer from more than an expanded waistline," Lady Eleanor had grumbled when she heard the excuse. "My brother is foolish to permit the duchess her pettiness." None of those in attendance to the conversation responded, but Carter recognized the consensus among his associates: Lady Eleanor spoke earnestly.

"I am unclear as to Swenton's absence," Carter admitted. "The baron sent me a message prior to Christmastide saying he had been called to Vienna to tend an ill friend."

"His mother?" The marquis asked what they all assumed.

Worthing cautioned, "None of us know for certain the woman John regularly visited was his mother."

Lexford suggested, "Swenton will share when he thinks the time right." The viscount and Mercy Kimbolt had welcomed a son in December. The birth secured Kimbolt's title, and the viscount had never been more relaxed.

Carter caught a glimpse of Charleton's coach through the bare trees. "Finally," he murmured and turned for the door.

"I suppose the baronet's betrothed has arrived," Crowden taunted.

Carter called over his shoulder. "Even you cannot ruin my mood, Crowden." He heard the women entering the main hall from an adjoining drawing room, but Carter did not slow down. He meant to enjoy Lucinda's presence on his arm. To inhale her scent. To feel her skin beneath his lips. They would all greet her carriage, but Carter meant to be the first person she saw. When the coach came to a halt, Carter waved off Charleton's footman to open the door and set the steps.

"Sir Carter!" Simon called in excitement.

He lifted the boy from the carriage and set him upon the ground. "I am pleased to see you," he said as he ruffled the boy's tight curls. "You have grown. I expect you to be taller than I." The words brought a smile to the boy's lips.

"I have a pony, and Mr. Higgins has taught me to ride."

Carter caught the child's shoulder in an encouraging grasp. "Then we must ride together soon."

He looked up to see Lucinda smiling lovingly upon the scene. Carter's heart lurched before speeding up to double time. He stood there, transfixed, drinking in her beauty. "Assist your betrothed to the ground," Worthing whispered with amusement before giving Carter a nudge with his elbow.

Carter stumbled forward and extended his hand. "Mrs. Warren," he said on a rasp.

"Sir Carter," she said sweetly. Carter made the mistake of looking into her eyes. Heaven help him. He wished to send everyone, but her, away.

A clearing of Charleton's throat forced their movement. Carter assisted Lucinda to the ground, placing her hand upon his arm. God! How he had missed the pressure of her palm against his forearm "Welcome, Lord Charleton," he and Worthing said together.

"Double my pleasure," he grumbled as he took several stiff steps.

Ladies Worthing and Linworth caught the earl's arm. "Come in from the cold, my Lord," Worthing's mother said cordially. "It has been a most damp summer and now a like winter. I hope the weather changes to sunshine soon."

Carter permitted the others to precede them. He knew the serene mask upon Lucinda's countenance hid her passion, as well as her anxiety. "I thought this day would never arrive," he whispered into Lucinda's ear.

She blushed, but she tilted her chin upward. "I thought it a dream until I saw you waiting on Uncle's carriage."

"This time tomorrow, you will be Lady Lowery, and I will be the happiest of men."

At ten of the clock, they had spoken their vows before family and friends. Lawrence had stood with Carter, while Lord Charleton had escorted Lucinda to the altar. She was beautiful in a light blue gown of silk—simple but elegant, and the sun for which Lady Linworth searched rose in Lucinda's eyes—golden flecks of light radiating from deep within her soul. His heart filled with hope and his body with desire. In his need for perfection, Carter often second-guessed his decisions, but not the one to marry Lucinda.

While Doctor Perry read from the Book of Common Prayer, Carter had reflected on how he had been the only one from his unit to have married by common license—to have waited a reasonable time to marry—to have honored his betrothed with the respect of not anticipating their vows nor had he teased Lucinda with more than several intimate kisses. He would never criticize the others, each of his friends had had his reasons for how he had conducted his courtship, but Carter had always known he would treat the woman, who would be his wife, with deep esteem.

"It is time to depart," he whispered. They had enjoyed the hospitality the Linworths had extended during the wedding breakfast. "The sky has darkened, and we will likely know snow." Unlike Law and Bella's wedding journey, Carter could not be away from London for months. He meant to leisurely escort Lucinda south to spend time at Huntingborne before he returned to his position in London.

"Permit me to speak my farewells to my uncle and Simon. Mr. Watkins has placed my bags upon your coach." She squeezed Carter's hand. "I shan't be long."

Carter turned first to his mother and the baron. "I will send word when Lady Lowery and I have arrived in Kent."

His mother kissed Carter's cheek. "I am so proud of you," she whispered softly. "No mother could ask for a better son. "

"As am I," the baron added brusquely. He extended his hand, and Carter willing clasped it. He and the baron would never know comfort in their opinions, but they would know love.

"Thank you, Sir." He caught his mother's hand tightly. "Are you to Staffordshire and Field Hall when you depart from here?"

"Your mother will travel on to be with Maria during your sister's lying in," the baron explained. "I will return to Blake's Run with your brother and Lady Hellsman."

Carter chuckled. "It has been a season of momentous occasions for the Blakehells. First, Louisa presented McLauren with another daughter, followed closely by the appearance of Nicholas and the securing of the barony, and now my marriage to Lucinda. All remaining is Maria's delivery of Sheffield's second child."

His mother sighed wistfully. "We are blessed most assuredly." A second kiss to her cheek bid the woman who was the family's rock a farewell.

He made his way about the room: his Realm friends, Law and Bella, as well as Delia and Viscount Duff. He expressed his gratitude to Worthing's parents and to the wives of the Realm for their attention to the ceremony's details.

Finally, he found Pennington. "You may reach me at Huntingborne if you require my assistance," he said privately.

Pennington smiled easily. "The world will go on without you, Lowery. Enjoy your wife. Start a family. Know you are not indispensable."

Carter frowned. "Yours is not the most inspirational advice I have ever heard."

"Yet, it is the most honest advice. What makes the difference is what we leave behind. You should have a dozen children who will bring you joy and carry forth your name. That should be your destiny. What you do for England through the Home Office may be forgotten, but not what you teach your children. Change England through them."

Carter considered Pennington's advice. The Realm's leader had taught him everything Carter knew of intrigue and of responsibility. He nodded his gratitude. "Then I will rejoin you in London in a fortnight."

Despite the heavy snow, Mr. Watkins had managed to maneuver the coach well, but Carter had insisted they stop at the next available inn. He would not risk Lucinda's life, that of his servants, nor of his animals.

"Yes, Sir?" The rotund innkeeper asked as he rushed forward to greet them.

Carter slid his calling card across the table. "Lady Lowery and I require one of your best rooms."

The innkeeper read the card and smiled broadly. "Of course, Sir. I imagine with the weather we will be quite crowded this evening, but you and your lady are early enough to claim your choice of rooms."

Carter shot Lucinda a quick glance, and his lovely wife blushed. "We will require privacy," he said and slipped a coin across the table. "I trust your judgment."

"This way, Sir." The innkeeper led them to a large room, which overlooked the back of the inn. Carter appreciated the lack of noise from the arriving carriages.

"We will require a meal a bit later. Your lady's best. Also your finest wine delivered immediately. My men will also require lodging from the storm."

"I will see to it personally, Sir Carter." With that, he left them alone.

They had spent time without chaperones previously–had traveled together–had seen each other at his worst, but this moment was different. She belonged to him, and the word *mine* tapped out a soft tattoo in his brain. "Come here, Wife," he said with a seductive note.

In the carriage, they had exchanged several heated kisses, and he had run his hand up her leg, dangerously close to her most private place, but her husband had showed great control; however, now he need not know restraint. He was the man she loved, and Lucinda had wanted to know Carter Lowery for what seemed forever, but at the moment, she could think only how she would likely disillusion him.

"Come here, Wife," he said seductively. Lucinda tentatively extended her hand in his direction. He caught her fingers and gave a little tug. She went willingly into his embrace. "I will not hurt you, Lucinda," he whispered as he kissed her temple. An aching desire spread through her loins.

Her husband lifted her into his arms, cradling her upon his lap as he sat in a nearby chair. Carter's mouth claimed hers, and Lucinda melted into him. The months apart had brought her great apprehension. More than once she had asked herself, "What if Sir Carter realizes he has made a mistake?" But he had showed no signs of a lessening of his desire for her. To fill her days in Lancashire, Lucinda had read numerous books regarding England's historical and political past. She meant to make Sir Carter a worthy mate–to speak with confidence. She had also sneaked her uncle's books dealing with the intimacy between a man and a woman. Those books she had devoured and had returned to several times. In addition to pleasing Carter by supporting his career, Lucinda meant to please him in bed also.

"I love you," he whispered as their lips parted.

Carter meant to know her slowly–to teach Lucinda of intimacies. "I love you," he whispered. "I am your husband, not your master." He peppered her cheek and neck with nips and kisses. "We must live our lives as partners." His tongue circled the soft indentation at the base of Lucinda's neck. Her breath hitched, and white-hot passion shot through his veins. He set her from him where he could look upon her countenance. His finger traced the delicate line of her jaw and the silky cream of her skin. "Do you understand my hopes for us, Lucinda?"

Her eyes held her growing desire: She shook her head in the negative. "Not in the least," she murmured before laying her head upon his chest.

Carter chuckled. "I planned this great speech on how we must learn to trust each other–to please each other–how this first time may not be perfect." His words might have made more sense if his wife had not run her tongue around his ear and down his neck.

"Carter," she murmured. "Bella warned me you plan every detail of every day, but you should know I learn best by doing."

A cold sweat broke upon his brow. "You are the most...the most...tempting woman..." Carter could not finish his thoughts; Lucinda's softly swollen lips were too enticing.

His heart lurched. A tremor of desire shot through him. "Lucinda, I mean to carry you to the bed. If you are not prepared for my attentions, say so now."

Carter had thought she might balk–might beg for more time. Instead, Lucinda pulled herself closer, pressing her breasts to the plane of his chest, and then she kissed him deeply. "Make me yours forever, Carter," she murmured.

He hardened completely, his erection straining against his breeches. Without another word, Carter lifted her to him to stand. Lucinda buried her face into the crook of his neck, her warm breath tantalizing Carter's skin. His wife meant freely to give herself over to him–to do what he desired: to trust him. Blood pumping boldly through his veins, Carter carried her to the bed. He thought to ask her if she wished to undress in private, but one glance to Lucinda's glazed expression said otherwise.

I learn best by doing, she had declared. In that case, Carter would teach her not to fear his intimacies. He set her feet upon the floor before him. As he kissed her forehead, Carter worked the small pearl buttons, which ran down the front of her gown. Her eyes followed his hands' movements, and she blushed, but she did not turn away.

Carter spread the cloth to expose her corset, which lifted her globes higher. Carter could not remove his eyes from the possibilities. He draped the cloth over first one shoulder and then the other to permit her gown to pool at her feet. Lucinda's breath quickened, and Carter grew uncomfortably harder. "You are so beautiful," he whispered hoarsely. She stood before him, the gauzy silk of her gown barely covering her luscious curves.

He stripped away his jacket and waistcoat before sending his cravat flying. Thankfully, Lucinda did not appear shocked. Of course, she had viewed men's bodies when she had tended soldiers during the war. Perhaps he had prepared himself for a reaction she would not portray. Lucinda was an innocent, but a woman with experience most ladies of the *ton* would never know. It was a confusing reality. Thusly, Carter abandoned all his preconceived ideas regarding his wife. Tugging his shirttail free, he pulled the cloth over his head to stand before her partially clothed.

Carter looked his fill and permitted Lucinda the same privilege. Her skin pinked, but his wife's eyes held the same hunger as his. "Touch me," he said on a rasp.

While her fingers trailed lines of fire across his chest, Carter removed the pins from her hair and permitted the mass of gold to drape over her shoulders and down her back. Her hair was not as heavy as Carter had expected, but it was much longer than he realized—hanging to well past her waist. He cupped her jaw and bent to kiss her tenderly. "I am blessed among men." He kissed her a second time, more demanding. Lucinda's palms stroked his bare chest and back. "I wish to see all of you," he whispered close to her ear, and his wife nodded her agreement.

Once again his hands returned to her clothing. He unlaced her corset and sent it in the direction of his cravat. Her breasts were full, her nipples standing pertly at attention beneath her chemise. Carter impatiently slipped the cloth over her shoulders and down her back. Except for her stockings and slippers, Lucinda stood before him, naked. He ran his hands over her skin, not touching her intimately, but claiming her as his. Then he cupped her hips and nudged her closer.

"May I?" she asked quietly as she reached for the placket of his breeches. His wife was a bold one. Carter should have realized she would be so. Lucinda had rushed into danger to save him. How could he ever think of her as timid? Her courage brought him complete acceptance.

"You may always touch me—anytime you desire."

Lucinda laughed self-consciously. "You do not think me odd?" The back of her hand brushed against his erection, and Carter closed his eyes to the pleasure.

"I think you glorious," he groaned, catching her hand and placing the palm over his throbbing manhood. His hips thrust into her palm while he held her against him. She was awkward, but it was exquisitely heady to have a wife willing to explore his body. He sculpted her arms, her back, and her hips.

Carter caught her in his embrace and led her down to the counterpane. His mouth found hers—demanding her surrender. Their tongues dueled—breaths mingled—her heat becoming his.

Sliding down her body, her tongue laved first one nipple and then the other. He captured each in his mouth to suck softly. His body afire. Carter meant to go slowly, but the images, which had tormented him over the past three months, set his blood to boiling. In his dreams, he had made love to Lucinda in every possible manner.

Her passion grabbed him—thrust him into a tumult of yearning. Carter returned to her mouth, his kiss hot and insistent. Raw need coursed through him. He hitched her leg about his waist so his tumefaction lay along the swell of her abdomen. She panted with anticipation.

With each kiss, Lucinda rocked against him. Skin against skin, and Carter fought hard not to spill his seed. "I want you, Lindy," he growled.

Desire had invaded his brain. He slid his mouth over her neck—her shoulders—her breasts—her abdomen. Carter felt his world collapsing in upon this moment—this woman. Nothing in his life had prepared him for this need. No training. Only instincts. He listened to the sound of her breath sliding in and out of her chest. The sound of Lucinda's heartbeat, so in tune with his.

He raised himself on all fours where he might gaze upon her fully. She was all woman, and she was his. Her cheeks blushed red, but Lucinda did not turn her gaze from his. Instead, her eyes slid to his protruding sex, as if fascinated by his manhood. A shudder of raw need shook him to his core.

"You are more beautiful than I ever imagined," he confessed. Her nipples called to him. They strained against her flesh, and Carter lowered his forearm to the bed and took possession. He slid the other hand along her flesh, seeking Lucinda's most private place. With his fist, he bumped her legs apart to open her to him. As he laved the ruched peak of her breast with his tongue, his fingers traced her wetness along the folds of her sex.

His blood sizzled with desire, but he meant to prepare her for his entrance. Drawing her breast into his mouth, Carter suckled her while his thumb found her bud, massaging it gently–tantalizing her. He stroked her folds, separating them, before entering her with first one finger and then two. She clenched her internal muscles, as her hips rose to meet each of his thrusts. Along with his, Carter could feel her need rising, and then she was writhing, pushing against his palm, her inner muscles tightening around his fingers. Carter milked her response until she cried out his name.

When she stilled, Carter crawled up her body to kiss her tenderly. "I hope you enjoyed your first taste of pleasure," he whispered. "When it comes again, I mean to be inside you."

A flame flickered in the honey umber of her eyes. "Love me, Carter."

He raised himself above her. "Always," he promised. His erection twitched with lust. He strained not to explode as he angled his hips closer. Carter positioned her legs where he could enter her with the least discomfort for her. He placed his swollen head against Lucinda's damp opening. It took all his well-honed patience not to thrust deeply into her. Their eyes met and held.

Inch by inch, he entered her. Sweat covered his brow as Carter exercised control he did not think possible. He pulled out and entered her again, setting up a leisurely pace, allowing her to feel the width and breadth of his manhood. Lucinda responded. Her moisture covered his length, driving him to complete distraction. He squeezed his eyes shut, silently begging for control.

He felt the thin membrane, which protected her innocence. With a hard, but fluid, thrust, Carter broke through. Lucinda was truly his. No other man would ever know her in this manner. It was exhilarating to consider. Carter lowered his head to kiss her neck, but he never paused his manipulations. "You have bewitched me, Lucinda Lowery," he whispered against her skin. "I was nothing until there was you."

A groan announced her desire. "I have loved you since Waterloo," she professed breathlessly. In her euphoria, his wife had uttered the first admittance of their being on the battleground together. She would learn to trust him, and Carter gloried in the knowledge.

Carter lifted her hips to him, holding her where he could sink completely into his wife. "God, Lindy!" he growled.

His pace increased, pounding into her, demanding Lucinda's complete surrender. A muffled cry of his name told him she desired him as much as he did her. A stilling of her hips announced another climax, her muscles tightening around him. Each thrust brought him closer; throwing his head back, Carter abandoned his self control to the ecstasy of knowing her. A shuddered brought his seed erupting inside her—inside Lucinda. His wife. Finally, Carter released her legs so she might lie flat, before he collapsed upon her. His sweat mixing with hers.

He did not know how long they lay as such, but Carter became aware of how his large form had swallowed her petite one. With effort, he rolled to his side and cradled her to him. "That was…" she said on a husky whisper.

Carter chuckled, "Exactly."

Her fingertips traced his lips. "I spent three and twenty years waiting for heaven," she murmured against his skin.

"And I five and twenty." He kissed her hair and inhaled deeply of her very feminine scent.

Lucinda raised her head. A look of self-chastisement graced her lips. "I do not even know your birthday," she confessed. "When did you celebrate another year?"

Carter kissed the tip of her nose. "The night of the prince's party. If not for you, it might have been my last birthday. When you admitted your love, I found myself thinking it was a glorious day, after all. I lay bleeding and exhausted, but I had found a home, one no one could deny me."

"I know nothing of being a good wife or of how to be a competent mother, but I promise always to put you first."

"We will deal well together. If we are honest, even when we disagree, our love will grow richer."

She snuggled closer. "Must we disagree?"

Carter lifted her chin to brush his lips across hers. "I fear we are both accustomed to speaking our minds. Ours will be a magnificent battle of wills, but I would have it no other way."

She crawled up his body. "Is it time for our second battle?" she asked as she ran her tongue across his nipple. Carter hissed in his breath. "I believe it is my turn to win."

Carter sighed heavily. "Do your worst, Lady Lowery. I am your prisoner of love."

Finis

In rivers, the water that you touch is the last of what has passed
and the first that which comes; so with present time.

\- Leonardo da Vinci

Other Books by Regina Jeffers

Jane Austen-Inspired Novels from Ulysses Press:

Darcy's Passions: Pride and Prejudice Retold Through His Eyes

Darcy's Temptation: A Pride and Prejudice Sequel

Captain Wentworth's Persuasion: Jane Austen's Classic Retold Through His Eyes

Vampire Darcy's Desire: A Pride and Prejudice Paranormal Adventure

The Phantom of Pemberley: A Pride and Prejudice Mystery

Christmas at Pemberley: A Pride and Prejudice Sequel

The Disappearance of Georgiana Darcy: A Pride and Prejudice Mystery

The Mysterious Death of Mr. Darcy: A Pride and Prejudice Mystery

"The Pemberley Ball" (a short story in *The Road to Pemberley* anthology)

Regency Romance from Ulysses Press:

The Scandal of Lady Eleanor – Book 1 of the Realm Series

Regency and Contemporary Romance from White Soup Press:

A Touch of Velvet – Book 2 of the Realm Series

A Touch of Cashémere – Book 3 of the Realm Series

A Touch of Grace – Book 4 of the Realm Series

A Touch of Mercy – Book 5 of the Realm Series

A Touch of Love – Book 6 of the Realm Series

His: Two Regency Novellas (includes "His American Heartsong," a Realm series novella and "His Irish Eve," a sequel to *The Phantom of Pemberley*)

The First Wives' Club – Book 1 of the First Wives' Trilogy

Second Chances: The Courtship Wars

Honor and Hope: A Contemporary Romantica Based on Pride and Prejudice

Historical Notes

Lord Sidmouth

Henry Addington, 1st Viscount Sidmouth, was a British statesman and Prime Minister of the United Kingdom from 1801 to 1804. Elected to the House of Commons as an MP for Devizes, Addington became Speaker of the House in 1789. In March 1801, William Pitt the Younger resigned as Prime Minister, and Addington assumed the position. However, in May 1804, an alliance of Pitt, Charles James Fox, and William Wyndham Grenville, 1st Baron Grenville, took advantage of Addington's inability to manage a Parliamentary majority and drove Addington from office.

Yet, Addington remained a political force serving as Lord President of the Council from 1804 to 1806 and in the Ministry of All the Talents as Lord Privy Seal and again as Lord President in 1807. In 1805, he was created Viscount Sidmouth.

In June 1812, Addington became Home Secretary. During his reign, Sidmouth countered revolutionary opposition and was responsible for the suspension of *habeas corpus* in 1817 (the setting for *A Touch of Love*), as well as the passage of the Six Acts in 1819. His term saw the Peterloo Massacre of 1819 (the setting for "His Irish Eve" from *His: Two Regency Novellas*). He left office in 1822.

Pentrich Rising

The Pentrich rising was an armed uprising in 1817, which started among the workers in the village of Pentrich, Derbyshire. It began on 9 June 1817. A gathering of 200-300 men (stockingers, quarrymen, and iron workers) led by Jeremiah Brandreth set out from South Wingfield to march to Nottingham. They were lightly armed with pikes, scythes, and a few guns, which they had hidden in a local quarry prior to the march. They carried with them a set of mixed complaints against the government.

When they reached Giltbrook, twenty soldiers of the 15th Regiment of Light Dragoons met their force. The revolutionaries scattered: Forty were taken into custody, but the leaders were not captured for several months. Eventually, three men–Jeremiah Brandreth, Isaac Ludlam, and William Turner–were hanged and beheaded at Derby Gaol for their participation in the uprising.

Jews in England During the Reign of George III

Like the Deputies appointed to protect the civil rights of Protestant Dissenters, the Spanish and Portuguese Jewry, who had taken refuge in England, periodically nominated *deputados* to keep the Jewish community aware of the political developments, which could affect Jewish interests. Therefore, when George III ascended to the throne, a standing committee was formed to express loyalty to the new king, while keeping a close eye on political changes.

However, the Ashkenazi sect–those of Judaeo-German extraction–lodged a formal protest, expressing their fear of neglect. They nominated the German Secret Committee for Public Affairs to serve their particular interests. Eventually, the King's government insisted the *Deputados* regularly communicate with the Committee of the Dutch Jews' Synagogues. This joint venture formed the basis for the London Committee of Deputies of British Jews.

The Jews in England had increased twelve fold over the seventy years following the Glorious Revolution and numbered between 6000-8000, most of whom lived in London. The more anglicized (but only 25% of the total population) nation were those from Spain and Portugal (Sephardic). The Ashkenazim were less assimilated (with several notable exceptions) and belonged to the lower classes. Many Jews chose to forsake their religion and take advantage of the opportunities available to those who submitted to conversion.

The process of assimilation brought English into the public school curriculum of Sephardic Jews. Sermons appeared in English translations. Even the publication of the Jewish prayer book into English occurred in 1770. Yet, the foreign character of the community was maintained by the constant influx of new arrivals.

London attracted more of the displaced Continental Jews than did other English cities, most settling in the East End or the West beyond Temple Bar.

The well to do found employment or developed institutions dealing in commerce, jewelry, brokerage or stocks. Those of the middle class became silversmiths, watchmakers, and shopkeepers. Lower still were tailors, hatters, glass engravers, pencil makers, etc. Lowest of all were those without job skills or money. These took on the roles of peddlers or traders of old clothes, often referred to as the "Rag Men."

Eventually, this population of peddlers spread out across England, bringing "treasures" (buckles, buttons, lace, tobacco, cutlery, toys, etc.) to the isolated rural population. Jews of the organized provincial centers aligned with one of the London conventiclers, generally the Great Synagogue.

At the height of the expansion, the Ashkenazim community was hampered by the steady flow of poor Jews, who were often of a criminal element. A series of crimes, culminating in a brutal murder in Chelsea, caused the community to disassociate itself from the malefactors.

Introducing Book 7 of the Realm Series

A Touch of Honor

John Swenton released the knocker to the apartments in a less than stylish section of Vienna. It tore at his heart she had fallen so low. A year had passed since he had last laid eyes upon her–actually sixteen months, one week, and four days–and John's heart quickened with the possibility. He had dreamed of her every night since he bid her farewell upon the docks at Hull.

He had come to Vienna, not to call upon her again, but to say his farewells to Baroness Fiona Caroline Swenton, his mother, but he had been too late. As she had always done, the baroness had made her exit with no regard for how it might affect him. Another woman would have fought her illness until her only child had arrived upon her doorstep, but Lady Fiona had never known maternal heartstrings.

When he had arrived too late to sit by Lady Fiona's bedside, John had made arrangements to have his mother's body exhumed. He meant to see her remains buried in the Swenton family cemetery behind Marwood Manor. He was certain Lady Fiona would not appreciate the gesture, but John knew his father's ghost would approve. Jeremiah Swenton had died, figuratively, the day his wife had walked away from him and their young son. She had performed her duty of producing an heir, and the lady wished nothing more of their company. John had often imagined the late baron had simply held onto life until John was of age and could assume the barony without legal complications. It had not been an easy life for either of them, but somehow they had survived the shame and the scandal.

"Yes, Sir?" A striking red headed pixie appeared as the door swung wide. She was dressed as a lady, rather than a servant, and for a moment, John wondered if he had the wrong directions. Her skin was pale and creamy, with a sprinkle of freckles across her nose, and despite his purpose in calling upon the household, John felt an unusual twinge of awareness.

Swallowing hard against his unconscious response to the woman, he bowed stiffly. "Baron Swenton for Miss Aldridge."

"Baron Swenton?" The girl's smile widened. "Please come in, Sir." She stepped back to permit him access. Closing the door behind him, she said, "I am pleased for the acquaintance, Sir. Miss Aldridge speaks kindly of you." John liked the idea of knowing Baron Ashton's niece occasionally thought of him, and in a positive manner. He thought of her every day and every night. "Please permit me to accept your hat and gloves, Baron." John obediently obeyed. "I am Miss Neville."

Realization dawned. This was the lady he had hired to keep him informed of Miss Aldridge's needs. She was reportedly of good family, but had been left alone due to family mishaps. His man of business had made the arrangements, and upon initial impression, John had approved of the hire. As requested as part of her settlement with his man of business, the lady had dutifully sent him two letters in the previous five months outlining her employment and sharing many of the "secrets" of Miss Aldridge's household. He did not think kindly on his actions in this matter, but as propriety kept him from corresponding with Miss Satiné directly, he had chosen the only course available to him. He wondered if Miss Neville had requested his presence in Vienna in a third or even a fourth letter to his home. He had been from Marwood for some three months—first, with the art theft investigation, and then with travel during the winter across the Continent.

"Ah, Miss Neville," he said with a second bow of respect. "I was not expecting Miss Aldridge's companion to act as man servant." He relaxed, his smile without humor. "I was in the city," John explained, "on family business, and I had hoped to have the company of Miss Aldridge. Please excuse my forwardness."

A flare of panic crossed Miss Neville's countenance, and John wondered if he had overstepped the lines of propriety beyond reason. Naturally, his fascination with Satiné Aldridge did not mean the lady would return his regard. "I fear, Baron, Miss Aldridge is not receiving."

John felt the pang of disappointment. "Of…of course," he said through tight lips. It had been foolish of him to pin his hopes on this visit. "If it is acceptable, I will leave my card. I should have thought…" He paused to collect his composure. "If you would ferry my message to your mistress, I would be most appreciative. I mean to depart for England at week's end. Please ask Miss Aldridge if I might call upon her before then. You may reach me at Auersperg. Prince Vinzens has extended his hospitality."

The lady appeared decidedly intrigued, but with an equally noticeable wary expression, she responded, "I am certain Miss Aldridge would enjoy having Prince Auersperg's acquaintance, but I should have explained more adequately: Miss Satiné has taken to her bed. I do not expect her to be available for visits or for social events for several weeks to come."

John drew in a deep breath to disguise the tension clutching at his chest. *Was Miss Aldridge seriously ill? Could he lose her before he had had the opportunity to declare his intentions?* "Has a physician seen to the lady's care?" he pleaded. He struggled with the desire to know what had occurred.

Miss Neville gestured him to a nearby sitting room. She closed the door to keep their conversation private. Neither of them chose to sit. The lady wrung her hands anxiously. "I am at sixes and sevens, Baron." Mixed with the fretful overtones in her voice, Swenton noted the twinge of an Irish accent. Many in York held Irish roots, and he was accustomed to the soft roll of the vowels and even a few of the consonants. "Although I serve Miss Aldridge, I am aware you are most assuredly my employer, and I am indebted to you for your generosity." John had pretended to act with Baron Ashton's approval when he had placed Miss Neville in Miss Aldridge's household. He fully understood others would not approve of his presumptuousness, but it was the means he had for information on the woman he loved. Miss Neville presented him a rueful shake of her head. "I hold an allegiance to both you and Miss Aldridge."

Swenton's mouth thinned with displeasure. "I will not sack you if you keep your mistress's confidences, but you must know I hold Miss Aldridge with great regard. If the lady has need of my protection, I would perform my duty gladly."

The blue sapphire of her eyes flashed. *With annoyance or admiration?* he wondered. She worried her bottom lip in indecision. Finally, with a sigh of resignation, she explained, "When first I came to Miss Aldridge, all appeared well, but as I confided in my last letter, over the past three months, Miss Aldridge has become more withdrawn, barely leaving her rooms. Her appetite has become nonexistent."

John stilled. "Was there nothing to be done for the lady?" He sucked in a deep breath and mentally braced himself for Miss Neville's next pronouncement.

Anxiety sounded in Miss Neville's tone. "Miss Aldridge's illness was not one medicine could cure. Only time will do so." She pressed her fingertips to her mouth as if she wished to snatch back her words. Averting her eyes, she continued, "This is not a conversation for strangers, especially strangers not of the same gender."

He responded in a tight voice. "Yet, I insist, Miss Neville."

She regarded him intently, and John cursed his weakness: The one where he had always sought love where none existed. He had hoped this visit would lay the basis for Miss Aldridge's return to England, as well as preparing the way for him to woo the woman with a proper proposal. To date, he was the only one among his associates who had yet to claim a bit of happiness.

Miss Neville momentarily glanced away before meeting his gaze with her firm one. "Miss Aldridge's lack of appetite was self-imposed," she explained. "My mistress worried for her figure."

A barbed smile formed on his lips. "I cannot imagine Miss Aldridge's stature would tolerate anything less than perfection," he declared with confidence.

"And I am certain Miss Aldridge sought perfection when none was to be had," she countered.

His voice had a harder edge than he intended. "Perhaps you had best explain without all the niceties, Miss Neville. I tend to be a plain spoken man."

Her expression sobered before the woman nodded curtly. "Miss Aldridge has kept a scandalous secret from all her dear friends and family. Her withdrawal was to disguise the fact she was enceinte. Miss Satiné delivered a son a fortnight past."

 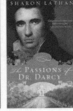   
    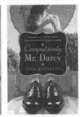
  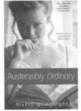  

Made in the USA
San Bernardino, CA
01 February 2015